Return to Redemption Ridge

Sequel to *Redemption Ridge*

Lottie Brent Boggan

Return to Redemption Ridge

Sequel to Redemption Ridge

Lottie Brent Boggan

Dragon Breath Press

Ridgeland, Mississippi

ISBN: 978-0-9990692-5-7

SYNOPSIS

Brucie Claymore left Redemption Ridge when she was thirteen, but she carried dark secrets with her. Now, after many years and life in Boston as the wife of Herschel Von Dieter and mother to Memory and Dale, unexpected hardship and tragedy force the family to return to Redemption Ridge, Mississippi, not for a visit, but permanently.

Both Memory and Dale suffer from post-traumatic stress disorder, but for different reasons. Dale's affliction is referred to as "shellshock," a result of World War I and the devastating loss of life under his command. Memory's problem doesn't have a name, but childhood memories of being raped assault her mind as she rages against the change, although she has recently been widowed. But, perhaps, redemption awaits both brother and sister in Mississippi—as well as their mother who also must finally confront her darkest secret, another child as a result of being raped by the man she thought was a father—a child hellbent on revenge and claiming what she sees as her inheritance.

Also, awaiting the Claymore descendants at Redemption Ridge—ghosts who need their souls to be set free. Can Memory and Dale succeed upon their return in helping Vernell and Captain Bruce Claymore, their true grandfather and supposed Confederate traitor, "find their peace"?

OTHER BOOKS BY LOTTIE BRENT BOGGAN

Redemption Ridge

Streams of Mercy

Saleta's Secrets

Mr. Honeycut

Come up Churning and Keep Your Buckets High

Mad Dogs and Moonshine

Fireflies in Fruit Jars

From the Sleeping Porch

https://amzn.to/2DgGGsB

DEDICATION

To the Gentle Man across the street and our Beloved Girls

DISCLAIMER

The following work is fiction. Any resemblance to any person, living or dead, is coincidence.

ACKNOWLEDGEMENTS

Gratitude and thanks go to my very talented grandson, Robert Brent Boggan, who penned the poems for *Return to Redemption Ridge*.

Grace, thanks and peace to my wonderful boys, Bob and Bill, and their wives, Gail and Binnie Jo, who are always so kind, thoughtful, and very patient with me, their mother-in-law.

Love to my grandchildren, the greats and our wonderful multi-layered family: Michelle, Carter, Aden, Kimberly, Brent, Maddie, Christian, Baylee, Wyatt Henry, Peyton, Katie and Eric, Kiera, John David, Addybelle and Shannon, Cecelia and Mike, Pat, Trace, Jan, Jennifer and Mark, Katelyn, Lainey, Matt and Kim, Logan, Riley, Alvin and Becky, Homer, Gene and Shelly, John and Frances, Lindsey, Kyle, Pat and Jody.

Gratefulness to Christopher Chambers, the gifted artist who did my cover. (juroddesigns.com)

Deep appreciation goes to Janet Taylor-Perry. I could not have walked through these dark valleys, climbed hills, rocky ridges and found redemption without her patience, dedication and perseverance.

As always, I am grateful to my writing friends who are so supportive of me: Judy, C.C., Edrie, Philip, Lydia, Jackie, Melanie, Carole, Vivian, Lee, Ruth, Carlene, Darden, John, Glen and the Madison Writers Group.

PROLOGUE

I tried to be true to myself and true to my cause, albeit a lost battle. I hurt no man except in the heat of conflict. My war, my fight, I'm not sure if it was right or wrong. Just weigh my ways, and the burden of my heart on the fragile scales of justice; if I was honorable to the end. Judge me for that, my God, not for the ways and whims of that terrible war. As God was my witness, I did no wrong.

I want to return to You, my Lord. Too long I have waited as months have spooled into years. All around I smell decay; powdery bones floating close to the ground are taunted by the lapping waters of Noble Creek.

Those here beside me whom I have loved. I feel your spirits. You walk beside me. We know these fields. The ridges. The hills and valleys, the creeks and the rivers. The cannons are forever stilled. As if they had never been more than the heavy pulse beat of a fainting, fading heart. Now, over all there is the cocksure crow of a rooster at dawn, the lonesome cry of the owl just at twilight.

The woods are mysterious and elusive, like grasping the dark deep words of a country preacher bent on hellfire and destruction. And, oh, that the truth, only Your truth, not sermon words, could be known, henceforth and forevermore.

The lives of these my people, then their people, all who lived in glory and others who died in shame. Promises. The tunes they sang of others who broke promises. Then promises they broke. Yet there was honor. Hope. Always hope.

I've said hello and goodbye to the seasons, heard the birdsongs of spring and smelled the scent of flowers on the wind. Days when the sun sets slower, I hear steel plows break and turn stone-hard dirt on hot summer days. The rust and gold forests of fall keep solemn watch over dried and bristly stubbled fields. I watch winter's icy haze embrace the rounded hills of Redemption Ridge and feel freezing winds challenge the swaying sycamores, oaks and willows that are guarding, always guarding Redemption Ridge, shielding its secrets from the world.

And yet, forever beckoning, the land and the money. Time has purified a portion of the money. It was used for good. For my children. Lamont, Brucie.

Still, the brooding land waits. For the sins of the fathers to be wiped away. There is still atonement. There are yet prices to be paid.

Will all my people ever return? I do pray so. How can they know their name, is my name? Not by rite of penned ritual, but by rite of flowing blood. What will it take, oh, God? How can I reach them? I need my name cleared, their name, not tainted. Until then, my peace may never be. I need my eternal rest.

Maybe one of the offspring of Brucie or Lamont will be the one to make amends, salvation to make this ground hallowed. Lamont's children? It could be. Or it may well be that my soldiered grandson will return and be the instrument of my eternal peace. He is the one who wandered these hills and wept over these graves. Maybe he'll see me in a shaft of dusty sunlight, or in a sparkling of moonshine as I see the molting bodies of the dead all around me.

And, oh, the stories they could tell. But that's for another soul. Not this one.

Now, hasten the day, dear Savior, when I shall sleep forever in the soil of Redemption Ridge.

Always I pray for peace. For my people. And for redemption. Then, perhaps my ghosts who have haunted me through these long years will fade away, and I shall weep no more.

Then, maybe, God willing, a new day will begin at Redemption Ridge.

Captain Bruce Claymore
Confederate States of America

CHAPTER 1

The hands of love
Wear bloody gloves,
Fondle strangers, made
Strange by the war.
Memory's hands are also red,
Picked up in a wet room
She strangled through.

They slip from her brother,
Slip from a man with a
Shock of red.

Wednesday Night, December, 1919

"Don't worry, Papa," Memory said, her blue eyes flashing. "I'll take care of Dale." When she hung up the hall phone, she saw the pair of fur-lined leather gloves on a marble-top table close to the front door. The gloves were ones that her brother had worn all the way through his time on the French front.

"Oh, Dale. What were you thinking?" She bit her full, pouty bottom lip in anger. "We've had an early snowfall and it's freezing outside. Someday you're going to hurt yourself or somebody else. I'm sick and tired of this." *Your brother is lost,* she reminded herself. *And yes, I do love him. I hurt with him. It's not easy, but I have to be strong for his sake.*

She put on her coat and hat and stuffed Dale's gloves into her coat pocket. She went outside and holding on to the iron rail so she wouldn't slip on the icy steps, got into the motorcar.

This was the second time this month she'd had their chauffer, Milton, drive her to Long Wharf, a part of Boston she wouldn't have visited otherwise.

Luckily, she spotted her brother right away. "There he is." Memory pointed to a streetlight that cast an amber glow in front of a tavern. "Dale's good friend, Mr. Jenson Cooper, called and told us Dale had been kicked out of the Lame Duck and this is where he'd be."

"Mr. Cooper's usually the one who tries to keep Mr. Dale on the straight and narrow," Milton said thoughtfully, "and he does a right smart job of it." The chauffeur pushed in the clutch, shifted to a low gear and carefully steered toward the curb.

"He usually goes around with Dale, but he's been tied up for a few days with some kind of veterans' meeting out of the city," Memory said.

She was relieved to see that the street was deserted except for her brother and two other people. A heavyset, short lady stood out front of a pub, and a tall, gray-haired, older gentleman grasped her arm with one hand, the other one raised to Dale. Even at a distance, if she hadn't known who he was, she could tell that the young man in a tattered, snow-flecked army overcoat was drunk or under the influence of something. *He's probably gotten hold of some of that illegal whiskey and bad cough medicine that makes him act funny,* she thought. In the past, if she had passed anybody like this on the street, she would have turned her back. Right now, she fluctuated between feeling helpless and angry. Her life was messed up too, but her brother was making it worse for both of them. For a brief moment her inclination was to stay in the motorcar.

Memory's breath cradled in her throat. She felt as if she were drowning. It was on the tip of her tongue to tell Milton to go on, but when she saw Dale touch the lady's shoulder, she decided. *Old habits of looking after a younger brother die hard.*

"Stop."

She pushed down the door handle, jumped out before the motorcar came to a complete stop and began making her way through piles of slushy snow to where the three people stood.

"Get away." The lady talking to Dale wore a puzzled, I-can-hardly remember-your-name look on her face.

"I knew you'd be here, Marianne," he said.

"Leave me alone," she said. "Leave me alone, Dale Von Dieter."

"You have no right to marry this man. You were engaged to my buddy, Samuel Stanton. I introduced you that time Samuel and

Jenson Cooper came from Mississippi to stay with me. He loved you. I vowed I'd bring him back to you."

She brought one hand up to her face as if to fend off a blow. "Samuel was shot."

"I was like his older brother. Jenson Cooper was my big buddy. Samuel was my little buddy back in Mississippi. They were both next to me in the trenches. You need to hear how it was." It seemed as if Dale had forgotten where he was. He looked up at the overcast brooding sky as if searching for something only he could see. "It rained all the time. We had a rough go of it. It wasn't just the shelling. Not just the gas. It was the runs. The influenza. We were tired. We were wet and cold. We coughed constantly."

He shivered, patted the silver whiskey flask in his pocket then drew his arms close around his body. "All we could think about was getting warm. I'd remember us talking about the heat when our family would visit Mississippi in the summer. The sun was so hot on your head you'd think you were roasting in Hades. And all these years later, sitting in the trenches, our teeth making more noise than drums in a band, it was a comfort of sorts to talk about that heat. It seemed to warm our very bones."

"You're not making sense," the man said, his breath puffing out in a cloud of steam. "Come on, Marianne; you've listened to enough of this. Get in the car."

"Wait just a minute," Dale said. "We were scared. My men sobbed for their families. I had heard those cries before back in Mississippi. When I was there in the summer, we slept on mattresses on the screened porch. Sometimes over the sounds of the katydids, whippoorwills and tree frogs, I could hear moans and sighs coming from an old Confederate battleground, Redemption Ridge." He clutched his fists. "My mama said it was the wind soughing in the pine trees, but I knew better. It was dying men on that battlefield calling for their mamas, wives and sweethearts."

"Marianne," the man said, "he's crazy."

"Samuel cried for you. I thought he'd make it. His legs had been cut off. He took shrapnel in the head." Dale's voice had a pleading sound to it. "He was carried to surgery. Didn't make it. I kept his legs. His legs came home."

13

"Get away from me!" the woman cried. "They buried him in France, in St. Dizier,"

"Most of him they did." Dale nodded. "This much I do know. I have some small part of him here. To carry home, where he begged to go."

"That's enough." The tall man elbowed Dale, almost knocking him over. "Come on, Marianne." He pulled her toward a parked motorcar.

"I know he was shot." Dale turned his head down into the bend of his elbow, wiped his mouth and then straightened. "God, I'm cold. God, we're all cold."

His face chiseled like a Greek statue, his eyes the blue-gray color of a winter storm, he continued to seek understanding, forgiveness.

Memory stood by Dale's side. "You look like you're freezing." She touched his arm, then pulled his gloves from her coat pocket. "Here," she said. "Put these on. Let's go home."

He snatched the gloves from her hand. "No," he groaned. "They have Samuel's blood on them." He cocked his arm and flung them at the couple. "He loved you. I hope you look at these every day. Think of Samuel when you do."

"You bastard. This is a lady. You don't treat ladies this way." The man grabbed up the gloves, threw them back and pushed his date into the car. "I have important friends in this city. You'll live to regret this."

"I didn't want to hurt anybody." Dale dropped his head into his hands.

"You're drunk, Dale. I've come to take you home." Memory picked up the gloves. "You need to sober up. I don't want you to embarrass me anymore."

"I just wanted her to understand. I tried to tell them in there"— He raised his head and cocked his chin toward a nearby tavern— "but they put me out."

Memory glared at the man with Marianne. "Gentlemen don't use crude language in front of a lady. I'm a lady too."

The car door slammed. The woman who seemed to swing between frightened and angry couldn't be seen now. The man with her swaggered arrogantly to the other side of the motorcar. "Your father may be an important man about Boston, but you will live to regret treating my fiancée in this manner, Mr. Dale Von Dieter. If we see a policeman, we're sending him after you."

"Don't. He's sick. Sometimes he thinks he's still back in the war. It's eating him alive." Her voice trembling, Memory put her hand across Dale's back. "I'll handle him," she called as the couple drove away.

She took her brother's arm and steered him toward their car. "Let's get him home, Milton."

"Our father may be a murderer." Dale glared at Memory.

"You've gotten that mixed up."

"He hurt our soldiers. He built warships in Scotland and has an armaments factory in Germany."

Out in the bay, a muzzled foghorn blew it's mournful, lonely call. "Evil needs to be stopped." Dale put his hands over his ears. "I hear a voice wafting from the end of the trench. One I've heard before. My men are dead. The guilty must pay," Dale snarled.

The stars are messages
from the treeline,
bullet holes in
the plank wall
of a chapel,
desperate
rings of light
to squint at prayers by.

"I'm well aware that you studied English at Ole Miss," Memory said. "And we thought you might someday marry your Mississippi sweetheart, Sam Stanton's sister, Laura Lee. But life isn't written in rhyme and meter. You're not making sense. Our father didn't do anything. You've got it all wrong in your head. Thanks to a great-aunt, his family owned part of a ship building company in Scotland. Our grandparents owned that steel factory in Germany. Now, get in the motorcar. Milton's taking us home."

The chauffeur adjusted the crank in their Ford Model T town car and started the motor. Memory took a deep breath as he drove slowly on the slick, snow-covered streets. She carried a picture inside her head of Dale as a little boy. Her holding him, fighting off another boy who had shoved her brother down. "I'll always fight for you," she whispered as Milton stopped at the entrance to the Von Dieter home, stepped from the car and opened the gate. When he started forward again, the motorcar slid sideways on the icy pavement, but Milton turned the wheel in the direction of the slide. The automobile straightened and he drove on up the winding drive to the front of the brick house.

"Come here, son." Their mother stood outside in front of the tall mahogany doors. Dale weaved and almost fell as they mounted the verandah steps. Brucie held her arm out, but he shook it off.

"I have no tears left in me," Dale muttered as he stumbled toward his room. "My father's a murderer. He helped kill my men."

***

Thursday noon

Right after lunch Dale pulled his sister aside just before she started up the staircase to her room. "Nasty rumors are floating around about your husband. If the wealthy Senator Peter Shields finds out what he's been doing behind his back with that policeman relative of his, Liam McRae, he'll kill Thornton. This family needs to do something."

"I don't want to hear it." Seeing her brother's face covered in a five-o'clock shadow, Memory reasoned he was still hung over from the night before. "I don't know what you're talking about, and neither do you." She didn't try to disguise her irritation with him. "And, where's that running buddy of yours, Jenson Cooper? Has he headed back to Mississippi yet?"

"He's around." Dale put his hand over his mouth, strangling a cough. He caught his breath and then reached back and slipped off a canvas haversack kit threaded across his shoulders. He opened it and took out a tarnished, silver cigarette case. He reached into his pants pocket and pulled out a match. He lit a cigarette and sucked in deeply. "Your husband thinks he can get away with anything. Thornton may get all of us in trouble," he continued in a raspy voice. "Are you still penning a log? Writing about him and this family?" He shook his head. "It's time for this family to wake up. Before it's too late for all of us."

"It runs in the family—someday you may become the family's premier poet," she said.

Although Dale had only been home from France a few weeks, he had not been himself since he returned from the Great War, and Memory was angry over the way it was affecting not only him, but her life as well. Mentally, he was a depressed, sick young man, and he made violent emotional swings, often ending in fantasies. He had been sprayed with mustard gas, but not as much as the men who fought under him. Because he was an officer in the war, he had been responsible for sending some of his friends into an ungodly nightmare, while others had been buried alive in the French trenches. He'd been through hell. Their mother, Brucie, made allowances for what Dale was doing with his life. "The term is shellshocked, and he's suffering," she said more times than Memory could count.

Memory was worn out with it. *My life isn't a bed of roses either. No happy, wishing-well thoughts. I can close my eyes,* she thought. *A stench of sweat overcomes me. A face looms. Breath leaves my lungs. My body yields to I do not know what.* She often felt like saying to her mother. *I strangle.*

Off balance, Dale swayed, then flattened himself against the wall. "Thornton's playing with fire," he said. "It's hard for the Senator to walk good with only one leg, and he's become pretty dependent on Liam McRae. So much so, that he's even set him up in a house on the edge of town. McRae's gotten out of line before, but he's family. The Senator will forgive his cousin's sins, but your husband better watch it. McRae will always do the dirty work, and the Senator will always take him back. I think if the truth were known, both of these men have something on each other. No matter about that though. If he doesn't straighten up, Thornton may end up a dead dog."

"He's not doing anything, and nobody knows what you're talking about," Memory muttered. Truth to tell, she was sick and tired of both of them. She felt like she was living on borrowed time with her husband, and her brother was an embarrassment and a deadweight. Last night had been the worst time she'd had with Dale yet.

Now, standing in front of his sister in the hall, Dale looked a lot better than he did last night. "Your husband needs to do some listening," he said. "That powerful Senator who Thornton works for may have to use crutches or a cane to get around on his wooden leg. But he says one thing about how his left leg got cut off, and there are disturbing rumors that say something else."

"I don't believe much of what I hear," Memory said.

"For your own protection, you and Thornton might want to do some checking. According to Senator Shields, he lost that leg in a streetcar accident. Says he saved a child from being run over. What other people who aren't beholden to the Senator say though, is late one night he was down on the waterfront, drunk and doing something weird. According to that account, it had to do with a troubled veteran sailor suddenly missing some of his body parts. The sailor had a buddy who took exception to what had happened. He chloroformed the Senator and sawed off his leg. Then he held a commemorative ceremony. The Senator's extremity was tossed into the bay for fish bait."

Memory shifted uncomfortably.

"And if that policeman cousin of his, hadn't come along, the good Senator might not be here today," Dale went on. "A few days later though, when the ship sailed away, one of the crew was missing. To this very day, no one knows for sure what happened to the man. The troubled sailor, if there ever was one, couldn't talk. The story was, he was hanging from the rafters in a brothel down on the waterfront. The tips of his fingers had been cut off with a cigar trimmer and his tongue sliced out. The official line, or so they say, was that he killed himself. But I'm here to tell you, he couldn't cut his fingers and chop out his own tongue. Again, all of this is rumor. My sources also say Liam McRae and the Senator each have something on the other one. And this may be part of it."

Dale hesitated as if trying to make up his mind whether or not to go on. "One of these days, when I feel better, I'm going to run down that rumor," he said. "And, of course, it's well-known that the Senator's an excellent poker player. He makes a big deal of putting his winnings into that wooden leg of his and then he donates the money to 'his men,' the wounded veterans.

"But in the meantime, as vindictive as the Senator is, the rest of our family will be in trouble if Thornton doesn't straighten up."

"I'll say something to my husband," Memory said, wanting to get her brother off her back. "But I don't know what you're talking about. Thornton's worked hard, and Senator Shields has been good to him." She had heard something of those malicious rumors but didn't believe them. The Senator was one of the best-known men in Boston, and honestly, sometimes she kind of liked to throw his name around.

Dale clutched the lapels of the army greatcoat he enshrouded himself in most of the time, pulled it tighter and walked unsteadily through the hall. He swung open the heavily carved door. His combat boots sloshed as he tromped down the icy steps.

Turning away, she walked up the graceful staircase that swept up to a top floor landing. Memory shook her head as she went to her bedroom. Even though she and Thornton weren't getting along, as she had done so often now, she put her brother's ramblings about her husband down to his war memories and his drinking.

She was getting ready to change clothes and dress for their evening meal when there was a tapping on her door. "Miss Memory." Elnora, the downstairs maid stuck her head in the room. "Your husband called, and he said for me not to set him a place at the dinner table tonight. He'll be working."

"Again?" Memory bit her bottom lip. "I'm not surprised, and I really don't give a fig," she whispered to herself. "I'm sure Thornton's doing some important state business for the Senator," she answered.

***

Thursday evening

Memory had dropped out of Wheaton College before she graduated when she met Thornton. They had been married for almost four years, but there were problems from the beginning. Thornton worked for McAllister's Hardware Company; about a year ago there was talk about large sums of money missing from a cash drawer in his department. The two of them were renting rooms fairly close to the Von Dieter's home, but when Thornton lost his job, they gave them up. His elderly parents had passed away several years ago, so since the firing, they lived with her parents, the Von Dieters. Memory's mother, Brucie, a very kind person, was tolerant of Thornton, but her father, Herschel, had a hard time with rumors of stolen money and of his son-in-law being out of work for several months. In the early fall things began looking up. Thornton was hired; not a job this time, but he was given a position on the staff of the well-known Senator Peter Shields, a much-respected elder statesman who had gained nationwide recognition because of his work with veterans. According to talk around Boston, Thornton, one of the "smart boys" was moving up and making a name for himself. He was one of the Senator's inner circle. He seemed to have been hand-picked by the politician to give him special aid and assistance because of the trouble the Senator sometimes had with his artificial limb, going back to that streetcar accident.

Thornton was not that much older than many of the returned veterans. He and the Senator's policeman cousin, Liam McRae, seemed to have a natural rapport with some of the troubled young men. Thornton's rapport did not include a friendly relationship with his brother-in-law, Dale.

Memory came down the steps dressed for dinner just as her father walked out of the library with a brandy in his hand.

"Thornton got in touch with Elnora," she said. "He has a very important meeting with an out-of-work client this evening, so he won't be joining us for dinner."

"Vell, that seems to be happening quite a bit lately." Herschel Von Dieter held open the parlor door for his daughter, and when he did, he spied a business card on the floor. He bent over, picked it up and read:

<u>Senator Peter Shields</u>
My door's always open.
Just come on in.
You'll be welcome.

"Ah," Von Dieter said. "This makes me feel better." He pointed to a handwritten note which had been added to the bottom of the card, *"See you at six thirty."*

"This has got to be it. I asked Thornton to set up a meeting for Dale. I believe your brother has made an appointment vith the Senator. Your brother needs to be a man. If anybody can help him and us, it'll be Peter Shields."

When Memory wasn't exasperated about her brother's situation, she allowed herself to give credit to Jenson Cooper, where credit was due. "No," she said. "I think you're heading in the wrong direction. Cooper has really looked after him since they got back from the war. I wouldn't count on the Senator."

Jenson was not much older than Memory. She had a few vague but pleasant memories of those long-ago years when they spent their summers at Redemption Ridge. Now that they were both grown, calling him Mr. Cooper sounded strange to her ears, but she was a married woman. "Mr. Cooper's been staying with friends, trying to help Dale get his life back together."

"Before he vas murdered, his grandfather, old Sheriff Bramlett did all right. He invested in land and cotton, but Jenson Cooper vasn't to 'the manor born.' I don't trust any of your mother's old friends," Von Dieter said. "He'll be history soon. I'll grant you this, though. Guess it vas nice of him vhen he heard Dale vas enlisting to sign up vith him."

He cleared his throat. "I'm sure he'll be heading back south. He still has family in Mississippi. Mr. Cooper's grandfather's dead, but he helped your mother over some hard times." He checked his watch. "Almost six." He tapped the card then laid it on the hall table. "Ve should have some input in this meeting. I need you to go vith me. All your brother needs to do is to be a man," he said, a familiar, irritating note of self-righteousness in his voice.

This is not a good idea, Memory told herself. Dale had worshipped his father when he was a child, but that had ended abruptly with the war. Unfortunately, he had gotten some strange ideas in his head about Von Dieter manufacturing war materials. *And whiskey and that strong cough medicine Dale drinks makes it worse.*

"I keep telling him that. Dale vill listen to you, if he'll hear anybody. Your mother has a church circle meeting so ve've no set time for dinner.

"If ve leave now"—Her father's voice cut into her thoughts—"ve can be there right before your brother's appointment."

"Dale didn't say anything to me about seeing the Senator." She had just received some photographs from a friend who had taken a Cunard cruise and all she wanted to do right now was look at them and make a decision on when she and Thornton could go, then catch her father at the right time.

"He might not vant us to know, but he's asking for help. I feel ve should be there." His jaw set, Von Dieter's blue eyes narrowed into a familiar determined look. "I vant to find out vhat to do for your brother," he said. "If you care about him, you'll go vith me. The Senator has influence all over Boston."

An awkward silence hung between them, and it seemed as if neither one would budge. *I might as well give in*, Memory realized, *if I'm going to ask father to help pay for a cruise.*

"Okay." She slipped her hat, coat and gloves off the back of a chair in the entry hall. As they turned to leave, she picked up the business card and slid it into her coat pocket. She heard the rumble of the motorcar; their chauffeur, who had already been summoned, waited in the front drive. They circled through the driveway onto Beacon Street. Once Milton was out of the neighborhood, he drove through several streets to State Street, then got onto Atlantic Avenue. Memory had bad feelings about this venture, an almost overwhelming sense of foreboding, as if things would never be the same. *This is silly,* she thought. There was nothing she could put her finger on, but she felt there was something wrong. She and her mother, Brucie, were known among their friends as having second-sight and right now a voice in her head screamed, *Don't go. You won't like what you see.*

"I don't think we should do this," she said as they pulled to a stop under a streetlight in front of the Senator's office. There was no answer from her father. He had gotten out ahead of her and, moving like a soldier on parade, was already striding toward the entrance. Memory pulled the card from her pocket. The other side was face up, and she saw more writing in the same hand.

The esteemed public servant, and our employer, Senator Peter Shields, is out of town, and I asked my police captain for the day off. Looking forward to having some fun with you. Be sure and bring the baby oil. Always, L.

Her heart pounding, "Wait," Memory called, running to catch her father. "I don't know who this is, but it's not Dale."

She was close behind, but Von Dieter was already in the Senator's office. She heard a jingly sound and saw that her father had stumbled over a pair of silver-spurred riding boots in front of a closed door. He almost fell but he managed to right himself, and shoved the door open just as Memory caught up with him. "Oh God," he said, his lips barely moving. He grabbed his daughter's elbow as she came in. He tried to swing her around, but she saw what her father tried to hide from her. Thornton and another man with a storm of red hair lay nude upon the sofa in a spooned position.

Uneven footsteps pounded behind them. Someone without a plumb gait burst through the door, almost knocking Memory and her father over.

Silhouetted from an overhead light, a thick-chested, dark figure swaying on crutches shoved them aside as if they had been nothing more than a small tree branch that was in the way. "I'll kill you, Thornton!" Senator Shields shouted, slashing down with one crutch. "Damn you. You're mine."

As Von Dieter pulled his daughter on down an icy sidewalk and toward their motorcar, behind her she heard the sound of glass shattering.

On the drive home, her father gasped several times as if he had been punched in the stomach and then he sat hunched over. They said nothing to each other. She felt by the way he acted he wasn't sure she had seen the sordid scene. Or if he did, he chose to ignore it as he often did unpleasant things. It seemed as if for Von Dieter, if he didn't pay attention to bad things, they would disappear.

The scene in the Senator's office flooded Memory with a mixture of anger and relief. A faint smiled flickered across her lips.

***

Before midnight Memory moved from the room she shared with Thornton to another floor. She left a note on his pillow. "You'll never touch me again."

The next morning at breakfast, mouth set in an angry grimace, her thunderbolt eyes cast down, she sat across from him. "If it eases your mind," he said, "from the very beginning I never wanted to touch you."

When she looked up, she saw that Thornton had a puffy left cheek and a large purple ring circled his blood-shot right eye. His lower lip was almost twice its normal size.

He held up her note and tore it into shreds.

"Aren't you a pretty boy?" she said.

He pointed to his face. "I slipped on the steps."

"Stay out of my way," she whispered. "I'm done."

"I was done before we ever started," he said, "and from now on I'll do as I damn well please." But there was a quivery, I'm-walking-on-thin-ice timbre in his usually self-assured voice.

Later that afternoon as she was putting her clothes into an armoire, Dale came into her new room smoking a cigarette and in a drunken stupor. "Something bad's going to happen. Word's out all along the waterfront. The peg-legged Senator's going to kill your husband." He drew in a deep breath and threw his head back as if his cares and worries would fade like the smoke drifting toward the ceiling. "Our ever-loving father's threatened to expose the Senator's little den of iniquity. The honorable Hersehel Von Dieter doesn't know who he's messing with. Mr. McRae, that pretty boy, redheaded cousin of the Senator can get out of line, but woe be unto anyone else who crosses the Senator. Peter Shields has the final say on anything that happens in Boston. He and the powers that be will strangle us."

Dale's body stiffened. He snapped his fingers. "Pass the word. When I say charge, we go over the top."

Memory wanted to take her brother by the shoulders and shake some sense into him. "Stop it." She shoved him out the door. "You're thinking crazy, and you're not in France."

Her mother had been hinting that they might go to Redemption Ridge and stay there. That was not what Memory had on her mind. Now that this marital war was almost over, she was ready for that overseas cruise. "I'm ready to board a ship. I need a ray of light in my life. A rainbow in this dark sky."

And, the way she felt right now, she'd find a way to set sail. Without her husband.

CHAPTER 2

His funeral was
A cold marriage.
The details weren't public,
But his two wounds
Were bright as eyes
In her privacy.

A chance meeting
Between woman and beast,
A cold wedding
In the wilderness.

Her future prowls the
Ridge like a panther,
Long thought gone
From Mississippi.

Friday Night, January 30, 1920

Memory pushed the red velvet drapes aside, leaned on the antique library table and looked out the window. Sparkling as if sprinkled with diamonds, ten inches of new-fallen snow blanketed the ground. She traced her initials in the condensation. MEVD, then shook her head. *No. Still, MVDH.*

Memory pulled out a chair, sat down and took a silver nail file with a pearl handle from her beaded bag. Pushing up her blouse sleeve she began to dig into her arm as if she were tunneling out a worrisome insect.

"Ouch." She sighed deeply, laid down the nail file and dabbed the blood with a pink handkerchief she always kept with her. She twisted thick strands of her gold-tinged auburn hair into a tight bun on the back of her neck and secured it with hairpins.

That done, she sighed, unlocked the top middle drawer and lifted a Bible from the drawer. It fell open to the page with her wedding certificate. *My problems didn't begin when I changed my last name from Von Dieter to Hastings. They started long before then.*

Memory took out her leather-bound journal that lay under the Bible and once again began to write.

My brother. The War. The gassings. Those were the crowning blows for Dale. My brother, the crown prince, the poet laureate of this family, had never worried about anything in his life. Until France and the trenches. He returned, not a crown prince, but a wounded warrior.

My mother. Oh, to God, if I could tell her I do know some of her story. That time will come though. Of that, I'm certain.

And, my misery? Someday God will unlock the mystery to me. Until then, I can only know my hell began with something that looked like a crushed strawberry. I see it in my dreams. It fills my mouth. It chokes me.

And husband Thornton? He was only a bystander.

***

As Memory expected, her mother, Brucie, had given her the obligatory, uncomfortable, mother-daughter talk before the wedding vows were taken. From the beginning, almost from the moment she and Thornton Percy Hastings III, exchanged rings, it wasn't moonshine and rosewater perfume for her. Memory didn't tell her mother that although the marriage had been consummated in the Biblical sense on their wedding night, Thornton had returned to their marital bed only a few times since. On those occasions he was usually drunk. There were other disappointments she had to endure. She had been raised to be her "daddy's girl" and expected to get her way, but this came to an abrupt halt when she became a Mrs. The ground rules were that Thornton was the one to be catered to and to be pleased. Brucie was very intuitive. Memory could tell by the way her mother looked at her that she knew something was wrong. She tried to bring it up a time or two, but Memory shied away from discussing her problems. After almost four years, she had accommodated and taken the path of least resistance with Thornton. She hadn't cared too much what happened in her marriage.

She laid the wedding certificate aside and lifted an envelope under it. She raised the flap and turned the envelope upside down. Several newspaper clippings fell out, a front-page write-up about the murder, the obituary, and a public service announcement.

The murder article had been in the headlines a short time ago and had covered most of the front page, but Memory just glanced at it. She had read this piece of news so many times it was seared into her mind. According to Boston police, the motive in Thornton Percy Hastings's death was robbery, pure and simple. The dastardly deed had taken place right after the Greenfield Park Zoo closed. There were a lot of desperate poor people and drifters on the streets since the war ended. The thieves vanished into the dark and according to the police there was no way to track them. The few friends Memory had left took the crime at face value; what they read in the papers and heard on the radio was the way it happened. It was simpler for them. She knew better. Although they might have doubts, she wasn't at liberty to straighten them out. Her lips were sealed. Explosive secrets and influential people lay behind her husband's death.

Of course, the family knew there was much more to the story. The gruesome details of her husband's death were not recounted. There was no way for her family to prove it, but word on the streets was that Thornton's rich, influential lover, Senator Peter Shields had greased the palms of someone on the police force to take care of an embarrassing personal problem. The killer had slammed Thornton onto the spread-point picket railings around the Greenfield Zoo. It was done slowly. Thornton was pushed down onto the black metal spikes and rocked from side to side, slowly, one side at a time. The wounds were boiled and burned. Boric acid had been poured into each open puncture. None of this was mentioned at the funeral, only that a well-known, well-thought-of Boston citizen had been robbed and murdered and that the investigation into his death was ongoing.

Memory put the murder account back into the envelope. She then smoothed out Thornton's obituary and began to read.

On Friday, January twenty-third, in the year of our Lord nineteen hundred and twenty, Thornton Percy Hastings III, a member of one of the most respected families in our city passed on to Glory. The obsequies were held in the Emmanuel Episcopal Church. As two o'clock drew near, which was the hour fixed for the funeral, a large crowd gathered in the building and spilled over onto the street. The prayers in the church were recited by the Rector Plakin and his assistant, Rector O'Keeffe. They also officiated at the solemn ceremonies at the graveside, adding a feeling of refinement to this solemn, heartrending and perplexing occasion.

The police continue to search the area of the Greenfield Zoo for possible vagrants who may have been the perpetrators, not only robbing Mr. Hastings of some of his worldly goods, but of depriving him of his very life. Senator Peter Shields has taken a personal interest in this dastardly deed and has instructed the police chief to put Sergeant Liam McRae in charge of this ongoing investigation.

There were many beautiful wreaths placed on the grave and when the internment had taken place all knelt and prayed for the repose of the soul of the dead. At the same hour, all the entrances to the Greenfield Zoo were closed for the whole duration of this solemn occasion, as were temporary feedings of the animals.

Mr. Herschel Von Dieter, Mr. Hastings's venerated father-in-law said, "God was good, especially to my daughter, Memory Elaine Hastings. He sent sunshine to us, on this, a day of extreme sadness to our family. God was good."

From the time Thornton was murdered, Mr. Von Dieter, known to be a very stoic man, always in control of his feelings, surprisingly, had shed reams of tears. The whole tragedy was a two-edged sword. The tears were not just because of Thornton's ungodly murder. Von Dieter had threatened to reveal rumors not only about his son-in-law and his lovers, but also the Senator's shady life. Namely, that of a sinful dalliance with a policeman. With that, war was declared. Senator Shields would fight back and unfortunately, he had all the ammunition. Even before Thornton's murder, rumors began to spread about Herschel Von Dieter owning munitions and mustard gas factories in Germany during the Great War. Which, even though it was not true, Memory's father had been helpless to dispel.

It was apparent the Senator was out to destroy the whole Von Dieter family. Spoken only in whispers by those present at the funeral but understood by many was that not only was his son-in-law dead, the family's reputation was gone. Von Dieter had lost most of his money in a few short weeks. For years, his overseas ship-building business with Germany and Scotland had flourished. It ground to a halt with Germany during the war but had picked up considerably since mid-November. Almost overnight, thanks to the Senator, his business dealings in the state of Massachusetts slammed shut. The public servant who had been in the shadow of their lives became a deadly menace to the Von Dieters. Sentiment was strong in Boston social circles against the whole family.

Memory looked at the obituary again. More than once she thought the write-up had been kind to Thornton Percy. She put her fingers on the line, *"passed on to Glory."*

"I'm not so sure about that," she said. "I don't like what you've done to my family, Thornton Percy Hastings the Third. Thank God there won't be a fourth." She put the obituary back into the envelope.

"But Senator, even with destroying a family's reputation and even with a killing, you weren't quite done with us, were you? You and your high-powered connections rubbed it in."

She held up the last piece that was in the envelope; a public service announcement. "The Greenfield City Zoo will be closed for the weekend in remembrance of the death of Thornton Percy Hastings, III. Everyone in the area is advised to be alert for the murder suspects."

Memory started to put the announcement into the envelope with the murder write-up and the obituary, but she stopped. Instead she took a moment and thought back to the day of Thornton's funeral. Services done, everyone but her parents had gone. She was just about to join them in the library that day when she heard her mother and father talking.

Something in the tone of her father's voice alerted her to wait a moment before she went in. "Dale must be more careful," she heard him say. "He goes down to the vaterfront, vhere some of those good-for-nothing ex-soldiers hang out, and he gets drunk. He stops people, trying to get them vorked up over the var. The var's over and done vith. If he keeps this up, the police vill be vatching for him.

"And that's not all." Her father's voice trembled. "I received a terrible phone call a short vhile ago vhen ve got in from the cemetery. The caller had a message for me." He cleared his throat as if it were hard for him to speak, and then went on. "I could be after you next. Or your son. In vorse vays than a tarnished reputation. So, keep your mouth shut. And make sure your son does too."

Memory felt sick. She leaned against the wall and put her face in her hands.

"I'm desperate, Brucie," her father said. "All I know to do is sail to Germany. Then England and Scotland. Make my contacts again and start over. Vhile in Dusseldorf I'm sure I can find some specialized help for Dale. Certainly better than vhat I can find in this country. Most of all, I need to see about some of my business holdings.

"You've alvays taken care of our family, Brucie," he said, as if that settled things. "I know you'll continue to do so."

"I'll take care of things here the best I can." Brucie spoke in a subdued voice. "We might return to Mississippi. To Redemption Ridge."

"No," Memory breathed angrily to herself. "I don't want to go to Mississippi." Guilt gnawed at her for just a moment. It was natural that her mother would want to return; it seemed as if Redemption Ridge was in her very bones. Getting away from Boston might be best for her brother, but it wasn't what she wanted. Maybe when spring came, and if there was somehow, suddenly, enough money she and some of her friends could make a grand tour of Europe. She wanted a new start. There was much sadness and anger she needed to put behind her. She started to go into the room, but her father spoke again.

"And now, there's something else. I hardly even know how to tell you this. That vasn't all the man told me," her father said in a strangled voice. "For more reasons than vun, it vas good ve had a closed coffin. Thornton's sexual organs vere cut off vhile he vas still alive. The panthers had a feast last veekend."

Memory ran down the hall and onto the back porch. She threw open the door, ran down the steps, fell onto the icy snow and retched, over and over again.

***

Memory picked up a picture in a carved rosewood frame of Thornton made on their wedding day. His thick, dark-brown hair swooped down in a curve over one eye. He had a habit of flipping it away from his face. Just as often, he had flipped her from his life. She took the picture from the frame and laid it on the desk. She put the murder write up, the obituary, and photo together, and carefully folded them into a smaller and smaller square. She placed them into the envelope and licked it shut.

She bent over and reached into her bag. She took out her nail file and dug under her left thumbnail. "Ouch," she whispered and dropped the nail file back into her bag.

She got up from the chair, stretched and looked out the window. A pale sun had almost set; afternoon had fallen to a shadowy darkness. She walked to the fireplace and stirred the embers with a poker.

"Well thanks to you, Mr. Thornton Percy Hastings the Third, there'll probably be no Cunard sailing for me this spring," she muttered. A pouty expression on her face, she pressed down with the toe of one foot, as if she were trying to kill something alive and crawling in their Aubusson carpet. "Maybe never. And all these black clothes I have to wear right now make my skin look as sallow as a chicken bone." She sighed and threw the envelope into the flames. "I don't want to go to Redemption Ridge. But I may have no choice."

Memory had left out one piece that had been in the envelope, the newspaper notice about the zoo being closed. She picked up a

33

pen and wrote across the bottom, "Henceforth and forevermore, this part of my life is over." She put it into the Bible, right where she felt it should be, by Psalm thirty-one, verse seventeen. *"My bones are pierced in me at night, and my gnawing pains take no rest."*

CHAPTER 3

Sounds ring out in Boston
Hearts beat
Of brick and steel.
Balls dropped in the dark
Knocking down spines
Like stones in a
Tin Shaft

Fewer memories in Mississippi?
Or just
Younger fewer angles
As faltering steps stumble
On their lonesome journey
To a closed armoire
With fewer keys

Monday Morning, February 16

Memory smelled the scent of gardenias as her mother swept past her and sank onto a velvet loveseat in the front parlor. She noticed that Brucie clutched the same dog-eared letter to her breast she had seen her carrying around for several days. She set the letter beside her and flattened her hand across it as if to make sure it stayed where she'd put it.

"We may need to go to Mississippi," Brucie said in a firm, don't-argue-with-me voice. "I don't know for how long. I told you about this letter from Lamont. Redemption Ridge has no overseer. He and his wife left in the middle of the night and took some of the old family silver with them. It may not be seemly for us to leave Boston right now, but we may have no choice but to travel South. To take care of business."

"What about Papa?" Memory asked.

"You and I both know he had a hard time facing what was going on here. But more importantly, your father's overseas trying to get money from some of his investments. Maybe sell what we have there. All our income in this country has been shut down. Nothing of the Von Dieters' can be unloaded, not only in Boston Harbor, but on the whole East Coast."

"He should have gotten rid of his business in Germany years ago," Memory said. "Before that awful war."

"Young lady, for years that factory supported you in a fine style. We made a lot of money off our overseas investments," Memory's mother reminded her.

"Dale thinks father secretly produced mustard gas in the one in Dusseldorf," Memory mumbled.

"Your brother is dead wrong." Brucie reached up and rubbed her head.

"And speaking of your brother, Bruce Tisdale Von Dieter. We're probably going to need for Milton to crank the motorcar. You and I'll have to go look for him. Again," she said. "I have a feeling that he's down in that bad section of town, getting into who in the world knows what. Every now and then he mumbles something about taking care of his friend's legs. Says it's up to him to get them home. It doesn't make sense."

"I'm sick to death of this family," Memory said. "Call Jenson Cooper. He follows Dale around like a lost puppy most of the time."

A vigilant guard dog, more likely. He looked after Dale when you all were just little kids at Redemption Ridge. Brucie took a long breath and slowly let it out. *So much has been taken out of our hands.*

Right now, with her husband, Herschel, in Germany, he seemed far removed from her life. *My family may not agree with my plans, but I'm going to do what I think best.*

"We've had a lot of tragedy lately," Brucie said. "More than our share. Thornton's murder just a few short weeks ago. Your brother's mental condition." She looked thoughtful, as if searching for the answer to a question. "And thanks to Senator Peter Shields we're ruined here. With your father sailing off for no telling how long, I have to do something to help all of us.

"This move. It may well be a blessing in disguise," she said, half to herself and half to her daughter. "It may be permanent."

Memory tossed her hair from her face. "God help me, the last place I want to go to is Mississippi."

"Don't take the Lord's name in vain."

"Why don't you just send Dale to Redemption Ridge when Jenson Cooper decides to go back home?" Memory asked. She knew Jenson and her brother were very close. Dale had opted not to go to college in Boston but was talking about returning to Mississippi where he and Jenson had attended the University of Mississippi together. They both lacked only one year of graduating. Jenson had meant a lot to Dale, and when Memory allowed herself to think about it, also to her. He had been a part of their childhood during their summers at Redemption Ridge. Not just for Dale, but for her too. She was aware that loyalty to her brother overrode anything Jenson might personally want to do, but he was there for all of them. And now that he'd come back into their lives, there was something unsettling about the way he looked at her, as if he remembered way back to when they were children and he had stolen a few innocent kisses from her. Now, she was a new widow. Stolen kisses would not be innocent. Even to this day, she remembered how they had felt, how his lips had tasted. She almost wished for the clock to turn back to the days that could have been. Even when they were kids, Jenson's kisses had been more exciting than Thornton's had ever been. And now she knew hers had not meant much to Thornton.

"Mr. Cooper has a lot of respect for Dale," Brucie said. "I am so blessed that for the moment he's willing to help him live through this nervous condition. Back when they were children, being older, Jenson always took it upon himself to look after Dale. Now that they're grown, and were together in the war, he's well aware of the kind of man your brother has become."

"From where I'm sitting, unless something changes, the two of them need to hop a freight and leave here. Mr. Cooper needs to start chopping cotton, running a plantation," Memory said. But she didn't really mean her words. Jenson's broad shoulders suggested strength, and he was a handsome man, she admitted to herself.

Probably the best-looking man she'd ever laid eyes on. She was just worn out with everything and everybody. "And, I need to get on with my life here in Boston."

"Your brother. He's not in any condition to take over anything, Memory Elaine." Brucie's voice gave away how upset she was. "I'm worried sick about both of you. Maybe this is what we as a family need, to return to our roots. I just have to go with what my heart tells me."

"So, it won't be a surprise and so you'll know where I stand, I'm really thinking about not going," Memory said, just loud enough for Brucie to hear. She saw her mother close her eyes and duck her chin as if she'd been hit, but she was going to go full steam ahead with her plans. "I've got my whole life ahead of me now. My friends are probably sledding and going to hot chocolate parties. Down there in Mississippi there's nothing but brown slush from all that rain. They have stray cats. They have fleas. I hate it. And I've some catching up to do here in Boston."

***

Brucie nervously pleated and unpleated a thick wool scarf draped across her shoulders. *I have so much to take care of,* she thought to herself. She had her hand out to turn the chifforobe key, when she caught a glimpse of herself in the mirror. She pressed her forehead against the cool glass, afraid of what she'd see, then she stepped back. She had had so much on her mind she'd not paid any attention to the way she looked in months. Despite everything they had been through, it did make her feel better to see that although she felt a lot older than her fifty-seven years, she still had very few wrinkles; she had not aged overnight. Her thick wavy hair was invaded by only a few strands of gray. Her russet hair rolled into a tight ball, she unpinned it and flung her head. *I don't care how I look. That's the least of my worries.*

Elnora, one of the few maids still employed by the Von Dieter family, came into the room just as Brucie opened the chifforobe door.

"I'll be going through clothes and getting rid of those I won't be using," Brucie said. "Then I'll see what I'm carrying to Mississippi. We won't be gone long. But I have business to take care of.

"I'm putting those I'm not taking in that trunk at the foot of the bed."

As she handed stacks of clothes to Elnora, Brucie was aware that the young, thick-hipped maid's rustling skirt and quick movements gave away her impatient feelings. Not only did she have trouble with her children, almost open rebellion was brewing in the air with what household help she had left.

"The way I see it, we have no choice," she said. "And Miss Memory may think she won't be going, but she's wrong. She won't get her way on this."

With the two of them working, it didn't take long to fill the trunk. Brucie closed the lid and snapped the iron locks on either side. Elnora then turned the large key in the middle. She pulled the trunk close to a big walnut armoire next to the bedroom door, and wiped the key on her apron. She handed it to Brucie who put it into her skirt pocket. Elnora started to leave the room, but Brucie waved her back. "If you would, I'd like to go through some of our summer clothes. They're in the armoire. Now would be as good a time as any, to take them out of mothballs and air them out."

Elnora moved over and unlocked both doors to the wardrobe. She then stepped back, tapped her feet and blew out an exasperated breath as if she didn't like what she saw. A pouty look on her face, she carried several armloads of skirts, blouses and coats to the bed and dropped them on the blue silk spread.

"When we arrive down south, we'll have need of lighter clothes. Even if we're just there for a month or two." As if she were already thinking ahead, Brucie threw her heavy scarf into a chair.

"With as much snow as we've had here in Boston, right now, Mississippi sounds like the promised land," she said. *And not just because of the warm weather*. What her husband and family didn't know was, that even though they were out of money here in Boston, Brucie had hidden financial assets in Franklin, Mississippi. Long years ago, when she was just a thirteen-year-old child and Brucie's Cousin Sarah brought her to live in Boston, she and her old childhood friend, Lamont, were aware of hidden treasure from their dead father, the disgraced Confederate Captain, Bruce Claymore. Cousin Sarah had seen that a small amount of these assets was used and invested wisely. Although she had been dead for years, Brucie had breathed many times, "Thank you, Cousin Sarah."

On his own, Lamont had also carefully bought up a few businesses and more land for the two of them, all in the name of Brucie Tisdale Von Dieter. Brucie and Lamont knew it wouldn't be seemly for a white lady and a colored man to own property together, so their transactions had been handled by a trusted lawyer back in Franklin.

"It's all happened so fast. I'm not sure how long we're staying, but I should know by the first of next week exactly when we're leaving," Brucie said.

I'm crumbling inside, she thought, *but trying to go through the motions of keeping up what appearances I can.* A few days ago, when she received Lamont's letter, she thought about it for only a short while.

On her own, she had made an important decision, and she had sent their chauffer to the post office with her answer to Lamont. When Milton drove away, Brucie felt as if she had not only her life, but also her family's lives in her hands.

Lamont, she had written. *Yes. I will come. I always felt in my bones that someday I would come home, and now the time seems right for me and mine to return to Redemption Ridge. My two children, Memory and Dale, are young adults, but already life hasn't been too kind to them. I feel a call deep within me to go back to where it all began. But I will extend this stay for a long as I can. We do have business to take care of. In so many ways.*

As you said, the two of us are getting older, and we have seen and lived through so many changes. Good and bad. Other than my children, there's no one on this green earth I feel closer to than you. You, my friend, have done more for this family than I could ever imagine, and have done it well.

Your mother always took such good care of both of us. I will miss Vernell to my dying day. Of course, as you and I both know, there is that bond between us.

She almost added that blood bond. Our father, Bruce Claymore's blood, but decided against it. It was an unspoken, but strong, link between her and Lamont Randall.

It's all been set in motion, she thought. *Lamont should have received my letter by now.*

Elnora's voice broke into her thoughts. "Ma'am." The maid tilted her nose up and her lips formed into a slight sneer. "I jest wonder what Mr. Von Dieter's gonna say ta ya when he finds oot ya all have packed up, closed this house, an' moved away from here. Best tell yer children what yer up to."

"It won't be a surprise," Brucie answered, even though that was not the whole truth. "We've talked about it many times. I'm not sure when my husband's coming back from Germany, but he'll join us when he does."

She was aware that quite some time ago her once respectful Irish maid had lost esteem for the whole Von Dieter family, as had what was left of the household staff, save Milton. Brucie had never given many directions on running the house, but just the fact that she was around insured certain standards would be upheld. That was no longer true. The beds were made late, or not at all. Their meals were no longer on time, and a heavy coating of dust lay over most of the furniture. Most of all, Brucie wasn't used to being treated with disdain.

"I've seen them bill collectors hangin' 'round." Although Elnora muttered the words, Brucie heard what she said. She was tempted to dismiss the maid then and there but decided instead to ignore the haughty tone in her voice and her remark. She had enough money in their Boston bank account to take care of food and travel expenses and to pay what was left of their household staff. For the time being, she still needed Elnora to pack up and help close their house for good.

She turned away so that the maid couldn't see her face. There was a harsh, unspoken realty to Brucie and her children about moving back to Mississippi. She hadn't exactly told a lie, but she wasn't all that sure when her husband would be coming back from Europe. He did have pressing business interests to take care of in Dusseldorf and Edinburgh. But since those malicious rumors had been spread about Herschel here in Boston, he had drawn into himself. The whole family had been deeply hurt. There was also the growing resentment Dale had toward his father. Memory was also showing signs of it. So, Herschel had been more than ready to leave.

Brucie went to the hearth of their bedroom fireplace, picked up a poker and stirred the ashes. "You don't know where Memory is, do you?"

An irritated look on her face, Elnora put her hands on her hips. "Last I seen of yer daughter, she was downstairs."

"I'm worried about both my children. Being in those horrible French trenches didn't just make my son sick," Brucie mused, more to herself than to the maid. "It nearly killed him. Dale's not the same person he used to be."

"Uh-huh." Elnora shrugged her shoulders and raised her hand to her mouth. "An' him, Jaysus," she muttered behind her fist. "If he don't kill himself or somebody else one of these days, I'm goin' ta be surprised."

Brucie trembled with frustration. She had just about had enough of the maid's insolence. Maybe, despite how much she needed Elnora, it was time to let her go. Again, she urged herself to have patience. It wouldn't be for too much longer. "That's enough for now," she said. "You can go on downstairs."

"That's not quite everythin' oot of the armoire. There's jest one more thing that needs tendin' to." Rocking from side to side and walking as if her shoes were packed with heavy rocks, Elnora went back to the armoire. She bent over and ran her hand under something on the bottom shelf. She scooped up a small bundle and set it on top of the closed steamer trunk. "I've seen this before," she said smugly. "There's a rotten quilt. An' some baby clothes wrapped in it." Her voice rose, almost as if she had something to be excited about.

The dropped fireplace poker rang out on the brick hearth, like a metal hammer striking iron. Brucie lurched toward Elnora, but before she could stop her, the maid had untied a ragged pink satin ribbon. When she did, squares of rotting purple velvet sachet bags tumbled to the floor. The faint smell of old rose sachet mingled with the acrid odor of mothballs, casting a funeral pall over the bedroom.

"Oh, ma'am. I'm so sorry," Elnora said. But the look she gave Brucie out of her cornflower-blue eyes showed anything but contrition. "Who does this belong to?" she asked.

Unconsciously Brucie backed away, fingering her wedding ring. "I don't know," she said in a trembly voice.

Elnora held up a tarnished silver cup. "There's baby hair in here," she said. "An' engravin' on the side."

"Put it back in the blanket. It belongs in the blanket."

"'Thelma Jewel Claymore. 1877,'" Elnora read. Her back ramrod straight, her chin angled as if she were now the mistress of the manor, she gave Brucie a questioning look. "I knew ya were a Mississippi Claymore, ya da C.W. Claymore an' yer mum Miss Charlotte, but ya haven't ever said anythin' about a little sister. Yer older, but she'd be a middle-aged woman now."

"No. No. No. Her name isn't Claymore." *Why, oh why, did I keep that?* Brucie wondered. *That was another life, one of despair and grief.* She swayed on her feet. She grabbed the back of a velvet slipper chair and sank down into it before her legs gave way on her. She patted her chest. As she had done so often, gathering a black velvet ribbon hanging around her neck, Brucie caressed a gold cross twined with gold hairs.

"She was never a Claymore." Her voice caught in her throat and she barely got the words out. "Her name is Thelma Jewel Cl-Bledsoe," she whispered.

"Uh-hum." A tight, self-satisfied smile on her face, Elnora side-stepped through the door.

"She belongs to Clementine Bledsoe, Cousin Sarah's niece. She lives in California," Brucie said as she slid to the floor and curled into a ball. "I don't even know what she looks like," she sobbed.

CHAPTER 4

The groundwork for shock is
Laid by earth in the child's
Educated impulse to startle.

A bite is the shortest line;
Rarified along the vagus.
How old is this small machine?

A sudden peal in a French cathedral
Impels a candle behind the sternum,
Fusing, in memorial, a thimble full of
Blood.

Monday afternoon, February 23

Dale wiggled his toes. "My feet burn." He bent over, raised one leg at a time and dried his almost frozen feet on the hem of his overcoat. "I may be right in front of sanctified ground, but I'm going to say it anyhow. I hope that whoever stole my boots while I was asleep burns in Hell." He straightened and wrapped his coat around him. His body jerking against the cold he curled up on a wrought iron bench outside the dimly lit cathedral.

Bam!

"Oh, God!" Dale threw his arms around his head. He took several frightened breaths before he realized what he had heard. "That's no gun." The motor to a nearby car backfiring had sounded like a gunshot. After a few seconds of quiet the motor roared like the accelerator was stuck. "It's too loud," Dale said. Stretched out, he began to shake all over, whether from the cold, loud noises or the unwanted thoughts that kept tormenting him, he didn't know or care. One was as real and intrusive to him as another.

A horn blast assaulted his senses.

Dale cupped his hands over his ears.

My feet are wet and cold. My toes feel like they will fall off. He sat up and looked behind him. No cathedral. He shook his head. "Where am I?

"Here. Here," he said. "I'm in a muddy trench. I look for my men."

The guns roar. My thoughts are all a-tangle. We make it back. We make it back from a death trap. We fall to safety. To our mud-slimed haven.

Sunken trenches are wet lipped. The wind blasts over us. Slides down into the trench. Chaps my cheeks. My lips are dry. My hair stiff like an ear of dried corn. The mud. It's cold and wet. The close air chokes. Gas creeps. Gas slinks down like a hole-hidey snake. Ready to strike. The gas looks for my company. My men. It finds my men. Gas burns. Their skin blisters. But we are safe. For now.

Just in front, flame bursts light the sky. My head hurts. White rockets streak. Shadows of stretchers. Behind us, boys from my company, wounded, but alive, carried by tight-limbed, thin-lipped men.

Nonstop. A burst of machine gun fire. Death lines dash the field. On my side, we lie low. In our rat-crawly home. A stones throw away, a form moves. Half raises.

"Help me."

I know the voice. One of mine. My young/old friend. Private Samuel Stanton.

"Come get me. I'm cold. My arm hurts. I can't see."

"I'm here," I call. "Your captain."

Someone slithers behind him. A metal flash strokes the evening light.

Screams. A figure snakes away. A flagpole wavers. No. No. A leg.

"Oh, God. My legs." Samuel weeps. "Take me home," he sobs.

Bullets are a death stream.

"Don't let me die."

He doesn't need to be alone. "I'll get you. Soon."

A line of machine gun fire bolts across his path. Again. Again. Again. An aimed-for target lies between.

Silence falls. Echoes are stilled.

Crouching, I dash. His shoulders hug a shell hole. A red pool bathes the ground. I turn my soldier over. Roll my arms through his. I pull a bloody lump. My men reach. He's tossed into the trench, like a thrown sandbag. A stretcher comes. We get him to surgery. "My arm has a hole," he sobs. "I lost my legs. Take me home. I'm blind."

"I'm here," I say. "I'll stay."

"Tell me what you see," he pleads. His breath catches like a small baby. "I wanta go home. If you'll get my legs I can walk. Run. Climb. Where we did. The cemetery. Redemption Ridge."

I talk to him. "You have my word. I'll get you home. Wait awhile. Until then, we're going to another place," I say. "Where you can see." Slowly he turns his head toward my voice. We go away together. I tell him about creeks in the summer. The whirling water soothes and kisses cold toes like the brush of soft damp moss. A mask covers his face. "Oh," he breathes. I tell him I see the cotton fields back in Mississippi. I want him to remember what they look like. When the cotton bolls are full and ripe, they're puffed bigger than a snowman's head would be up north. He's not crying now. I remind him that early in the morning, we slipped away from a sleeping porch before the grownups were awake. Ran across dew sparkly, blond-tipped green grass. Climbed a chinaberry tree all the way to the top. Watched the sun ease over the horizon like a shy child peeping to see if he should come on up. Soon, even in the early morning, it's so hot your head burns. Your brains could scorch.

He's quiet. He's either sleeping or dead. If he's dead I talk on to his corpse.

It's cool in the chinaberry tree at Redemption Ridge. A breeze rakes branches. The wind whispers. Then it blows loud. It hurts my ears. The wind howls. I climb down from the tree to get away.

Shells seek me out. The world I loved is gone.

I sense it. Young Private Samuel. He's somewhere else now. He has, laid him down to sleep.

I pray the Lord, his soul to keep.

Frightened horses scream and screech. All night. God, make them quit. If I can make the screaming stop, I, too, can sleep.

Why are you here? You're not angry with anyone, Dale. "I am now," I counter whisper. "I am now."

A sense of already being dead won't leave me. I pinch my skin. It hurts. I'm still alive.

A bell rings. All clear. Everything grows quiet. I hear no moans or spattered gunfire.

This battle's done. It's deep in the night.

A clanging bell pealed through the stillness. *The fight is over,* he realized. *I'm somewhere else.*

"A damn church bell. I'm in Boston. I'm frozen." Dale felt like a failure. "They may have buried part of you in St. Dizier, Samuel. Somewhere. But, later, I got your legs. Gave them to my cook. To put with the fresh meat. To bring what I could home. Someday, part of you will walk Redemption Ridge again. Like you wanted to. You lived but died in surgery."

Dale was so cold he was almost having rigors. *Greenfield Holy Name Cathedral's behind me,* he remembered. He sat up. *It'll be warm in the church. People are there. Maybe the Monsignor will lay his hands on me. Heal me.*

The bell pealed again.

"Oh, no," Dale said. "The gun sounds. Not again. I don't want to remember. I don't want to go back. I don't want to hear those other words coming at me again." He put his hands over his ears.

"Evil needs to be stopped.

"My men are dead," Dale breathed. "The guilty must pay," he said through clenched teeth.

***

"Well, my father could afford to sail to Europe, but couldn't manage to send me on a cruise. And he can afford to move us to Mississippi," Memory fussed. "I want to go somewhere grand and wonderful. Ever since I met Thornton, everything's been rotten."

Overwhelmed at the way her life was going, she felt like screaming but she stopped herself and blurted aloud, "I won't go to Tallouga County, Mississippi. Not forever, anyhow." She fingered her long, thick hair...gave it a hard yank as if to emphasize her thoughts. "You can't make me live down in that hot, backward state."

She glanced at a fashion magazine on the beside table. She lifted a lock of long auburn hair. *I'll make some changes if I have to go. And I'll start with this. A new bob. I'll at least be fashionable and it will be cooler.*

From a bedside table she picked up a dainty, china figurine, an Elizabethan lady in a shepherdess dress. She cocked her wrist. Frustrated, she slung the figurine across the room. It hit the wall and broke into pale pink and blue smithereens. "I'm not living in Mississippi!" she screamed. "So, there."

She looked at the marriage bed and suddenly had an image of herself rolling over, away from Thornton. She reached for her large, beaded handbag that now held her journal. Writing in it had become a habit.

I used to think marriage meant love, she began. But to me it meant giving up pieces of myself one slice at a time.

Her eyes brimmed with tears. "Thornton dead. A widow. I'll never have a child," she whispered. "No man will ever want me. I'll never know what it's like to hold my baby. To feel that first, gasping breath."

And Mississippi. It's not just the heat and the slow-talking and slow-moving people that bother me. Nightmares. And when I allow myself to think about it, there's something about an old well in the back pasture. Where Dale, Jenson and I and some of the others used to sit around and tell ghost stories. Something bad happened there.

She had tagged it from the time she was around thirteen years old and for some reason she was by herself.

Frog skin. Knobby kneecaps. A gray stubbled beard. Noises like a snorting pig.

Memory set the pen down. That was as far as she could ever get. It was as if a fog were rolling in. But there were answers in the shadows to their old homeplace. Maybe she didn't want to know the answers, but then again, maybe she needed to know them.

"You're being ridiculous," she said. "You've just been through something really awful with Thornton." Once again, she began to write.

And it has nothing to do with Redemption Ridge. But that's the last place you want to live. Your friends are here.

"Mississippi isn't where I want to start putting my life back together," she said.

I don't know many people in Franklin, she wrote. I just didn't like it down there. Those mosquitoes seemed as large as a dinner plate. To this very day I can hear those mosquitoes whining.

They have ticks that dig their head into your skin and bite. The people eat squirrels, raw turnips and chitterlings. They talk funny. The men wear union suits and the women dip snuff and wear poke bonnets made out of croaker sacks.

She folded the papers shut. "We sure as heck can't pay for a whole new wardrobe of hot-weather clothes for me," she said. "I'm telling my mother right now. Thornton wouldn't let me, but it's time for me to have my life. Before this goes any further and before I get any older."

Dressed in the black of widowhood, Memory stormed out of her bedroom and started toward her mother's room. Her long full skirts had more starch in them than their Christmas tablecloth. Rustling when she walked and her shoulders squared, she was ready to do battle. She was right at Brucie's door when she heard loud, unfamiliar voices in the front hall and on a lower note her brother speaking. She spun around and hurried to the stairs.

By the time she got down the steps, Elnora was talking to two men in dark uniforms.

Memory's heart missed a beat when she realized they were policemen.

One, a short, bulldog-shaped man gripped her brother's arm. The other, a young, lean-bodied policeman stood a little back.

"Monsignor called from the sanctuary," the chunky man said. "Some people stopped this vagrant from coming into the church. He was barefooted and confused. He scared some good, churchgoing people," he barked. "The Monsignor knows who he is. He's given them trouble before."

"The Monsignor gave us your address," the younger man said. "Here on Beacon Street."

The stocky man looked slightly shamed. "But in this neighborhood, and looking at this home, I believe the Monsignor made a mistake."

"He didn't make a mistake," Memory said. "This is my brother, and this is his home."

"I wanted to go into the cathedral." Dale was unsteady on his feet, his face flushed, and his eyes glazed like they were covered in a sheet of thin ice. He tried to pull away, but the policeman held on to him. "Maybe pray with the people and tell them some things they need to hear. But I knew they probably wouldn't listen. This is not where I should be with my message. If I were somewhere else, if I were in the South, they might hear me."

Memory was hurt by the look of sadness and longing on her brother's face. She felt an urge to reach out and touch him, but he went on before she could.

"Sometimes my mama can almost work magic. I wish you'd get her to take me on to Mississippi, Sister," he whispered. "They'll let me through the iron gate and on into the still waters and the green pastures there. And I have part of my friend with me. I brought some of Samuel back home. Someday. Someday take to Mississippi." *But what about me*? he agonized. *My medicine? My whiskey?*

Memory took a couple of deep, shaky breaths. *This is the worst Dale has been yet.*

"Once I get through the cemetery gate, I can talk to them out at Redemption Ridge. Those men under there will know what to do. They'll be company for Samuel."

"I guess you're talking about that old Confederate cemetery," she said. "And the dead soldiers buried there."

"Yes, yes, yes. They've fought the fight. They'll tell me how. I need to know how to save my men. I could go back and do it."

"I wish you'd get those dead men at Redemption Ridge and that Samuel Stanton off your mind." Despair filled Memory's heart. "Their war's over and yours is too," she said.

Although she didn't see or hear her mother, suddenly she felt Brucie beside her.

"What can I do for you gentlemen?" she asked.

"This is my mother," Dale answered. "Mrs. Von Dieter."

"You're the one I'm supposed to see." The thin policeman had a smug sound to his voice.

"I know you from somewhere." Dale looked at the handsome policeman as if just now realizing he was there. "My mother's a lady. Please treat her that way."

"We've never met before," the man said. A slight smile on his lips, he held up a box wrapped in white tissue paper and tied with twine. Memory had a bad feeling and she could tell by the way her mother moved slightly away from the blue-coated man that Brucie did too. He shook his head as if flinging off raindrops and when he did, there was something slightly familiar to Memory about his thick shock of curly red hair. In some ways he reminded her of Thornton. All but his green eyes. They put her in mind of stalking animals she had seen at the zoo.

"The Monsignor told us to make sure we gave this to Mrs. Von Dieter."

"That's I. This is my son, and I'll take care of him now," Brucie said. "I do thank you for bringing him home."

"I was told to make sure this was in your hands before we go." Although his voice was smooth and slightly high-pitched, there was a tone of arrogance behind the younger man's words as he held out the package. Brucie took it from him. He rubbed his hand down the side of his dark pants as if he were wiping off a stubborn stain. When he did Memory heard a tinkling sound and noticed he had on ornate brown boots with silver spurs. She thought she had seen those boots before, but just then Brucie tightened her shoulders and handed the package to Memory. She pushed down on the front latch.

"And now, goodnight and Godspeed, gentlemen."

Brucie closed and locked the door behind the policemen. "Let's go into the library." Tears that were a mixture of resignation and sorrow streamed down her cheeks as she grasped Dale's shoulder and steered him to the other room.

"You might not want to see what's in that box." Dale wrapped his arm around his body and sank down onto a sofa. "We've angered the wrong people. One of them was here tonight," he muttered. "I can guess who that's coming from. It won't be a gift you'd want."

"You may have to open it, Memory Elaine," Brucie said. "All of a sudden, I'm dizzy in the head. I'm going to have to go to my room and lie down."

Memory knew that her mother was unusually perceptive and must have sensed something wrong. She was not one who ran away from unpleasantness. Instead, she was one who tried to smooth it down for others.

"The package smells bad," Memory said. "Like it might have some old, rotten meat that's been left out in the sun a long time." She set down the box. "There's a folded note glued to the top." She lifted the note and opened it. *"Go back to Germany,"* she read. *"Where you people belong. For future reference, I still have the other glove. The right hand is a perfect fit for somebody else in your family."*

Goosebumps ran up Memory's arms. She stared at the box a minute, then she shrugged her shoulders indifferently, picked up a letter opener, and slit the cord. "Humph! This doesn't scare me." She tore the crinkly paper away and lifted the top off the box.

She held up a piece of wood with a large round stem on the end. "This looks like part of a fancy walking stick with a quartz clock handle on the end," she said. "But there's something still up under it in the box that stinks."

"Well, I think we can guess who this gift came from." Dale shook his head and pointed. "The stem's been whittled and there's something shiny threaded on it." He closed his eyes and collapsed in a miserable heap. "I don't want to see this."

Memory had a sinking feeling in the pit of her stomach. Her heart pounding, her eyes widened in alarm. "What I'm seeing here on this cut down piece of a walking cane looks like Thornton's wedding ring." Her skin felt clammy, her voice trembled. "I thought it was buried with him.

"And there's something wrapped up in a black cloth under here." She took a deep breath and gagged.

"Oh, God!"

She threw the box to the floor and fled the room. A familiar, fur-lined leather glove with a decaying, bloodied hand nailed to it flew out and hit the floor.

CHAPTER 5

**The sweet, sweet taste
Of revenge upon
His tongue.
Commanded unto death
By the spirit of the trench.
To make sure the
Devil takes the
Hindmost.
And sent him home a legless stench**

Monday night, February 23

Dale woke to a stench so strong that in his confused state he thought he had been swallowed alive by an odor. Unsure of where he was, he had a hard time catching his breath; remembered terror and the odor of his friends' rotting bodies came back to him. Slowly, he returned from the gray mist of a deep, nightmarish dream. "Oh, Samuel." Dale's back and legs hurt; blood pounded in his temples. "God. I've got to do something. I held you with my glove. And Thornton's rotten hand next to your last drops of blood. There is evil to the core in this room. It stinks."

He put his hand over his nose, stumbled from the library into the hall and sank to the floor. "I don't know what I'll do, but I will take care of this," he vowed. The feeling of helplessness was strong, and he realized there would be no help or comfort from the law or the church.

"It's time to get yourself together," he said. "The good Senator is the law around here. He has to be stopped."

Dale reached into his back pocket, patted a silver flask that held his whiskey, picked a haversack off the hatrack and slipped in a container of cough syrup. "Oh God. I'd rather get drunk now. But for what I need to do it's better to be sober." He got up from the floor, stumbled to a large Boston fern, and poured out the rest of his drink. "That's it for now Bruce Tisdale Von Dieter. You've got to get your head clear. Then you can plot your revenge.

"Whatever I do to the Senator needs to change his life. It should be very painful."

He had the operator ring his buddy, Jenson Cooper. When they first returned from overseas, in order to make a little money, Jenson had worked for the Senator for a short while. Dale told Jenson what he had in mind and that he would need his help.

"You can count me in. As you know, I despise the man," Jenson said. "He's brought pain and misery to lots of people. It's time for him to get a dose of his own medicine." He chuckled. "I know where everything is in his office. I'll give him a dose of laudanum in his drink that'll put out his lights until this time tomorrow. Then, you and I can do what you suggested. When you came down to Redemption Ridge for all those summers, you were like the little brother I never had." He caught his breath and sighed. "But that was nothing. You took good care of all your men under horrible conditions, me included. It'll give me great pleasure to help you, Captain. And lucky me! To be the one to get back at that rat, Peter Shields.

"As you know, I've taken care of our friend's legs. The Senator's not even aware of it, but they're in his ice cellar."

After he hung up the phone Dale stripped to his underclothes. "Ready or not, it's time to completely clear my head." He shoved open the front door. The cold crisp air blasted his body. Before he could change his mind, he ran down the steps, and spread eagled in the snow. "Ahhh," he cried, feeling like he'd been thrown head first into an icy river. Jolted wide awake, he rolled over several times then he jumped up and ran back into the house. Shaking all over, he dried himself on some towels he had brought into the hall and hurriedly slipped on his clothes. Trembling, his lungs aching, he stretched out on the cold hall floor to wait. He would have been more comfortable in the library, but he didn't want to be in the room with Thornton's rotten hand any more than he had to. He bided his time and sometime after midnight, felt he was sober enough to begin his quest for revenge.

Dale decided to go upstairs to Thornton and Memory's old room. He wanted some part of Thornton to be there when he got back at the Senator. He never had any use for his dead brother-in-law, and he knew Thornton had hurt his sister.

Being careful not to make any noise, he walked up the edge of the stairs next to the railing. When he opened the door to Thornton and Memory's room, it was dark and musty smelling. Dale set down a suede pouch and a small leather suitcase he'd brought in with him. He dug through a bureau drawer until he found what he wanted. He lifted out a white satin ascot the Senator had given Thornton for his birthday. "For now, I don't want you to get messed up," he said as he dropped the ascot into the suede pouch and put it into the suitcase. Holding the suitcase, he left the bedroom and eased back down the steps. He opened the library door.

"Whew!" Now that he was good awake and sober, the stench that flooded his nostrils was even stronger than before. Dale took a step back, gagged and clamped his hand across his nose. He ducked his head, and without looking at it, picked up the glove. He dropped it into the suitcase, and then flipped the latches.

"My friend's blood was on my glove," he agonized. "God willing, to the best of my ability, his memory needs to be avenged. I probably need to rest a little." He shook his head. "I've got his legs taken care of. There's no way I can stay in a room with Thornton's decaying hand in my glove. The Senator has contaminated something holy." He checked his pocket watch. "Late." He went across the hall into the parlor, made himself comfortable in an oversize chair, and closed his eyes. Dale slept lightly but kept a check on the time. The black hour hand crept forward as the seconds and minutes glided through their journey. Finally, it was close to two o'clock.

He picked up the phone. When the operator answered, he had her ring for a cab.

"I'll be waiting outside."

"When this is done," he said to himself. "I'm giving myself a pat on the back. Stone cold sober. But not for long." *I'll have earned the right to do anything to make me feel better.* "Ánd the devil can take the hindmost. So put that in your pipe and smoke it."

***

Tuesday morning

A silvery, faint dawn was beginning to lighten the sky as Dale and Jenson left the butcher shop and went out into the bitter cold. Even though Dale had been the senior officer, it was comforting for his friend, Jenson, to be with him now, even as it had been when they were in combat. Dale had always looked up to Jenson, a muscular man with thick dark eyebrows above soft, kind, honey-brown eyes. "Chicken feet, pig guts, beef brains, chitterlings, and deer livers are a good combination to stop a snake in the grass," Dale said. Even with the chopped meat and bone splinters wrapped in sheets of white butcher paper and then secured in a suitcase saturated with clove oil, a strong odor of old garbage surrounded the two men. Breathing through their mouths they walked with their heads turned away from what they were carrying.

"His office isn't far," Jenson said. "I know where he keeps his key."

In a short while they stood outside the Senator's office. Jenson pulled a key from under an old fern stand and slipped it into the keyhole.

The building was dark. The Senator kept a bed in a small room next to his office. He spent most of what he called his "working nights" there. "To be close by and handy in case any of my men need me," he always said, as if he considered himself to be a guardian angel of some sort, always at the ready.

Loud stuttering snores came from behind the closed door. For a moment, Dale was frightened. Instead of harsh snores, "Rat-a-tat-tat," were the sounds he heard.

"Those goddamned machine guns. They're blasting the heads off of my men." He dashed forward toward the noise.

Strong arms grabbed him. "Captain! Are you all right, Sir?"

"My men," Dale groaned. "They're slaughtering them."

"I'm here," Jenson put a comforting hand across Dale's shoulders. "Catch your breath. We're at Senator Peter Shields's office. That man snores like a firing machine gun. When I worked for him, that's what it always sounded like to me."

Dale shook his head. He took a deep breath and forced himself to wait for his head to clear. In a few seconds, as it sometimes did, the feeling passed, and he came back to reality. He knew he had to go through with his plan. He waved at Jenson and the two men picked their way through the reception room.

Outside the bedroom door, sitting on his desk as if waiting for the Senator to slip it on and go about his business, was his wooden leg. Propped against a table at the end of his couch were a cane and a pair of crutches.

"When I'm done, he won't ever wear that limb again," Jenson said. "Most of the time his stump is raw." He swiped a hand across his chin. "He soaks his bandage in colloidal silver cream. As you saw, I know where he hides a key. Like you suggested, when I came by here earlier and made sure he was down for the count I mixed rat poison and acid in that leg cream he sets such store in. Right at this moment, it's plastered against his stump. And hopefully rotting it," he said, a note of cheerfulness in his voice, as if he were going to a long-awaited party. "Fired me when I wouldn't be one of his boys," he grunted in disgust. "I've shown him."

Jenson slowly shook his head. "And words out. I heard from a source who works for the Senator. He knows we're onto him. Thornton."

"I really don't care. Let's just be extra careful. Did you get Samuel's remains from the ice cellar?" Dale asked

"No. But I'll look after our friend until we get him home."

"For now, let's take care of that rotten bastard," Dale said.

"You might want to lower your voice a little, Captain. Don't forget. The good Senator's in the next room."

"He's been snoring like a buzz saw. And either way, awake or not, I don't give a rip," Dale said.

"He might get a message out of what I have in mind. A message he's needed to hear for a long time. Your sins will catch up with you." He tilted his head to one side. "Tell you what. I don't want to just decorate, and then leave our creation here.

"Let's take the peg leg with us. It needs to be seen and worshipped. We can walk to the Greenfield Holy Name Cathedral. It's not too far from here and close to the zoo where Thornton was killed."

Jenson picked a brass name plate off the desk.

Senator Peter Shields. The Soldiers Friend. Day and Night. Night and Day. I'm always here for you.

"This'll make sure everybody knows who that wooden leg belongs to," Jenson said. "And after that, I'll take care of our buddy, Samuel."

"We might be able to use the Senator's cane," Dale said, propping the Senator's crutches against the side of the desk, "but I'll leave these crutches so he can get out and be seen. And I pray to almighty God, that something will strike this man down."

"Justice will be done, Captain Von Dieter," Jenson Cooper said. "And, if God doesn't see to it, I will."

***

The two men eased down the aisle of the empty cathedral, Dale with his haversack across his back and carrying the Senator's wooden leg and Jenson his cane and the suitcase. Dale set the peg leg at the foot of the altar.

"The Senator had this walking piece special made, and from what I was told it took several months," Jenson said. "Looky here." He reached into the prosthetic and took out a large wad of money. "His poker winnings. He must have won big last night. He puts it out that he gives this money to "his boys," but that's a lie. It goes to his "special" boys. To make sure they show up when he gets a notion for them. This here will go to some of my wounded friends that the Senator won't give the time of day to," he said, stuffing the cash into his pants pocket. "And I'm here to tell you, that's no lie."

"It's time to enhance the Senator's peg," Dale said. "Here goes." He dumped the smelly meat and splintered bone fragments into the leg. Then he pulled a tall narrow bottle from the case he'd brought in and poured blood in on top of the other nasty mixture. He took the Senator's cane and poked the blood, meat and bones around in the leg.

"The old boy'll be hobbling around town on crutches from now on," Jenson chuckled, "if he can get around at all.

"But let's not put it all in the wooden leg," he said. "I think I'll go back to the Senator's apartment. I gave him enough laudanum, he won't wake up until tomorrow. I'll smear a little bit of what's there on the altar, along with the acid and rat poison cream I slathered across his stump."

Dale had swiped pen and ink from the Senator's office. He took the white satin ascot his dead brother-in-law, Thornton, had been so proud of from its protective pouch. "I remember some of the words I heard when I was in the trenches. To this day, they ring in my ears." Very carefully he printed, "Hell's dust chokes our veins."

A German flag cut into a five-pointed star was placed on a table in front of the altar. Painstakingly, the two men centered the leg in the middle of the banner. Aromatic candles were placed at each of the star points.

"Here. Peter Shields. Everybody needs to know who this honors." Jenson placed the brass office sign with the Senators name in front of the altar.

"Day or night, he's here for some of his men. Those that give him pleasure," Jenson said.

"I'm done," Dale said. "Now it's my time to kick back, pay homage to our men and enjoy this in my own way." Smiling, he lifted a small container from his haversack. "No looney bin for me. I'll get my good feelings back with this right here." *But Mississiippi? What can I do*? ran through his mind. He shook away his feelings and genuflected in front of the leg. He crossed himself, stood and took deep swallows of his cough medicine. For a moment Dale had the overwhelming feeling he was being watched. As if he were commanded to do so, he raised his eyes. When he looked, he not only saw, but felt the gaze of the martyred Christ on the cross looking down on him. *Am I being reproached?*

Dale could swear he heard a soft voice saying, "As much as you have done it."

"No, blessed Savior. I won't ask for forgiveness. I'm doing this not against you, but for my men."

A door slammed shut somewhere in the cathedral.

Dale put his hands over his ears. "A gun went off," he said. "I'm wet and cold in this muck and mire.

"Someone gave me a scrap of paper and told me to write these words where other men could see.

"My men are dead," he breathed. Once again, he took up his pen.

But still I hear the echo of your cries.
Will they ever go away?
What passing bells for those who die as cattle
Only the monstrous anger of the guns.
Only the stuttering rifles' rapid rattle.

"Soon. Cooper can get our friend's legs from the cellar. I'll return them to Mississippi. Home."

Evil needs to be stopped, he wrote on the ascot.

***

It went unreported in the newspaper, but early morning worshippers at the Greenfield Holy Name Cathedral were greeted not by a cross or a decorator designed flower arrangement, but by a smelly wooden leg centered on the altar. The artificial limb sat on a pentagram made from a German flag. Aromatic candles burned from each corner. A used military glove with a decaying hand nailed to it adorned the stump opening. Fleshy lumps that at first were thought to be large, rotten toes but later identified as bull balls had been glued to the last three fingers. A strip of wrapped bailing wire secured one, long stemmed, blood-red, thorny rose to the thumb and forefinger.

***

Tuesday afternoon

The whine and clang of a streetcar assaulted the Senator's senses. It took him a few minutes, before he realized where he was. He was alive in his office. He must have been there last night and much of today. He hurt all over. Numb with pain, his body in shock, and nearly senseless from drugs, he rolled over and fell back into a coma-like sleep. Sometime later, crying, mewling sounds woke Peter Shields. Curled tightly on his side, it took him a few minutes to know what was going on. He held still until he could get his wits about him. When he did, he was horrified to realize he was the one making the noises. The side of his face was coated with something sticky. He touched his chin. He lay in a pool of vomit. In the past he had often experienced a dull, phantom pain where his left leg had once been. Now, flaming, hot claws dug through his stump, as though it was on fire. Hours must have passed since he'd moved. Not only was he in agony, his lower parts smelled worse than the vomit. He wore no pants, but a slimy putrid bandage taped onto his stump was thick with a smelly cream. The top of his leg, the Oriental rug underneath him and the bandage were soaked with urine.

A bright shaft of evening sun streamed through an undraped window. Groaning, Peter Shields gathered his wits about him. He reached down, tore the bandage off and flung it across the room. A wet goo oozed onto the Oriental carpet. He rolled from his back to his side. Pushing up on his elbow, holding his body weight on his spread hands, he rose up. His body stiff, muscles aching, he moaned, "Oh, God." Gripping the arm of a couch, he mustered all his willpower and raised himself. He collapsed onto plump sofa cushions. It took the Senator a few seconds, but he caught his breath and ooched forward.

He grasped his crutches and pushed himself up. He managed to struggle into his pants.

Clamping the crutches under his arm, rocking like a porch swing that had been given strong shoves, he flung himself through the office.

His breathing ragged, Peter Shields stumbled out the door. "You'll pay," he yelled. "You bastard. I know it was you, Dale Von Dieter."

Eaten with anger, tottering and swaying he lurched toward a friend's office. The Senator, peg-legged on his crutches, into the street and onto the trolley tracks. Peter Shields didn't see the fast moving, swishing trolley.

Down at the far end of the street, riding on a roan horse, a young policeman, a swag of auburn curls crawling from underneath his helmet, spotted the Senator. He jabbed his spurs into the horse's side and galloped toward him.

"Stop!"

"Von Dieter," the Senator screamed. "Coo..."

The frantic, clanging bell of a streetcar swallowed his words. The policeman didn't make it in time.

"Goddamn, Von Dieter'll die for this," the policeman yelled, his fist slamming the horse's neck.

CHAPTER 6

**In her own twilight,
Cherry-wood pillars of the parlor,**

**Brucie could almost
Replace her surroundings
With the fey Belleau woods.**

**The particulars of horror
Escaped her, but she was at
The cusp of empathy.**

**A thundering racehorse
Carried her mind south,
A cavalry charge's thin
Impression.**

Thursday, February 26

The doorbell chimed.

Brucie thought her imagination was playing tricks on her and pulled the covers up over her ears. The doorbell chimed again. When she finally realized what she was hearing she sat straight up in bed. The bell pealed, not once, but over and over. It took several moments to clear her head; then heart pounding, she reached toward her nightstand. She turned on the bedside light and looked at the clock. Six-fifteen. Whatever or whoever was downstairs at their front door, she knew, this wouldn't be a good thing.

She grabbed her dressing gown, tied the sash and slid into her bedroom slippers. Weak with apprehension and holding onto the banister because she was afraid of falling, she made her way down the steps and to the entry.

Her voice trembling, "Who is it?" she managed to ask.

"It's Jenson Cooper, ma'am," a deep male voice answered. "We brought our Captain Dale home."

Brucie had a sinking sensation in the pit of her stomach. Hands shaking, it took her several seconds to slide the large round knob of their dead bolt and open the door. In the pale morning light, she made out the slumped form of her son between two disheveled men.

"Miss Brucie," the familiar voice of Jenson Cooper spoke haltingly, "I'm sorry." He shifted his feet uncomfortably. "I do apologize for bringing Captain Von Dieter home in this shape. This here with me"—He nodded toward a small, weary-looking man—"is Private Zebulon Booth. I usually do better than this by my captain."

"Come in," Brucie whispered. She fingered a gold cross around her neck, given to her by Vernell, and supposedly twined with the golden hairs of Captain Bruce Claymore. "I've been worried sick about my son."

Holding Dale up, the two men, their uniforms covered by battered army greatcoats stepped into the hall. They eased him into a massive, heavily carved chair. Brucie bent over, put her hand under Dale's chin and raised his head. When she did, she smelled a strong odor of something like overripe rose petals.

"Captain needs to sleep this off," Jenson said.

My son's drunk and out of his head, Brucie realized, as she had so many times lately. *I thought better of Jenson than this. He's always been a good friend, but if he really cared for Dale this wouldn't have happened.*

As if he were reading her mind, Cooper spoke up.

"I'm sorry. I wish I could say I'd done the best I could," he said in a clumsy way. What he didn't tell her was, he had gone to the Senator's refrigerated cellar. The limbs of Private Stanton that Dale had protected for so long were gone. "But that might not be the whole truth. The Captain and I, we did us some dirty work at the Greenfield Cathedral day before yesterday." He glanced at her apologetically, then turned his head down and coughed into his shoulder. Brucie waited impatiently until the man caught his breath. "After that, I left Captain Dale in a back room at the Lame Duck Tavern."

A back room where he drinks whiskey and some of that that cough medicine that makes him act funny. And I've been told, there's sometimes pills he swallows.

Brucie was tempted to say something, but once again, she cautioned herself not to speak. Nothing would be gained from it.

Like the snowflakes outside building up into snow drifts, the silence in the hall deepened and thickened. No one said anything for a few minutes as they all assessed one another, then Jenson Cooper cleared his throat. "A couple of hours ago the owner sent somebody after me to come and get my Captain."

Brucie looked at first one man then the other. *He's not at fault,* she reasoned to herself. *Dale's his own man and he can be hardheaded.* "We'll put him in the library," she said. "You know the way, Jenson." Each man put their arm around Dale, and supporting his weight, they followed Brucie as she led them down the hall.

She opened the library door, stepped aside to let the men carry Dale into the room and inclined her hand toward a sofa. His two comrades slid him down.

"It may be a while before he'll be back to himself." Jenson lifted Dale's legs and gently stretched them out. "The Captain and I have looked after each other most of our lives. He saved my life at Belleau Woods and I might have been letting him down the other night. I did what he wanted. Seemed like a right good idea at the time, but looking back, maybe not." *And another mistake I may have made. Telling Senator Peter Shields about Samuel's remains in his ice cellar. He tells that redheaded cop crony of his everything.* He reached to the back of the couch, lifted an afghan, shook it out, and spread it over Dale. "If I may be so bold, though. I will say this." He wiped his hand across his mouth. "There are some pretty mean folks around here. I think it might be best for you all to take the Captain away until some bad things die down around these parts. I'll help, any way I can. If you go back to Redemption Ridge, I'll be going home for good before too much longer."

Jenson looked a little hesitant, then he spoke up. "I've already started looking into my travel arrangements. Haven't tied the date down yet, but I'll leave on the Boston to Chicago train. From there to Memphis and Jackson." He nodded his head. "After that, l catch a branch line on to Franklin.

"I'd be honored to include y'all in any arrangements I make, Miss Brucie," Jenson said. "It's past time for me to go home."

"I don't know yet what we're going to do," Brucie answered.

Dale pushed up on his elbows. He leaned his weight on his left side, lifted his shaking right arm, and pointed as if he were about to squeeze a trigger. "I've got a bead on you," he threatened. "Leave my men alone!" His voice rose. He collapsed and lay motionless for a minute. "Ah," he whispered, "but when their fallen bodies lie in repose, there will never be more glorious heroes than these, when they enter God's domain."

"My poor, poetic, friend." Jenson shook his head. "He's not himself now. Hasn't been since we got back. What's eating on him I think is kinda like a cottonmouth you don't see. You step on the tail, and its gonna whip around and sink its fangs into you. And then poison creeps up your spine." He tightened his mouth, then seemed to make his mind up about something. "He pulled me to safety. Not once, but twice." His face seemed to light up with admiration as he spoke about his friend. "Each time risking his own life to save mine." He ran his hands through his thick, dark hair. "If you're any kind of a man, you don't forget that. If you'll just say the word, I'll be pleasured to help any way I can." He bowed his head. "I can hold on going back home. I'll stay right here with my Captain. As long as he needs me."

"Jenson, I'm sure you two men need some sleep. If you will stay with Dale now, until I can decide what to do, I'll have blankets and pillows brought in here," she said. "So, you can rest."

"No, I'm fine," Jenson said. "The sun's already winked her big yellow eye over the harbor."

"When Dale's like this, sometimes its several days before he's himself again." Brucie put her hand over her mouth as if she were going to say something else, then she took it down. "That'll give me time to weigh the pros and cons. To make up my mind what to do.

"For now. If you'd bring your friend to the dining room, in some small way, I'd like to thank you," she nodded toward the man with Jenson Cooper. "If you two gentlemen will follow me, I'll have Elnora serve you some breakfast shortly. We'll leave my son here," she said. "He'll be fine."

"Zeb." Jenson held up his hand. "Don't forget, you got you a missus," he said. "After you eat, you better get on home."

Zebulon's mouth curved into a gap-toothed grin. "I'm my own man," he mumbled. "But I guess I'd best leave before too much longer."

"I'm not even thinking," Brucie said. "I'll certainly have our chauffeur drive you wherever you need to go."

They followed her to the kitchen. "I'd be much obliged, ma'am. But you don't have to feed me."

"It's my pleasure." She pointed to a marble-topped, mahogany sideboard. "Elnora already has coffee prepared. Cups, cream and sugar are out. If you need anything, ring the bell there on the table," she said after seeing that the men were seated. "I'll run upstairs and slip on some decent clothes."

Mouth open in a large circle, Zeb threw his head back and looked up at a massive crystal chandelier. A small child watching a circus performance of wild animals couldn't have been anymore intrigued. "I'll be swan. If there was to come up a breeze, I believe we might have us some sparkly sleet come down on our heads."

Brucie smiled. "You all tell Elnora what you'd like for breakfast. I'll freshen up and be back down shortly. You've been very faithful to Dale. In so many ways. I do thank you, from the bottom of my heart."

"He's been my friend for almost as long as I can remember. It's always my pleasure to help you and my Captain, ma'am," said Jenson. "It's an honor. When machine guns were swinging around, cutting down his men no more than if they were just sickling cuts of hay, I saw that man there slide over an icy trench like he had on a pair of bladed skates. He jumped over that mucky trench and took out a whole machine gun nest. Single-handed. And those of his that had been shot." His voice trembled. "He felt every death. I'd go to the ends of the earth for this man."

Just then Elnora came in holding a dish of hot biscuits and a large silver platter filled with ham and bacon. While the men were being served and eating their breakfast Brucie went upstairs and hurriedly dressed. When she was done, she went into the library to check on Dale and was relieved to see there had been no significant change; he was still in a deep slumber. Other than that, which she expected, he seemed to be all right and not aware that she was anywhere around.

A little shaky, Brucie sank into a chair. Even though the library was warm, she hugged herself protectively. She became aware of the steady ticking of the grandfather clock in the hall.

What do I do?

Before she could answer her own question, Elnora brought Brucie a cup of hot tea. She appreciated it, although it was a bit out of character after the way the Irish maid had been acting.

"Ye're lookin' a wee bit peaked, my lady," Elnora said. "An' them gentlemen's...them's almost done."

"Thanks." Brucie smiled and took the cup. "I needed this."

A short while later, Jenson and the other soldier, Zeb, stopped in to tell Brucie good-bye.

"Thank you so much for breakfast," Jenson said. "And if it's okay with you, Miss Brucie, I'll be back later this afternoon to check on my Captain."

After they left, Dale roused a moment and stumbled to the toilet. He walked back in and sank onto the sofa not far from where Brucie sat. He stretched out, folded his hands and rested his head on them and passed out. The house was quiet, but Brucie was uneasy. She set down her cup of tea, got up, and walked to the large curved window.

"I love to run my hand over so much in this house and its gardens." She pulled open the thick drapes, leaned against the big bay window and allowed herself to consider what she would leave behind if she left here forever.

A full city block of manicured lawn stretched out before her, starting on Beacon Hill Street and sweeping back toward the house. Such beautiful grounds. And the house...she had spent many pleasant hours in this library, with its olive stained oak paneling and the long wall covered with books she loved to touch and read. The large brick fireplace filled with shard-shaped flames brought her both comfort and pleasure.

She turned away from the bank of windows accentuated by rose satin curtains lined in shimmery gold and walked to the door. Unconsciously she tipped her head in acknowledgement of the stately parlor across the hall. The room, with its cherry paneling, antique furniture, and leaded glass windows was Herschel's sanctuary. A reflecting pool lay beyond the French doors.

"I've come a long way," she said, "since wading in the muddy waters of Noble Creek."

She sighed and gazed down thinking of the warm goop oozing between her toes and how good it felt way back when she was a child.

She turned and studied the grand curving staircase in the front hall off to her right that led up to the bedrooms, her dressing room, and its onyx bathroom.

A moan from Dale brought her back to the here and now.

Brucie swung around and glanced at her sleeping, disturbed son.

What if I had left here and we'd lived out our days at Redemption Ridge?

"What should I do now?" she asked herself aloud, with a shake of her head. "I need to own up to it. I've been gone from there for years, but did I ever leave Mississippi behind? Is it home? If so, is that good or bad? Which way do I jump? Back to the beginning in Mississippi? Or do I stay here?"

Dale pointed at his lips.

"Are you trying to tell me something?" Brucie asked.

When he didn't answer, she sank back into her troublesome thoughts.

Mississippi…times past…and yet what's to come? The way our lives are going, it may well be the future. Is that what I want for me and mine? Living down south is so different from here. So many things to consider. My feelings are warring like a pair of racehorse stallions.

"Primed and ready to burst through the gate," she murmured aloud. "A Boston thoroughbred."

"Flasher."

"Yes." Brucie smiled down at her son. "You do hear me, Dale. Your daddy's thoroughbred. The other one. A randy Mississippi quarter horse."

"Thunder," Dale whispered.

"Yes." Her voice broke. "That was your horse's name."

He said nothing else.

"Don't worry," she continued, walking to him and taking a deep breath. "I'll take into account what we'd leave behind and what we'll face there if we go. Those two feelings speed inside me neck and neck. Like the thoroughbred dashing ahead and the other one closing the gap. Neither can overtake the other. I'm also thinking of your sister, who has no horse in this race. We need a winner. So, think, son. Take this. One by one. Help me. Use your head."

"My head. Hurts." He ran his fingers across his forehead.

"I don't ask for help often. I need you to listen to what I'm saying. Bostonians are busy people. I've noticed that since I first came here. Even before your father and I were married. They bustle about as if they're always on important business. The city reeks of steam engines, oil, and fish. The ladies dress in hats, gloves and furs, and people shop in department stores spread out like yard children. And I've been right there with the best of them.

"You step outside the stores, and the streets teem with people." She bent and smoothed Dale's hair. "You have to wait for trolleys, taxicabs, and chauffeur-driven vehicles. Cars honk like braying donkeys." She laughed lightly. "They sound just like the old plow mules back home.

"But on the other side of the coin, how often I have thrilled to the sounds of booted heels on marble floors in fancy drawing rooms. And you. And your sister. You both love the better things in life, such as the taste of fine wine, served in hand blown Venetian glass.

"Our world. Self-assured people who perch on French sofas while servants pour steeped hot tea from bone china pitchers into fragile, fluted cups." She shook her head. "I will say this: their voices are loud and flat, and they all talk at once as if vying for attention."

She shook her shoulders as if casting off part of what she would be leaving behind.

"You may not be saying much, Dale, but I feel like you're hearing every word I say." A smile flitted over her lips. "We have high church here. Worshipers wear velvet, furs, and jewels, and after service we're chauffeured to high tea or dinner at the Parker House, Jacob Wirth's, or Young's, just so we can see and be seen.

"My children. Been there. Friends with high social standing. Very much the thing for us to do."

Dale shifted on the sofa, but otherwise didn't acknowledge her words.

"Even with all that, let's compare the two places," Brucie continued. "Back home in Franklin, the stores—McMahon's Seed and Feed, Fly's Drugstore, Warren's Hardware, the Blessed Rest Funeral Home, and Mrs. Netter's Boarding House—are all family owned. And the streets aren't crowded. There are no clamorous sounds, no chattering, clattering trolleys to disturb the town. Just the neighing of horses and the occasional labored chug-chug of an automobile or a loud ooga. I'm trying to make up my mind. You know what I see?"

"No?" Dale breathed out the word as a question.

"I'm picturing in my mind the neck of the purebred stallion lengthening. He gains speed and takes a slight lead. Yet the quarter horse races close behind. His body swathed in sweat, his nostrils flaring and his eyes blazing. He bunches his withers and stretches his legs. Which shall it be?"

"Thunder," Dale murmured.

"Yes, yes, yes." Brucie picked up the hand-cranked black music box she'd brought from Redemption Ridge. She wound it up and let her imagination drift with the haunting music of the old Civil War song, *Aura Lee*. "He's not fancy like the Boston purebred stallion."

"Soul."

"Yes. Your Thunder. He didn't have registration. No fancy pedigree. But he had soul." Brucie smoothed her skirt. "And yet there's so much more to consider, both good and bad. Out in the country, you stroll through dog-trot cabins, sleeping porches, yard kitchens, and outhouses." She sighed. "In larger homes, like Redemption Ridge, they have verandahs, parlors and dining rooms. Big bedrooms, indoor kitchens and baths."

Dale started to get up but lay back down instead.

"Tallouga County is quiet," Brucie told him. "Often the only noises competing with the slow creak of rockers, echoing footsteps on the porch and the crowing of roosters and mooing of cows is the bleak whistle of a train in the distance."

Brucie's thoughts continued to race as she picked up her Royal Doulton china cup and sipped her tea. *Where do I belong? Do my feelings count?*

"This tea is cold." She shook her head. "Cold and tasteless."

"Coffee," Dale said.

"Ah, coffee," she said quietly. "Early morning, before sunup, you wake to the smell of strong, black coffee. Down home, the coffee served in chipped cups will burn your tongue."

Dale licked his lips.

"Hungry?" she asked.

He shook his head.

"Fine, then let me tell you about the food," she went on. "Unless it's hunting season or the men are out working the fields, they have a heavy noon dinner. Leftovers for supper. Often, it's cornbread crumbled into a bowl of buttermilk or milk fresh from the cow, but for some folks, out back, moonshine swigged from a jug."

Dale made sideways motions with his hands, as if trying to rub out a spot.

"Ah. That struck a chord." Brucie looked toward the window as if hoping to see a familiar scene outside. She tightened her body, then looked back at her son. Her face grew softer. "The people I grew up with had a slow, languorous way of talking.

Most of their conversations didn't include history, foreign affairs, or finances, but they did like to pontificate about local politics."

Dale continued to move his hands.

"You'd make a great politician," she said. "Still can. You have a way with words. Or, on the other side of the coin, maybe even a preacher. Presbyterian, of course."

The music box had run down. She reached for it, then changed her mind, sat beside Dale and closed her eyes.

"Come Sunday, in Tallouga County, Mississippi, the Sabbath Day is different. Church bells peal out 'come and worship, come and worship' all morning long."

"Free from sin," Dale mumbled.

"Yes." Brucie opened her eyes and leaned forward. "Inside the church house, hand-held funeral-home fans swish in rhythm. People are either being washed with the unseen waters of religious righteousness or quietly drowning in their sins."

Dale raised one shaking hand. Brucie couldn't tell if he was agreeing with or protesting what she'd said. She went on.

"They'll have a bevy of souls to pray over. Some in the town churches, and others out in the country at protracted brush arbor meetings. Hopefully, henceforth and evermore, a glorious tally of souls will be saved." She lightened the tone of her voice. "After church, we usually have Sunday dinner at home, and we invite visitors. They always protest, but they come."

She gave a short laugh and smiled as if remembering who the people were.

"And we'd ask Laura Lee," he whispered.

"Ah, yes. Your Mississippi girlfriend. We always thought— never mind."

Brucie ducked her chin. "Are you sure you don't want something to eat?" she asked. "Elnora will be leaving soon. I'm sure there's something left from breakfast."

He shook his head.

"I guess that means no, but I get hungry right now just thinking about southern cooking. The kitchens are always hot and pungent with the aromas of peas, butterbeans, collards, country hams, fried chicken, and cornbread. Sideboards and tables groan with food, and they wash it all down with sun-brewed iced tea. And for dessert after those Sunday dinners"—She licked her lips—"they have cobblers, pies, homemade ice cream, and cakes served with coffee—milk coffee for the children.

"I'm getting carried away, but I still remember those summer days so vividly," she said. "Once dinner was over and the visitors left, we always had an uneven procession onto the porch. First, you children and the men, followed by the cooks and the cleanup help. Shortly after that, you youngsters went outside to climb trees or play tag."

"King of the Mountain," Dale said softly. "And the King needs his whiskey. And sometimes his medicines."

She smiled again. "Yes. And you were usually it. Unless Memory played with you all. Then she often won."

Dale's body tightened, and he nodded as if agreeing with her.

"The grownups would drift off to the bedrooms or the sleeping porch to nap. We often fell asleep to echoes of an aging choir singing, "Would you be free from your burden of sin?"

"Power in the Blood," he whispered as if he were praying.

"Yes. You're right, son. There is."

Dale rolled over and faced away from Brucie.

"I'll talk with Elnora, make sure she's gotten everything cleaned up. I'll go and tend to a few things in the kitchen," she said as she got up. "I'll be back shortly."

***

A sharp cry echoed from the library.

Brucie raced back inside and found Dale struggling with an invisible enemy.

"Cover. Give me cover," he moaned, twisting on the couch. "I can get him back."

She put her hand on his forehead, leaned over, and stroked his cheek as she had when he was a little boy. After a moment, he settled down and his breathing became steady and even.

"Bloody," he whispered.

"It's all right," Brucie crooned. "I'll decide what to do. Soon."

He sighed. Relieved that he had calmed, Brucie glanced toward the large Bible Von Dieter had placed on the desk. A Bible that had seldom been opened.

"At home, the Good Book is always open, and the pages are worn," she murmured, walking to it. Part of the morning paper and a sofa cushion lay across the Holy Book. She cringed and tossed the items aside as if expecting lightning to strike. "No. It's sacrilegious."

She stroked the black leather Bible as if it were a beloved pet.

"I've never really fit in here in Boston. It's a showplace, not a home." She glanced toward her son who had slipped into a dream world all his own. "You may have a better chance of making it in Mississippi. Many of our people are dead, but on our visits back home you always seemed to feel as if their spirits were still alive to you."

Dale made a clicking sound with his tongue, as if trying to tell her something.

"In some ways, maybe they are," she finally said. "To both of us."

Brucie took his hands in hers.

"Oh, but Memory…" A sense of loss and frustration slid through Brucie as she thought of her daughter. She shook her head. "Your sister's visits home tell a different story."

A bad feeling nagged at the back of Brucie's mind. *Memory is always miserable down there. Says she tries. Still, she wants everybody around her pitiful too.*

"Something's off kilter at Redemption Ridge with your sister," she murmured aloud.

"Yes," Dale whispered. "Ask her."

"No. Memory tilts at windmills just like I did." *Except no one ever got after my child like Daddy Claymore did me.* Her stomach tightened into a knot. *Please, no, Lord.* "Even so, I have unfinished business back home. Business I may not finish in my lifetime."

She picked up the music box she'd brought from her old birthplace. She wound it tightly, sat back in her chair and closed her eyes.

"I'm the lady of this house." Brucie took a deep breath and allowed herself to reflect on what she would be leaving behind. When she did, her emotions crashed into each other as she compared Boston and Redemption Ridge.

"What am I doing?" she scolded herself. *What Herschel and I have created here brings me comfort. It's as peaceful and soothing as stroking the soft velvet coat of one of our thoroughbred horses. Redemption Ridge wasn't always kind to me. From the moment Cousin Sarah and I stepped off the train at South Station, I have been in awe of this city and its history. I'll be giving up the world I've come to know and treasure.* She shook her head.

She wiped tears from both of her cheeks.

"A maid with gold hair," Dale sang softly, as if to himself.

"Sunshine came along with thee and swallows in the air, Laura Lee."

Brucie opened her eyes and leaned forward, drinking in her son's soft tenor. "Ah. Your own sweetheart, Laura Lee."

"Boston. A place."

Redemption Ridge waits. It flows through my veins

"She may be waiting, too," Brucie said. "We've got to make haste. We're going home."

***

Elnora had left for the day. Jenson Cooper knocked, and the library door creaked open. He poked his head inside and acknowledged Brucie and Dale.

"Just checking on y'all before I go on to my room on Calder Street." He directed his gaze at Dale. "Looks like my Captain's resting easy."

"Yes," Brucie said. "You did say you were making plans to return to Mississippi, didn't you?" she asked.

"I did. I have tentative reservations to leave Boston on March 20th, so I'll be settled in by Easter."

"That sounds like a good plan, Jenson."

The grandfather clock chimed in the hall.

"It's a quarter past the hour." Brucie met his eyes. "Would you include us in your reservations?"

"Home by Easter," Dale murmured. "The quarter horse."

"Crossed the finish line," Brucie completed his thought.

***

A man wearing a worn butler's vest and tan wool pants walked into the Uerige Brewery in Dusseldorf just as a waiter poured beer into Von Dieter's pewter stein. The man lingered in the doorway for several minutes, as if unsure of himself. Von Dieter recognized him as Ernst Abram but waited to see what he would do.

When Abram finally met Von Dieter's eyes, he nodded and made his way through the boisterous crowd to the other man's table. He paused beside it and shuffled his feet back and forth on the dark stained wood floor.

"Prost!" Von Dieter downed a healthy swallow of frothy black beer and set the stein on the table. After emitting a cough, he belched quietly behind his clenched fist.

Abram didn't speak.

"Vell, vhat do you vant, Ernst?" Von Dieter ran his fingers over the table, furrowed his brow, and looked up as if the man were interrupting an important conversation. "I'm vaiting."

The cowed-looking man held out a telegram.

Von Dieter raised the pair of pince-nez glasses hanging from a chain around his neck and perched them on his nose. Then he took the telegram.

Senator Peter Shields dead.
Stop. Will leave for Redemption
Ridge soon. Stop. Brucie. Stop.

CHAPTER 7

**Lineage is a bad dream truth,
A shame to be pressed,
Held in secret against the chest.**

**A family secret slips
Into the river like a cut
Stone, a quiet fire should go out
in the right light
Like ducks in a row, everything in place
Evil wins. There is no grace**

Monday, March 1

Liam McRae rang the doorbell, snatched his bobby helmet from his head, held it behind his back and assumed a very respectful position.

"As I live and breathe," Elnora the Irish maid said as she showed the redheaded policeman into the entry hall. *Ohh, he is so handsome.* "Ya probably don't have no recall of me," Elnora said. "But I do of you. Ya'd be the policeman I seen over here the other night with Mr. Dale." She licked her lips. "When I called, I really didn't know as ta how ya'd be interested in what I had ta say. But, before he left, I heard Mr. Von Dieter tell the missus he thought ya had somethin' ta do with Mr. Thornton's death. An' he was hot under the collar. Makin' noises he was. Sayin' somethin' he was, aboot goin' ta the authorities."

"You said you had something for me," McRae said, his voice curt. "For the time being, until I get some loose ends tied up, I'm still with the Boston police force, and I don't have a lot of time." He pulled out his pocket watch and glanced at it. "Unless it's important."

"Well, I'm here ta tell ya, it jest might be that." Elnora rolled her top lip down as far as she could to hide the brown spots on her front teeth. "The head of the house, Mr. Von Dieter, is in Germany.

The rest of the family is gone fer the mornin'," she said. "I'm terminated from livin' here an' have moved in with my auntie. The missus is makin' arrangements ta leave in a few weeks. Movin' somewhere down south, ta Mississippi. A place called Redemption Ridge. Now, if ye're interested in a little somethin' on the family, I have a thing or two yamight be a-usin'," she said. "It might jest be a-costin' ya somethin', though."

"Depends on what I'd be buying."

"Oh, ya'd be a-wantin' it," Elnora laughed. "It might be I'd have ta dole it to ya a little at a time." She fluffed the ends of her hair.

"I'm here to tell ya, everybody's got their secrets." She gave him a coy smile. "An' it seems that the snubby-nosed, high-tailed, Mrs. Von Dieter's got 'em more than most folks. We have ta go ta the pantry." She crooked her finger over her shoulder. "But it jest might be, I'll be a-showin' ya a tad of the family secrets." She turned and led Liam toward the kitchen. "I don't usually take gentlemen ta nothin' but the parlor," she said in a flirty voice as he followed her.

"These here." Elnora nodded toward a pantry shelf which held two closed and latched leather boxes. "The missus done throwed 'em out. But me, I took 'em an' put 'em aside. Ya never know what might come in handy. I had me an idea what she was a-throwin' away. Some old baby clothes." She looked at Liam as if he should be reading her mind. When he didn't say anything, she went on. "But I'm not nobody's fool. They have somethin' ta do with somebody Mrs. Von Dieter would jest as soon forget aboot. By the name of Thelma Jewel." Elnora had a smirk on her face. "Because of what I heard Mr. Von Dieter sayin' aboot ya an' aboot how Mr. Thornton, God rest his soul, died, I jest thought ya might be interested. Get the jump on Mr. Von Dieter, before he gets ta ya." She swayed her hips from side to side, tilted her head, and her top lip pulled down, she smiled at Liam. "There's more than jest a smatterin' of baby dresses. I got me a note too. One fer sure the missus won't want nobody ta read. Aboot a baby girl, it tis. Raised in another place. I got me names an' addresses. They might be worth somethin' ta ya. Then again, I jest might have ta sell what I got ta the highest bidder."

Liam rocked back on his heels. "I'm interested."

Elnora opened a box and held up a letter. "Mrs. Von Dieter'd pay a pretty penny fer me not ta show this ta somebody. Seems Miss Memory an' Mr. Dale might have another sister oot there somewhere." She licked her lips. "One nobody knows nothin' aboot. An' here in me hand, I got proof. I know who she is. An' *where* she is. There's more where this come from."

Liam took a deep breath. "Miss Elnora. I'd like to get to know you better. Why don't I buy you dinner? You're a pretty Irish lass, not one of those women of the night." He rested his hand on her shoulder. "The kind that I, a God-fearing man, wouldn't have anything to do with. When's your night off?" he asked. "I know a quiet place on the waterfront where you'd be welcome. Unless you have other plans."

"Oh, I could work it into me schedule," Elnora said. "Are ya askin' me oot?"

"That I am, pretty lady. I'm known to be a man of action. How about tonight?" He put his hand under Elnora's chin and raised her face. "If you catch a cab. I'll pay for it."

Elnora's heart raced. "If it fits with my auntie's plans, I'll be pleasured ta." She tried to appear nonchalant. *Lordy, lordy. I feel like dancin' a jig.*

Liam pulled a card from his coat pocket. "Here's the address, The Whistling Kat. And if you don't say anything to anybody, I can get us a little libation to indulge in.

"I live close by," he said. "We'll go to my place later and get to know each other better. Why don't you let me have that note? I'll give it back to you when I see you."

"No. I'm keepin' it. But it might be that I'll read it ta ya tonight." Elnora swished her shoulders from side to side and pocketed the note.

Liam McRae gave her a dazzling, wide-mouthed smile. "Seven sounds good to me."

***

Elnora gave the driver the pub's address. The taxi slowed down on a dark street and stopped near the water, in front of The Whistling Kat where Liam McRae waited. Pulling her worn coat tight around her shoulders, Elnora followed him as he steered her to the back. He let down a small drape that shielded their booth.

"Give me what you said you had." He reached out his hand.

"First, I want me somethin' ta eat," she said.

"Fish and chips are coming. We'll have us a beer. You can show me what you've got, and then we'll go to my place for the rest of the night." Liam gave her a smile. His green eyes glittering, he reached out his hand. "Why don't I read what you have?"

"No, no," Elnora said. "I got ta have me some money fer this here. I need ta strike me a bargain." *I ain't a fool. I got ta first make sure it's me he's courtin'. Not jest a piece o' paper.*

Done with the fish and chips, and after two steins of beer, Elnora plunged her hand into her coat pocket, pulled out a page of cream-colored stationery, adorned with vines and lavender roses, and began reading.

June 17, 1918

Dear Mrs. Von Dieter,

Lord knows. I've tried. Thelma Jewel was not an easy child to raise, but with your support and with your help, I have done the best I could. You have always been there for us.

Now as to why I'm sending this letter. I find that my thinking goes off track sometimes. My health seems to have been on the decline in the past few months, and as you know, there is the ongoing matter of Thelma Jewel's daughter, Gertie Mae, and her special needs. I will always remain somewhat uncertain about the lineage of this girl. As I have told you, according to Thelma Jewel, some years back she and a Swedish fisherman wed on a Friday, and he drowned in San Francisco Bay on Sunday. Also according to Thelma Jewel, she did not like the foreign way his name sounded, Hans Eidsvik; therefore, she elected to keep Bledsoe, her registered birth name.

Along those lines, I have noticed that there is more evidence of the damage that was done to Gertie Mae's lower body. According to Thelma Jewel, (I was in another part of our home at the time) when Gertie Mae was around eight years old, she fell from the top of the steps all the way down to the bottom. As I have made you aware, her legs have been out of line since that day. I set aside the money you so graciously sent. The physician's recommendation was for her to go under the knife for the leg condition when she becomes a young woman. That time will soon be upon us, but alas, the funds are not to be found. Thelma Jewel, who also has access to that account, has assured me that she invested the money well and wisely. Funds will be available when they are needed.

Along with my health issues, I do think you should be very aware of a new development I was beginning to feel. Now that Thelma Jewel is in her early forties, she had become increasingly suspicious of her lineage. I have found her crawling through the attic, going through old boxes and papers that I have meant to take care of for years. You and I are in perfect accord. She is better off with her familiar life here in California, and you and I both felt that Thelma Jewel should never know you are her real mother. But that has changed to some degree. Enclosed you will find a disturbing note from Thelma Jewel. Sometimes she does not seem to be able to see things quite as clearly as she should.

Let us now be honest with one another. Thelma Jewel is a rather large-bodied woman, and she has no friends. At her age, and with the special conditions of Gertie Mae, I feel no suitors will be coming around.

I am an old woman now and am feeling that my days are numbered. Because of your future dealings with Thelma Jewel, I must pass this on to you.

Thelma Jewel will soon bring me my chamomile tea. Sometimes I wonder what she flavors it with. Oftentimes, a bitter taste is left on my tongue.

With Thelma Jewel's underhanded assistance, I fear I am on an unwanted fast road to Glory. I strongly suspect that she could be lacing my tea, but either way, I am an old woman and not long for this world. I mention this so you may become aware of what Thelma Jewel is capable of.

As you know, the house is in my name, to be passed on to Thelma Jewel at my death, with a modest monthly income. I am sure you will look after Thelma Jewel and Gertie Mae from afar.

I am closing for now.

Yours,
Clementine Bledsoe

P.S.

I am enclosing a very disturbing missive I found. To the effect, that Thelma Jewel knows of her parentage.

"Interesting," Liam said. "Where is this Thelma Jewel?"

Ye're drunk, girl, Elnora cautioned herself. "That might be all I can tell ya," she said. "Fer now." Her tongue was thicker than cold gruel, her voice sounding as if she were talking through a tin can.

"Have some more Guinness, Elnora."

Keep yer wits aboot ya. "I'm goin' ta my auntie's house." Elnora stood and weaving made her way to the front of the pub. The next thing she knew for certain, she woke up in the cab snoring in front of her aunt's house. The note was gone. *But it don't do Mr. McRae no good,* she consoled herself. *He don't know who these people are.*

Friday, March 5

Elnora's life wasn't going the way she wanted it to; she would soon be unemployed. The Von Dieters were leaving for Mississippi in a few weeks, her aunt was pressuring her for money and she hadn't heard from Liam. She was desperate to see him again. "Bless my soul, I've got ta do somethin'," Elnora said. She rang the police station and told the answering Sergeant to get word to Liam McRae that Elnora Peavey had some important information for him.

A few minutes later, the downstairs hall phone rang. When Elnora picked it up and heard Liam's voice, her heart skipped several beats.

"I might still know a few things," she informed him. "It might really be worth somethin' ta the right person, Mr. Liam McRae. The best is yet ta come. Fer somebody. I found me a few names and addresses.

"An' as to Mr. Dale. I got me an empty bottle of some medicine he takes. An' a small bottle of them pills he hides. I might could bring that with me."

"Elnora, the best is yet to come for you too," he said. "I haven't been well the last few days, but I'm better, and we need to see each other. I'll do like before. I'll send a cab around. Bring what you've got."

***

"I have something special for you, my lady," Liam said when Elnora got out of the cab. He carried a large canvas bag over his shoulder, his boot spurs made clicking noises that sounded like rain on a metal roof as he steered her toward the bay. "I've got a friend's boat here. I'm taking us on a little romantic boat ride."

Moonlight made shimmering silver streaks across the waves as they drew closer to the water.

Elnora's heart beat fast. "I might be a-showin' what I have ta ya tonight, an' then again, I might not." She stopped walking. "I don't feel so well. Maybe we better not go out on the water."

"This won't take long," Liam said. "We'll drink a few beers, maybe have some of what I have here in the bag to eat and call it a night."

"What aboot yer place?"

"Oh yes. My place. We'll do that last. First, I just might have a proposal for you."

Maybe I've been wrong. He jest might be fixin' ta be my beau.

For a moment, she was excited. Then, her stomach growled. "What aboot them fish an' chips? I ain't eaten nothin' yet."

"I got our Guinness and some supper here in this bag. A special treat for a special lady." Liam got into the boat first, reached for the canvas sack and set it in the back of the boat. He held out his hand to help her. "Careful, careful," he said. The boat shuddered as Elnora stepped into it.

"I've got some rocks in here to keep us steady," Liam said. When Elnora was seated, he reached into the bag, took out two ceramic mugs, a small keg of beer, and poured her a drink. "What do you have for me?"

Elnora reached into her coat pocket, gave him an empty glass bottle, a pill jar and showed him a letter. "There's some things in this here fer me ta know, an' you ta find out. It'll cost ya."

Liam turned on his vest pocket flashlight. He took out a roll of bills, counted out ten dollars and put the money into her outstretched hand. She gave him the folded paper.

"I, Thelma Jewel Bledsoe (Claymore)," he read out loud, **"found what the woman who lied and raised me (for an unspecified sum of money) has been hiding. I am the Illegitimate daughter of one Brucie Von Dieter (Claymore) from Redemption Ridge, Mississippi. Sent me away to be raised by a distant relative. Someday I would like to lay claim to my name and my rights. And get revenge for what has been done to me."**

"This here in my pocket," Elnora said. "I got me an address an' a telephone number ya can ring. Ya gets them afterwards."

"Address and a telephone number. That's what I need." Liam flexed his fingers several times as if he wanted to grab hold of something. "If what you've been telling me is true, and I have no reason to believe it's not, I'll bury the Von Dieter family with this. All I want is where to find Miss Thelma Jewel Bledsoe. I'm getting sweet revenge for my friend, Senator Peter Shields."

Elnora's mouth opened and closed. She couldn't think of anything to say. This was not exactly what she had expected. Her heart missed a beat. As a gust of wind rocked the boat, she grabbed hold of the side.

No, no. She shook her head. *Mrs. Von Dieter wasn't all that bad to me. I jest want me a little money. Not ta hurt nobody.*

"Then ya ain't gettin' this here address an' no telephone number to ring," she answered. "I jest want me a little lay-by money."

She stood as tall her five-foot three-inch body would stretch and stuck her tongue out. She reached into her coat pocket and held up a piece of stationery.

Liam jumped up, wrenched the paper from her hand and crammed it into his pocket. He grabbed Elnora, jerked her close and kissed her. "You've got fish breath. You need to take a swim," he said. "You're dirty."

He shoved her backward. She tumbled into the water.

"Oh, Gawd!" she screamed.

Liam pushed her under. Making soft, sad noises, she struggled to the surface, but he clamped his hand over her head. He held her down until the water stopped churning. "Now that didn't hurt me a bit." Breathing heavily, he lifted her lifeless body back onto the boat and opened the canvas bag. "Beddy 'bye, Miss Elnora." Liam threaded her legs, torso, arms and then her head into the bag. He picked up the scattered stones and shoved them on and around Elnora. He looped a rope around the top and tied a knot. Very carefully, so as not to tip over the rowboat, he lifted the sack, rolled it into the bay and wiped his hands. "You got me wet, bitch," he grumbled. He checked his pocket and pulled out a note he had written to make sure it hadn't gotten wet.

Friday, March 5

Mrs. Von Dieter,

> *I realize that you will still be in Boston until sometime after the middle of March, at which time you and yours are leaving for Mississippi, but I regret to inform you that because of things that have come up in my life, as of today, I can no longer work for you.*

Elnora

"I'll leave that note in their mailbox," Liam said. "The Von Dieters will think she wrote it, and they won't come looking for her. And nobody'll pay any attention to a missing Irish maid." He picked up his ceramic mug, threw his head back, and swigged down the rest of the beer.

Liam then switched his flashlight on and reached into his coat pocket for the crushed stationery. He laid it on his knee, smoothed it out and read the upper left-hand corner. The name was the same. *Thelma Jewel Bledsoe. 731 Dexter Street, San Francisco, California.*

"I've got some California friends on the police force. They'll be hearing from me." Liam wiped the back of his hand across his mouth. "The fastest I can, I'm making contact with one Miss Thelma Jewel Bledsoe. I think the lady and I can do some business together."

He gazed toward the water and grinned.

CHAPTER 8

A fake smile held in place
The guest sits in a crowded room,
Where windows look out to nowhere

An image unspooled in
Thelma's mind in time with the
metronomic hiss of a train:

Serpents coiling,
Swallowing jewels and
her girl's dumb marble eyes
as if robin eggs.

Thelma's tongue flickers
Revenge tastes sweet

Friday, March 19

She was a plain woman, but Thelma Jewel didn't seem to be aware of how she looked to other people. She gave off an air of self-satisfaction. She dabbed at her broad face, shook out her napkin and tucked it under her chin, spreading it over her large breasts. A small lumpy child, leaning to one side sat next to her. The child's red hair hung in soft ringlets over the collar of her shapeless black and gray tweed dress. Her eyes neither brown nor black, stared at something on the tablecloth only she could see.

"Gertie Mae." Her mother popped her on the leg. "Sit up straight."

"You said you'd take me out and buy me a pretty if I got dressed. I want to catch the train back to California," she whined.

"Hush up, crybaby. Don't you get uppity with me. You can listen to them trains until the moon turns pink, but we are not going anywhere right now." Thelma Jewel put her finger on the side of her mouth. "From my mouth, to God's ear, I'm here to get what's owed to us," she spit out in a loud whisper. "And getting me some payback in the process."

The girl rolled her small lips together and dropped her head.

Then, teacup held in the air, her short nose slightly raised as if she smelled an offensive odor, Thelma Jewel looked around as if she were expecting a servant to dash over and see that she got whatever it was she wanted.

"If you wanting some more cawfee," a lady from another table ventured, "it's over there on the buffet table, but it's probably cold. You have to help yourself."

"Well, I never." Thelma Jewel's lips crimped as if they had tasted something sour. "Well, we've just got off the train and arrived from the West," she said, "and I guess from everything I've heard about these people down here, I should have known how things would be."

She shook her head, her double chins moving in small waves. "We stopped off in Hot Springs, Arkansas. They know how to treat quality folks over there. Service to their betters was certainly superior there."

She removed the napkin from her neck and dabbed at her cheeks, which were a bright red, as if sunburned. "When I get things taken care of at Redemption Ridge, I might just spend the rest of my days sitting there on that verandah of the Arlington Hotel, rubbing shoulders with the hoi poiloi of Hot Springs, Arkansas. I'm sure no one from these parts would be able to appreciate it, though." Thelma Jewel pushed aside a pair of glasses dangling from a beaded crystal chain, pulled a small red velvet sack from her bosom, lifted out a bejeweled, round watch and checked the time. She skimmed her fat thumb over the rhinestones circling the watch. *Someday these here are going to be the real thing. Diamonds.*

"Well, I never," she said to her daughter. "That Mr. Turnipseed called and said he'd be here at eight o'clock. Here it is, almost half past now. You can't depend on anybody nowadays."

She had hardly gotten the words out of her mouth before she looked up and saw a square-shaped stranger raising a finger in her direction and then tapping his chest. She nodded, and he came to their table.

The short man rocked from side to side. He took off his hat, held it in his hand and patted down a few straw-colored strands of hair.

"Miss Thelmer Jewel, I presume."

"One and the same."

"I'm Mr. Mudge Turnipseed." He gestured to an empty chair at her table with smudged, stubby fingers. "I understand the Von Dieters'll be here in a few days."

"So, I've heard."

"An' who, may I ask is this little lady with you?"

"This is Gertie Mae. The light of my life. The one I told you about."

"Tha's what I thought."

The child wore long, white, rolled up socks and scuffed patent leather laced-up shoes. She kicked one foot up and down as if something were trying to bite her foot.

"Pearl." The short man called and gestured to a colored woman cleaning one of the round tables. "Y'all got any more fatback an' gravy back there?"

"Reckon so." The woman pushed her lips out. "My name ain't Pearl."

"Well, what you waitin' on. Go git me some, Pearl."

"I've got to pee," Gertie Mae said.

"It's an inside workin' flush," Mudge said to Thelma Jewel. "Mrs. Netter ain't behind the times."

"I never considered that it wouldn't be, or we would have found other accommodations. Gertie Mae, you're a big girl. The toilet's at the end of the hall."

Gertie Mae stood. When she walked toward the door it was easy to see one leg angled away from the other one, making her appear bandy-legged and splay-footed.

"Is that what you meant by special?" Mudge pointed. "She's got her a little bit of heft an' looks like she's crippled up to me."

Thelma Jewel wiped her heavy jowls. "She's a special child. A very smart girl. She could almost say the whole alphabet by the time she was seven years old." She raised her glasses and set them on her nose. "Now, I am at a point in time where I need to make a decision about my daughter."

Mudge rocked forward and back in his chair as if he were rowing a boat.

"Not so sure what that means," he said, "but I've done found you a place you kin board her. I'll see that she's treated right. I own part of it. It'll cost you eight dollars a month, but as I told you on the telephone, the church I go to has a kinda school, The Divine Deliverance Holiness Church and School for Boys and Girls. They'll feed your dorter an' see that she changes her underwear ever few days. The boys at the school git to bathe on Friday an' the girls on Saturday. The school people don't want them smellin' bad at church on Sunday. I kin have one of them darkies from there git a mule an' pick her up later in the day."

Thelma Jewel nodded her head. "Agreed. Once I have Gertie Mae off my hands, for the time being I shall be unencumbered, and my life will be on the upscale." She put her watch back into the velvet sack. "You and I can get on to collecting what we're both owed by those Von Dieter people.

"Starting with Brucie Von Dieter," she said. "We both know they're kin to the old Claymore family of Redemption Ridge."

My mother by birth. Thelma Jewel almost said the words out loud.

She does not claim me. I don't claim her. She clenched her fist. *Just what she has. That land and them jewels Mrs. Bledsoe babbled about. She didn't make sense a lot of time. Talking about the witches brushing cobwebs out of her brain and such.*

Thelma Jewel narrowed her eyes. *But when she got to railing about the Claymore land and jewels hidden somewhere out in that cemetery, I believed her. And she had it set up in her head they were somewhere around my namesake, Thelma Grace Claymore.* Thelma Jewel primly tucked her napkin back around her neck and once again spread it over her large bosom. *I'm not telling this Mr. Mudge about them though. They'll be mine. And I'm not sharing with nobody.*

"So, let us definitely proceed ahead with our plans," she said.

"Of course," Mudge said. "What's our plans?" he asked. "An' what's in this fer me?" He sneezed. A small trickle ran from his nose. He raised a corner of the tablecloth, wiped it and then grinned. It was a hand-puppet smile; there was no depth to it. "Mrs. Brucie Von Dieter was a Claymore," he said. "An' them Claymores owes my family, the Turnipseeds, too. Not sure what. But I know they owe, an' I aim to collect on the debt."

"I will help you. I'm sure it will be a fight," Thelma Jewel said, "But I'm up to it. And I may want to exact some very special revenge. To make these people suffer what I, the Good Lord's humble servant, have had to endure." Her expression indicated she had lived through many hard times. "We will do this together," she said. "I will pay you and make it worth your while." Her lips pursed, she went on. "First though, I must see what the lay of the land is. I intend to get back what was stolen from me." She looked down at the table and didn't speak for a minute. *I've got it in me to take care of these people. And you too, if I have to.*

She raised her head and pasted a sad look on her face. "With some charitable help, from you, Mr. Turnipseed, I shall prevail in this rightful and shameful cause."

"Mudge," he said. "It's jest Mudge."

"Mudge it shall be," she answered. *But I'm not sharing with anybody*, she reminded herself. *I took care of that woman, Mrs. Bledsoe. Bet she rued the day she ever saw me.* Thelma Jewel dropped her head, wiped an unseen tear with the edge of her napkin. She covered her mouth with her hand as if what she was thinking was too powerful to speak of. She looked up and smiled sadly. "My late husband. I didn't keep his name but went back to my own. Bledsoe." *Not my husband. Just somebody I had me a one night's bed sharing with. Can't even pronounce his name. Didn't know anything about the man. Don't care a fig he's floating out in the bay somewhere.* "The dear man has passed on to his glory and is buried somewhere deep in some foreign soil.

"I do expect, very soon, to come into a vast sum from his estate." *All he left me was a case of the crabs and Gertie Mae. Mrs. Bledsoe's estate does not leave me enough to live in the manor I intend to have. My money's going to come from Brucie Claymore Von Dieter.*

"So, I will make it worth your while to help me," she said. "I'll get them back," Thelma Jewel muttered. "Those Claymores."

"A widder lady, you say?" Mudge drummed his smudged fingernails on the table. "Down the line, if you need one, I know me a good lawyer man. One what goes to my church. Make sure you git everythin' tha's comin' to you. From them damn Claymore's." Mudge rocked his shoulders. "Sorry fer the cussin.' Sometimes seems I jest can't help myself." A small smile spread across his face.

Already a rich widder lady. An her due some Claymore money. He rolled his bottom lip into his mouth and ran his tongue over it. *An' a little girl to boot. Without them splayed legs, an' them roller-wheel eyes, she wouldn't be too bad to speak of.*

"Speakin' o' church." He leaned across the table. "Whyn't you allow me to escort you to a special service we got comin' up?"

"In California I was a churched woman. Not mainstream, I must say."

"Likewise. I'm a churched man. More of the Holy Rolly type of persuasion. We do have us some real intense meetin's. Now, those people at The Divine Deliverance Holiness Church an' School fer Boys an' Girls, what I go to, I'm proud to say. They are filled with the Holy Ghost. They're the ones what have the school Gertie Mae'll be goin' to. If you'll join us, come Easter Sunday, I think you'll find our special service will raise you to new heights of glory."

He looked around the room, almost as if to make sure no one else was within earshot and whispered, "You might be interested in comin' around to one of them brush arbor meetin's. You'll see somethin' I bet you ain't ever seed in California."

Thelma Jewel ran her fingers through a thin pouf of henna-dyed hair. She leaned forward and slid her hand down into her bag and felt the cold tip of the small derringer she carried with her.

"You might git to see a little snake handlin'," Mudge added. "We got us a special celebration comin' up."

"Snake handling! Well, I never." Thelma Jewel ran her tongue over her teeth. "What time do your services start?" she asked.

CHAPTER 9

**In the mirror aging through imagination,
Wearing your mother's age:**

**Reflected generations spider-web,
Threatening to wild these idols.**

Such would be a fierce chase out of oneself.

Monday, March 22, on the train from Chicago to Memphis

Memory woke when sunup was only a splinter of light at the bottom of their partially-raised shade. Brucie was already up and gone. *Knowing my mother, she's probably already dressed for the day and is somewhere drinking a cup of coffee. And there's no reason. We don't have to be in a hurry. I'm glad we spent Saturday night and most of Sunday in a hotel in Chicago. We weren't so tired when we boarded late last night.*

She put on a gray gabardine skirt and matching jacket and combed her hair. She took a moment to lean back against the wall of her unmade berth and think about the last few days. They'd only been gone from Boston since Saturday, but it seemed as if they had been on the train for a week. She knew her mother had high hopes for this move to the South making a real change in Dale's life. Besides, Brucie had made it clear she was, at long-last, on her way home. At the very least, Memory had mixed feelings, and she began to have a different take on her return to Mississippi. From the moment the decaying hand, probably belonging to her dead husband, had been delivered to their house, she knew she had to leave Boston. Added to that was her brother's downward spiral and the death of the infamous Senator Peter Shields. If she had anything to do with it, this unwanted jaunt to Redemption Ridge would only be a temporary exile for her. When the train pulled out of South Station in Boston, she made it a point to let her mother know she was going only because Dale needed her, that what her mother perceived as their dangerous situation back home played no part in her decision. She felt since Senator Peter Shields was dead, he would be no big deal around Boston anymore. Any repercussions from his death would soon blow over.

She'd keep in touch with what few friends she had left, and when Dale was settled in down south, she'd pack and leave. She might well take a cruise. After the cruise was done, then she would find somewhere else to live. She picked up a menu from the Cunard cruise line a friend had sent her and ran her finger over the words describing a lovely French dinner. *Right now, Lausanne, Switzerland, has a nice ring to it. Wherever, it certainly won't be Tallouga County, Mississippi.*

As she had done so often, she reached into her beaded purse and drew out her nail file. She slipped her jacket off and began digging into the fleshy part of her upper arm.

Everything in her life had changed. She had only been a widow a short while, and in all truthfulness, she was sorry about Thornton being dead, but she hadn't been too unhappy about being single again. Her head ringing with the clickety-clack of the wheels, the noises of the train ride had gotten to her. Memory was miserable and ready to do everything she could to direct the blame for her unhappiness somewhere, and her mother made a good target. Her mother would be back in their compartment soon, so she dropped her nail file back into her bag, dried blood droplets from her arm with a deep pink handkerchief and put her jacket on. She had timed it right.

Dressed for the day in a black-and-gray tweed suit, with a wide-brimmed black velvet hat on her head, Brucie came back into the drawing room. She set down a heavy reticule. Memory noticed that every step she took, like a faithful dog on a short leash, she had kept the bag swinging against her hip. "We'll be having a late lunch, so I've asked our porter to bring us coffee and rolls."

"I feel like moving to Mississippi is the end of the line for this family," Memory said. "When summer comes, I'm thinking about taking that Cunard cruise I told you about."

"Where do you think your money's going to come from for such an expensive trip?"

Memory clamped her lips shut and decided to let that remark ride, for now.

There was a muffled noise, like clothes rubbed over a washboard as the train sped across a rough section of track.

Brucie checked her watch. "Where's Brother?"

Memory heard an unfamiliar tremor in her mother's usually self-assured voice. *You're sounding old. That makes me uncomfortable.* She saw lines she had never noticed before. It was like seeing her mother in a cracked mirror. At the moment, Memory had too much on her own mind to worry about anybody else. *Besides, if it wasn't for her mother, they wouldn't be headed to that God-awful hot and humid place.*

"This train ride isn't ever going to be over. And what's coming next will be worse."

While Brucie folded a few clothes and put them into her suitcase, Memory spread her skirt across the seat, picked up a tattered *Saturday Evening Post* and began thumbing the pages.

This was her world as it used to be. The way she wanted her world to be again. Summers spent at a beachside resort on Cape Cod. Shopping at Macy's or going to Ziegfield Follies at the Globe Theatre in New York.

She wanted no part of what she remembered of Redemption Ridge. She was afraid of what might lie ahead of her.

Memory rolled the magazine up and pointed it at her mother as if she had an invisible blackboard in front of her. "I don't intend to stay in that God-forsaken place forever. I'll never forget the summers we spent in that backward state. Mosquitoes were big as a skillet and buzzed like chicken legs frying in hot grease," she said in a mocking voice. "I hate the heat. Besides, everybody talks like they've got a mouthful of warm taffy."

Brucie unfastened the top button of her suit and ran her finger under the collar of her gray silk blouse.

"I've never liked the town of Franklin, or your place out there in the country at Redemption Ridge."

"It's not my place. It's our place."

"No, no, no. You're wrong." Memory glanced sideways at her mother. "Redemption Ridge is *your* place."

"Dale likes it. Your brother will have a chance to start over."

Memory took a deep breath and rolled her eyes. "Well, isn't that the cat's meow? The male always comes first. You probably hope I'll find some old rich landowner, marry again and not bother anybody."

"Give it time," Brucie tried to reassure Memory. "You'll fit in just fine."

Memory flung her head in exasperation, swishing her thick bobbed hair around her head. "Why didn't you just send Dale down there?"

Brucie took in a breath and sighed. Her voice was so low Memory could hardly hear her. "If I don't do something, your brother's either going to die, or he's going to kill another human being. It's just a matter of time. Right now, we need each other."

"I've been quiet long enough and played the part of the good little girl." Memory had her guns ready and loaded for this. "I'm not going to take it sitting down. Now, you'll hear how I feel. You said it." She raised both hands, as if she were surrendering to something or to somebody. "The words came out of your own mouth. There in a nutshell is the way it always is. The king's son rules."

Brucie gave her a weak smile and shook her head sadly. "Somehow, you have the idea that because Dale is the son, he's favored over you. Not true. We'll all have a chance. To start again," she added lamely.

"It's not just the male-female thing. What in the name of God am I supposed to do down there? Do you expect me to snap beans and cook cornbread and black-eyed peas?" Memory set the magazine down and made pulling motions with her fingers. "Milk cows?" She looked around the train compartment then raised the hem of her skirt and brushed it across the seat as if it were a cleaning rag. "Or clean out a privy? Who's going to tote in the firewood? Don't look for me to use a scrub-board out in the side yard." She held out both hands. "I like my fingernails shaped. I like my fingernails long."

Brucie seemed to have no power of speech left. She shook her head in disbelief at her daughter's tone of voice, at what she was saying

"This is where I came from." Memory raised the magazine and pointed to a page of well-dressed women. "Not Franklin, Mississippi. I swear. Some of the more fashionable women in Tallouga County sew up flour sacks for their Sunday-go-to-meeting clothes. Anything remotely resembling fashion or the way we've lived our lives up East, in God's country, certainly does not exist down there in Mississippi."

She stared at her mother. "The first and only time I went to a country church meeting, those old women of the Divine Deliverance Holiness Church hated me. They were whooping, 'Faith alone can move mountains.' I made the mistake of standing up and giving my testimony and saying, 'the only hill I've ever moved in Mississippi was an ant hill; and that wasn't because of faith. It was because of my big toe. And I got stung all over my legs."

"That's not our kind of church, and you know it. I think your imagination's running away with you." Brucie's cheeks narrowed in what could have been either anger or despair. She dropped her head down and covered her eyes with her hand. Memory saw her reaction, but she wasn't done.

"Well, that's neither here nor there. But there are worse people in that neck of the woods. Those that live down by the river. The ones I heard about that handle snakes. I guess you'd like to see me praying on stage and kissing a water moccasin."

"No. We never had anything to do with those people. That's those crazy Potters and Turnipseeds. For all I know, they've killed each other with those snakes." Brucie raised her head. "They eat dirt. They live in treehouses. They interbreed with each other."

"That's the kind of stuff I'm talking about. And last I heard, somebody said we were kin to some of them."

Brucie raised her hands in an I-give-up motion. "It's getting late. What about your brother?" she asked again.

"You told him last night we'd meet in the diner and have a late lunch." Memory yawned. "He's a grown man. Don't worry. He'll make it off the train just fine."

"Don't you think you need to check on him?"

"You're paying Jenson Cooper to look out for him. He's probably out on the caboose now."

"It's awfully cold for him to be out in the weather smoking a cigarette."

Memory shook her head. "Well, you might not want to admit it, but cold as it is, if he's out in the weather, it'll be something stronger than cigarettes he'll be enjoying," she muttered. "Jenson will look after Dale. And by the time we get brother dear settled in at Redemption Ridge, Mr. Cooper may well have earned his money. And then some."

She popped her hand against her leg. "Money I could have used for the cruise I wanted to go on."

Brucie's body tightened as if Memory's words offended her in some way as the train steamed across scrabbly, dry land. Memory rolled the magazine she had been looking at as if it were a megaphone and put it to her lips. "Come one, come all. See the once rich Boston heiress. No, I mean poor white, Tallouga County trash, Miss Memory Von Dieter Hastings. She can make the barnyard pigs to slow waltz while she's feeding them their slop. She can tame snakes, while in the background a choir sings, 'Only Believe.'" She made a hissing sound. "It's a family talent."

"No. No. No. Don't talk about snakes anymore," Brucie said sharply. "That's how come our old barn burned down. That's how come Daddy Claymore, who'd had a stroke, died. Cousin Book Turnipseed, his paid caretaker, had been terminated. Angry, he sneaked back to Redemption Ridge. He brought a bag of moccasins with him. He wheeled Daddy Claymore to our barn and was tormenting him." Brucie stopped talking for a minute, but her lips moved, as if in silent prayer. Then she seemed to gather herself together and went on. "One of Book's cousins was there and saw it all. Book tripped and dropped the box. In a heartbeat, those snakes were all over both of them."

Memory's eyes flashed. "What you just told me about the Potters, Turnipseeds and Tallouga County, Mississippi, says it better than I could ever dream up." She flung the magazine to the floor and stomped out of the compartment.

"Stop." Brucie's voice had a catch in it. "It's not the way you're making it sound."

In a huff, Memory stood and started to walk toward the end of the car but the corridor stretching in front of her seemed endless, and the way she was thinking right now, led to who knew what or where.

"I didn't handle that well," she said. "But like it or not, that's the way I feel." Rocking in rhythm with the train's motion, which seemed to throb with as much anger as she felt inside, Memory dropped her head down and sat in a vacant seat.

The whistle blew out a high, arrogant scream at the sky as the train slowly circled through a curved stretch of rail. Feeling bad about the confrontation with her mother, it took several minutes but she was finally able to get herself together.

She took a deep breath, pushed the drawing room door open and went back in. Brucie had her head in her hands. There was a long uncomfortable silence between the two of them. Memory knew that she had hurt her mother. But she was hurting. Too much had happened. She and Thornton had never had much of a marriage, but even so, her life had completely changed. And in some ways, she did miss her husband. They liked to wander through museums, go to plays, the movies and have dinner at fine restaurants.

For a moment Brucie said nothing, and Memory was afraid she would have to apologize, which she really wanted no part of.

Then Brucie raised her head. "Let's change the subject," she said. "Maybe one of these days we'll get it all figured out and be normal again. I heard the clock a short while ago. It's a little after one. Your brother should have been here."

"That suits me," Memory said. "Right now, I'm hungry and hard to please."

The train screeched to a crawl as it went through a small town. "Dale will join us in his own good time." Her shrill voice was almost in perfect pitch with the train whistle. "Let's go eat." She pulled a beaver cloche hat over her fashionable hairstyle, the new, bobbed cut. "If Dale's hungry, he'll find us."

CHAPTER 10

Somewhere, these pictures are kept
Brucie thinks,
Somewhere these pictures are kept.

Secrets from the old days
Hidden from her children
Only hers to see

Reality was to be hidden

Brucie sees jewels bright as seeds
Planted in the fertile depths of
Redemption Ridge.
They have ripened into memories.

Somewhere, these pictures are kept
Dale thinks
Somewhere, these pictures are kept.

Daylight was
A grim Capture

Shelling in the night
Was the thousand eyes.
The eternal watch.

Monday, March 22, Breakfast

"If your brother doesn't show up soon, I don't know what we should do," Brucie said as she and Memory stepped into the dining car.

"You worry too much," Memory snorted.

A waiter picked a starched linen napkin off a small table and draped it over his arm. He made a half bow and motioned the ladies to follow him. He seated Memory and Brucie and then handed them a menu. Brucie pushed the large reticule she had brought to the diner under the table, then she put one foot on it as if she were pressing a piano pedal to the floor.

The waiter set out pats of butter on small white china plates and filled their water glasses. "Would you ladies like anything to drink?" he asked.

"I'd love some hot tea," Brucie said. "And if we can order off the breakfast menu, that's what I'd like."

"Make that two of us," Memory said.

The waiter left and returned in a few seconds with another menu. Brucie and Memory scanned it and placed their orders.

"I wish Dale would come on and join us," Brucie said.

An unhappy look on her face, Memory rolled her eyes and didn't answer.

"I'm going home," Brucie said. "It feels right. For all of us."

"Speak for yourself," Memory mumbled.

Oh God, Brucie pled. *Please give me wisdom and strength. I'll need it for what's to come.*

The two of them were quiet for a time before Memory raised the edge of the tablecloth and nodded toward the big bag under her mother's foot. "Why'd you bring that to the diner?"

"I've got important papers in here. Things you should know about Redemption Ridge," Brucie said. "And I'm carrying a few jewels," she added in what seemed to be an afterthought.

"Redemption Ridge is the last place we should have run." Memory sighed. "I think Papa will be very unhappy with this move." She got her compact out and reapplied her lipstick. "He may not even come back from Germany. That might not be all bad."

Brucie stirred her tea and settled back in her chair. "He'll join us as soon as he can." If only she could be as certain of this as her voice sounded. She leaned over, ruffled through the papers, lifted one of the bundles from the reticule and laid a large, yellowed document tied in thick string on the table. She stared at it a moment and placed her hands across it as if it were as precious to her as the Holy Bible. "While we're waiting for our breakfast, let me show you one thing you need to know about. These are deeds to the house and to land and property in Tallouga County. We're in far better shape in Franklin, Mississippi, than we were in Boston. Land and old family property were deeded to Lamont and me back in the eighteen eighties." She raised her hand and waved the waiter over. "I'd like a little more." She pointed to her teacup.

"Cousin Sarah took care of the legal work for the two of us," Brucie went on. "I've said very little, but Lamont's managed our affairs all these years and has done it well. He and I also inherited some very valuable jewelry. Years ago, a piece at a time as we needed it, Lamont took some for both of us out of our hiding place." The waiter set down another cup of tea. Brucie nodded, took a sip and continued. "Everything's much cheaper around Franklin than in Boston. That's why I've been able to fix our house and for Lamont to buy a few small businesses in and around Franklin. And overall, most of it was used for the good of Tallouga County. You're old enough for me to tell you where the jewelry is." Brucie noticed that Memory looked irritated, and as expected, it wasn't but a moment before her daughter began to speak her mind.

"I'm not interested unless it'll buy me a summer in Europe. I haven't lost anything out there in Tallouga County. I'll never forget those hot and boring summers we spent there. Not only that, your buddy, Lamont"—Memory's voice carried a small hint of resentment—"always told you and us, what to do. And you did what he said. Sometimes it seemed like you two thought alike," she said accusingly.

The waiter brought eggs, toast and patty sausages to the table. "You don't know the half of it, young lady," Brucie said once the man had moved away. She almost went on with the truth but stopped herself. *Be cautious.* She searched Memory's face for the answer to a puzzle of when and how much to tell. She saw no clues, only a closed face. *Now's not the time to share those days. There's so much I can't tell.* "Lamont and I grew up together," she said carefully. "I have told you this many times."

Absentmindedly Brucie ate some of her eggs. *Around thirteen. That's when I found out why Lamont Randall and I were so much alike.* She frowned, thinking about those yesteryears. "Soon."

"What?" Memory asked.

"Nothing. We'll talk about it later."

Sometimes her childhood was clearer to Brucie than the hours that she had just lived through. *Lamont and his issue. Our blood kin. We're half-brother and sister. Someday I'll tell you. Soon, Memory.*

She leaned back. "I've said enough for now."

"There's still a family scandal there," Memory said.

To Brucie, Memory's demeanor seemed like a dog with a bone; her daughter wanted to chew on their family history for a while longer.

"You're part of it. People in that little town talk behind your back," Memory said. "They say you've gotten above your raising. I already know a lot more than you think I do. Or than I want to know."

"There are long stories behind any Tallouga County gossip you might have heard." Brucie's eyes narrowed. "When the time is right, I'll tell you what happened."

"Try me now, while we're on this endless, boring train ride."

"Now's not the time. But you should know this. In many ways, our maid Vernell was more of a mother to me than my own mother." Tears filled Brucie's eyes. "I don't know what I'd have done without her." Remembering how it was, grateful feelings overtook her.

She gazed at Memory as if she wanted her to understand what she was feeling. *Thank you, Jesus, Daddy Claymore was not my father. Vernell. She told me who it was. Daddy Claymore's half-brother.* It was on the tip of Brucie's tongue to say what was on her heart, but she decided against it. *But his half-brother, the handsome, disgraced Confederate officer, Bruce Claymore. Father to me. Father to Lamont. They say he was some kind of a ladies' man. I believe it.*

"Vernell's name needs to be cleared." A frown crossed Memory's face; she had a rigid set to her jaw.

"Half the people in that country town still like to think she was a murderess." Memory could not disguise the accusation ringing in her voice.

Brucie cautioned herself not to say anything she would regret.

"It was such a horrible crime that when they hanged her, her body had to be hidden. Nobody even knows where she's buried." Memory smiled thinly. "And every time this comes up, you look like you know some big dark secret."

"You've heard me say this before. Vernell was hanged for killing my sister, Thelma Grace. But she didn't do it." Brucie looked down at her hands. "Oh, how I remember burying Vernell. Lamont and I, and the long-dead Sheriff Bramlett knew what happened. We knew, and God rest her soul, where Vernell's grave is.

"And, I must say, the more I'm around Jenson Cooper, the more he reminds me of his grandfather. He's like the sheriff in so many ways. Back then Sheriff Bramlett took care of Vernell the best he could. So, no one would disturb her grave. There were many secrets we had to keep." Brucie bit her lips to keep from speaking. *Where my real father's bones rest. There, in the casket, with Vernell's. And Lamont's twin baby sister, Sunnie Flo. Our jewels close by. Most of them gone now. Many used for charity. A home for the old soldiers. A church. New jail.*

"So much time has passed. It shouldn't matter now. But still, it's probably best for me to keep my peace about some things. That'll be for another day. There are things still not spoken of."

She raised the shade by their table almost to the top. Nice and warm here in the train, outside it was a grim, gloomy day. Wispy clouds the color of a hoot owl's wing tumbled through the sky.

"You've never made it a secret that Vernell was trying to protect someone," Memory said.

Brucie took a sudden sharp breath. Vernell was the gateway to her past. In the months and years following, more times than she could count, she was haunted by what had happened to her. "As you know, Vernell was protecting me." Once again, she agonized to herself on this day, so many years later, as she had done over and over. "She thought I killed my sister. She took the blame. And then, when the truth came out, it was too late for her."

She wiped her lips with her napkin. "You've heard it piecemeal before. It wasn't Vernell, nor Daddy Claymore, but that carpetbagger scum, Warner Sledge, who stabbed my sister, Thelma Grace." She looked down at the floor. "By the time Sheriff Bramlet found out who it was, Vernell was already dead. Rather than have a town blanketed in shame, because of some self-righteous church people hanging Vernell, it was best to just let it stay as it was. And the sheriff had taken care of Mr. Sledge." Struggling to control her feelings, Brucie bowed her head and turned away from the window. *Could I have done anything,* she wondered now, as she had done so often through the years. "I don't want to talk about it." *Time softens. Sometimes old scandals and sins are healed.*

The wail of the train whistle broke into her thoughts. "Well, let's think about what's ahead. I know it was hard to lose Thornton. Especially the awful way your husband died. Your whole future has changed, but you have a long life ahead of you."

As usually happened when Brucie mentioned the loss of Memory's husband, she noticed her daughter had a slightly irritated look on her face and made no reply. Even though they were alike in so many ways, Brucie could often see the judgmental Von Dieter side coming out in her daughter. Trying to understand Memory was like trying to capture a will-o'-the-wisp with a wide-stringed butterfly net.

"I do need to talk to you and your brother about Redemption Ridge. About Vernell and the old place. So often I think there are unsettled spirits there."

A flash of rotting teeth and fish breath flashed through Memory's mind. "Oh God," she whispered. "I have my own evil spirits. They're waiting there. At Redemption Ridge."

"You've mentioned that before. I don't understand." But despite her words a hot, shameful flush washed over Brucie.

"You're supposed to be in touch with the other world spirits and what's happening." Memory shook her head as if she wanted to move on with their conversation

"That part of my life is over."

"Maybe then you do need to talk to us. But not about the old spirits." Memory wished her mother would be honest about the past. "There's a lot you didn't tell Dale and me about many things. Dangerous things."

Brucie took a sip of her tea

"Thank you, Cousin Sarah, for letting us know," Memory muttered. "Because of you, the neighbors told us our half-sister is a murderess," she said under her breath.

A distracted look on her face, Brucie put the cup down and was just before buttering a roll when she heard the chair next to her being pulled out.

She was relieved to see Dale and also for Memory to have something else on her mind besides Vernell and the evil that had happened to her and to others she cared about. "Glad you joined us. What would you like, son?"

"Nothing."

Beneath them, steam hissed like an angry, spitting cat. There was a screech. With a jerk, the train slowly pulled out of a station.

Dale held the sides of his chair with both hands as if he were about to fall out of it.

Even though it was warm, Brucie shivered. Dale had a grainy beard that was not becoming to him and it was easy to see that he was unsteady and didn't seem to know for sure where he was. He hummed a tune under his breath,

> *So, prepare, Say a Prayer*
> *Send the word, Send the word to beware*
> *We'll be over. We're coming over...*

"You look like you could stand a shave, and you stink like a Boston Brewery." Memory's face hardened. "You need to get your head on straight and remember, the war's over." Even though her tea was already milky white and almost cold, she poured more cream into her cup.

"I smell bacon frying." Dale looked around as if searching for someone or trying to figure out where he was. "That's what they fed us for breakfast yesterday. Just before we attacked the Germans. We were fed a good country breakfast. Like the way we used to eat back in Mississippi. Except, no grits." He took several deep breaths that quickened into shallow panting. "I can't breathe in here. My heart wounds are bleeding. They sent us out on a suicide mission. I had to lead my men."

Dale shifted uneasily in his chair. "I don't want to go to sleep. When I do, I'm not sure if I'm going to wake up. Or, if I want to. Please, hear this." He seemed to appeal to the two ladies for their understanding of what had happened. "We had to retreat. Samuel was crawling back toward our trench. He had been hit in the arm and grazed above his eye. He slowed us down. We had to leave him."

Brucie was relieved that the clinking of dishes, conversations from nearby tables and clacking of wheels skimming across the metal track probably made it difficult for other people to hear what her son was saying. She put her hand on Dale's knee to calm him, but he kept talking.

"I felt his fear. His agony. 'You can, you can make it,' I hollered. The machine guns kept raking across my men." Dale raised his hands in a blocking motion. "Like the bullets were trying to give them haircuts. Almost everybody else had made it. Trying not to be hit again, not to be a target, Samuel fell toward a shell hole."

Brucie noticed that a few people turned their heads in their direction. "Lower your voice. Please."

Dale cocked his head in a half nod. "Two bodies were already glued into the frozen, mud-slimed pit. He couldn't slide in. He piled on top. Rats ran out. A German soldier crawling right behind him grabbed his legs. I heard Samuel scream, 'Help me.'" Dale's voice had become high and shrill; he sounded like a yelping puppy.

Memory picked up a spoon and drummed it onto the tabletop. "People are looking at you."

"The Kraut sliced his legs off with his saber. The Heinie squirmed away with his bloody trophies. If the dead men in that hole had been alive, they would have drowned. Samuel's blood blanketed the shell hole." Dale's voice broke. "'Cut my throat.'

Samuel's cries echoed over the battlefield. 'Oh, God, cut my throat.' I couldn't, but I cried with him."

He ran his hand across his chin. "I waited. My turn came. And I made it across and back with my friend. I scrubbed him over ice. Ice pricks. Red. They laced his body. Red shoelaces."

Memory waved her hand. "Why don't we talk about something else? People are listening to you. This isn't exactly dinner-table conversation."

On some level Dale seemed to understand. He continued, but he was speaking almost in a whisper now. "Shell holes. We bumped. We bumped over dead bodies. Caught on blown-off arms."

Memory reached across the table to touch her brother's hand, but he kept on with his nightmares. "Eyeballs resting on cheeks as if they were tired of looking at the slaughter."

Dale's eyes were glassy; he didn't look at either his mother or his sister. "He bled out. But it was on our side."

"Two days later we turned the tide."

"People in this diner are giving us funny looks," Memory warned.

A tiny agonized sound slipped from Dale's throat. "We invaded their command post. Samuel's legs. They were using them for a latrine doorstop." Moving quickly, he pushed back from the table. "I'm sick to my stomach. I can't stay." He stood. "My men need me." Weaving, bumping into tables, he blundered away from his mother and his sister.

As if the car were a theater and the diners an audience waiting for the curtain to be raised, a hush fell over the room. The only noise was an occasional clink of dishes, the soft clacking of wheels skimming over metal tracks. Brucie felt something bizarre was getting ready to happen, and she was powerless to stop it.

Stumbling down the aisle Dale tripped over someone's foot. He flung his arms out, fell and grabbed at a tablecloth, snatching it loose. A loud noise broke the car's silence. A vase of crimson roses, silverware, food and dishes crashed to the floor.

"Watch out buster," an angry voice called.

"Not again," Dale moaned. "Don't let them come off." He rolled to his side and grabbed the startled man's foot. He held it, then as if climbing a short rope, his hands went on up the man's ankle and calf. Dale jerked. The man fell from his chair and slammed to the floor. Dale wrapped his arms around his thighs. "I'm no conchie. I was there for my men. I stayed. You're in my company. I'll save them, man," he said. "I'll save them," his voice slurred.

No one in the car moved. On his back, the man's arms flailed. His mouth worked furiously, but no words came out. He got himself together, doubled his fist and butted the side of Dale's face with one hand.

"I'll get you home," Dale said. "You're one of mine."

"I know, I know." Seemingly from nowhere, Jenson Cooper appeared. "I'll help." He bent over and put his hand on Dale's back.

"Get off him, crazy man," a voice from the rear of the car called. A waiter who had come in with a tray of food dropped it. Fists doubled, he ran toward the front of the car.

From a nearby table a heavy-set man with an upswept handlebar mustache sprang forward. "Stop." He flung his arms out, blocking the charging waiter. "I was there too. At Chateau Thierry."

"Captain Von Dieter was at Chateau Thierry and Belleau Woods," Jenson said loudly, as if that explained everything and there was no need to say anything else.

When Jenson spoke, Dale didn't release his finger-grip, but his body relaxed. "I have it, Sergeant," he said. "We can give him his legs back. I'll hold him so you can do it."

The tackled man rained a few one-handed punches anywhere on Dale he could. Jenson caught the man's hand, then pried Dale loose from him.

The mustached stranger released his grip on the waiter who bent over and helped the man who had been jerked from the chair to his feet.

Holding Dale's arm Jenson Cooper led him to an empty seat and table at the far end of the car. He pulled out a chair. "Get yourself together, Captain. I'm here. You'll be *home* soon. Let's sit and catch our breath a minute." He turned and faced the other diners.

Tallouga County. Where will I get my liquor? My cough medicine? Dale agonized.

"He has nightmares all night. He sleepwalks," Jenson said as if explaining a simple arithmetic problem to a roomful of children. "He marches, one foot in front of the other." Jenson dug in his pockets. He laid cigarette paper on the table, filled it with tobacco, rolled and spit on it. "He struggles to breathe at night. That's how it is sometimes. It was hard to breathe in the gas mask." He flipped a match with his thumbnail. "He remembers."

Except for the clickety-clack of rails and a slight rattle of dishes, once again the dining car fell still. For a few moments, the sergeant had an audience. "He's slipped back into another time and place," he said. "He can't get easy.

"Shellshock, the doctors call it. I've seen him like this before. It doesn't last long. He should start to come out of it soon."

"God a'mighty," the man who had been thrown to the floor said in a clipped Boston accent. "He's dangerous. Get him outta here. Before I telegraph the police at the next stop we come to and have him thrown off this train."

"He was an officer," Jenson said. "In the name of all that's holy, you best think about the way you're feeling." His tone forgiving, he sounded like a minister absolving his congregation of their sins after they had celebrated the Lord's Supper.

The stranger who had held back the waiter snapped Dale a salute, a strong amen to what Jenson said. Then he turned and faced the other diners. "He saved you people from the Heinies."

Brucie stood. Walking as if she were wounded and swaying with the motion of the train, she stopped by the people that Dale had disturbed. "He was in The War," she said to the man who by now was on his feet and brushing off his trousers leg. She couldn't help but notice the look on the other people's faces in the dining car. It was like it wouldn't have been hard for them to start throwing dishes at her son; in olden times, it could have been a stoning. "He was fighting for peace. You should be on your hands and knees. He was a hero." She brushed tears away with the back of her hand. Her lips and chin trembling, she left the dining car.

Her emotions frayed, Memory sucked in a sharp breath and flung her napkin to the floor. Quick and angry looking as a small child, her cheeks flushed, threatening to trip on a white ruffled petticoat daggling from under her long skirt, Memory bounced down the aisle. "You people are not helping," she called over her shoulder. She sweated. Her hair, smoothed under her new cloche, began dripping and wadded into small tangled tendrils.

"This train ride won't ever be over!" Memory jerked the door open. "This gets on my nerves something awful. We don't know what else to do to help him. Everybody's tried."

Pausing just outside the door, she heard a commotion behind her as a chair fell over. She refused to look back, but she heard a familiar voice say, "I found your legs. The guilty must pay. Evil comes from the parlor. Evil needs to be stopped."

CHAPTER 11

**The past is a kind of south
to be traveled to a lower latitude
closer to memory.**

**Halfway between Memphis and Jackson
a secret becomes a bitter strawberry
in Memory's mouth.**

Monday, March 22

Panting and out of breath, Brucie looked down at her hands. *I'm tired. Too much to think about.* "We'll soon be in Mississippi." She closed her eyes and immediately saw a familiar scene, the old cemetery at Redemption Ridge. She felt a soft warmth, like a breath, caress her neck; she heard a sigh.

Miss Thelmer Jewel. She's on her way too. She's gone make you some trouble. You jest remember. You done the bestest you could by her. I'll be a waitin' fer you to home.

Opening her eyes, Brucie put her hand over her heart. "Oh, Vernell. You're always with me. I only wish I could see you," she said softly. "Maybe."

The roomette door flung open. "I'm sick of this." Memory stomped into the compartment. "I'm ready to get off this train. As far as I'm concerned, Redemption Ridge is the other end of nowhere."

Brucie drew in a deep, easy breath. *I didn't even know I was sleepy, but I must have dropped off.* "It was just a dream," she said softly, reminding herself of where she was.

"We'll help each other." She bit her lip. "I'm coming home." From the time they had turned south she felt as if she were crossing the boundaries into another country, one where she was comfortable. The train reduced speed as it rounded a long curve; a high shrill whistle pierced the stillness. Cows raised their heads in slow motion with a "what are you doing here" look on their faces.

A few children who were probably walking to school waved at them.

It was as if this part of the world had frozen in time; looking out the windows, Brucie could believe it.

They passed barns and homes needing paint. As the train once again put on brakes, a breeze made by the turning wheels lifted nearby weeds and bushes, brushing them into a slow hello wave. *With the slower speed, we're probably coming into some small town for a mail catch,* Brucie realized.

"Our lives will be better," she said. "Just look. There's nothing as tranquil as a southern scene, almost winding back to another century. It's like nothing has changed. This could have been right after The War."

"It's boring," Memory said. "I'd rather be winding in the here and now, over waves on the high seas. And the only war I care about just ended."

Brucie tuned out Memory's answer the best she could. In a few minutes they picked up speed; they were running on a straight stretch. The rails hummed so loud it reminded Brucie of the swarming noise she used to hear in the country around beehives.

The nearer the train carried them to Redemption Ridge where the old homeplace was, Brucie's life in Massachusetts seemed to fade, to belong to another person, someone she barely knew. *I've never let go. Those early memories. More real to me than riding this train.*

"It shouldn't be but a little more than another couple of hours before we make Jackson," she said. "We have to wait until tomorrow to take the branch line on to Franklin. And before we get off the train, you'd better put your coat on. We're usually here in the summer. Even though we're in the south, the March wind down here can cut to the bone."

An unhappy look on her face, Memory got up and took a coat out of the grip she had kept in the compartment with her. She closed the suitcase and snapped the locks shut.

A cold draft blew through their compartment when Dale burst through the door and stumbled to the window. "It's dark in here.

Like a grave." He pushed the shade all the way up, with as much force as if he were upper cutting someone's chin.

"I need to see what's going on. The fight rages." He pointed to the window. "Even if you can't see, it's out there."

"If you want to get off this train and hop a freight in the other direction, I'll go with you," Memory said. "We might just find that fight you're talking about. We might even get in the middle of it. Better there than here, though."

"Trust me." Dale nodded his head. "It's out there. Everywhere."

"Oh, jeez." Memory stomped her foot. "There's nothing out there but scrubby trees, pig sties and some spavined mules looking at us. Get off your high horse and come back down to earth." She got close and leaned to her brother. "Among other things, we just might run into that murdering half-sister I told you about."

"You don't understand. We're fighting a battle." He lowered his head and closed his eyes. "We're in dire straits. This family doesn't even know it. I've got to take care of my men. I've got to bring them home. It's what the voices tell me to do. It's what God wants me to do."

He sat on the edge of the seat, next to his mother. Brucie leaned forward and smoothed his hair. "I sent your father a wire, and I've heard back from him. He'll be joining us in Mississippi. Soon," she said hesitantly.

"Any time's too soon for me." Dale tipped his head to the side as if he were trying to roll something from his ear. "He's hated me since I joined the army and fought against his beloved fatherland. I don't want to hear anything he has to say."

Like a turtle sensing danger, he hunched his shoulders forward and seemed to draw into himself. "I don't exactly see him as the knight in shining armor coming to our rescue. He's with the enemy."

"Once we get settled at Redemption Ridge," Brucie answered softly, "you'll realize how wrong you are. We'll all help you. Lamont and your sister. And me." She hesitated and then said, "And Laura Lee Stanton meant a lot to you."

"She still does," Dale said. "But I didn't save her brother."

The train shimmied across an uneven stretch of track as it hurtled on toward Jackson, slamming Dale against the seat. "You're the general, Mrs. Von Dieter. We're riding the rails, but I think I'll go outside and count them for a while." He stood, pulled his coat open, and stretched one leg out. His eyes blank, he fumbled deep through his trouser pockets and seemed to find what he was searching for. He coughed, then lurched out of their compartment.

"He was probably reaching for that cough medicine or for some of those pills that make him act crazy. He's going to the caboose. He'll get back to what he'd already started," Memory said. "One way or the other he wants to get drunk enough not to care about what happened to him in France or to people he cared about. And what might happen to him now."

There was a moment's silence after she finished speaking. Out of the corner of Memory's eye she saw her mother's mouth tighten.

"Fumes from that mustard gas still plague him," Brucie said. "Once he gets a change of scenery and some fresh air into his lungs, he'll be himself again."

"You use that as an excuse. It's just easier for you to say that's the reason why he's been acting strange since he got back from the war than to admit he's ready for the looney bin." Memory picked up a book she had been reading, *A Family Secret,* by a southern female, Eliza Frances Andrews. "For your sake, I'm trying to indoctrinate myself into the way I'm supposed to think and act. But it'll take more than this train trip to make it happen. I've got too much Von Dieter in me."

"We won't be on this train too much longer. You might want to try and make the best of it." Brucie reached into her reticule and pulled out an afghan she had been working on.

Memory closed the book. "We need to shake some of that old dirt out of our family rugs," she said.

Brucie sighed and closed her eyes.

Memory reached down for her beaded bag and pulled out a covered ink well and pen. Once again, she began writing in her journal.

My mother and I, we need to clear the air. And if it pleases you, oh God, let me know when the time is right!

My mother thinks life will be better when we reach Redemption Ridge. What about the family ghosts that rise and fall, slip and slide over the hills and between the gravestones?

Memory's head ached. When do I let my mother know that her secret is now also, my millstone, she wrote? That Brother and I know there's another daughter? The one she had by Daddy Claymore? He had his way with her. Father, yet not father.

There's a Thelma Jewel out there somewhere. Named for mother's sister, Thelma Grace. Like her aunt, Thelma Grace, she could be a murderess.

Memory chewed the end of her pen, then once again dipped the point into the inkwell.

How misnamed. Grace. I hardly think the word describes that murderer. No, murderess. Thelma Damned, she should have been called. Killing her own mother.

Memory felt, rather than saw Brucie looking at her.

I'll finish this up quickly, she wrote. Thank you, God, that Cousin Sarah told those neighbors that if she were no longer alive, to make sure I knew about their suspicions. My mother would be in denial about her daughter. They knew, they knew, that Thelma Jewel had poisoned Mrs. Bledsoe. Two old ladies both of them sick, and they didn't know what to do about it. Thema Jewel. She murdered Mrs. Bledsoe. I also told my brother. Thanks to them, Dale and I both know.

There is so much rotten, rotting beneath the clay hills of our old homeplace.

The train's whistle gave a high, piercing wail; its speed stuttered and slowed as they went through a small town.

> **But, there's more. With me. What about that choking strawberry that fills my throat? It nearly drowns me. And, it's only at Redemption Ridge.**

Memory leaned her shoulders forward as if to keep her mother from seeing what she'd written. She straightened the paper, then dipped her pen one last time.

> **Is this a new beginning? Or a sad and frightful ending? Only time will tell.**
> **These are my secret thoughts; I will never let anyone else read my words.**

She closed her journal and reached for her purse and her nail file.

"Memphis," the conductor called out.

CHAPTER 12

The file slid under her fingernail,
Much better than nails on a
chalkboard.

The train shook under her,

It was dark in the car.
The shadows cleaned the lines
Of furniture, casting them about
Like bones in a charnel house

The smell of meat was as poignant as
The sensation of the sharp file
breaking the skin.

Home was a long way home
And she was nowhere near
Free of the underworld

Monday, March 22, coming into Jackson

Memory felt unsettled. It wasn't because of the jousting with words she and her mother had had this whole trip. Vague shadows seemed to drift about their roomette; she sensed trouble was very close. "This is not good," she whispered. Sometimes her mother seemed to anticipate events before they happened. Back in Mississippi, Memory had picked up from more than one person that Brucie had been known throughout Tallouga County for this. And many people didn't think it was a good thing. Some believed it was of the devil. Memory had noticed it mostly happened when her mother was in Mississippi, it was not as strong when she was in Boston.

She began swinging one foot sideways as if she were doing battle with small animals nipping her ankles, all her anger seemed to have gone. A few regrets were left about her old life, and she felt an accustomed apprehension for what was ahead in the new.

"I'm uneasy," Brucie said as if she too were feeling something strange was about to happen. "I don't know why, but there's nothing we can do about it. Be ready."

Her words reinforced Memory's troubled thoughts. The two women leaned back in their seats; Brucie with her fists clenched, and Memory tapping her fingers as if she were sending messages with them. The clucking sounds of the rails seemed to mark the minutes. The two of them waited as if for an answer to a question neither of them wanted to hear.

Memory twisted her body so Brucie wouldn't see what she was doing. She reached into her handbag and lifted out her silver nail file. Cautiously, she dug the sharp point into the skin on the underside of her wrist.

The door slid open, and Jenson Cooper guided Dale into their compartment. Memory dabbed her arm with a handkerchief, dropped the file back into her purse and pulled her sleeve down.

"Whatever it is, it'll be soon." Brucie spoke quickly and pressed her lips together.

Memory shivered. *I don't like the way this seems to be going.* The sinister undercurrents that continued to shadow their lives since Dale returned from the war seemed to be moving in a different direction; they were all in danger of drowning from the backwash of his nightmares. Memory closed her eyes. When she did her throat tightened; she felt as if she were strangling. Bruised, rotten strawberries floated tantalizingly, as if they would consume her. *No, no,* she scolded herself. *You're imagining things.* She reached up and squeezed her left breast until she almost cried out in pain. She was on the train. Not drowning in a pool of rotten fruit. She could open her eyes.

***

A short while later an unpleasant odor seeped through their roomette.

At first, lost in his own troubled thoughts Dale paid no attention. He brushed it off as an overflow from the gentleman's toilet down the car from them, but the smell became stronger, more like dead and drying flowers at a funeral. They heard an unexpected knock. Jenson slid the compartment door open. Their porter, a large-bodied man whose uniformed buttoned coat strained to cover his belly, held the door ajar with his booted foot. His head turned to the side, a look of I'm-only-doing-this-because-I-have-to, the attendant held a large wooden box with a dozen red, wilting roses tied on as far away from his body as he could. "I have a gift for you," he said in a loud voice. "Part of this here has been in a bag of ice in the refrigerator car. Back way after we left Chicago, a man paid me an' said he'd take care of it some way special."

In just a few moments the stench settled in. So malodorous it could have been an untended chamber pot left outside for days in the dead of summer. The foul smell invading the roomette made it hard to breathe.

"But my glory!" The porter opened his mouth in a wide O. "Dead or fresh picked, I ain't never smelled no roses like these ones here."

A wave of nausea washed over Dale; the thrum of the train wheels sounded like the pulse pounding in his head.

"A young, redheaded gent done paid me. He knew where all you left this here box. Before I give you his present, though, first I been told to have one of you men," a shifty craftiness about the porter's eyes, he nodded in Dale's direction, "to read a poem 'the redheaded devil' done wrote. That's what he called hisself to me. An, then I am to give this present to the young lady, here."

He untied a black velvet bow around the flowers, set them on a seat and put a folded piece of paper in Dale's hand. "I'm to open this here box an' put it right here in the middle of where you all are setting." He took out a claw hammer hooked onto his belt, began forcing the top off the box and pulling loose the thin wooden slats.

Dale's eyes slightly glazed, weak in the knees and breathing through his mouth, he read:

"Moving down south—you think it's so fine?
But there's some things, you just can't leave behind.
You left this in my church, a holy place
And, someday soon, you'll see my face.
But for now, this is yours in remembrance of me.
I'll show up again, just you wait and see.
The Avenging Ghost"

Dale dropped the note as if it burned his fingers.

By this time the porter finished un-nailing the top. He ran his hands down the sides of the box and folded back green florist paper. He then raised and tilted the large box. Everyone in the roomette could see a tin bucket packed with ice. In the bucket, a worn canvas bag holding the remains of two human legs were surrounded by long, flesh-colored wooden shards. The wood strips were mottled with specks resembling green spittle. What looked to be a decayed human hand crowned the legs.

"What it is?" Brucie gagged.

"Those are our friend's legs," Dale said reverently.

"Dear God!" Jenson shook his head. "As I live and breathe. Those wood strips stuck to our friend's legs. Senator Peter Shields. His peg leg. Something my captain and I took care of back in Boston." He rubbed his chin. "I thought."

The train whipped around a small sharp bend. The porter pitched forward and hit the crate. The box and a tin bucket holding the bones tipped onto the floor. Finger bones coated with a few shredding leather fibers and wattles of skin spilled out.

Memory sank onto the seat. "That glove," she gasped. "Thornton's hand. I'll never forget the night it was brought to our house. It smells horrible." She covered her mouth as if she were going to vomit. "

A pool of sweat glistened on Dale's face; tears streaked his cheeks. "My friend wanted me to take care of him. I let him down. I made his sister Laura Lee a promise. I'd take care of him. Oh, God. What do I do?" he moaned. "What do I do? "

He tightened his shoulders. "I told you. I will get part of you home. Back to Redemption Ridge." He wiped tears away. "To a spot there in the ground, with your name on it.

"When I do, you can run from that hell-hole, shell hole," he said, his voice unsteady with the pain he felt.

The bag holding Samuel's extremities slid, disgorging some of the rotten strips of wood, as if his remains were trying to escape from them.

"I'll take care of this." Jenson stepped between Dale and the debris on the floor. "Our friend's remains have been in the refrigerator car on ice all this time. 'Til right now. I'll make sure they'll stay that way until we get to Redemption Ridge." *Thank God they turned up, even if desecrated.*

He nodded toward Dale. "Upon my life, we'll take care of Samuel." He pulled the bag forward and kneaded it with his fingers. "I messed up once, but it won't happen again. What's left of our comrade will get a proper burial. I think I know who's behind this. He won't get away with it."

Jenson gave the porter a hard look. "Where'd you get this?"

"A man gave it to me." The porter's eyes shifted. He spoke through the bar of fingers over his mouth and nose. "He said the captain would want it. He paid me real good to get this to Captain Von Dieter. He said it's to stay with him."

"Our dugout smells." Dale staggered to the window. "They're out there." He pressed his hands against the glass. "I'd like to smash this window. Find and kill them before they kill us. They'll plow up our sad bones." His hands moved in a swinging motion, as if he had a rag in his hand and were cleaning a wide expanse of glass.

"He's a looney," the porter said. "We ain't in no dugout. It's that goddamn hand that's putrid."

"You're a nothing." Jenson punched a finger hard, against the porter's puffy chest. If he hadn't been leaning against the compartment wall, the man would have fallen.

"You make me sick. I know what my Captain went through. He had to send good men to certain death. And he was right there with them."

Jenson reached down and gave Memory's hand a gentle squeeze. "Why don't you move your people to an aisle seat?" he asked softly. "It's not far now. We just have a short while 'til we make Jackson. Tomorrow we catch the branch line on to Tallouga, County. We'll be off this train soon. I'll deal with this man."

He moved over and put his arm around Dale's shoulders. "I'll clean up Samuel's legs and keep them for you, my captain. We want no part of Peter Shields's wooden limb or someone else's rotten hand touching our friend. Why don't you see to your mother and sister? They're the ones who need you right now."

"I don't know if I can walk," Memory said. "I'm trembling all over." But despite what she said she took Dale's arm and with Brucie close behind they went out into the train aisle.

"Okay, we're going to take care of this." Jenson shoved the hand out of the way with his foot.

"Now." He gripped the porter's arm. "You will gently lift the legs."

"Uh-huh. I can't." The porter made a grating, hocking noise in the back of his throat, puffed his cheeks out, and leaned over as if he were going to spit.

"Don't you dare!" Jenson whipped a Colt .45 revolver from under his coat. "Now open that bag. You will clean up the mess around our soldier friend's remains. I'll shoot your foot off if you drop any part of those legs. I won't allow my friend's remains to be contaminated. Not by Thornton Hastings's nasty hand. And certainly not by any part of Senator Peter Shields's stump. I'll see to what's left of Samuel Stanton. I'll keep it up until he's resting in Redemption Ridge soil."

Trembling all over, the ashen-faced porter did as commanded

"I see a few splinters on my friend's legs," Jenson bit out. "Pull them off. Dump them down there by those rotten fingers with splotches of leather stuck to them."

The porter gagged. "I don't think I can," his voice cracked.

"I don't give a rip what you think you can and can't do." Jenson raised the pistol. "Just do it. Double time."

Breathing deeply through his mouth, the porter plucked a few strands of wood from the decaying legs. Several times he turned his head away and gagged. His face white as goose down, he moved as if to leave the compartment.

"You're not done. Very carefully, very easily, close the military bag holding my friends remains. Then say the Lord's Prayer.

The porter froze. "Huh?" he squeaked out

"You heard me." Jenson jammed the pistol into the porter's neck. "I want your head bowed and your eyes closed."

"Our Father," the porter began as he trembled out the prayerful words and finished with a barely audible "amen."

"Where is he?" Jenson cocked the pistol. "Where's the son of a bitch who did this?"

"He paid me in the Chicago station," the porter strangled out the words. "A right good sum."

"Is he on this train?"

"I don't know."

"If he is, or isn't, wherever he is, I'll find him." Jenson holstered his gun. "When I do, he's a dead man. Here's the goddamn box. Take it. Burn it. Get your ass outta here."

He shoved the porter through the door, cradled the haversack in his arms and left the compartment.

Shoulders hunched, the porter hurriedly cleaned up, then stumbled down the aisle. "I don't care none if you find him or not. He paid me right smart," he said to himself. "Now, I've gotta get thet box outta here and hide it. And keep him outta your eyesight 'til all of you folks get off the train in Franklin." The porter rubbed his throat. "Ain't much left, but he said he'd see to it that the good Captain would eat what was in that box. If it was the last meal that man ever had."

"Jackson," a voice called from the far end of the car. "All out for Jackson."

"I've got us rooms at The Royal Hotel," Brucie said. "The branch line left hours ago, so we're spending the night here."

Memory reached into her purse for her nail file. "I bet it was that bastard policeman friend of the Senator who did this."

No one watching, she slid the nail file under her thumbnail. She pushed.

"Redemption Ridge," she gasped. "Tomorrow. We'll be there tomorrow."

CHAPTER 13

A peach tree forked from a wet place
in the field;
Sudden dendrite rooted in a long, soft
peal
Dale's war was against timeless
locality.
He stretched from his wet toes as a boy
to the (fruit.)

Stretched so far he ripped along the
seam
Of his first love, leaving his legs like
Gruesome, internally reflected water
(In the shades of that peach tree
On Redemption Ridge.)

The rest of him rose on the lack of
itself
To heights high enough to
reconnoiter the lay
Of Chateau Thierry. Men lay
everywhere, crushed
Away from their grooved pits.
Phosgene hissed like weather from
a snake.

Steam mingled in the railcar with
incensed smoke.
Inertia changed the path of his
reverie.

Tuesday, March 23

After he had helped the Von Dieters settle into their seats on the branch line to Franklin, Jenson Cooper went to check and be sure their trunks were in the baggage car. Memory scrunched her lips into a scowl. Brucie nervously twisted her wedding ring around her finger; Dale slid down on the seat and began jiggling his legs.

The seats on this small branch line from Jackson were narrow and hard, but Brucie was so relieved to be on Mississippi soil and easing through familiar land she could have been stretched out on a feather mattress on the sleeping porch. They'd had a long, stressful journey from Boston. As the train slowed for a snaking curve and blasted out a screeching whistle, she knew almost to the second how long before it stopped in Franklin. *It'll be better there.* Then she remembered her husband's words.

"If you leave Boston, you'll be using Dale as an excuse to go to Redemption Ridge," Von Dieter had said to his wife before he left for Germany. "I don't think this backvard place in the middle of novhere vill be good for that boy."

He had indicated if Dale needed any help for his nervous condition, he wanted his son treated in Germany, not America. "There'll be time enough to address that later. Ve are, vhere ve are, for now. And his so-called, 'condition,' is nothing but a self-induced veakness. He just needs to grow up. You need to quit coddling him."

I'll prove you wrong, Brucie had thought. *You had your own excuse to do what you wanted. To return to Germany. I'm not sure how I feel about you coming back either.*

She suddenly felt sick to her stomach. She rested her head against the seat and closed her eyes. She was almost asleep when the words, *Thelma Jewel,* rang in her ears; she felt a hand on her shoulder. *Thelma Jewel.* Again. The voice sounded like Vernell.

She looked around. Only she, Memory, and Dale were in the compartment.

Thelma Jewel. She'll be there.

"No. No, Vernell," Brucie said. She no longer felt a hand but was aware of a familiar presence.

But what do I do if Thelma Jewel is at Redemption Ridge? she wondered. If so, she was fearful for what might be ahead. For all of them.

***

An edgy look on his face, Dale stared out the window.

I'm going to do better. Try and get hold of myself. "But, right now, with what's gone on, be damned to everything and everybody. I can't sit here like this." *I'm wound up inside.* "I need to go to the toilet. I remember all this boring scenery from past trips."

He almost felt like a turncoat when he said these words, because he didn't feel as if he really believed them. He didn't know for sure what he thought or believed. *I have happy memories from being down here, but maybe they're wrong. I have been wrong about so much.* Instead of going to the toilet he went toward the caboose and stood between it and the car he had just left. Used to the Boston chill and dressed for it, for a minute, even though this was the Deep South, he was as cold as he had ever been in Boston. The March wind whipping around the sides of the train almost took his breath away. Dale drew his coat tighter. He gazed out toward a stretch of flat, yellow-stubbled, Mississippi countryside. Overhead, he saw movement. The train shimmied. He steadied himself and then glanced up again. Circling, spread-winged buzzards drifted with the wind currents as if they were dancing and dipping to waltz-time music. *Is there a message in this for me?* he wondered. "Are you trying to tell me something, God?" he asked.

A short while later, Jenson came and stood beside him. Dale had yesterday's scene with his friend Samuel's legs being corrupted by Thornton's decaying hand and splinters from Peter Shields's wooden leg on his mind. Something about this was eating at him. More than just the incident itself.

In a few minutes the wheels gave out a grinding wheeze and then turned into a hum as the train slowed going through a small town.

"Turkey Trot. Remember that name?" Jenson turned to his friend. "You've been through here before. In fact, in the dear dead days almost beyond recall, I do believe you and I hunted here."

"Kind of like Panther Burn, a little further north. Where else on God's green earth would you have a town named for a burning panther or a trotting turkey?" Dale had some of his old animation in his voice. "Nowhere but Mississippi."

"You're beginning to sound like yourself." Jenson smiled. "Maybe this move south will be just what you and your sister need, Captain." He put his hand on Dale's back. "We're almost to Redemption Ridge. Let go of the war. You fought the good fight."

"Maybe so. Maybe not. Maybe, I can't let go."

"Why don't you start thinking different? Turn back to who you were before the war?" Both men swayed as the train picked up speed and moved on through Turkey Trot.

"I can't seem to give it up. I've been wondering, although I doubt you have any answers. How in the world did somebody know how to get hold of what was left of Samuel Stanton?" Dale asked, his voice low and calm. But a burning need to have an answer to the question lay behind his words.

The train had regained its full-out running speed. Barreling around a sharp curve, Jenson Cooper flung out both arms to keep from pitching to the side. He leaned against the train, and he looked up at the sky as if asking for divine guidance. It was a little harder to hear now—he leaned close to Dale. "I always told you I had taken care of what was left of our friend until we headed back South. I was responsible for his remains being left in the Senator's ice cellar. I didn't say anything to you, but during the short time I worked for Peter Shields, I thought he was a good man. Right before Thanksgiving, one night when we were at a party for returning soldiers, I was pretty much in my cups." He stared down at his feet. "Without thinking, I told Senator Peter Shields where our buddy's remains were, down in his ice cellar. That soon, we'd be returning what little was left of him to his home. Then forgot I had said anything. Of course, it wasn't long before the Senator's true colors came out, and I found out he was nothing but a conniving bastard, strictly looking after himself. I quit working for him. It never occurred to me that he'd even remember our conversation." Jenson swallowed hard. "But I began wondering and did some asking around. After I left, he told a Boston policeman, Liam McRae, about Samuel's remains. I've been meaning to tell you that for a while now. I'm sure that Boston policeman's had his eye on us this whole time. I've had my eye on him too. I'm doing some checking on him."

Dale's head snapped back. "You told the Senator? I wish I'd known it," he said, an expression of anger and disbelief on his face. "We'd have done things differently." His ears began to ring; a heavy pulse thrummed in his temples. He felt the here and now, the today, start to slip away.

The train slowed, going over a bridge. Somewhere in a nearby stand of water oaks gunfire exploded. The blast of a shotgun reverberated and then echoed again.

"Which one of my men? Which one bit the bullet?" Dale yelled. "Or was it more than one?" Grasping a metal bar, he jerked his shoulder sideways and slung his leg out to jump off the train. "I'm coming."

Jenson grabbed Dale's chest.

"Stop it! That's somebody out hunting."

"Oh, God! I can't save them." Dale's body slumped.

The train engine snorted, once, twice. A tongue of smoke spewed from the stack.

Jenson pulled him back close to the train door. "We're not in France. They're not shooting your men."

Dale shoved him away. He bent over, taking in deep, trembling breaths. "You can go on to your family. My God constrains me." He raised up. "I have a duty to be with my suffering men."

Images of certain death he had sent men to burned Dale's brain. "You're in one piece. I don't need you. My life's going in a different direction. Leave me the hell alone."

An awkward silence fell between them.

"You made it. My people across there are getting slaughtered. Hell could be waiting just over the next hill. I sent them. I need to go with them."

"We need each other, Captain," Jenson said. "The living need you."

"I'm not your Captain anymore. You betrayed me. You ratted to the Senator."

Eyes almost closed, brow etched in deep lines, Jenson wheeled around and snatched open the metal door to their car. "Okay, Sir."

A small part of Dale knew he'd made a mistake, but the rest of him was more determined than ever. His mouth set in a tight line, he pulled out his silver whiskey flask. He raised it to the sky as if making a toast, held his head back and took a deep drink. "What have I done?" he asked. "I'm nobody's Captain now. I have to earn it again. My men won't have me, unless I save them."

The rails squealed like the screams of wounded soldiers—the death screeches of those being slaughtered. Dale saw the face of one of his men. Blown off. No mouth. A gaping hole. One ear pasted where his lips were. *Suffer my little children. Where are the green pastures? God,* he pled. *You make your tired, dying children to lie down in flea infested ground.* Pictures flipped through his head. *Bombs. Bayonets. Machine guns.* He gripped the rail. He heard a noise behind him and almost in slow motion glanced over his shoulder. A tall stranger had come through the caboose door and stood opposite him.

Dale couldn't make out much about the man except that he wore a bobby hat and a dark uniform of some kind. A bandana covered most of the stranger's face. "I don't think I've ever seen you before," he said. "That cloth over your face. We could use it for a tourniquet, but it won't stop the gas." He lifted a cupped hand to his forehead. "Can you see our people out there in front of us? I need help for my men," he pleaded. "Can you call in fire cover?" Off balance, he almost fell, but he flung out his arms and grabbed the steps railing.

"Don't bother to call for cover, only God can help you. And He won't answer your ring," the man said. "I've got you in my sights, Captain.

"You're still alive, you coward. You sent your men to their deaths."

Dale saw his eyes. *Those eyes. Those green eyes. Greener than a blow fly's belly. I've seen you before.*

Tendrils of red hair had escaped from under the man's helmet. Careful not to disturb the bandana over his face, he reached up and pushed them back under.

> **Not thick red hair**
> **That's not what this is about**
> **It's your bloody, bloody brains**
> **Man, they're threading out.**

Oh God," Dale cried. The pictures in his mind grew darker.

"Your brains," he tried to say. "Your blood-soaked brains are spilling. I'll help." No words came out, he couldn't move his lips.

"I've got you in my sights, soldier boy. I'm going back to my car," the man said. "Before I left to come here, I buried my dear friend. Senator Peter Shields. I went by your house. I talked to your old maid, Elnora." He folded his arms in front of him.

"Your mama had another baby girl. You have a sister, Captain. That baby girl's grown up and has one of her own." He put his finger up to his mouth as if he were playing a childhood game of I have a secret. "She knows about Redemption Ridge."

"And, I know about her. She mur…" but Dale couldn't get his tongue around the word, murdered.

Liam McRae crammed an envelope into Dale's coat. "This is from her, to you, you bastard. Something she wants you to have." He reached behind him and grabbed the door that led to the caboose. "She knows its part hers. She has some claims. I'll help her see to them. We'll have some fun out there on that old battleground. She'll be there with bells on, ready to take care of you." He slid the door open. "See you and yours later. Around the cemetery."

And I'll take care of you too, he thought. *That drinking buddy of mine and his Mississippi cousin. Dead man. No, Dedmon. All set up. He can get hold of some moonshine and you'll guzzle some of that. I've got hold of that cough syrup you like and some of those pills.*

The bloody brains and the smell of metal and steam were too much for Dale. His legs unsteady, he was aware that he must position himself; he could slide off the steps and fall from the train. For a moment, he was tempted. But he must still get what was left of his friend home. He had promised. Because of so much open space on the caboose platform, he grabbed a bar and held on as he slowly slid down. Once down, his body stretched from one end of the small platform to the other; his hips rode the sharp seam of the metal coupling between the caboose and a train car. Dale had the dry heaves, and he vomited off the side of the car. But he was alert enough to know not to let go of the bar he had grabbed. He lay in a miserable heap, bouncing and scrubbing the platform with his body as he was slung from side to side with the train's movements. In a few moments, he raised his head, wiped bile from his mouth with the back of his hand and got to his knees.

Brown stubbled grass drifted by in a dizzying wave. Bare tree limbs seemed to wag bony fingers at him in a no-no motion as the train coiled around a curve. From some dim recesses of Dale's mind, from the many trips made on the branch line in the past, he became aware that the train was nearing Franklin, Mississippi. Nausea passed, his head a little clearer, still holding on for dear life, he rose to his feet.

***

The brakes and wheels hissed. Tears blurred Brucie's eyes so much she could barely see the station through the mist, but as the wheels ground and the train slammed to a stop, she could see enough to tell that the old depot was still in need of paint and repair. The station hadn't changed and the town was probably still encapsulated in the same scenery as when she left.

"Well, there it is," Brucie said to Memory. "Franklin, Mississippi, Tallouga County. I've been gone from this life for a long time." She picked up her reticule. "This is where it all began."

Her heart beat rapidly. "And this is where it will end for me," she whispered.

"What?" Memory asked in her clipped Boston accent. "I didn't hear you."

"Nothing. Just talking to myself." Brucie peered out the window. Leaning against the dirty, grayed wooden building, she saw Lamont. *Of course, there's always, Lamont.*

"Our trunks will be unloaded from the baggage car. I'm sure Lamont's made arrangements to get us on to Redemption Ridge." She looked anxiously around the car. "Where's your brother?"

"Jenson will see to him."

Brucie caught the familiarity. "Mr. Cooper has family here and he's been gone for a long time," she said. "He might be ready to move on with his life."

Maybe I should have had a different take on things, Memory thought. *Let Jenson know how much I think of him. What would we have done without Jenson Cooper?* She almost asked her mother that question out loud but stopped herself. She'd been aware he watched her closely, but now she owned up to her feelings. And he was also probably the best looking man she'd ever seen. Did it take coming to Mississippi for her to see it? Why hadn't she noticed him in this way before?

***

Standing apart from the depot crowd, Lamont waited near the end of the tracks. Next to him his older son, Minyard, hopped up and down on his tiptoes, watching for the train. Every now and then Lamont glanced to the side trying to catch Topper's eye, but with the boy squatting next to the building and engrossed in a dice game, he wouldn't look up at him. Ignoring his father was beginning to be an annoying, everyday occurrence. That, and other things, which Lamont couldn't quite put his finger on.

"I'll take care of your hide when we get home," he muttered to himself.

He checked the telegram he had in his hand one more time. *Coming in on Thursday. Arriving on the two eleven. Need to be met at the station. Brucie.*

He'd had a few phone conversations with Brucie so he knew they were moving back to Redemption Ridge and that household goods would arrive later. He'd lit the furnace, and his wife, Bertha, had food in the house until Brucie could get into town and shop.

Way around a bend, Lamont spied a stream of gray smoke spiraling into the clouds. The whistle blew out a long, shrill note. Lamont pulled out his pocket watch and checked the time. "Two eleven in the afternoon," he said. "The Westbound Limited's almost on time. She's coming into Franklin."

CHAPTER 14

Shadows gathered round the depot,
Wingless, fluttering.

How far had they come,
Come so long they stretched the coast.

Tall, gangly, loud if they could be.
These are the fates that cannot abide

Tuesday, March 24

Head down, Liam crept to the rear of the train, stopping short of the caboose. He set down a wooden box tucked beneath his arms, took off his bobby helmet then slid down and checked his watch; from what the porter had told him he still had a pretty good ride on the branch line until they made it to Franklin. Bored, while he waited, he reread a letter from Thelma Jewel.

Mr. McRae,

It was nothing short of divine Providence for me to receive your telephone call at this particular moment in time. The woman by whom I have been raised passed on to Glory some several months ago. Knowing that she would soon meet her Maker, I thought it best to prepare for her demise and to do some investigating into my past history. In our attic, I found old documents that were thought to be disposed of but which have revealed to me how sorely I have been treated by my birth mother, a woman of means, one Mrs. Brucie Claymore Von Dieter, originally from Redemption Ridge, out from Franklin, Mississippi. As a helpless infant I was cast aside by Mrs. Von Dieter as if I had been no better than a homeless orphan and have been banished from the life my daughter, Gertie Mae, and I deserve.

I have property and was left some money by Mrs. Bledsoe, the woman who raised me, but the life I deserve out west can be very costly. The woman who had been hired to look after me had been deathly ill for quite some time and was in the self-serving process of using up what I would need to live on to maintain my accustomed comfort. The fever mostly took her a little at a time. I am a woman who believes sometimes a little help to the other side is the kind, the Christian thing to do, and in Jesus name, I took care of this step-woman to the best of my ability and my beliefs. I must say, I have been sorely treated by neighbors and whatever friends this woman had. They have elected to have nothing to do with me. For several reasons, I don't care to go into what they are. But because of the looks I get, and the accusatory words whispered behind hands spread across suspicious faces, I think for all concerned that it is best that I leave the state of California as soon as possible.

So, on my own, with those old documents in hand, before I heard from yours truly, I had already contacted several far-off acquaintances relating to my Mississippi history and parentage (Some of whom I'm sure Mrs. Von Dieter would not want me to know about). I have set in place plans and am moving myself and my darling daughter, Gertie Mae, to Mississippi. Gertie Mae will have special needs, and I have found them to be more fulfilled in a suitable church than in any other place. We are more in keeping with a Holiness doctrine than the staid Baptist, Methodist, or Presbyterian faith.

Finding a few names from Tallouga County in the attic documents, I have already put in motion plans for a place for us to stay. I have been in contact with the offspring of one Book Turnipseed, a former employee of the Claymore family. Suffice it to say, Mr. Turnipseed's line and lineage have nothing good to report on any of my forebears. There were heart-stopping rumors from the past as to what had happened to more than one person who encountered the residents of Redemption Ridge. My namesake, Thelma

Grace Claymore, I have found out, was supposedly murdered by a Yankee carpetbagger. But, to this day there has been more than one story about her untimely death. I have been informed other people have also questioned this.

They have also questioned another murder that was committed right back of the old homeplace at Redemption Ridge. The dastardly drowning of an old woman in the family well, a Miss Pet Binkie. Both of those murders were ascribed to one man, one Yankee carpetbagger, Mr. Warner Sledge. But I do wonder. There were others who stood to gain from both murders. And I have my suspicions as to a family member killing my namesake, Thelma Grace. Supposedly, a fortune in jewels was ripped from her dead hands when the dastardly deed was done. And who stood to gain from this killing? And where are those jewels? Hmm. I do wonder.

As I have previously stated, other people have also questioned this. Well, we shall see. There is a day of reckoning. And maybe with some help, I can hasten same.

From what you have told me of your arrival later in the month, you will find that I will already have been settled in for a few days and making certain that my daughter and I are taken care of.

From my mouth to God's ear, I will meet with you in Mississippi on my soon-to-be-claimed, ancestral grounds.

You mentioned the Irish maid, Elnora. I told you I felt a need to contact the Irish housekeeper. You said she was no longer available. And that there is no way for me to contact her. Well, I will just have to let that go. But. I do wonder where she could be…

Yours in perpetuity,
Thelma Jewel Bledsoe
(soon to be changed to Claymore,
the firstborn daughter of one
Mrs. Brucie Claymore Von Dieter)

"She's ahead of me," Liam said. "Wonder what mischief that good lady has been up to? Glad we're in cahoots. She'll not be as easy to handle as Elnora."

***

Angry-sounding steam hissed from under the cars. Lamont slid the telegram from Brucie into his pocket. "Sounds like rats in a trap." He put his hands over his ears as the brakes squealed; the coaches swayed like foot-rocked cradles and the train wheels slowed to a crawl.

With a loud screech, the train came to a complete stop. Then, it slowly backed up. While it was in reverse and reattaching the cars, the train porter held onto a bar and swung off the number three car. He dashed into the depot.

Standing just outside the building, a scowling, tall dark man with black hair stiff as a wire clothes brush beckoned to the porter. "I'm Dedmon. Lucius Dedmon. You the one? You rang me from Jackson. Said you had a deal."

"Ain't got but a second. Here it is." The porter thrust a ceramic jug and a small pill box into Lucius Dedmon's hands. "The man what's doing this said there'd be more coming."

"And here you are." Dedmon covered his palm with two dimes. "Thanks to you, I'll take care of Mr. Von Dieter. Whoever Mr. McRae is, he's gonna be satisfied with what I do."

A high-pitched squeal announced brakes locked. Huffing, the porter ran back to the third car and swung up,

Dedmon looked around the platform. He stepped into the station and beckoned the ticket agent over. "I see Topper Randall out there rollin' dice with somebody." He gave the ticket agent a handful of pennies. "This here's for you. I need you to have Topper meet me right inside the station. Don't nobody need to see it."

"You're the one. What some folks call the voodoo man," the agent breathed, wiping his hands down his pants legs.

Cars secured, the train jerked to a final stop and the porter quickly grabbed a stand of portable wooden steps. He dusted the steps with a small brush, reached up and began helping the passengers down.

The voice of a lone vendor on the platform calling out, "Peanuts," grew shriller. People crowding around waiting to catch the train or to meet friends and relatives talked to one another at the top of their voices like they had very important things to say and a very short time to say them. Off to the side, Lamont and his son, Minyard, stood close to the building.

The agent came from the station. He ran his thumbs under his straps, hitched up his coveralls and looked around. He raised his hand and managed to catch Topper's eye. He held up a penny and beckoned. Topper pointed to himself. The agent nodded.

Topper thumbed his bottom lip, then made up his mind—the man wanted him. He got up from the dice game and digging deep in his nose as if searching for hidden treasure, he slouched over to where the coveralled agent stood. The man gave Topper two more pennies. Bending slightly, he covered the side of his mouth with his hand and gave him a paper bag holding the jug and a small box. "This here's for you to give to Mr. Von Dieter," he whispered into Topper's ear. "He's coming in on the train. Mr. Lucius Dedmon'll see you right inside the station and tell you what he wants that you should do." He put his finger to his lips in a shushing motion.

Keeping an eye on his boys, Lamont noticed Minyard's twin brother, Topper, talking to a thin man wearing coveralls. People were beginning to walk down the platform toward the depot. He wanted to watch for Brucie so turning back toward the train he missed seeing the ticket agent slip money, and a bag into his son's hands and Topper dashing into the station.

Brucie hesitated at the top of the train step. She searched the crowd trying to locate her son, but she couldn't see him because Dale was on the small open space between the car they had been on and the one right behind it.

Dale was nauseated, the smell of metal and steam was too much for his upset stomach. For a moment he had the dry heaves and then he leaned over on the side away from the depot and vomited off the side of the car.

With silver spurs jingling on his brown leather boots, Liam McRae tightened a blue bandana covering the lower part of his face, pushed his helmet down on his head and sprang from the train. He landed on his feet and moved to a small hill. He wiped his hands on the sides of his pants legs and ducked behind a small patch of scrub bush.

Brucie smoothed her skirt. Taking the porter's raised hand, she and Memory went down the steps. She stood on the platform, and as she did so often, she patted her chest as if to make sure her cross from Vernell still rested next to her heart.

There was a glare; squinting into the sun, it was hard for Brucie to see, and Lamont spied her before she saw him. He took off his straw hat and swung it in the air. Then as if she had seen something that pleasured her very much, Brucie smiled and gave Lamont a big hand-wave.

Stepping back outside the station, Topper pursed his lips, did a quick, happy shuffle, and fingered the money in his pants pocket. "Mist Dedmon an' me doin' some business," he whispered. Walking with a jaunty step he went back to the boys he had just left.

"It's been a while since we've seen 'em, but that over there is Miss Brucie," Lamont said to Minyard. "You remember her." Close behind Brucie, Lamont saw a younger version of his childhood friend. "And her daughter, Miss Memory, all growed up."

He glanced over toward Topper. "You. Topper. Get over here, boy," he called.

Topper frowned and scuffed his feet as if he wanted to kick something. He ran his hand into his pants pocket, then, a smug smile on his face, he shrugged his shoulders and ambled toward his father.

"Come on now," Lamont said. "We gotta get Miss Brucie and her family on out to Redemption Ridge. You and Minyard. Can't barely tell one from the other. But the way you act, you all are different as day and night. I wants you boys to show her some respect. You hear me?"

"I am, Daddy," Minyard answered.

"You too, Topper." Lamont shook his finger. "Mind out now. You hear me?"

While he waited to see what the Von Dieters were going to do, Liam pushed his helmet back on his head, untied his bandana and slipped it down. He stretched back against a rotten tree trunk and smiling to himself, recalled in great detail the telephone conversation he had had shortly before Thelma Jewel left for Redemption Ridge.

"Mr. McRae," she had said, not trying to hide the pleasure dripping from her voice. "My daughter, Gertie Mae, and I can hardly wait for you to join us in Franklin, Mississippi. I will stop off in Hot Springs Village, Arkansas, for a few days and we should arrive in Franklin sometime around the twentieth of March. I am sure my presence will become known to one and all in the country town, and I will soon be in need of some higher-class company than the rural people I will encounter in this backward state.

"Our plans will be to meet with a Mr. Mudge Turnipseed. I will be in temporary residence at Mrs. Netter's Boarding House, an old established home in downtown Franklin. I must say, it will not be up to our usual standards, but until we can come into our rightful place in this community, we can and will make do.

"And," she added. "My daughter Gertie Mae is a special child. So that I may best take care of her talents and blessed needs, I have heard of a home affiliated with the Divine Deliverance Holiness Church out in the country. The Divine Deliverance Holiness Home for Boys and Girls. 'We do meet their needs and see that they are fed daily and cleaned on a weekly schedule.'"

Liam recalled Thelma Jewel's parting words; they had played a sweet melody in his ears. "Whatever it takes and whomever we can use," she said. "It is now time for me to claim as my own, rights which should legally and morally have belonged to me and my daughter, Gertie Mae. Knowing that you will also be leaving Boston for Tallouga County, Mississippi, and will probably be traveling with, but unbeknownst to, the Von Dieters I am mailing you a communication. If you could, by any means deliver the missive to one of those who mistakenly consider themselves the only legal inhabitants of Redemption Ridge, I would forever be in

146

your debt. I would like them to know retribution awaits. But from whom? Hmm. They will have to ponder that matter."

"It's for sure I'll see you soon," Liam had said after he hung up the phone.

A few days after the phone call, he received the note from Thelma Jewel to pass on to a Von Dieter. "I got that taken care of on the train, Miss Thelma Jewel," he laughed to himself. "It's done. Not sure if he's read it or not, though. But I did what you told me." He folded his bandana, pushed it into his pocket and waited.

***

His stomach emptied, Dale felt some better. "You've got to move," he said. He saw his mother and Memory, but he didn't want them to see him.

Swaying, he took a few deep breaths, pushed out a few sighs and in just a matter of seconds felt strong enough to swing off the train. His legs weak, he staggered and almost fell, but managed to stay on his feet. Shivering and miserable, he wiped his mouth. He stumbled away from the crowd, then to keep from falling over, he braced himself against a wooden post.

Hat in his hand, Lamont made his way through the crowd and took Brucie's elbow.

"Miss Brucie."

"You're always here," she said softly. "I've missed you."

"You were comin'. Of course, I'd be here," he said, almost indignantly, as if she didn't even need to speak the words.

"I got the Blessed Rest Funeral Home's hearse for today," he said. "It'll ride good and hold folks comfortable. I took everything out the back and put me some benches in. We'll do the trunks in a buckboard. "

"Oh, Lamont," Brucie said. "What a good idea. You've taken care of so much." She reached out to touch his shoulder. "We may have to use this hearse on more than this one occasion. I do think, I do, that soon, Mr. Von Dieter will motor on down from Boston. He, or someone still in our home, will see to the rest of our personal belongings. We'll be shipping more of our belongings by rail."

"Yes ma'am," he said. "That's what I thought you'd probably have to do."

Swinging her purse with one hand, and swishing her skirt with the other, looking around like a butterfly searching for a place to light, Memory walked over and stood by her mother.

"As I live and breathe." Lamont pointed his finger. "This here's Miss Memory. She's growed into a fine lookin' lady. Almost pretty as her mother." He glanced around. "Where's the young Mr. Von Dieter?"

"He'll be with us in a minute." A look of uncertainty crossed Brucie's face. "I'm sure you remember Mr. Jenson Cooper from right here in Franklin. He rode down with us. He and Dale were in The War together and he's been a companion to Dale since they got back. Right now, he's helping with our baggage. I'm sure he knows where my son is."

"Jenson Cooper." Lamont nodded his head knowingly. "He's kin to the old Sheriff Bramlett. I know his people from way back. They're fine folks."

One car down from where Memory and Brucie unloaded, Jenson had been setting aside his luggage and following an old habit, he was taking care of the Von Dieters'. He looked up to see Memory talking to her mother and Lamont. For a brief moment, he allowed himself to think about what might be, what he hoped for. "I've waited. Someday, you will be mine." He shook his head. *But we'll be going our separate ways soon,* he acknowledged. *Me to my family; Memory out to Redemption Ridge. And Von Dieter will be returning soon.* "Hell, what are you thinking?" he scolded himself. "She's Boston born and bred. All the way through."

Memory turned to look for Dale and when she did, she noticed Jenson standing on the outskirts of the crowd with the Von Dieters' baggage pushed against the side of the building. He must have left the train ahead of them. The two of them saw each other at the same time.

On this trip, Memory was more aware of him than she'd ever been. Of his broad shoulders that offered strength, and of the comfort she had taken from him in the past few months without being aware of it.

They stared for an instant, each seemed to have unasked questions in their eyes. Boston days were gone, and childhood remembrances came back to Memory of the summers they had spent at Redemption Ridge. "You've always been there, Jenson," she whispered. "Always helped. All of us." *I've been seeing you through the prism of a child's eyes. A privileged child at that.*

His expression pleasant, yet guarded, Jenson turned away first.

Memory's heart raced. *What's wrong?* Her emotions ran the gamut from trust, to apprehension, to melancholy. Some part of her admitted that from the very beginning, she could hardly bear to have Thornton touch her, but now, in this moment, she longed to feel Jenson's arms around her.

Drawing herself up to her full height of five feet four inches, "Mr. Cooper," Memory called, having no thought of what she'd say to him.

Jenson looked around as if he heard something, but her soft voice was lost in the raucous throng around the platform. He shouldered his way through the crowd, walked over and tapped Lamont's shoulder. "That over there"—He nodded to a stack of belongings—"is the Von Dieters'. I'm taking care of my Captain's belongings. Dale's over there by the far end of the station." He pointed over his shoulder. "He might need a little help from you."

Memory stood close enough to hear him say, "They're in your hands, now."

Her heart sank. She didn't want him to leave. She wanted to ask, "When will I see you again?" But the words hung in her throat. For months now she had taken him for granted, being around whenever she or her family needed him. His face, she had often thought easy to read, was now a mask. Something was different.

Jenson drew closer. He looked down at Memory. She gave the appearance of fragile beauty, but inside, he knew she was tough as nails. "Memory, I..." He fought with himself and stopped in mid-sentence. He almost said, "I don't want to leave you." Instead, he leaned back and crossed his arms over his chest. "See y'all later," he said, his lips thin, his voice tight. Spinning on his heel, his boots made a gritty sound as he walked away.

Memory fought an urge to run after Jenson. Security, and she didn't know what else, seemed to leave with him.

"Where's Dale?" she heard Lamont ask.

"Dale!" She had had enough of everything and everybody toadying to her brother.

"No telling where he is," she huffed. "Mr. Cooper's hired to look after my mixed-up baby brother. We all have to watch out for Son." Memory snatched her hat off and puffed her cheeks out. "Son hasn't been the same since The War. I still care, but right now I'm getting to where"—She tossed her head and slung sharp words over her shoulder—"somedays, I just don't give a rip." She plopped a hand on her hip. "Where's a porter to carry our belongings?" she asked haughtily. "I haven't ever seen such in my life."

"You'd better come off your high horse, young lady," Brucie commanded. "It's been a while, but you've been here many times. It's a change. I know better than anybody you've had a hard time these last few months. But Redemption Ridge gives us all a chance to start over. As soon as we see your brother, we're on our way."

Memory knew to back off. She'd said more than enough.

"There's Mist Dale." Lamont took Brucie's arm. With Memory and his boys following, they headed toward Dale who, his back to the crowd, held on to a wooden post.

Minyard and Topper walked a little way behind their father. Topper picked at a front tooth; he seemed to find something, looked at it and then he flipped a dark speck from his finger. "Why's he leaning against the post like he's holding it up?" He pointed at Dale. "I remember him. Is he crazy now?" he asked.

"Shut your mouth," Minyard snapped. "He's okay. They said he got too much gas in the war and needed to come here to git hisself straight. We'll help him."

CHAPTER 15

The procession unwound, a patterned throng
Of black ants. Hats were the only swatches of color,
Fragments of leaves, clutched in the mandibles from
A Mississippi wood.

The hearse crawled on, fat, full of purpose
And self-importance. Here was the queen,
The life and death of the celebration.

They marched afield, a dance of death
Hands were mouths, linked together
In strange desire.

Tuesday, March 23

With Jenson Cooper gone, Memory felt sad and restless. Not wanting to be close to her family for a moment, she spotted a peanut vendor and thought something to nibble on might get her mind on other things.

Slipping her hat back on, she moved away from the others and bought a sack of peanuts. Memory cracked open a couple of peanuts and popped them into her mouth. She ate several handfuls, but the husks hung in her throat. She wadded the sack and moved toward the train to throw the sack onto the rails. When she did, out of the corner of her eye, she thought she saw a flash of metal on a hill right past the caboose.

"Nothing." But a shiver ran through her body, the same kind people say that means someone's walking over your grave.

Dale heard the train whistle blow and saw smoke billowing from underneath the train. For a few moments a burning, metallic odor and hot steam blowing across the concrete was almost stronger than he could bear. "My God," he cried into the chilly March wind, his breath curling away in a small misty cloud. "I smell it," he choked out. "Gas! Creeping through the trenches.

Where are our planes?" His words strangled, he coughed out, "We need air cover." He pushed away from the post and held out his arms as if he expected something to be placed in them.

Dropping her reticule, Brucie ran to his side. "It's all right," she cried. "You're home. It'll be all right."

"Oh, Miss Brucie." Lamont trailed closely behind Brucie. "What's wrong? What can I do?"

"I've been pinning all my hopes that coming back here might save my son's life," Brucie said, her eyes glistening with tears. "It was that war, Lamont. Dale was gassed over there in the French trenches. He hasn't been the same since." Her hand trembling, she pressed down the side of her already smooth skirt.

Memory wanted to take her brother and shake some sense into him. She moved close to Dale and when she did an unexpected compassion snagged her conscience. She put her arm across his shoulder. "Those pills you take and that alcohol and cough syrup you sneak around and drink have hold of you right now," she said slowly. "But out here in the country, hopefully you'll have a hard time finding what you like and make some changes. It's not your fault you're like this."

Hesitant to join Lamont, Topper and Minyard hung back, but both could see something unusual was going on with their father and the Von Dieters. Topper's mouth opened in a dry grin. "That white man's crazy. He's walking like he needs to go to the outhouse. Him, I'm gonna like. I'm gonna have fun doing things with him." He started to say, "I got something for him and something to tell him. I'm gonna make me some money." He thought better of it though.

Minyard saw a familiar brutality in the set of his brother's mouth and the hardness of his eyes, a meanness he had to live with. "If he gets mixed up with the likes of you, the good Lord best look after him." He shook his head. "That'd be his only hope."

Lamont turned his head in his son's direction and signaled them.

"My boys'll pick up your trunks," he said to Brucie. "While we got us some daylight, we might best be goin' on. I borrowed you all a hearse from your funeral home to carry you and your peoples on out to Redemption Ridge. I've also got us a buckboard."

As they passed through the station, Dale noticed a scarred-face, worn-out looking man wearing a faded and torn private's uniform sitting on one of the wooden benches. Dirty bandages covered the top of the man's face, he held crutches in one hand and a sign in the other. A tin cup with a few pennies sat on the bench next to him. *My eyes were shot out in the war. Please feed me. I'm hungry.*

For just a second, Dale saw, not a stranger, but someone who could have been one of his men. He heard a train whistle.

"I'm stopping in the lavatory," he said to Memory. "I'll catch up in a minute." *Death came while I was riding the train. I couldn't protect them.* He walked away, and pulled the door shut. Breathing hard, he closed his eyes. *The train rails in France were not next to us,* he remembered. *You are in Mississippi, not France,* he reminded himself, bending over, trying to ease a painful knot in his chest.

***

Outside the station, Lamont, Brucie and Memory stepped around the usual older men who were sitting on cane chairs and benches in front of the depot and solving the world's problems.

"'Fore I forget it, Miss Brucie. This here's for you." Lamont gave Brucie the telegram the station master had given him a short while before.

She read silently. "Well. My husband will be coming in just before Easter." She rolled her lips shut.

"Miss Brucie." Lamont pointed a little way down the street. "That there in front of the Square is the hearse from your Blessed Rest Funeral Home."

"Our funeral home," she corrected quietly.

Lamont put a finger to his lips. "Known only to me and you and Lawyer Man Stanton," he reminded her. "Colored folks in the back, white folks in the front.

153

"Me, Minyard and Topper will load up your trunks and ride in that buckboard there behind the hearse. We'll unload when we get to your house."

"Lamont. The two of us. We're family. We're in business. That hearse belongs to both of us. You and I, we ride together." She touched his shoulder then her own.

Fine wrinkles in Lamont's face deepened like plowed furrows. "Yes, ma'am." He smiled and tapped his hat brim. "Us ownin' that funeral home business together stays betwixt us two, though. You'd best remember it."

Memory was limping a little behind her mother and Lamont. Her shoe hurt her foot, and she thought she might have gotten something in it. She stopped, raised her leg, took off her shoe and shook it while Lamont and her mother walked slowly on ahead.

"There's so much more than business between the two of us," Brucie said. "Remember who our father is. I sometimes feel as if Bruce and your mother, Vernell, look down on us. "

"I think they'd give us a head nod. Seeing as to how you've come back to Mississippi and brought your children."

A peanut shell fell out of Memory's shoe. She slipped it back on, hurried down the sidewalk and caught up with Lamont and her mother just in time to hear Brucie say softly. "It's like coming home to me, when I see you."

"I'm not sure what that means, but nothing about this place is like home to me," Memory muttered. She was going to say something so they could hear her, but Lamont was pointing at the hearse which was right in front of them

"One of the embalmers, Shank, is gonna drive us. He's a grandson to that old murdering, one-armed man, Ollie Potter." Lamont gave a half laugh, but it was one that had no humor in it. "Old man Potter's been gone more years than I can remember. Shank's daddy, God rest his bad soul, was one of those Potter boys we knew."

"Can you trust anyone named Potter?" Brucie asked.

"I didn't have much choice. Not many people around here want to touch dead folks. But for some reason they don't seem to bother Shank or his brother, Trestle, none. But knowing they're Potters, I keep a close eye on them. Sometimes"—Lamont bit his bottom lip—"I think they might do a little voodoo or practice some black magic every now and then.

"But I don't forget, and keep it very much in my mind's eye," he went on. "You and I know old man Potter had a lot to do with the mob that hung my mama. I watch this one close. I couldn't find an embalmer even in Jackson, and Shank and Trestle works for cheap."

"That inbred Potter family goes go way back with being bad people. Just watch yourself," Brucie said. "When Old Papa Claymore put them off the place, they lived in a tree house down by the river. Old Man Potter could steal more with one arm, than a paid thief could with two arms and five people helping him."

***

"Captain." There was a pounding outside the lavatory and the soothing, familiar sound of Jenson Cooper's voice was like a late afternoon breeze sweeping across the French hedgerows.

"I'm in Mississippi," Dale reminded himself.

"I thought I'd check on you before I left for home. Let's go on outside. It smells bad in here," Jenson said, opening the lavatory door a crack. "Worse than those slop jars and holes in the trenches."

Jenson reached out his hand to close the door behind them, and then bent over. He carefully picked up a wooden crate holding the tin bucket with ice and Samuel's legs. "You and I. We go too far back and mean too much to each other for us to have any kind of disagreement. From the time you and I were little boys and you came down here from Boston, it was like we were brothers." A feeling of nostalgia washed over him. "And back then, Miss Memory could have been my sister. She may have forgotten it, but sometimes, I did look after her. I think in ways, she'd just as soon forget."

Dale took a step forward then stopped. "There's somebody here we need to help. That man sitting down over there"—He pointed to the old soldier sitting in the station—"He has no eyes. We need to do something."

He slammed himself in the chest with his fist. "I want to do something."

"We can't help him. You can't take care of the world," Jenson said. "We have Private Samuel's legs. They were lost, but we found them.

"Why don't you put up your whiskey and cough syrup for now?" he asked. With those words he and Dale exchanged uneasy glances. "They play with your mind too much. And you probably won't be able to get what you like around here." He set the crate down, held the door open and waved his hand in a let's-go motion.

"I saw your family. By now, they should be about ready to board a wagon."

"Oh, God," Dale breathed as he and Jenson stepped onto the sidewalk. No spurts of machine gun fire. No smell of burning flesh.

"I may have a chance."

"My brother's picking me up. He should be here any minute to load up me and my trunks. I need to get on. I'm taking care of this here." Jenson pointed to the box at his feet. "You and I, we'll give our friend's remains a proper burial. Until then, he'll be in the icehouse." He tapped Dale's arm and gave him a gentle nudge. "You go on. I'll be out in a day or two to see y'all." He arranged his baggage and sat down on a bench with some of the old men while he waited for his ride.

Jenson propped his feet on one of the trunks and realized it was one of the Von Dieters'. Uneasy about Dale, *This'll give me a good excuse to run out and make sure they're all okay,* he told himself.

Brucie, Memory, and Lamont had crossed the street. Just short of the Square, the hearse, with the words, Blessed Rest Funeral Home written on the side in large gold letters was pulled to the curb.

"Come on, Miss Brucie." Lamont raised his hand and directed her to where a bony man with a nose so large a coat could be hung on it, leaned on the front of the vehicle and was fast asleep.

Lamont shook his head and sighed. "This here's the wagon we all are gonna ride in. I see Mist Dale coming from the depot now."

He gave the driver a gentle shove. The man jumped awake and swiped the back of his arm across his drooling mouth.

"Miss Brucie. Miss Memory. This here's Mr. Shank Potter," Lamont said.

His Adam's apple jerking like a bouncing ball, the man jumped awake and snatched off a tattered straw hat. A large birthmark the color of a crushed strawberry and looking like pulpy rotten flesh spread over his forehead and down one cheek. He smiled, showing large top dentures, then rolled his lips in trying to cover a pink-gummed bottom mouth, with a few jagged, brown teeth. No one else seemed to pay any attention but Memory noticed it, shivered and backed up. *You're staring. Stop it,* she told herself. *People can't help the way they look. But that nose. Dear God. I think I've seen that nose in an old nightmare somewhere.*

"Potter." Brucie frowned. "I knew your grandfather. And, as I recall, you were around the place one summer taking care of some of the livestock."

Memory could tell by the tone of her mother's voice and the disdain on her face that Brucie considered Shank Potter to be the lowest of the low. White trash. And having acknowledged him, there was nothing else she wanted to say.

"Don't reckon as to how I remember none of that," he mumbled.

Brucie had already turned away and with Lamont's help had stepped into the hearse and was lowering herself onto one of the benches.

Hanging a little way back from them, Dale seemed undecided about what to do.

"Come on," Memory waved in his direction. "I need you with me."

Dale held up both his hands in a blocking motion. "I'm not getting into that hearse," he said. "Some of my men may be on the train over there. They may be still alive. If they are, we might be able to help them. Get them to a first aid shelter, even if they're riding in a death wagon."

"You're not in France. We're in Mississippi," Memory replied through clenched teeth. "I've about had enough of this nonsense. You have to get in. You can do it. It's just to get us to the house."

"Come on, Mist Dale," Lamont said. "Follow me. You can ride in the buckboard with my boys, Topper and Minyard. Another Potter's driving that one. Shank's brother, Trestle."

Dale drew in a deep, relieved sigh. "I am here. I am in Franklin, Mississippi," he said, as if it were a completely new thought to him. "I can do that."

Lamont walked back with Dale and gestured to the buckboard. "These here are my sons, Topper and Minyard," he said. "And that one there"—He jerked his head in the direction of the driver, a wide-mouthed, sallow-skinned man, who could have been as young as Dale or as old as Lamont—"is Trestle Potter."

Memory had a strange feeling they were being watched from somewhere off to the side. She traced a fingertip under the narrow leather belt to her over blouse, stepped away from the hearse and glanced toward a scrubby hillside just past the train's caboose.

Liam McRae, still hidden, parted a bristly brown branch.

Again, Memory thought she saw a metallic glint.

Liam rose.

Memory stood on tiptoe. She felt a tightness in her chest and sucked in her breath She saw a figure with a shock of thick red hair streaming from a metal helmet. Her knees grew wobbly.

"That looks like somebody I've seen before. Somebody from Boston," she murmured to herself. Her fingers trembling, she slung the peanuts to the ground. "Oh, forget it. My mind's playing tricks on me. It's a stowaway. Not anybody I know."

Liam saw Memory look in his direction. He slid down.

Brucie leaned out of the back of the hearse. "Get in, Memory," she called

Stop it, Memory scolded herself. *As usual, your imagination's running away with itself.*

She still didn't feel right but put aside her misgivings when she saw her brother standing by the buckboard. Knowing he would be riding with Lamont's children made her feel better, and she turned toward the hearse. Shank Potter appeared by Memory's side, took her elbow and helped her up the step where she sank onto a small leather bench next to her mother.

For a moment Memory was slightly breathless, as if she'd fallen down a steep hill. She shook her head as if trying to fling away something too terrible to recall. She opened her mouth to speak, but she couldn't remember the words she wanted to say. Finally, she managed to mumble, "There's something about Shank Potter that makes me feel sick to my stomach."

"He's ordinary, but the man can't help the way he looks," Brucie answered as Lamont sat in a cane chair behind them.

"He's scary." Every part of Memory wanted to run away from this man, and she had no idea why.

"It's good to be home," Brucie said as they pulled onto Main Street. "We can begin again. We have the land. Always the land," she said over the noise of the train blowing out steam. "I know your father will be with us soon."

Liam spread the bushes in front of him. All the Franklin passengers were off the train, the few who were saying their goodbyes and going on hurriedly boarded. Soon, the train wheels made grinding sounds as the Westbound Limited pulled away from the depot.

No one watching. Time to go. Liam flung his helmet down, picked up his wooden box, bounded across the tracks and sprinted through the depot.

Out in front of the station, head ducked, still being careful not to be noticed, he looked, but for a minute didn't see the Von Dieters.

Then he spotted the long black funeral car and a buckboard pulling away. His unblinking eyes gleamed with anger. "Someday they'll carry one of you off in that same vehicle," he said. "And I'll be watching when you have your final ride in The Blessed Rest Funeral Home hearse, Mr. Dale Von Dieter."

CHAPTER 16

Red, red, red.
Red in the shape of Mississippi.
Red in the sinuous remembrance of
rape.

There is blood in the air here, guilt too.
Some devil is after the truth in a
careworn Good Book.
Some djinn leads Memory to memory.
Soon Redemption Ridge will experience
A reckoning. All it will take is a
Mischief breeze or a sudden religious
Impulse

Tuesday, March 23

The town of Franklin wore the look of an old man who had been working in the fields too long. Not many people were out except around the depot, and not many of them had left on the train or had been meeting someone. It was just an air in the small town—never knowing when something might happen. Just sit and hope whether good or bad, just to have something to talk about.

The few stores and buildings had a down-home look and down-home names: Heddie's Emporium, McMahon's Seed and Feed, Fly's Drugstore, Blessed Rest Funeral Home, Mrs. Netter's Boarding House, New Merchants and Farmers Bank, Adkins Meat Market, Harmon's Merchantile.

"It's good to be home," Brucie said, just loud enough for Memory to hear.

Memory still felt a need to feel alive. Even though she was almost compelled to reach for her nail file, fearing she might be seen by Lamont, who sat behind her, she thought better of it. Looking at the country town, and thinking of the city she'd just left, Memory wondered what this place held for her now that they'd be living here. She was relieved that Mr. Shank Potter, whoever he was, sat way up front, away from Brucie, Lamont and her. For some unknown reason the sight of the man sent chills over her. Just before she climbed into the hearse, she had stared at his face a moment and felt as if she was seeing an old stage play. *That birthmark. Something like that filled my eyes one time.*

She shook her head. *What a nightmare I must have had. Looking up, I thought a red mark would be the last thing I'd ever see. Then, there was water. Everywhere. In my ears. My nose. My mouth.* She shook her head, trying to clear up her thoughts. *Why in the world would I remember a nightmare from who knows when about a red birthmark? I don't know anybody who has one. Until now.*

Since the summer she was thirteen, Memory would get sick to her stomach at the thought of returning to Mississippi for a visit, much less being forced to live there. She didn't know where this discomfort came from, and she never spoke of it; but each time she was here in Franklin, she had spells where she felt as if she were suffocating. In the past, even though there were wonderful times, she would count the days until they returned to Boston. Now everything had changed. "I might as well make up my mind," she murmured. "It's all different." *Leaving may not be part of the picture. Like it or not, this might be home.*

Lamont leaned forward and tapped Brucie on the shoulder. "The town hasn't changed too much since y'all been here last.

"You gonna recognize most everything," he said. They drove slowly on through downtown Franklin, past the First Baptist Church and the Crossroads Methodist across the street, then picked up a little speed as they drove on to where a few stately old houses lined both sides of Main Street.

"Families here had roots," Brucie said. "Even though I've been gone many years, I've never been able to let go of my ties."

"My roots are up east with streetcars, art galleries and Packard touring cars." Memory gestured out the open window. "Not here with ticks, water moccasins and rat-tailed possums."

When the hearse reached the end of Franklin, the street slanted down. Then they turned slightly east onto Old Farm Road, and there was a drastic change from the neat homes and yards.

On either side of Old Farm Road, trickles of wood smoke twisted from brick chimneys sagging away from weather beaten gray shacks. Scrawny, stretching dogs lay on small porches or in the dirt yards. A few chinaberry trees grew nearby, and small ponds stagnated under a thin layer of greenish scum. Spread out from many of the houses, small fields that had not been planted or cultivated in several years lay fallow or overgrown with broom-sedge.

As the hearse moved on toward Redemption Ridge, they passed a few people on the road who waved, then stepped off into a sandy ditch or small, washed-away places to let them by.

"We're not far from home now." Brucie placed her hand over her heart as if her chest hurt.

"I've told you and Dale a little bit of family history before, but you've probably forgotten. When the time is right, there are more things I need to tell you and Son," Brucie said slowly, reluctantly.

Lamont shook his head. "You needs to let it loose. It's way past tellin' time, Miss Brucie."

"There's not much to tell or understand." Brucie smiled. Her eyes told another story; her words edged with bitterness.

Lamont leaned forward and gave Brucie a hard, reproachful look, something Memory had never seen him do. "There's lots you could say, if you was of a mind to."

"You're right," Memory whispered.

Brucie glanced out the window. "I dream about your mother a lot," she said. "Sometimes I almost expect a resurrected Vernell to appear."

"My mama was a fine woman. I'm talkin' about your peoples."

Brucie dropped her head. Even with Lamont's remark it seemed as if she wasn't ready to speak of what might be hurtful family matters.

"My brother and I both know and understand more about the Claymores than you think we do," Memory whispered, half to her mother and half to herself. She had always been curious about their family history, but it had really been aroused some years ago when she overhead Brucie talking to Cousin Sarah about unspeakable family matters. From that conversation and others, she had heard she had gotten bits of information about the Confederate Captain Bruce Claymore and some of the family's deep, dark secrets, but many questions still gnawed at her.

Looking for answers and knowing her mother wouldn't want to talk about it, later that afternoon Memory and Dale had approached Cousin Sarah in her sitting room.

Memory still had a mental picture of her and Dale being with Cousin Sarah those long months ago, shortly before Dale went off to fight a war. "We need to know more about our family. Starting with our grandfather." Through the years Memory had pieced together enough to know that her mother had been terribly mistreated by her father.

That afternoon, Cousin Sarah had stared at Memory and Dale as if trying to judge whether or not they could bear to hear hurtful truths about their family's past. Then she seemed to come to a decision and when she spoke, some of her words hit Memory like a lightning strike.

"I've been praying for this moment. It's time for you to know some of the facts," the family matriarch had said. "You"—She nodded to Dale—"are soon shipping out to go overseas and fight, to save the world. After much prayer, I've come to the conclusion there are some things it's best for you to know before you leave the country. What I have to say begins and ends with family."

She hesitated, and from the look in Cousin Sarah's eyes, Memory knew they were going to become privy to hurtful secrets, maybe some she didn't want to hear.

"I will come as clean as I can at this moment in time. There is even yet another family bloodline that should be straightened out. Oh, what tangled webs we weave," she said.

"I will say this. Your mother and Lamont. There's more to their friendship than meets the eye. But this is up to your mother to tell you as she sees fit.

"Much of what I'm passing on to you, I was told by Lamont's long-dead mother, Vernell. I would believe anything Vernell told me as being the God's truth."

Cousin Sarah took a deep breath, shifted her weight uncomfortably and smoothed her skirt. "Bruce Claymore, known to be the handsomest man in Tallouga County, was C.W.'s half-brother.

"This I want you to know before we go any further. Your grandfather was not that lecherous, C.W. Claymore—Daddy Claymore as he was known in the family.

"Captain Bruce Claymore. You've heard of him all your life." Cousin Sarah rocked forward in her chair. "He was not only your dear mother's namesake. He was her blood father."

Memory had been standing. Even now she could remember her legs went weak and she had to sit down before Cousin Sarah could go on.

What Cousin Sarah told her and Dale that day was like one of the old fairytales she had read when she was a child.

"Depending on which side of one legend I'm sure you'd like to believe," Cousin Sarah had said, "Bruce Claymore was either a traitor, or a hero. I wish I could say that the truth will set you free, but it doesn't always work that way.

"It was known that Bruce had in his possession a fortune in jewels collected from people all over Tallouga County for the Confederate cause. There were lies about him, that he was keeping the fortune for himself.

"Now branded as a traitor by many, he should have been a hero. He was trying to get through to the Port of Orleans with them when he was murdered. And in the town, it wasn't known by whom. "

Cousin Sarah became silent a moment, then she went on. "Now we will get to Daddy Claymore, the grief he has caused to so many, and the evil that was in the man.

"There's no question in my mind that C.W. murdered his half-brother, Captain Bruce, thinking he would find the fortune. I have seen a signed confession by none other than C.W. to that effect. As if he suspicioned something happening, Bruce had taken precautions with the fortune. Supposedly, only two people knew where the jewels were.

"Vernell and Bruce. Of course, they're both long gone. But Vernell made sure someone else knew. Sheriff Homer Bramlett."

Cousin Sarah paused as if to let her words sink in. "There is proof of what I have said. Proof of the murder. And of a location for the Confederate fortune, which, even down until this very day has been searched for all over Tallouga County.

"The murder confession and the proof," she said, "Sheriff Homer Bramlett, Jenson Cooper's grandfather, recorded it securely in a family Bible. The Bible was passed from his hands into those of Lamont Randall when he was a boy. It has been at his house for, lo, these many years. Lamont was instructed to return it to your family when he was older and felt the time was ripe."

Cousin Sarah moved to the edge of her chair. "The two of you are adults. You, Dale, are going off to war. I may not be here when you return." She laid her hand across her chest as she said this. "Someday you will be man of the house at Redemption Ridge, Dale.

"The Bible should not fall into Herschel Von Dieter's hands. I will inform Lamont to put the Bible with its confession from Daddy Claymore and the location of the treasure in some safe place."

Memory remembered that Cousin Sarah acted as if she didn't want to go on. She had risen and walked to a window. Finally, she said, "There's more."

She put her hand on a chair as if to steady herself, then sank into it.

"Your mother was misused. By the evil C.W. What was done by him. It should have been cause for a stoning. And the most disturbing thing. This may well affect you two. "

The silence in the room became long and uncomfortable. A look of distress on her face, she finally went on. "There was, what the country folks call a 'lay-by baby,' who is also in the picture. Even until this very hour. Your mother was only a child herself. She could not raise her. This other Claymore lives in faraway

California and was raised by a Mrs. Bledsoe. I have recently received two letters, one from Mrs. Bledsoe and another signed by two neighbors of hers. They were concerned about the safety of their friend. That if anything happens to her, perhaps, the authorities should be called in. My understanding is that you may also receive one, Memory.

"And, that's enough for now." She had waved at Memory and Dale. "I need you to leave. I'm bone tired and need to rest."

Unspoken words, unanswered questions hung in the room as Memory and Dale walked out. Memory looked back and saw Cousin Sarah take a vial of pills from her skirt pocket.

Less than two months before Dale was due to come home from the war, Cousin Sarah died from consumption.

***

The summer Dale was at war, Brucie and Memory made a short visit to Redemption Ridge, leaving Thornton and Herschel behind in Boston.

Memory was around Lamont. For some unknown reason, before she could stop herself, the word 'Uncle' slipped out several times when she went to say something to him. She didn't know where it came from, it was as if words had been put into her mouth. Not 'Uncle' in a put down way, rather in a manner of speaking to a close relative. With no change in his facial expression, Lamont always answered her.

Today Memory felt a rush of frustration for what her mother hadn't spoken of about her past, and what she had been told by Cousin Sarah. Respecting her wishes, she and Dale had never mentioned any of it to their mother.

But, if I have to live here, there are a lot of things I want to find out.

"Whatever it takes," she whispered. "And the Good Lord willing, I will find out. Even if I have to resurrect some ghosts."

CHAPTER 17

Artillery bursts like Mississippi thunder
The sun is obscured by acrid clouds
That wait for lightning on the ground.

The Captain remembers the
Promise he made the young man.
A peach pit picked up in a
Deep, forgotten orchard of youth.

A shared memory walked with a cane
Along the hills of Tallouga County.
How these men fought,
How they died.
We would get there again.

The sirens howled, we climbed
The trench ladders into
No man's land and swept across
The wired field as ants
Under a magnifying glass.

The German fortifications were overrun,
The Captain kept his promise;
The door that was propped
Open with the young private's leg swung wildly,
He would walk the crest of his youth
In his dreams forever.

Tuesday, March 23

"Y'all jest have to hold your horses." Trestle Potter took a deep breath and shot a stream of tobacco juice into the street. He swiped his bent arm and smeared another layer of brown across his already dust-laden face. "I got me a case of the runs. We can't git goin' yet a while. An' I also got me somethin' to pick up."

Dale was beginning to feel somewhat like himself again and wanted to get on to Redemption Ridge. He frowned, took a deep breath and propped against a lamppost to wait while Trestle Potter took care of whatever he wanted to buy and whatever stomach problem he claimed to be having.

Minyard came up to Dale. "There's something I'm needing to tell you," he said. "My Daddy, he said make sure you tell this to Mist Dale. There's a Bible put in your room. Where your clothes are gonna be. There's some words in there you need to be sure and see."

Minyard swung up into the buckboard to wait.

Topper's mouth lifted in a sly smile. "I got what I need," he said to himself. He moved over and stood by Dale.

"What Mist Potter means about his stomach"—Topper leaned his head to one side as if he were draining something from his ear—"he's got him a place to buy a stash of whiskey just over there behind that fire station. A one-legged, hair-lipped man sells a little moonshine outta his barn."

Dale ran his hand into his coat pocket for his bill holder. He felt an envelope. He pulled it out, slit the envelope open, and lifted out a note. He read a few lines from a message that made no sense to him.

> **To the manor born. Well, not exactly. I would suggest you all watch to see what appears on your doorstep. All in due time.**

Dale shook his head in bewilderment. *This means nothing to me. But wait,* he told himself. *Green eyes. Someone with green eyes and red hair. On the train. I know. He put this in my coat.*

An ill-tempered looking, tall dark man with stiff black hair beckoned to Topper from the other side of the street. Topper puffed air into his cheeks and crossed to where Lucius Dedmon stood.

"We're doing business," Dedmon mouthed. "Don't ever think about you crossing me. I'm the boss man." He gave him a small glass bottle. "I been told this here is what he likes. He'll be wanting some of that. I kin git him some more, over to Lou'siana."

Dale saw two men with their heads together. It looked as if Lamont's son and the man were talking over something very deep. It didn't involve him, so he didn't pay much attention.

In a few minutes tired of standing, he yawned, stretched then climbed into the buckboard. Topper walked back across the street, swung up behind Dale and took a seat next to Minyard who had fallen asleep.

Dale pulled out his pocket watch. Twenty minutes. He was just before climbing down from the buckboard to see if he could find another way to Redemption Ridge when Trestle came back, untethered the mules and climbed into the wagon.

"I was beginning to think we wouldn't get away from here until dark." Dale's fingers tightened on the bench and he leaned forward. When he did, he smelled a strong, peculiar scent and began coughing. It took him a second before he knew what it was. The odor from Trestle's body irritated his nose. Some of the old-timers in these parts washed themselves with kerosene to get rid of mites. His nose, more sensitive since the war, began seeping. *This is so bad, I could almost use my gas mask*, he thought.

Dale swiped his hand across his face, then grabbed the bench as Trestle flipped the reins and they plodded down the street.

They were passing by Fly's Drugstore when Dale felt a hand on his shoulder.

"I got something for you," Topper said. "From a friend."

Dale shook his head. *My friends are half a world away. They won't ever make it back home*. "Jenson Cooper is about the only friend I have here now."

"No, sir. You're dead wrong. Somebody in the station give me something and told me you might want it mighty bad." Topper grinned. He gave him a bottle of Bayer's Cough Syrup with heroin. "This here's a gift," he said. "Good stuff.

"We're gonna be friends. And I know where I can get you all the whiskey you want. And some more of that there."

"Home again, and all you could want," Dale said softly, looking around as they passed through town. "No place like Tallouga County, Mississippi."

It had been over three years since he had been to Franklin. *In some ways the past hasn't quite caught up with Tallouga County,* he thought, *and the future is off in the distance. Whatever happens, whatever comes, we have to make the best of it. Have to live with it. Life turns on itself. Renewed in its own timeframe. No matter how much we may want it to be ours.*

As soon as they turned onto the Old Farm gravel road it was if one book had been put down, and another, much older book, one with yellowed pages and hard-to-read loopy writing, had been picked up. The words were penned in a childish hand and script.

Narrow in parts where the gravel and dirt had sloughed off, the road was eroding in many places. It was easy to see that unless more gravel was hauled in, it wouldn't have taken too many rainy days for part of the road to slide on away and wash off into a slough.

They rode in silence. In a short while the buckboard rounded a large bend in the road. Off to the side Dale could see the sluggish waters of Noble Creek. He smelled a slightly brackish odor, dead fish, decaying leaves. A few tree limbs, bleached pale as bones, floated in the water. He shivered. "I've lived in Boston. And I don't have a lot of stock in those old country sayings, but I feel like a rabbit just ran over my grave," he said.

Just then a long, sleek, green roadster, made a slow turn from a narrow lane in front of them onto Old Farm Road. The driver came to a dead stop. Loud, udn, udn, udn, noises came from the automobile.

"Lawd Gawd a'mighty," Topper whistled. "It's that crazy Mudge Turnipseed. He's got more money than he's got sense. Hold your hats."

"A Turnipseed!" Dale managed to say. "No Turnipseed's ever had a pot to piss in. Much less drive a roadster like that."

"He's got him the gift and made hisself a pile o' money," Topper said. "He owns that Divine Deliverance Holiness Church.

Let him git ahold of some snake milk from that witchdoctor, Lucius Dedmon, and he can charm the warts off a wart hog."

Up ahead of them, the driver waved both arms in the air. Then he reached down and arranged something long and slithery around his neck. "Hiss, hiss," he hollered, "Comin' at you.'"

He blared the horn. He set the steering wheel as if he were piloting a large boat through dangerous waters. He pressed in the clutch and pulled down the gear shift. He pushed the accelerator all the way down, popped the clutch off, and the driver, a bulldog-faced man who wore touring glasses perched on his nose like a pollen-sucking butterfly, barreled toward them. Trestle yanked the reins, jerking the mules to the side.

"Gotcha," the driver yelled, aiming straight at them and then steering away at the last moment. "Sinners all. An' God loves ya. An' He can take your sickness away," he hollered over his shoulder.

Dale barely made out something long and black, like a string tie hanging around his neck. Except the tie slithered then quivered like a divining rod that had found water.

The buckboard jolted to a stop a few feet from a bend of Noble Creek. The right front wheel slid off and mired in the gravel. Part of the road had collapsed like a mouth with missing teeth. Trestle and Minyard went to work, and in a few minutes they had the buckboard back on the road.

"I'm gonna heist on to my place," Minyard said. "And I'll see you later, Mist Dale."

***

As they passed by a heavily wooded area of Redemption Ridge, where a bloody battle was fought during The War Between the States, thick air coiled around Dale's neck like an angry snake, ready to strike. He felt as if his frail hold on the here and now was disappearing with the wind-stirred dust. "Where are they taking my men?" he called out.

"You mean your folks what just left?" Topper asked. "That's them on up ahead of us."

171

"My men," Dale said. But there was uncertainty in his voice.

Perspiration broke out on Dale's forehead. They were covered in dust. Salty sweat burned his eyes; it was hard for him to draw breath into his irritated lungs; his throat felt as if he had swallowed glass. He covered the bottle with his hands as if he didn't want whoever or whatever might be out there to see him with it.

He smelled odors from his childhood. Muddy river water, the acrid smell of horse sweat, the gluey odor of dried cow's milk.

It seemed as if he heard sighs and voices ringing out from the foot of the ridge. Sounds he'd heard before. *We're here. We're here. Please find us.* This was a sensation he'd felt when he was a summertime visiting child playing here at Redemption Ridge. Part of his past flashed before his eyes. Fragments filled his mind.

In his imagination he had glimpsed men from another war, had fought childish battles on these old fields. He had stumbled and played war games over the tombstones, swashbuckling with make-believe swords with his friends, Jenson Cooper and Samuel Stanton.

"Someone's breathing out there," he had told his sister several years back, just before he left for Ole Miss. Troublesome words, words he could barely hear had been whispered in his ears. "Help me find my peace."

"I hear them," he said. "The dead and forgotten men are calling out."

"You're crazy," Memory had laughed back then. "It's the wind in the trees." But Dale had wondered, *could it have been restless souls with tortured breaths coming from the cemetery and beyond?*

And now, years later, he was a different person than he was then. *That cough medicine. I could use more of it. And hopefully, some whiskey too,* Dale thought Then, somewhere near the colored cemetery he could swear he heard a thundering echo.

"Help me find my peace."

CHAPTER 18

**The tattered and debrided remains of
Vernell swayed.
This was a Christmas tree inverted.
Memory's mind collapsed, running
into the past, crushing delicate glass
ornaments in a strange music of want
and terror.**

Tuesday, March 23

Ahead of the wagon, a few miles from town, Memory made out the beginning of the ridge and the crumbling rusty iron fence encircling the old cemetery.

"You needs to let your children know who else is there, Miss Brucie," Lamont said as they drew nearer to Redemption Ridge. "It's part of who they are."

A long, uncomfortable silence followed. Instead of saying anything else, Brucie seemed to be waiting for someone to tell her what to do or say.

She looked out the window, clasped her hands together. "I'd like to stop a minute," she said. "Smell the country air."

"Why don't we pull over here, stretch our legs, and let you all look around." Lamont eased toward the front and tapped the window blocking the driver from the rest of the vehicle. "Here by the cemetery, hoe up a minute, Shank," he called.

When Shank swung to the side of the road and stopped, Lamont pushed the door open, stepped out and reached for Brucie.

"It doesn't look as big as I remembered," she said, stepping down with Memory, so close behind that their skirt hems brushed. "Sometimes it seems as if the whole world began here, and this is where, for me, it will probably end." Brucie arched her back and stretched.

Filled with leaning tombstones, moss-covered, large, ornate statues, and wooden crosses the cemetery was encompassed by the Civil War battleground. To one side of the white burying ground was the old colored cemetery; like the white, it was hardly used anymore and almost forgotten; most of the new cemeteries were in town and behind churches. Through time, the dead and dried grasses of both Redemption Ridge burying grounds had knotted, vined, twined, and trunk-choked one into the other. It was hard to tell where one burial ground ended and the other began.

Brucie raised her hand and pointed. "Over there. That's where my mother and my sister are buried. I think I'll see if our family markers are okay."

"From what you've said, and what I've heard about your sister, Thelma Grace, I'm glad you didn't name me for her," Memory said. As always when Thelma Grace's name was spoken, as if to confirm this, she noticed her mother winced.

Brucie shrugged her shoulders and pointed to the adjoining smaller, overgrown burial ground. "Over there's where Lamont's mother, Vernell is. Lamont and I were there when she was buried. It was another lifetime."

Memory stepped away from the hearse. "While you're looking after your folks, I'll mosey on the other side," she said. "See if I can stir up any old ghosties."

She rested her fingertips on the rusty gate and looked toward the colored section. "What secrets are hiding out here? She asked. Although there was a breeze, she felt warm all over. The air in the cemetery seemed to be thick. Was it heavy with the streaming tears of these forgotten people?

Cheeks burning, Memory wiped her sweating hands on her skirt. As she opened the gate and stepped into the cemetery, she half expected to see ghostly apparitions floating around the old burial grounds. Instead, she saw only years of neglect: untended grounds, slanting tombstones and sunken graves. Splotches of sunlight filtered through oak and pine trees; a breeze brushed Memory's face.

Forgotten people lay out there in front of her, unmarked and unknown in their graves. As she surveyed all the forgotten, even with no ghostly revelations or spirits flying through the air, Memory sensed they were there. She waited in the stillness for something to happen, but the scene in front of her was clear and serene. If she were just patient, someday, somehow, many of the family secrets might well come from these old burial sites.

She knew her grandfather, Captain Bruce Claymore and Lamont's mother, Vernell, were buried somewhere in this soil. Maybe even together.

"Where are you, my grandfather?" she asked, recalling Cousin Sarah's words about their family's history. "You're my kin, sir. If you're here, speak to me. Show me something."

Nothing.

"If only the dead could talk. For some reason, Vernell seems more real to me than you do. I feel she has things to tell me," Memory said, ready to move away from the graves, return to the hearse and head for the house.

As she hiked her skirt, overhead a murder of crows chattered into the air as if something had startled them. Behind her, she heard faint rising and falling sounds. At first, she thought it was the wind stirring the budding spring leaves.

The noise grew. A hard shiver went through Memory.

No. Not leaves. She stiffened. She willed herself not to run.

It sounded like soft sobs.

Stop it. This is otherworldly. It may be of the devil.

She held her breath in anticipation, but scene remained unchanged.

"I must be imagining things."

She made out words, *Help me find my peace.* She felt a presence.

The voice seemed to hover near the edge of the black cemetery, close to the white. She saw nothing.

Then, toward an old wooden bench, Memory heard soft moans and the sound of boards being nailed. She raised her eyes. Her heart missed a beat. Something hung from the gnarled limb of a large live oak tree sheltering the bench.

Stepping closer she made out a dangling rope. Knotted in the rope and slowly swinging in the breeze she saw what looked to be a crumpled, rotten dress. "Vernell! Oh dear, God. That is how she died," Memory breathed.

Help me find my peace.

There was a slight movement in the one of the tree limbs. She watched, half fascinated, half frightened as a pale bony hand reached down for the thready rope. "That hand. Trying to save her."

A little too much distance. The skeletal fingers couldn't grab the rope.

He's here. With me. Help us find our peace.

"Somebody else. Somebody else," Memory sobbed. Like a tornado blasting an attic to splinters, fear swept the scene in front of her away. Heart racing, she fled the burial grounds.

Lamont saw Memory running and sensed something was wrong. "Let's us get on outta here," he called to Shank Potter. He jerked open the door as Memory flung herself into the hearse and fell onto the leather bench next to her mother.

Dig, dig, she thought, reaching down for her comfort, the nail file.

No. Her purse was under her mother's feet.

"Not me," she sobbed quietly. "I'm no visiting angel. I'm not brave."

Heart pounding, Memory looked back, half expecting to hear a voice speaking or to see a bony hand reaching to open the hearse door.

No. Behind them, she made out horses pulling the buckboard her brother was in.

Memory shoved one clenched fist against her mouth. "I'm not brave," she muffled.

***

As they came up on the old cemetery, Dale saw the Blessed Rest Funeral Home hearse disappear over a hill. *Hearse. Different here. Over there. Ambulance. Hearse. One and the same over there.*

He remembered the ambulances, also used as death vehicles that had been part of the life he had left behind not too long ago. Some pulled by horses, other newer ones with motors. All of them carrying fellow soldiers, many of them screaming with pain, some already deathly quiet.

He knew he'd never see those men again in this life. But in some weird ways back in the fields, it had been a comfort to see them in the death wagon. Though they would soon be only a shallow mound resting in some foreign field, his men's names would be planted over their bodies. They would not be lost to eternity in an unknown, gummy, ratty-pilled spot. Maybe, praise God, even a cross would be raised. *I need to quit thinking about the past*, Dale told himself. *But I just can't.* Friends were buried in that thick, French clay. Many of them just kids, some as young as fifteen or sixteen. "I need to get out. There's something I need to see."

Trestle pulled to a stop.

Depression was a walnut-sized lump in Dale's throat as he walked through the gate his sister had left open a short while ago. As soon as he stepped into the cemetery, the guns he'd heard just moments before were silenced.

Instead of artillery guns, shrill-voiced crows jeered. Dale heard birds cry, "Here."

No...

"There."

Were they trying to tell him something?

CHAPTER 19

Redemption Ridge was ringed with trees.
Oaks, magnolias, pines.
In the hot breeze and sway they
became the neurons of displaced,
releasing memories and rustling sound,
changing colors, and mysterious pheromones.
The guests' memories were activated,
 too, for better or worse.

Tuesday, March 23

Once she was away from the Redemption Ridge burial ground, Memory began to feel like herself.

In a few moments, Lamont's property which adjoined Brucie's old homeplace, came into view. The fields were different from the others they had passed; they looked like a smooth lake stretching far as the eye could see. The broom-sedge had been burned off, rows of earth had been freshly plowed, and it was easy to see the fields and yard were well-tended.

"Your place looks lots better than anything we've seen since we left town," Brucie said.

Lamont nodded. "We've done some spring plowin' but are runnin' a little behind this year."

"Look up ahead, Memory." Brucie raised her hand. "You can see Lamont's house from here."

His neat, white framed house, which sat just off the road, was ringed with trimmed bushes, the gravel drive had been edged by wood planks.

"Right beyond, around the next bend, is your place," Lamont said as the road curved gently, and they reached the Claymore property.

The grounds were surrounded by stands of oaks, magnolias, pines. The old house sat back from the road on a small hill. Rays of afternoon sunlight spilled through the trees bathing the house in a soft glow.

During the years Brucie lived in Boston, she and Von Dieter had made many visits to Redemption Ridge. With Lamont's help and with a few pieces of the hidden treasure trove of jewelry only she and Lamont knew about, they had slowly remodeled the old homeplace. The inside was completely refurbished, the verandah replaced, an inside kitchen and toilets put in. Fresh shrubbery enhanced the yard, garden crops had been replanted out back.

"It looks good. It's been almost three years since I was here," Brucie said. "Not long after Dale left Ole Miss and enlisted in the army. You and I brought it back, Lamont. Maybe not to its 1857 glory, but close."

A glimmer of pride in his eyes, Lamont lowered his head and smiled.

"I like our new fence," Brucie said as Shank slowed down then stopped. He kept the motor running, slid down from his seat, slouched over and opened a gate to a white picket fence with unusually sharp points around the front and sides of the house.

"I don't," Memory said in a tone that let her mother know how she was feeling. "I don't remember a picket fence from the last time I was here."

My bones are pierced in me at night and my gnawing pains know no rest. Once again, the Biblical words rang in Memory's ears. Remembering the spears her husband, Thornton, had been impaled on, her breathing was flinty and quick. "I hate it."

Shank climbed back into the hearse, and with gravel crunching, they moved on through the gate and up the driveway which ran by the side of the house. Shank stopped a little to the side of a Model T Ford parked under a large oak tree. Lamont stepped out, reached back and helped Brucie and Memory from the hearse.

The March wind had picked up and was blowing the limbs; green leafy shoots burst out through the branches. The breeze lifted Memory's ankle-length pearl-gray skirt, and she had to clamp a hand on her head to keep her hat from blowing off. The hearse cast a long shadow across the yard.

"Whose automobile is that over there?" Brucie asked. "I wonder if Laura Lee, Dale's Mississippi girlfriend's, here."

"I reckon those here are the Presbyterian church ladies," Lamont said. "They sent word out that they were comin'. I went by your place early on to make sure they had got in okay and had everything they needed. I'll go on in and see can I do anything for them. When the buckboard gets here, we'll help unload. The boys and I'll go on home in the hearse. Trestle can ride back in the buckboard. Shank Potter said he had some business up the road to tend to, and he'd git a lift with one of the men he's meetin' up with."

Memory wrinkled her nose at the Potter name. She and Brucie came up the curved walkway leading from the driveway and climbed the porch steps to the house. The two of them stood motionless in front of the thick wooden door flanked by leaded glass windows.

"Come in here." Bertha, Lamont's wife, opened the door. "Me an' my Sassy girl'll tend to things. Whatever y'all need. Y'all home."

Brucie stretched her arms, and the two of them embraced.

"Sassy'll be over later this afternoon to help out."

When Memory and Brucie stepped into the large front hall, the house was redolent with the aroma of food. Soft voices came from the dining room and the kitchen to the left.

A fair-skinned, young lady wearing a long beige skirt covered by a green and white checked apron swooped toward them in the entry hall. "Memory it's so good y'all are back home." A petite lady with blond ringlets, she held her shoulders back and raised her chin as if she were trying to look taller.

"Lordy. Good to see you, Laurie Lee," Memory said. "Dale's missed you. And so have we." She almost said more but stopped herself.

"It's been a while. Thought y'all might have forgotten me."

"Oh, Laura Lee. It's been way too long, and, you're a sight for sore eyes," Brucie said. "I could never forget you. And not because you're Lawyer Matthew Stanton's granddaughter." What Brucie wanted to say, but of course she couldn't, she always had a faint hope that Dale and Laura Lee might someday become engaged.

And it wasn't just because she was so pretty. "We go way back with the Stanton family."

"Of course." Laura Lee's tone was warm and gracious. "I'm so glad y'all are back in Redemption Ridge. For so many reasons." She glanced down at the floor, then looked back up. "But right now, I wanted to let you know, the Ladies Circle of the Dry Creek Presbyterian Church wanted y'all to have a welcome-home meal from us tonight."

"How lovely." Brucie reached out her arms and hugged Laura Lee.

"Dale and my brother were such good friends. I think Samuel enrolled in Ole Miss because of Dale being there," Laurie Lee said. "And knowing Dale was studying English, he decided that's what he wanted to do." She stepped back and ducked her chin. "He used to quote poetry to me. Some of it, he wrote."

"I know." Brucie started to say, "You and Dale were sweet on each other," but she thought better of it.

Laura Lee caught her breath. "Of course, Brother didn't make it back home from The War. It hurts my heart to know he's buried over there somewhere in France, not here with his people."

"Well, maybe Dale has a few things to tell you," Memory said. Since Laura Lee didn't know her brother's remains had been brought home to Mississippi, it wasn't her place to tell her. That was up to Dale.

Laura Lee's face brightened. "But in my letters from Brother, we heard such good things about Dale. I know y'all are very proud of him. I probably should say, Captain Dale. I prayed for him every night," she said softly. She untied the apron from her wasp-thin waist and quickly folded it. "The dining room table's set for y'all. Food's out on the stove and on the kitchen table. I'll show you what we have in the kitchen, Miss Brucie. The other ladies are leaving now, and I won't be too far behind. My brother, Otis, rang a short while ago. He's coming out to pick me up, but he's running a tad behind. He saw Mr. Cooper at the train station. Mr. Cooper's borrowing his brother's car and bringing some of y'all's trunks by here after a while. And, Memory, if you or your mother need anything, please feel free to have the operator ring us."

Listening to the soft chatter of ladies' voices coming from the kitchen, and Laura Lee's musical southern drawl, a rhythm never heard in Boston, the full force of Memory's changed life hit. *Dear, Lord, what do I do? I don't know these people. It's like they've been resurrected from some other century. I'm caught in a time lapse between the past and the present.*

"Charmed, I'm sure." She tried to sound pleased, but she heard the questioning tone coloring her words.

As soon as her mother and Laura Lee left the parlor, Memory turned and looked around. It had been years since she'd been here and there were many changes. Despite the way Memory felt, she had to admit, the remodeled home looked lovely. The heart-of-pine floors had been refinished and were polished to a soft sheen. Flanking the fireplace, a large Oriental rug lay between a pair of walnut sofas ornately carved with roses and vines and covered in a deep purple velvet. Maple tables with marble tops were placed at either end of each sofa. The portrait of her mother, which had hung in the library in Boston, was now over the white marble fireplace mantle and looked as if belonged in this room. Von Dieter had commissioned it the first summer he and Brucie were married, and Memory had to admit to herself, even though she was often unhappy with her mother, Brucie was beautiful then, and she still was.

Memory was tired and just as she sank into one of the wing-back chairs on either side of the fireplace, Laura Lee and Brucie came from the kitchen.

"I'm going to sit out on the front porch with Laura Lee and wait for her ride," Brucie said. "We have some settling in to do, but I thought in a day or two we might go into Jackson and try and stock up on some things we'll be needing. Laura Lee's being a big help. She's reminding me of some things we could use." She took a long deep breath and hands trembling, she brushed her hair from her eyes. "But where is Dale?" she asked, her voice quivering with anxiety. "He should have been not too far behind us."

***

A light mist rose over the colored cemetery. "Death's backyard."

Dale took a sip of some of the medicine he'd just bought and pressed the bottle against his chest as if were a familiar pet that brought comfort to him. "I seek the truth, whatever that truth is."

"More than likely I can get you more of that there pain syrup and all of the whiskey you need, Mist Dale," Topper said. "From Mist Lucius Dedmon. He says he can get some over in Lousiana."

"Good. Just in case you and I have a time when we can't make contact. Why don't you put it behind the barn door?"

"Yes, sir. I'll set it up under a pile o' hay. You can go ahead and pay me for some now, if you've a mind to."

"How much?"

"Two dollars. For the both of them."

Dale took out his bill holder and counted out two ones.

Dale leaned against a tree toward the front of the cemetery, close to where an old line had been drawn with a fence, coloreds on one side, and white on the other. Through time they had almost blended, only strands of barbed wire claimed to separate the two.

A sudden breeze came up. The air seemed to have a different smell to it, an odor from the battlefields. Once smelled, never forgotten.

Looking down he made out mushy footprints.

"Wait here, Topper."

He swung his leg over a dangling stretch of the barbed wire and moved into the other burial ground. This land was close by the white cemetery but different. The terrain was rough. Dense underbrush tangled his ankles; vines knotted like twisted guts tripped Dale's feet as stiff, spiky weeds, nibbled his clothes.

He followed a faint trail that led toward the far back corner of the graveyard.

He saw movement; something seemed to hover over an old wooden bench, which had been a fixture ever since he could remember. Through a thicket of brush, he barely made out what looked to be the form of a gaunt figure beckoning to him.

The front of the man's shirt was black with dried blood.

"Help me find my peace."

"You're not fooling me. You've been dead for years, Captain Claymore."

"Help me find my peace. Avenge me." Dale heard lingering words, like an echo lost in a canyon.

Muscles tensed in Dale's body. He reminded himself that in no-man's land, the mind can play tricks on the brain.

Stumbling forward over a slight mound his knees buckled.

The world sank to a few yards of hard ground but Dale made no move to get up. His hands dug hard dirt. Men had bled and died here. From all over this country. Men in blue. Men in gray. In the midst of all the suffering, something had to matter.

Dale pushed to his knees, grabbed the bench arm to steady himself and slowly rose to his feet.

Off in the distance a horse whinnied. Nearby, a dreary tattoo, a woodpecker hacking a tree.

"I'm not strong enough for this." Blackbirds wound over Dale's head as he reached into his coat pocket for the syrup bottle. "I need to find my own peace."

Strains of a familiar melody seeped into his mind. "Through many dangers, toils, and snares, I have already come." He raised the bottle and took several deep swallows.

His head throbbed. "To thine ownself be true," a faraway voice called. A foul taste invaded his mouth.

"I'm leaving. I'm leaving now," he called over his shoulder, stumbling away.

Late afternoon sunlight spangle-danced through the trees as he retraced his footsteps, moving from one shadow to another. He saw only sunken graves. Carefully balancing himself he snagged his pants on the rusting barbed wire fence but made it safely back to where Topper waited.

"Let's get out of here and on to the house," Dale said. "This old battleground gives me the willies."

"I'll bet you'll get more of that there what you asked for," Topper said as they climbed into the buckboard.

SECOND CHANCE

1920

Once Miss Brucie an' her children, Memory Elaine an' Bruce Tisdale, Mr. Dale, set foot back in the ole home town, I know my peace is a comin'. But, not all at once. Oh, Lawd no. Glory didn't happen in one day. An' neither will my peace.

Oh, those long years ago I had already felt the winter in my bones when they took me out to that hangin' tree. I didn't even feel the rope. I jest leapt out to meet Mr. Bruce. But he was jest beyond, always jest beyond.

So, I've bided my time. Always reachin' an' yearnin,' sendin' courage to them folks I loved. Even though they can't see or hear me, I know sometimes they're a-feelin' my spirit. So, I have hovered over these hills, creeks an' fields for lo these many years. Always, lookin' after my peoples.

Sounds of rememberin' are all 'round me; the gentle nickerin' of foalin' mares, quackin' of Big Black River ducks, an the pantin' of hounds stretched acrost splintery porches.

Unable to touch or whisper, still I waited to make my presence known; sweatin' with those who toil, easin' the labor of mothers in childbirth. I hear an' suffer with the death throes of some. My days have groun' along like the slow turnin' of a cotton gin's wheel. An', like the turnin' an' blendin' of the threads of that wheel, I am bound to the memory of what was an' what must surely be. Some strands knotted an' rough, other threads as smooth as the mirrored glass in the old Claymore homeplace.

Always there was the pain, the cruelty. There was the evil creepin' along in the underbrush an' boilin' in the rancid creek water an' the Big Black River. Daddy Claymore an' his ruttin' ways. Thelma Grace's murder. Ollie Potter an' his offspring. Book Turnipseed. The hoodoo man. My hangin' from that tree. Evil, even down unto this very day. What Daddy Claymore done to Brucie. That lay-by of his. But sometimes there was the goodness sweepin' across the fields an' down through the hollows. There was the glory, the kindness. There was my son, Lamont, for love, an' his half-sister Brucie, who was liken to my very own. Through all the trouble I tried to see things clear, as they are...As they ought to be. Overall, always there was an' is the hope of redemption.

Now I pray to my God, that somewhere, in some space, I may be let loose. That I may join with Bruce again, an' to see my tormented Sunnie Flo, my poor little baby girl that I dragged behind me through those cotton fields those long, hot, summer days. An', yes, even though it might send me to Hell, I also pray I may step my foot down on Daddy Claymore's neck an' drag it unto the dust 'neath my feet.

There was my love, Bruce. Still his presence is with me. Only I, with Lamont an' Brucie, know where he rests. Will my time ever come? I could go back to the beginnin'. But that tale has already been told. We are in the here an' wait for the what will be.

"Oh, who sits weepin' on my grave,

An' will not let me sleep?"

The weeks an' the months have gathered on into years. Yet, I wait; yea, I yearn, for the season an' the time that is yet to come. When I will be released. It is soon. I want to carry my loved ones with me. To present them to God.

CHAPTER 20

Will this idol wild,
A stone set through a spider seam.
The legs support a
Shadow on its way to float a well.

Liminal ghouls from the
Tar sands of ancient memory
Step through a broken
Mirror into the present.

Tuesday, March 23

Although Laura Lee's voice was soft, slow, and melodic, Memory craved solitude. She was in no humor to be around anybody, dear friend, melodic voice or not. Just so she wouldn't seem rude and ungrateful, she offered the excuse that she wanted to go upstairs and unpack the case she'd carried on the train. Once upstairs, she didn't have much with her and the unpacking was done all too quickly. Still not wanting to make conversation, she went down the steps and sat by herself on the back porch. In a few minutes she heard noises from the front; a horse whinnying, people talking. *My brother's home. His home, not mine.*

* * *

Trestle pulled the reins to the left and turned the buckboard through the fence and into the Von Dieters' yard.

"I'll be out to see you," Topper said as he and Dale climbed from the buckboard. "Don't forget, Mist Von Dieter. We can do us some business together." He could hardly keep a smile off his face. *I'll heist me some of the whiskey and a little of that juice for myself,* he gloated.

"Just call me by my name. It's Dale. I prefer not to be called Mr. Von Dieter."

Topper nodded his head. "Yes, sir, Mist Dale." The front screen slammed, Lamont walked toward them, and Topper stepped back.

"Where's your brother?" Lamont asked.

"Minyard got out at our place. He's running late for milking the cows," Topper said.

"We can take the hearse. I need to check the oil," Lamont said. "Let Mr. Shank and Mr. Trestle go back to town in the buckboard. We'll go on home in a few minutes."

Lamont gave Topper a searching look. "Son. Where have y'all been?"

"Just getting to know Mist Dale like you'd a-wanted me to," Topper muttered, a sly smile on his face. *Gonna make me some money on that white man.* He looked down at the ground, ran circular patterns with the toe of his shoe, and moved closer to his father. "He kinda went roaming around in the cemetery all by hisself," he confessed.

"Dale," Brucie called out as she and Laura Lee came down the porch steps. Dale dropped a cigarette he'd just lit, then stubbed it out with his foot as if he were burying something and slowly headed toward them. "We were wondering where you all were," Brucie said.

Laura Lee who had been walking slightly behind Brucie moved forward and put her hand on Dale's arm. "It's good to see you." She stared at him, something like hope shining in her eyes. "It's been such a long time." She reached up and self-consciously tried to smooth a thick tangle of her blond curls. "I've thought about you so much. We had so many good times when you came here from Ole Miss."

There was a moment's silence. Memories of Laura Lee flared. *There was a time* Dale thought. *Even when I was in Boston. Before I went off.* "You're more beautiful than I remembered." He lowered his eyes. "That was another lifetime. I'm not supposed to be here," he said. "I am my brother's keeper. I failed. I didn't take care of your brother like I should. I knew they were spraying the battlefield with gunfire." He jammed his hands into his pockets. "I was giving orders. Dear God. I sent my men into a hornet's nest of gas, guns and wire. Samuel was one of them."

Laura Lee stared up at him. "Dale, you weren't responsible." She flattened her hand against her chest. "Nobody in my family blames you. And neither would Samuel. You were his hero," she said in a soft voice.

"Thank you for carrying him back to our side. I heard you risked your own life to do that. He was one of the lucky ones." Her words were filled with gratitude. "Because you did bring him back, hopefully, at least he has a burying spot and a cross raised over his head. I pray for him every day. Over there so far away from us."

Dale crossed his hands together and dropped his face into them. "Oh, my dear, Laura Lee, I have something to tell you," he said, his voice thick with the pain he felt. "I pray to God I have done the right thing. By you and by my friend."

He raised his head. "Your brother. You will be able to pray for him here. We brought him home. As much of him as we could. Home..." His voice broke off

"What?" A confused expression on her face, Laura Lee backed away as if she had been hit. Her legs giving way, she dropped to the ground. Breathing hard, Dale knelt beside her and cradled her head against his chest. "Part of him's buried in St. Dizier. I brought back what I could," he whispered. "He'll be buried here. At Redemption Ridge."

He had hardly gotten the words out of his mouth before a car drove up and Jenson Cooper got out. He opened the back door and reached to pull out one of the trunks, but when he saw Dale and Laura Lee, he ran to them.

***

Memory heard the others talking from the front. She wanted to be by herself a little longer but thought better about it. "Manners are everything down here. I need to be polite." Straightening her skirt, pulling her blouse down, she left the porch and walked around the side of the house. Part of the picket fence encircling the house cut in, separating the front and back yards. Memory stopped when she got to a latched gate and saw the peaked wooden spears.

Thornton, she thought. *Oh, God, I wanted him gone. Not skewered like a roasting pig. Not on spears. My bones are pierced in me,* rang in her ears. "I can, I can, go past those pickets," she moaned. "I can."

Just as she put her hand on the gatepost, she caught sight of Dale out in the yard, on his knees, holding on to Laura Lee.

Oh, God. My brother. "I can't take this right now." Even as she spoke these words Jenson Cooper moved to Dale's side.

Jenson Cooper. When he appears, it's always the right time. He looks after my brother. "I'll leave them be. I don't want to be around this right now."

Memory turned away too quick to see Dale stand; his face twisted in hurt for Laura Lee as he bent, kissed her forehead and helped raise her.

Wanting nothing to do with anybody, in the gathering gloom, Memory made her way toward the barn, thinking of the comforts the lowing of cows and the smell of hay would bring. Right outside the barn she could make out a stacked bale made ready for the next feeding. She sat on it, breathing deep gulps of the sweet aroma.

The setting sun threw long, dark shadows across the yard. She felt chilled. Even though she was used to Boston weather, this was a damp, penetrating cold.

She hadn't been there long when off to the side, out of the corner of her eye, Memory saw a slight movement. She barely made out a man, his face turned down and partially hidden by a leafy bush. His hand moved down to his loosely fitting overalls. He flexed his fingers as if he were trying to find something with them. He cradled his crotch, lifted it, then moved his fingers as if he were milking a cow. With the other hand he shoved away the bushes covering his face. When a burst of wind spread a few threads of stringy gray hair off his forehead, a strawberry patch birthmark blazed his face. Shank Potter tossed his head back. "She'll want it. I know she will."

He doesn't know I'm here. But he's blocking my way to the house.

In a panic, Memory sprang to her feet. Her mind reached for a time when Redemption Ridge had been safe. The old well. Jenson. Jenson, Dale, Laura Lee, me. A campfire. Ghost stories. She turned, carefully making her way toward a copse of trees.

Suddenly, she was against the old well. *I was here.*

The air was still.

We sat. Told stories.

Moonlight was a thin, bent, silver elbow. The night was the reverent quiet of a closed-up church after the congregation has left the building. Gasping, Memory touched the well. She flattened her hand and felt the cold, damp stones beneath her fingers. Instead of comfort from the old stories she and the other children had told in this place, she had a strange feeling of déjà vu; it put her in mind of a tombstone out in the cemetery, after a rain.

There was something she needed to remember. A faint recollection of what she had been told, that happened by this old well many, many years ago. It had taken place here, long before she had been born.

She remembered what she'd heard. That she'd forgotten. *I was a child. They told me. Don't drink the water. Miss Pet Binkie. She was murdered. Long time ago.*

She shuddered. *An old lady's body was in here.*

There was something else that happened in this place. Wickedness lay in that well. The water smelled of musk, a heavy body odor, something rotten.

Memory snatched her hand away from the stones and scrubbed it on her skirt.

To me. Bad. Here. No longer a child. I forgot.

Tonight, a humid wind blew in her face; chills ran over her. It was as if what had happened to her back then was a heartbeat away. *What? What happened?*

It was pitch black dark now. "Forget it. Go back. Go around him."

Memory turned toward the house. All of a sudden, she felt weak and light-headed. She had only gone a short distance before a wave of nausea hit her. Her legs gave way. Sobbing, she collapsed into a small dip in the land and lay with her head resting on a soft patch of fern. *As soon as I feel better, I'll get away from here*, she thought.

She heard sounds. Voices. She saw a faint light. Footsteps. Someone was coming toward the well. A kerosene-soaked lantern lit up the area. She flattened herself the best she could.

Torchlight danced ghostly shapes across the well's lichen covered stones. Four men. Their faces blurred in the dancing flames as if they'd been drawn with a child's dull colored crayon.

But she could see one she knew. She had gotten away from him a short while ago. Their driver, Shank. Beside him, a short man with a pug-dog face rocked from side to side like a little dog high-stepping through a briar patch. A tall, black man held the lantern in one hand. Standing close to him was a younger, shorter man carrying a wooden box with a thick leather strap. She saw a wiry haired, dark, lanky man. A soft rattle, like dice rolling in a tin cup came from the box. *Don't breathe. Don't breathe. Freeze,* Memory pleaded with herself.

She felt sick. She put her hand over her mouth. Although the few peanuts she had eaten earlier dribbled through her lips, she made no sound.

"Mistah Lucius Dedmon. I got your money here," the short man said. "I needs me a good 'un." His words ended in a high-pitched giggle. "Git me a fine one that'll set the Divine Deliverance Holiness Church sinners spinnin' on their ears."

"I found you one that'll scare the Be'Jesus into some a them churched sinners," the tall man named Lucius said.

"I got me somebody special. A high falutin' visitor who'll be at our celebration. She come all the way from California." The short man cackled. "She's stayin' in town at Mrs. Netter's but you jest wait. She's gonna set them Von Dieters what got their noses in the air a spinnin' through the swamp grass." The pug-faced man pointed and short-rocked.

"I'll take that air one you got in that box there."

"No, you ain't. Tattler the Rattler's mine, but after tonight, he kin be on loan for a short while," Lucius said. "This here's my son-in-law, Passel Skinotes. Show Mist Mudge our prize."

A humming sound from the box the man held seemed to ink an agreement with what he'd said.

"I orter git me somethin'," Shank whined. "'N I ain't into raddlers. Them noises rang in my ears like a dinner bell in a win' sterm." He pulled a small stack of paper from his pocket. "Mist Dedmon. I done got Mist Mudge Turnipseed to you," he said. "'N I can brang more churched peoples. From tree houses down by the Big Black."

"I ain't interested. Those people ain't got a pot to piss in. If they were given Sears catalogues to wipe their asses with, they'd still use their hands," Lucuis Dedmon said.

Shank Potter peeled off a square of cigarette paper; thumb-brushed tobacco from a small pouch into the paper. "I could use me a liddle money. My gullet needs greasin'." He flicked a match with his thumbnail, the flame danced slowly from side to side. He pushed his ill-fitting top dentures up, smoothed the tobacco with a thick finger, then rolled and licked the paper. "Lord knows. I ain't no tattletale. But if I ain't gone git no more money, then I jest might have to find it in me to tell Mist Lamont a few things."

"Mist Shank." The tall man waggled his tongue. "I hear you. That makes me know. I'm gone take care of you. Maybe a little bit later on tonight. But this I got here I'm gonter let Mudge Turnipseed borry." He pointed. His son-in-law held the box up as if it were a prize display.

Shank lifted the damp, sagging cigarette to his lips, rocked back on his heels and squatted on the wet ground. "His Turnipseed peoples ain't no bettern' mine," he whined.

"I'll take care of you later. I always take care of my debts. You'll get yours," the tall man said.

"If you don't take care of 'em, I will," his son-in-law, Passel, threatened under his breath.

A rattling sound came from the wooden cage. "We got Mist Mudge something in this here cage," Lucius said.

An icy breath crept across Memory's shoulders. She heard a thrashing, then a hissing sound. Shank sucked deep, then stood and flipped his cigarette into the well.

An arm shot out. Shank jerked back, tumbled and hit the ground.

"You best be careful. You might make Mr. Tattler the Rattler mad if that tobaccer was to land on him," Lucius said.

Memory was afraid to take a deep breath.

Lucius held the lamp down close to Shank's face. "Shank, you ain't got the Godly spirit beating in your heart. You best be careful around these here snakes. Me and my son-in-law, we'll treat you good this minute, but I'm doing my business with Mist Turnipseed."

Lucius turned away from Shank, wiped his hands on his pants and held out one hand while Mudge counted bills into it. "Nice doing business with you, Mr. Turnipseed." He peeled off a bill and gave it to his son-in-law. "Here you go, Mist Passel Skinotes." He looked up proudly. "We looks after each other. He tends to my business with me." He put the money into a shirt pocket, and again reached out his hand. Mudge met it with his.

"Gentleman to gentleman. Now, I gotta git on home. Past suppertime. An' it looks as how it might blow up a rain," Lucius said.

There was a rustling of footsteps. The voices faded. A small yellow smudge, like a firefly fading off into the dark, the light was gone.

Memory swiped her mouth across the sleeve of her blouse. The temperature had dropped. She was cold all over. To the bone. She struggled to her feet and rubbed her knees where the rough ground had scraped them.

Run.

CHAPTER 21

Symbology away from a dream,
This daughter flag spindled
Along timelines of driftwood.

An affected crucifixion,
Pressed for sea foam
And the smell of copper.
The hound of Mons
Doesn't hunt by sight.

Fine, swallowable bones
Float in a subtle mirror.
Simian ribs splay into trees
As they approach the lips of depth,
Allowing shadows into thirst.

Tuesday, March 23

"Tomorrow," Laura Lee said, gathering one side of her skirt, and stepping into the car. "We'll see y'all tomorrow."

"Don't leave," Dale started to say, but he stopped himself. He and Jenson Cooper waved goodbye from the yard, Brucie from the front porch. The car lights flickered and then were gone as Laura Lee and her brother, Otis, drove away.

Brucie drew her breath in sharply. She had a strong feeling she needed to know where her daughter was. The smell of danger was so thick in the air she could almost drown in it. Memory had always gone her own way, but right now, things were different. Brucie fingered the gold cross hanging around her neck, a movement that often brought her comfort. For just a moment, she felt a kinship with Captain Bruce Claymore and Vernell.

"Mr. Cooper, I'm going to the parlor," she called from the doorway. "If you have a moment, would you see me before you go?"

Jenson touched his head in a gesture of respect. "Yes ma'am. I plan to leave shortly."

"Jenson." Dale dropped his head as the two of them walked toward the house. "I know you'll think I'm crazy, but I saw him. In the cemetery. I know who it was. It was my grandfather, Bruce Claymore. Trying to tell me something." Dale felt a hot rush of shame. "Something, I'm not worthy to hear. He looked after his men."

They hesitated on the porch. Jenson pulled a leather key holder from his pocket and with each word he spoke, tapped the front porch railing with the car key. "Captain," he said. "You'd best leave that whiskey and that syrup alone. It's eating your heart and your guts away. Piece by piece."

"I'm fine," Dale said. "I just need some sleep. And not to hear these voices," he muttered as the two of them stepped into the house. "I think I'll get me a glass of buttermilk, and then I'm heading on to bed."

"Take care, Captain. I reckon I'll see your mother then go on home to my folks."

When Jenson stepped into the parlor, Brucie stood in front of the fireplace spreading apart a few dying embers with a metal poker in her hand.

"Where's Miss Memory?" Jenson asked.

"I'm not sure. That's why I wanted to see you. I'm a little worried," she answered. "We're all worn out from our trip. She's been coming to the country for years, but she's a city girl at heart. I have a funny feeling that something may be wrong. It's way past dark, and for some reason, she stayed out back until everyone left. I called, but she didn't answer."

"Do you have any idea which way she went?"

"No, I don't."

"Where's a flashlight? I'll take care of her, Miss Brucie."

"There should be one in the dining room sideboard. If not there, it would be sitting out on a shelf in the pantry."

"Don't you worry about a thing."

Jenson went to the dining room and searched the sideboard, but he found no flashlight. "The pantry," he said.

***

When she was at Redemption Ridge, in her bedroom, Brucie still preferred kerosene over electricity. She raised the lamp by her bed, turned up the yellow-orange flame and went to the window. The trees were too thick for her to see anything. An unwanted image snaked in about the old well out back. She felt something evil lurked around it. Years ago, a body had been found there. The town's spinster, Miss Pet Binkie, had been murdered and her body thrown in the well. "You're worn out and being silly. That was a lifetime ago."

Now that Brucie knew Dale was home, Jenson was checking on Memory, and the company gone, she gave in to her exhaustion and undressed.

Turning back the bed covers, she stretched out and fell asleep almost before her head hit the pillow.

Downstairs, it took Jenson a few minutes, but he found a flashlight on a shelf behind a can of bacon grease. When he moved the can, oily cockroaches scuttled from the top and down the sides. Startled, Jenson knocked the flashlight to the floor. "Lordy. I'd almost forgotten. Down here, roaches can grow as big as rats." He picked up the light and slid the button forward. Nothing happened. He shook the flashlight. *No batteries.* "Should be some out in the car."

***

The floorboards squeaked. Brucie jumped awake.

A sound she had often heard. Here in this very house. Footsteps. The same, yet different. *Not Daddy Claymore.*

"My imagination's running wild." She rolled over and shoved the covers into a thick line, as if they would act as a buffer between her and whoever or whatever was out there.

"She needs you."

She heard a bare whisper of what could have been a voice or a soft breeze rustling the leaves outside the window.

Brucie placed her hands over her racing heart. "Memory," she whispered. "Has something happened?

"No," she answered herself, willing it to be true.

"Out back."

The same soft voice.

"The well."

"Stop it. I'm imagining things." *This kind of night,* she thought. *Off kilter. Tired.* She put a pillow over her head, closed her eyes and curled into a ball. *I'm pulling a sack over my head.*

***

"Gotcha." A large hand shoved Memory toward the well. She hit the ground. She tasted dust. "Ahh," she cried.

Shank Potter straddled her. A sharp stick jabbed her right thigh.

He pinned her arms down with his legs. One scratchy hand covered her mouth. The other a breast.

She couldn't move.

Off to the side, hidden behind a tree, Shank's brother Trestle, shoved his pants down. Breathing heavily, he began moving his fingers back and forth. "Me too," he breathed. "Me too, brother," he said as he slid to the ground.

Shank Potter blew putrid hot breath onto Memory's neck.

Lips drawn back, his top dentures slipped loose, his mouth sounded like a cow chewing cud.

It came back to her.

Him. Before. He's done this before.

That night. Frog-skinned, blazoned, strawberry. Foul odor. She remembered. *Choking. Sweaty feet. Jagged, brittle nails.*

A swollen thing. Swung like a piece of water-filled rubber hose.

Stabbed. Swollen hose had stabbed. Between her legs. Again. Again. She had screamed with pain. Blood ran. She stung. A smelly hand filled her mouth. She could hardly breathe.

The pain. She had ridden waves of pain. A final, breathless, "Aw God." A push.

The man had hunched up on his all fours. "I ain't done. I ain't done."

"I will live," she'd screamed. She clawed. Her fingers had found a loose stone.

The frog-faced man raised his head as if he were offering prayers of thanksgiving.

He bent over. Again. Between her legs. His hot hose plunged. Strength surged through her body. Blood pounded in her ears.

She flung her hand up.

A snapping sound. Blood spurted. A fountain. The rock, coated red.

Choking, her attacker had writhed in the dust.

"My nose. You broke my godarn nose," he hollered.

Free.

"You tell, they'll kill me," he screamed. Memory had run for her life. The last words she'd heard, "They'll kill me," filled her ears. She knew. They would. If she told, he was a dead man.

That long-ago night she made a conscious choice. She had drowned what happened beneath the waters of the old well with Miss Pet Binkie's body.

Tonight, a wooden limb stabbed her right leg.

"Yer gonter ride me like a mule," Shank grunted.

Memory struggled one arm free from under his bony knee.

"Oh, no," she strangled out. "Not tonight. You won't."

He squeezed her face. Twisted it sideways. "I seen your laigs. I seen your skirt hiked up, like you was beggin' fer it. Here. I knowed you wuz here. Waitin'. Wantin' it."

The stick pierced her thigh. She gripped the spiny wood.

Shank forced her legs apart. She held the splintered tree branch, for dear life.

"Your one a them goldamn Claymores." He let go with one hand and peeled overall straps off his shoulders. "I almost made it feel good onct before. I kin do it this time fer sure." Pants riding his waist, he leaned on his left knee. "When I git through with you, yer gonter be swimmin'." He shucked his britches with one hand, the other he clamped across Memory's open mouth. "Drankin' well wadder."

The well. This time. He'll throw me in that well.

Her fingers knotted, gripping her makeshift weapon.

Binkie Water. Binkie Water. I'll drown in Binkie water.

"No." She slid her hand along the ground. The stick crackled.

"Ahh," a hoarse moan came from behind the other side of the well. Trestle Potter fingered his genitals. "I'll have ya too," he crowed, rolling on the ground. "Ahh."

His voice drowned out the sound of Memory dragging her wooden club.

She drew in a deep breath. She tightened her arm muscles. She jabbed the stick up.

"Oh, Gawd," Shank screamed.

CHAPTER 22

**Infernal rhythm of
Syllable
First crawling scree
of knowledge praise.**

**Death's reverend
Slated on a dais
for arrival, lust's
sacrifice.**

Tuesday night, March 23

"My pecker! Oh, Gawd, my pecker!"

Jenson Cooper's flashlight beam caught Memory on her knees, bloody stick still in her hand. Cradling his naked crotch, a screaming Shank Potter wallowed in pain. Rolling to his side, his tongue lolled as if he were trying to lick the grass.

"You bastard! I'll kill you!" Jenson jerked Shank to his feet and cracked the flashlight against his head. He slammed his fist into Shank Potter's face. Left...false teeth hit the ground. Right...a crushing noise; his jawbone crunched. Potter groaned, fingers apart, he fell backward, spearing one hand on his dentures, ripping and boning his fingers.

Jenson dropped to his knees. He grasped Shank's shoulders, pounding him up and down, Shank's head bobbing like a fishing cork.

"Stop," Memory screamed. "Stop! You're killing him! Jenson!"

At the sound of Memory's frantic plea, Jenson froze. He slowly released his grip on Shank and stared down at the unconscious man, then folded his face into his hands. "I've never killed an unarmed man. I was about to." He rolled the beaten man away, where he lay belly down on the ground. Contempt for

Shank Potter turned to disgust with himself and shock for what he had been about to do.

Jenson flattened one hand against Potter's back. "Thank God, he's still breathing. He'll never hurt you again, Memory." He pulled out a handkerchief and wiped his hands clean from Shank Potter's sweat. "I pledge you my word. I'll see to it that he never comes around you or this place again."

Memory sank down beside Jenson. His breath fast and deep, he made a strong effort to slow his breathing and get himself back in hand. When he had, he reached out and stroked Memory's cheeks. Gentle fingers lightly touched her chin and lifted her face. "You are my love. You always have been," he said, kissing the center of her forehead. He stood, lifting Memory to her feet as if she weighed no more than a small wounded animal. She rested her face against his chest, and when she did, she smelled old familiar scents from her childhood summers. Smells that made her feel safe. Sweat from long hours of playing in the sun. Skin slightly prickled and rubbed smooth with baby oil.

Her face buried next to his heart, Memory had a pleasant flashback of a summer when she was about eleven. Jenson had caught her face with both hands. "You're mine," he whispered, holding her close, planting a kiss on her salty lips, then dashing away. She had wiped her mouth, and pretended it made her mad. But really, it had pleased her; Memory's skin tingled from his touch. She had wanted more. And now—once again the taste of his manly sweat on her tongue, gave her pleasure and she took comfort from the strength she felt in his encircling arms.

Jenson spoke softly. "I've longed for this as far back as I can remember. Over there in France, it wasn't death I feared so much. Losing you forever was my greatest fear." He held her tight against his body. "Of never being able to say, 'I love you.' Of never being able to know that someday we'd be together. I've felt that way since the first day I laid eyes on you. You and I were meant for each other." He sighed. "I never even dreamed or wished Thornton dead, but somehow, I always knew that something would happen between you and him. Someday you'd be mine."

Memory shivered; words caught in her throat. Something akin to hope, an almost forgotten part of her life, stirred in her breast.

Jenson tilted her face up to his and kissed her, long and gently. "I'll never let you go."

"Oh, Lawdy," Shank Potter moaned as he rolled over.

Jenson sank down beside the miserable heap of humanity coiled at their feet. "I could very easily kill you, Potter. The taste of your death would be honey on my tongue. May God forgive me. I am so tempted." He tapped Shank's chest with a firm finger. "But for me, not a forever thought. Feasting on your death, that's not what I want."

No, he thought. *I want to savor the smell of life and of growing things. Not choke on the stench of rotting flesh. I want to hear horses straining against leather harnesses as they pull plows through the rich Mississippi dirt. I want the clear waters of Noble Creek to quench my thirst, not retch on the thick taste of bile in my throat as I did when our men choked on their last breath.* He put his hand across his own chest. "I want to see my friend's faces burned by the sun, not by the thick gas of death. I am sick of violence. I want no more of it." Jenson fell silent a moment as if collecting his thoughts. He stood and gave the injured man a gentle push with his foot. "It's a long road back from war and killing. I'm letting you live…for now. But for as long as you live, whenever you pass this lady on the street, turn your face away. If you don't, I *will* kill you."

He reached out and took Memory's hand. "Let's go home," he said, "and don't look back. There is no new blood on my hands."

"What about him?"

"I'll take care of you tonight." Jenson wrapped his arms protectively around Memory. "I'll worry about Shank Potter tomorrow."

Memory leaned against Jenson and stayed that way as they made their way toward the house. She drew his strength into her body and soul; a new hope sprang in her heart.

When they got near to the house, she could see a back porch light was on and her mother stood at the door. When Brucie saw Jenson and Memory together, she wiped tears from her eyes, covered her mouth with her hand, turned away and went toward her room.

Jenson walked Memory up the porch. Once again, he covered her lips with his. "You're mine," he said, moving away, his face bright with the hope he felt. "You always have been. We just had to make it happen. I'll be back out tomorrow just to check around that well and make sure we don't have a body there. Miss Brucie mentioned y'all were settling in for a couple of days." He opened the door. "Maybe going to Jackson to buy some things. So, I won't see you for a day or two. And then...Well. According to proper southern etiquette, it may be too soon. But, Miss Memory, I'm going to come calling."

"I do love you. I think I always have." The words were whispered so softly, Jenson wasn't sure what he had heard

Memory walked through the house, stood at the front door and watched until Jenson cranked the motor, drove down the driveway and turned onto Old Farm Road.

Exhausted, she made her way upstairs, changed into a gown and fell across the bed.

***

Tears streamed from Shank's eyes. Still in agony from Memory's cut to his penis, his broken shredded fingers and Jenson's angry punches, he curled into a ball again. "Oh Lawdy," he moaned. "He'p me git up. Somebody he'p me up." Just as he attempted his first feeble move, Shank heard footsteps crunching through the thick underbrush around him. Two figures, one carrying a kerosene lantern, the other a wooden box hanging from a thick leather strap materialized from the darkness. The lantern sent flickering orange shadows across Shank's face. A noise not unlike far off thunder came from the box.

"Well, well, well now. If it ain't Brother Shank a-waiting. Mist Shank, I told you, we'd take care of you." His son-in-law, Passel, at his side, Lucius Dedmon snickered and set the lantern down. Passel shifted the box from hand to hand. Shank fell back onto his back. He tried to sit up but didn't appear to have the strength.

Dedmon pinned the middle of Shank's chest with his foot. He cleared his throat, then spit a thick blob beside Shank Potter's head. Lucius pointed to Passel who raised the box up to the sky as if asking for a blessing.

"We are your servants," Lucius intoned. Passel smiled. Protesting noises beat inside the box. "Protect us."

Passel lowered the box and set it on the ground.

"'Stead of a finder's fee, whyn't we let you kiss this here?" Lucius asked in a soft, gentle voice. "Got Mr. Tattler the Ratter hisself fer you, Mist Shank." A continuous raspy rattle seemed to complete his thought.

Passel unlocked the top. Lucius eased the light over so he could see where the head was. The flickering light reflected gray black shades on Dedmon's skin. The only thing visible in the dark was the white of his eyes and the radiance of his ivory teeth. He set the lantern down. Passel raised the lid, inch by inch. "Oh, Jesus," Dedmon prayed. "We are Your humble servants." He carefully reached into the box and grasped the writhing snake behind its large, flat head.

"Guard me. Protect me." Dedmon and Passel sank to their knees. Holding the snake high, Lucius bowed his head. "You are my guide. I am in Your hands."

Shaking uncontrollably, Shank arched his back. His heels dug tunnels into the dirt. Fingers bent like claws, he scrabbled the ground. "Have mercy, Jesus," he hollered.

Sitting down on Shank's legs, carefully Lucius draped the snake around Shank's neck.

"Kiss, kiss." Dedmond smacked his lips together.

The sound of hissing drowned out Shank Potter's shrill cries.

"Let shouts of holy joy fill the skies. Hallelujah," Dedmon sang.

Shank's body lurched into spasms.

"The power of death has done its worst."

Shank Potter clutched his chest; he went rigid; all was quiet.

A few minutes later there was a loud splash.

"We didn't owe you nothing," Lucius said. "You white trash, Potter. Good work, Passel. This is what we do to those who try to cross us."

"You goldarn, Potter," Passel muttered. Hidden behind a tree, Trestle Potter stared angrily, helpless to do anything about what had been thrown into the dark abyss of the old well.

"Gawdamn," he said "Tha's my brother. She made it happen," he said. "I'm gonna git her. Jest like Shank did. An maybe even let a snike take her 'n' him ta hell 'n' back. 'N' you, Dedmon. You'll pay.

"Bastid," he spit out. "I'll have you too. I'll have you fust."

CHAPTER 23

**Faced with love
and its inverse
Memory mints a
Currency of chaotic intention.**

**She spends her coin
again and again,
Her broken renewal.**

Wednesday, 1:00 am, March 24

Filled with thoughts of what did happen and what could have, although she was worn out, for long hours after Memory crawled into bed, she was restless and fitful. Sleep was as elusive as trying to catch the hem of a Redemption Ridge ghost. History had almost repeated itself and Memory was seized by a fierce longing to try and understand some part of why she felt and acted as she did. Finally, she gave up any hope of going to sleep. "Too much has happened. It's after one o'clock in the morning, but while it's fresh on my mind, I need to write this down." She pushed the covers back and got up.

Because she had already unpacked some of her personal belongings it was easy for her to put her hands on them. She reached into her beaded bag, felt her nail file, then shook her head. Instead, she picked up a pen and paper, pulled a slipper chair to the bedside table and turned on the electric light. What had happened to her all those years ago was part and parcel of who she was, why she was, and maybe, who she now might become. Tonight, it had almost happened again.

Memory lifted her journal.

I feel compelled to tell the story, no, the stories, of these my people. Here in this journal. It will be recorded. When I feel it should be done, the best I can, and, perhaps, with the voice of Vernell whispering in my ear, I shall return to the past to build on and enhance where we are now.

Just across the way lies a Confederate battlefield and burial ground. I am here at our old homeplace, Redemption Ridge, Mississippi. This is a house of damaged goods. Maybe, every house that is a home is rife with secrets and with damage.

I can tell by the way my mother cuts her eyes at me she thinks me uncaring and unfeeling. From where I sit, not labeled an old Claymore curse, but a foreign affliction, one from my father's side of the family, a Von Dieter curse.

I am who I am. I don't trust men. My father. My brother. My dead husband, Thornton. But, Jenson? Yes. I trust Jenson.

Our story started even before this present life. There are tragedies going back to my mother and to the stories I wasn't meant to hear. But I did. Some of the secrets I've been told, and some I've figured out on my own. Daddy Claymore was not my mother's father by blood. There are tales that have been whispered about this man and what went on here, under those old roofs. There were those horrible, dreaded nights here at Redemption Ridge. When my mother, just a young girl, heard footsteps sliding down the hall. The tread maker, that rutting, vile man, Daddy Claymore coming to her bedroom. I would have killed him. Oh, what anguish my girl/mother endured on those nights from that man. Perhaps in this very spot where I now sit.

The torment came from him. From the man named as her father. But not her blood father. And what of the other Claymore, Bruce, the one now unspoken of in polite society? Daddy Claymore, thought to be full, but only half-brother, Bruce. The Confederate Captain. The shamed legend. The supposed traitor. And what of his cache of jewels, supposedly stolen from the Confederacy?

Bruce fathered two children with the emancipated slave, Vernell. Lamont and his twin sister, Sunnie Flo, were the offspring of Bruce and Vernell. And oh, the secrets that have been whispered down through the years about the damaged Sunnie Flo. She came into this world with a swollen head, a head thought to be full of knowledge and visions. Special powers. Hoodoo. Sorcery. Sunnie Flo didn't live long. After her death, not the live girl, but her child body, was used in ceremonies. Is it true? Who knows? Both my mother and Lamont, who would know her story, won't speak of this time. But even down to this very day there are lingering rumors about Sunnie Flo's body and her powers.

And not just Lamont and Sunnie Flo, but soon another child sprang from the loins of the handsome renegade, Bruce Claymore. Breaking her marriage vows, the beautiful southern belle, Charlotte Caroline Tisdale Claymore, secretly made love to Bruce on the banks of Noble Creek. With that another child was bred and my mother Brucie, became their secret offspring. My seed came, down through the years, not from Charlotte Caroline's husband, Daddy Claymore. She came from Bruce Claymore's loins.

But my mother, Brucie, child of Bruce and Charlotte Caroline, was always claimed by Daddy Claymore as his own. At that time, did he or anyone in the family know who her birth father was? Many years later our Cousin Sarah confirmed the whispers I had heard. Other than her, no one has ever spoken of this in my presence.

There were other family crimes and puzzles. Not just about my mother, but also about the murder of my grandmother, Charlotte Caroline and Daddy Claymore's older daughter, my mother's sister, Thelma Grace. Soon after Thelma Grace's burial, my mother was sent away to live in far-off Boston with her Cousin Sarah Bowman. Now, I know why. To await the birth of Thelma Jewel. Daddy Claymore's offspring.

There were many questions about the end a helpless Daddy Claymore came to. His body charred to cinders in a burning barn. Why, was Daddy Claymore, a paralyzed man who couldn't move, in that barn? How did he get there? Who set the fire? (Snakes?)

Those unspoken stories have been hushed. But they're there.

They fester and linger with Lamont, whom I have figured out, is my blood uncle. My mother, Brucie, his half-sister.

Memory set her pen down and ran her hand through tangles in her hair. She got up, went to the window and pulled the curtains aside. She looked out toward the pasture and the old well. So much had gone on only a short time ago. Now, everything was quiet. She sat back down, dipped her pen into an inkwell and continued writing.

As to where I am now. To this moment. Me and mine. Shank Potter. He set the tone for much of my life thus far.

And husband, Thornton? Wasn't meant to be. On some level, I didn't understand then, and barely understand now. I thought that by marrying Thornton, I might find my purpose in life. The marriage bed.

Too soon, I sensed that could not be. I would not surrender to some man's whim.

I didn't want my husband to touch me. And Thornton? He did not come to the marriage bed often. He was never smitten.

And that became all right.

Perhaps I knew all along. Bear children. Perhaps. But not ordained. No, it wasn't to be. But it could have been, should have been easier. I could have accommodated.

I was different because of that night all those years ago out by the old well. Thornton, he was, what he was. And I, from the tender age of thirteen, damaged goods. Neither of us would have changed. Neither of us cared to change. I was relieved when my husband was murdered. My Thornton problems they were solved. That relief, I'm ashamed to admit, says a lot about who I've become.

My mother had buried her long-ago nightmare. Daddy Claymore. I've lived with my buried horror. Not like my brother's. The fair-haired child, the son, The Sun. His had a name. Shellshock.

Here, on these shores far away from war torn France, the cannon shells are not shocking. But something in Dale has burst. He may not live. And I? I who have hidden my shame for years, will live. This I now know. Am I to be his, my brother's salvation? Before tonight. Maybe, was. My brother. I love him. His salvation belongs only to him.

My salvation is in question. Will it be Jenson? My savior? No. Maybe my lover, but not my savior.

Memory stood and stretched. She picked up the paper, held it close to her chest a moment, as if she were afraid someone would steal it. She set the paper down and again dipped her pen into the inkwell and continued writing.

Outside my open window I see the vague light of the coming sunrise. Only a few hours since that dreadful Shank Potter once again tried to have his way with me. This time, it wasn't to be. It didn't work. I'll tell this time. If he dies, my hands are not stained with his blood.

I've endured these creeping hours. I've listened to the ticking clock in my bedroom.

Restless and worn out, Memory stretched out on the bed. But still, she heard the monotonous tick of the clock. As she finally drifted into a fitful slumber, tick tock, became Jen-son...

CHAPTER 24

Bright green eyes,
Lights out from
a pattern primitive,
The warning of the
Serpent.

And small, warm,
Huddled in the eternal
Bramble of human
warfare, Dale watches
in a pair of eclipses.

Wednesday morning, 5:00 a.m., March 24

His family still asleep, Topper heard the distant rumble of thunder as he quietly bridled a mule in the early morning hours and headed for town. Several days ago, Lamont had told him he needed to go to McMahon Seed and Feed and buy fertilizer for the garden, so if his daddy caught him slipping out, Topper had his story ready for why he went to town. But fertilizer wasn't what he had on his mind. He figured that, like most folks round these parts, Mr. Dedmon drank his coffee early. He'd buy the fertilizer later.

When Topper got close to Dedmon's property, he hiked his legs up as far as he could on the mule's flank and tried to be very quiet. Not because of his dogs since they had already set up a racket in the backyard, but because he'd heard about snake cages and who knew what else could be lurking around Lucuis Dedmon's place. Some people called him the devil's voodoo man. And Topper wanted to get this visit finished in a hurry. He'd be selling whiskey, cough syrup and pills to Mr. Von Dieter, but he'd be holding on to a little bit of it for himself. If he was careful, some of it would be his for the taking and nobody'd be the wiser.

A light was on in the back of Dedmon's house. Topper hitched the mule to a tree, tiptoed carefully through the yard and tapped on the door. A few seconds later, Passel Skinotes led him to the kitchen.

Dedmon leaned back in his cane chair, and even though it was still over an hour before daybreak, he didn't seem surprised to see Topper.

"Mist Dedmon," Topper said respectfully. "I've come to get more cough medicine and pills from you."

Dedmon had what looked to be a piece of broom straw in his hand. Topper waited while he ran it between his front teeth, crumpled and threw it on the floor. Lucius nodded as if all along this had been his well-thought-out plan. "I believe you and me and my son-in-law can make us a little money here. The station agent said you'd be someone who could work with me. There are a couple of folks who have some kind of stake in this business having to do with Mist Dale Von Dieter. Not jest us, but a redheaded man from up Boston way. The Yankee man's come all the way down here to Tallouga County from up north."

What Lucius didn't say was that shortly after the train pulled away from the station yesterday afternoon, a stranger had talked to him on the street. He was a Boston policeman, a Mr. Liam McRae. The station agent got them together. Mr. McRae had briefly talked to him about Dale Von Dieter, how he wanted revenge on him for something he'd done. And that there would be some money in it. It wasn't just whiskey and the cough syrup the man was interested in him selling Dale; for a price, and a pretty good one, he might want to set up some kind of a crime scene with the policeman. It was obvious he had a bone to pick with Mr. Von Dieter. As long as he was paid, Lucius didn't care one way or the other.

"Look in that croaker sack in the pantry, boy." He pointed to Passel. "The one what says *Flour* on it," he said to his son-in-law, "then fetch me that stuff I showed you."

In just a minute Passel returned with a brown paper package. "Like I mentioned yesterday, us'll be in a little money-making business. You and me and Passel. We'll do us a seventy-thirty split. You can sell each of these here to the Von Dieter man for two dollars. I want you to hook him around your little finger.

When this here runs out, there'll be more. I got plenty of whiskey. If I'm not there"—He pointed to his son-in-law—"Passel'll take my place."

Dedmon held up the package. "I got me that source from up north. All you need. I'll set it up. But you have to take care of the selling end of it. And don't you cross me. I'll kill you in a heartbeat."

"No, sir."

"And now, you'd best git back on down the road. Weather ain't looking too good."

"I just wanna make me some money," Topper said. *And keep a little of this here whiskey for myself.*

"What if you have to kill somebody?" Dedmon asked.

"I'll do whatever you tell me," Topper said. "You're my boss man."

"And mine too," Passel said, his tone of voice intimating he would be very much a part of whatever went on.

***

8:00 a.m.

Tracer bullets skimmed low. Bombs whistled; exploded. Red hot flames rained down. An anguished cry rent the sky from the zigzag trench just to Dale's left. A scream, then a blast filled his ears. He jumped awake.

"God in heaven," he moaned. "Save my men."

Heart pounding, he rolled onto his side. For a minute he was surprised to find he was in a bed, not lying in an oozing, smelly, rat-filled trench sliding across the decaying body of someone he knew or hearing crackles as his boots crunched the brittle bones of some unnamed soldier.

Lightning flickered outside the window, the sound of thunder rumbling could well have been someone standing next to him and choking.

Screams. My men burning. He pushed up onto his elbows. *I can't take much of this. I thought, here, at Redemption Ridge, I might find peace.* "These battles, they may never end."

Dale swung his feet to the side of the bed and sat up. His coat hung on one of the brass posts at the foot. For some reason, for just a moment, he stopped himself before reaching into a pocket for his pills and syrup. In his mind's eye he replayed yesterday afternoon when they came from the train station and how he had felt when he saw the beautiful Laura Lee Stanton coming down the porch steps. He sensed she had looked at him in a special way. *But, was it pity? Disappointment? Or both?* He remembered the good times he and Laura Lee had together when he came home from Ole Miss. *What would she think about me now?*

"Who the hell gives a rip what anybody thinks? I'm past that."

Dale needed to use the toilet, but he didn't feel like going downstairs, so he reached under the bed for the chamber pot.

When he was through, he sat on the side of the bed. "Okay," he said. "Time to face the day. But first I need a little fortification." Reaching into his coat pocket, he felt an envelope resting under the cigarette case. He had a faint recollection of something that happened on the train. On the caboose. The branch line from Jackson to Franklin. Red hair. A large bandana covering a face. Green eyes staring into his. Those eyes. He had seen them before. *Back in Boston. Bright green, glistening like a stem of dew-kissed spring grass.* And he knew this person had something to do with Senator Peter Shields. "Jenson. He had suspicions about a Boston policeman. He'll know how to find out. I'll put him on it."

He peeled the envelope open and read.

You and your sister think you're to the manor born. Well, not exactly. Might be, you'll have a surprise. I would suggest you all watch to see what appears on your doorstep. Or you could go out to the cemetery. On a full moon night. And you might not live to tell it. I am owed!

Then he heard a voice speaking and that day in Boston with Cousin Sarah came back to mind.

"Your mama had another baby girl," she had told Memory and him. "A lay-by baby. She lives in California."

Dale wanted to deny it, to say the cough syrup and alcohol were singing an off-key song in his head, but he knew better. An unknown sister was no pipe dream. When he first heard the secret, he had a hard time accepting the idea that his upstanding mother would have a child out of wedlock, then a more painful realization hit him. *It wasn't her choice.*

Something else came to mind. He crammed the envelope into his coat pocket. *She will have claims. Get ready.*

"I need some bucking up. This welcome home isn't starting out so well." Many times in France when he didn't care if he lived or died, the thought of someday coming back to Redemption Ridge had kept him going. *Get with Topper.*

He wadded the note, cocked his arm to throw it into the chamber pot, then stopped himself. "Means nothing to me, but maybe I'd better show this to Memory."

Dale changed into fresh clothes, pulled out his pocket watch and checked the time. "Eight thirty. Going by Redemption Ridge time, the day's half over."

Even before he opened his door and went downstairs, he smelled coffee and knew someone who worked around the place, probably Lamont's wife, Bertha, would be preparing breakfast.

He saw his sister in the dining room drinking a cup of coffee. Right away, in some way he couldn't put his finger on, he sensed trouble. Memory looked different. Her newly bobbed, thick auburn hair was an unattractive tangle of tight curls, her eyes swollen as if she had been crying. She had a pinched look around her mouth. She had come downstairs, not dressed for the day but wearing a shapeless, gingham wrapper. Her sky-blue eyes, usually full of life, were as dull as a puddle of standing rainwater.

"Good morning, sleeping beauty." Dale tested the ground.

Memory's lips trembled. "Except for Jenson, it's hard for me to find good in anything right now."

This is something new? What now? Dale started to ask, but he thought better of it. There was a change in his sister's voice. He caught something almost hopeful when she said Jenson's name.

Memory frowned. "And along those lines, before I forget it, Mother got a telegram. Father will be here soon. He's driving in Easter weekend.

"We all agree on this one thing. Because of father and his German connections and what he lost in the war, we needed to leave Boston." She took a deep breath. "I hate to say it, but for many reasons, maybe it's best that we're here at Redemption Ridge. Still, I'm not sure how I feel about our father coming. To say the least, our lives will be more settled with him around."

She had hardly gotten the words out of her mouth before a thickly built, round-faced, silver-haired woman, Lamont's wife, Bertha, came into the dining room. She set down a bowl of hot biscuits wrapped in a white linen cloth, then began dusting the table with a rag. As he watched, Dale remembered Bertha from the past, her hands constantly busy. "What would you like, Mist Dale?"

He pulled a chair out and sat down. "I think I'll just have me a cup of coffee for now."

Bertha went to the sideboard, poured coffee from a silver server and set a cup on the table in front of Dale. He reached for a small crystal bowl and pitcher which were in the middle of the table, stirred in sugar and cream, then leaned back.

"If Topper's at his place, I'm going to saddle up a horse in a few minutes and ride over there," he said.

"No need to. He got here just a few minutes back," Bertha said. "He's out by the barn." She raised her apron and wiped her eyes. "Lamont an' me. We're natural worried about that boy. He ain't doin' right by himself. I'm right scared of what's down the road for him. I prays to the good Lord every night to keep my boy safe." She picked up the coffee pot. "I'll bring back some hot in a minute, Mist Dale. We've missed you folks."

Dale looked up at Bertha. It was as if all of a sudden, he were really seeing her as a person. *What's wrong with you, Dale?* His fingers moved in spasms, like a spider just finished weaving a web.

She's Topper's mother. She has feelings and dreams. Dale folded his hands. *Move Topper out of the sad part of your life.* "Soon. Soon," he whispered. "But right now, I need help. I'll find someone else though. Soon. I will redeem myself."

"What did you say?" Memory asked.

"It was nothing."

Dale reached into his pocket for a cigarette and when he did, once again he felt the wadded piece of paper he'd read earlier.

When he was sure Bertha couldn't hear them, he leaned forward.

"Memory. Somebody, not a good person, gave me something to read on the train, and you might want to look at it. It says we might have a surprise. And there might be something dangerous for us out at the old cemetery. I have a feeling it may be someone we've heard about. That half-sister, who it seems, murdered the woman who raised her. Mrs. Bledsoe." He spread the note "This won't take but a second."

Memory ran her fingers across the words as she skimmed the note. She shook her head then pushed it back. "This is the least of my worries. Too much has happened."

The room was thick with tension. Dale could feel it. It was like hearing the hellish whine of an incoming howitzer shell. The dime-sized piece of shrapnel might be the one that had his name engraved on it.

Memory pushed her cup and saucer back and shifted uneasily in her chair. "I've got several things on my mind. I need to get them off," she said, her mouth tight. "Something really bad went on here last night. I've debated whether or not to say anything to you. I had almost decided not to, but maybe for the sake of both of us I'd better tell you."

"Go ahead." Dale's body unconsciously came to attention. "Try me."

"I thought I needed you yesterday afternoon." Memory's voice was filled with unspoken bitterness. "But actually, when you all made it to the house, and I saw the condition you were in, I knew you'd be no help. And the way everything's played out, for once it's good you weren't yourself." She bit her lower lip. "Right after you got here from town, I saw something that even now I find hard to believe.

"You and I look after each other. We always have. If you had been there, you might have killed someone." Her face twisted in pain. "Shank Potter was out in the backyard."

She dropped her head down as if embarrassed to meet her brother's eyes. Dipping her finger in and out of the cream pitcher she made a procession of O's on the tabletop and stared at them as if somehow she might step into them and disappear into some other world. After a minute, she shook her head, sighed and looked up. "I saw him with his pants pulled down."

Dale's hands trembled. Hot coffee spilled onto the table.

"He was touching himself."

Overcome with emotion, Dale struggled to find words, but he found none.

"When I saw what he was doing, I ran," Memory continued. "I didn't know where I was going. I ended up by the old well."

Dale's face burned with embarrassment and shame because he hadn't been there to help.

"Seeing Shank Potter—that was horrible," Memory said. "I felt sick to my stomach. I felt like I was going to faint. I had to lie down before I fell."

"I am sorry. I'm so sorry," Dale said, anger and compassion thick in his voice.

Memory started to tell her brother that this was not the first time the Potter man had done something dreadful to her. It had happened before. Even worse. When she was barely more than a child.

She rubbed her hands across her face. "While I was there around that well, three men showed up. They didn't see me. There was a short fat man. They called him Mudge. I also recognized a colored man I'd seen on Main Street when we were leaving town yesterday. I just caught a glimpse of him, but even in the daylight the sight of that colored man caused shivers to run all over me. And that vile Shank Potter was there also." She sat perfectly still, as if she were once again hiding by the old well. "I held still. I was afraid to breathe. They were bad people." She squeezed her eyes shut and seemed to be gathering strength from some place within herself before she could go on. "I think they would have killed me if they'd known I saw them." She sighed. "What I've told you, that's not the worst of it. There's more."

A fear Dale was unaccustomed to seeing flashed across his sister's face.

"It has to do with a snake and that man they called Mudge." Memory stopped as if she needed to get herself together.

Dale pushed his hair back and covered his mouth with his hand. He recalled seeing the fat-faced man, Mudge Turnipseed, driving a green roadster on Old Farm Road. Him running them off the road. And something hanging around his neck.

For a moment Memory looked helpless. Tears filled her eyes. "I thought they were all gone. I was desperate to get back here." She gave a nervous little laugh. "I got up to leave." She covered her mouth with her fingers as if to stop the flow of words, then in a few seconds she took her hand down. "That's when Shank Potter attacked me."

Dale flinched as if he'd been hit. "He did what?"

"Shank Potter," her voice broke, "tried to have his way with me."

Guilt stabbed Dale like a knife. "I'll kill him." He sprang from his chair. He picked up a china serving dish and slammed it onto the table, shattering it to pieces.

"Jenson Cooper came."

Dale paced back and forth, back and forth, the sound of his shoes like a rhythm of gunfire.

"Stop it! You're too late for anything to do with this." Memory held her hand up in a blocking motion. "You weren't there. Jenson was. He took care of that horrible man." Her voice filled with gratitude toward Jenson Cooper, she went on, "He helped me get home. Jenson promised it would never happen again."

Dale braced himself against the table and stood in stunned silence. "Death has arrived," he said softly. "It tracked me from the killing fields of France to our Mississippi home." He slid back into his chair. "It stalks the fields of Redemption Ridge. Death has come to take us."

"Shut up," Memory said bitterly. "You have a fever in your head. You're fighting your battles. Only yours. I'm trying to tell you. We all have our wounds. I just didn't know what caused mine. Now, I do."

His head down, as if drained of any fight he had in him, Dale's eyes were deep wells of shame and anguish.

"My battle last night was real. Shank Potter. It began years ago. Here at Redemption Ridge, where we used to tell ghost stories. Out by that old well." Memory put her hand to her throat and then took it down. "Shank Potter." She called his name again.

"I won't say anything else for now. You're a big boy. You can probably figure out what happened. But, you and I, Dale. We've both fought hurts on two different battlegrounds. Yours was shellshock," she said. "Mine, it was people-shock."

She bowed her head. "I'm not telling you everything," she said, remembering how far back in time her hurt and shame went. *And now that I've owned up to it, in some ways my life never will be the same. One night when I was only thirteen years old.* "It wasn't all Thornton's fault we didn't get along," she said softly. "It didn't last long, but what happened to me, can change a life forever. I couldn't bear for Thornton to touch me. Our miserable marriage. For him too."

Dale balled his fingers into fists, sucked in a deep breath, then another. He raised both hands as if he were facing a firing squad. "Where's that God-awful scum, Shank Potter?"

"We left him out by the well, but Jenson left a note with Bertha. He returned real early this morning to check on Shank Potter. He was gone. He was in pretty bad shape when we left. He must have been well enough to leave on his own though, because Jenson saw no trace of him when he went back to look."

"Where's Jenson now?"

"Like us, he has a lot of settling in to do. He said he'd be getting in touch with us in a little while. Mother and I will spend a little time settling in. Tomorrow, the church ladies are taking me for the day. To shop or whatever we want to do."

Fears rolled from a dark corner of Dale's heart. He squeezed his eyes shut and put his hand over his face. "I believed I could return to this place I called home, and everything would be different. Even here, every time I try to run away from my nightmares, I collide with my past," he whispered.

The words of the ghost he had just imagined or had maybe seen the day before drifted through his mind. "Avenge me," Dale said aloud.

"Why did you say that? You don't sound like yourself." Memory's eyes narrowed. "What are you talking about?"

Dale shook his head as if trying to clear his thoughts. "Yesterday when we came in, we stopped by the cemetery. I thought I saw a ghostly suit of bones. The bones of the man Cousin Sarah said is our grandfather, Bruce Claymore."

"I'm not sure any of this is about Redemption Ridge and it's ghosts, Dale. You probably don't want to hear what I have to say, but maybe you're making up reasons to drink your liquor until you don't know what world you're in."

His sister's words stung.

Memory picked up a tablespoon and tapped the tabletop with it. "You need to get yourself together."

"I don't know how to fit back into my life, but when I get my head on straight, I'll see that nothing else bad happens here."

"This isn't about you." Memory's look seemed to be more about pity than anger. "There's nothing poetic or tragic about Shank Potter. No literary muses at Ole Miss would have penned what happened to me."

Dale grimaced. "This place. This place. I wanted it to be home. And Laura Lee. I have to earn her love back."

"That doesn't make sense. Have you noticed the way she looks at you?"

"I have a bad sense of everything coming to an end," he said, his voice hardly more than a whisper.

Shaking, stone faced and walking stiff, like a man going to face some unknown doom, Dale hurried to the dining room door. "We're exiles in our own land."

"Your land." Memory's breath caught in her throat. "It always has been. I'm still searching for mine."

After her brother left, Memory went into the living room. She sat down at the desk, lifted out her writings from her bag and ran the tips of her finger along the paper's edges. For a moment she was tempted to roll them up and throw them into the fireplace. "Do you really want to do this?" she asked. "What's the use? What good is it doing? What's happened, has happened. I can't change anything. Is this my home? Will I ever know where home is?"

But she thought of Jenson Cooper. And when she did, everything changed. She began writing.

You said, when you were a boy, late at night, you stood in the gravel drive outside our house. Watching for the light to go out in my bedroom.

Those nights in my bedroom when I, not knowing you were there, you were waiting. I had a hard time breathing. Then, when all was dark, you'd untie your horse's reins and gallop back to town.

I struggled.

You were, you are now and forever my heart's true love. Your arms around me last night were as thick and sturdy as the limbs of those live oaks that God adorned this land with. That I once thought, a God-forsaken place.

And now, at this moment, as long as I shall live, when I hear your motorcar coming up this drive, and the door opens and slams, I know, my moment has arrived.

CHAPTER 25

A small snake coiled around
A half-sunk re-bar stake
Near the abandoned well.

Like a caduceus in the midst
Of symbolic evolution, it
Broadcast a hard healing
From the earth.

Wednesday morning, March 24

The morning was gray, and even though Brucie's window was closed, the musty smell of rain filled the bedroom. *This is what I remember of March in Mississippi,* she thought when she woke. *Late last night the weather could go either way, like a child who stands on a steep creek bank and can't decide whether to jump in or run. Early this morning it decided to jump.* She stretched. If she had been in Boston, she would have felt guilty for still being in bed. Not at Redemption Ridge.

It's late but I don't have to be anywhere or do anything this morning. I can start unpacking and settling in after lunch. "That'll take some doing." She slid under the covers, closed her eyes and went back to sleep. When she woke again, she sat on the edge of the bed and tried to collect her thoughts; she remembered that it had been a night filled with dreams, but they were as elusive as chasing a hummingbird with a butterfly net.

Brucie got out of bed, opened a trunk she had brought from Boston, and unfolded some of the clothes she had worn to tea parties and church socials. "My life has changed. These dresses don't belong out here in the country. I don't ever want to see them again." She slipped out of her night clothes, went to a chifforobe filled with dresses, skirts and blouses she had left here through the years. She found one she had worn to a few church socials and funerals in Tallouga County; a faded long-sleeved navy-blue dress with white eyelet cuffs and collar. By the time Brucie was dressed, she felt every day of her fifty-seven years and an unexpected, unfamiliar let down came over her. She stood in front of the chifforobe mirror and really looked at herself, something she hadn't done for a long time. It was a shock. Her full head of hair was threaded with silver strands.

She touched her cheeks. They were lined with thin furrows. "Drat. I don't want to look like this." Then she stroked her golden-haired cross from Vernell. Even though she touched the hairs of Captain Bruce Claymore, she felt no better.

9:15

Finished with her coffee, Memory started up the stairs just as the hall phone rang.

She had hardly gotten, "Hello" out before Jenson Cooper said, "I love you more this morning, than I did last night. You are my darling, my beautiful Memory."

"Oh, Jenson. What a wonderful way for my morning to begin."

"Are you up for some slogging in the rain later on today? I thought I'd drive to Jackson in my brother's motorcar. Maybe look around and see about buying my own automobile. I have a little money set aside and it doesn't have to be a new car."

"I'd love to go anywhere with you."

Memory rushed upstairs and hurriedly rinsed off. Folded across a chair she saw the drab black skirt and high-necked white blouse with black piping she had laid out to wear.

"I'm doing something different today." She couldn't change the past, but she could command her future. "Done with the dowdy." She reached into a trunk she had brought from Boston and pulled out the brightest dress she could find. "Shank Potter, you'll never trample on my life again.

"Jenson just called me beautiful. His darling." Memory whirled around like a child. "How my life has changed. I've been through the shadow of evil and have survived it.

"I love Jenson Cooper." She blew a kiss into the air. "And I will fall in love with, Redemption Ridge."

***

9:30

Rain poured from the sky, thunder cracked nearby, but inside, the kitchen was warm from the gas stove and there was a homey odor of freshly polished wood floors and strong, brewing coffee. Brucie poured herself a cup and stirred in cream and sugar. She went into the parlor, unconsciously hand brushing a cushion on one of the sofa's before she sat down. "This weather could give me the mulleygrubs."

For Memory and Dale, you have to put a smile on your face, she reminded herself. *And when Herschel gets here, you really have to make sure everything's okay. He won't be happy with either of his children.*

"This is where it started." She moved a table lamp closer so she could see better, picked up an old family album from a maple table and began going through the scrapbook. She stopped turning the pages when she saw a small watercolor of Lamont's mother, Vernell, painted by a friend of Vernell.

Tears misted Brucie's eyes. In so many ways, Vernell had been more of a mother to Brucie than her own mother, Charlotte Caroline Tisdale Claymore, ever had been. In this painting, Vernell was bent over picking cotton. A sling across her back held Lamont. A shaft of sun touched, not the black whorls of his hair, but highlighted the copper-hued tones. Behind Vernell, lying on a quilt made of old clothes was Lamont's twin, the sickly baby, Sunnie Flo. Vernell had made a shade for her from old gunny sacks and sticks.

Brucie closed the album but it had made her think of something else she probably should take care of. "Should I talk to Lamont about what's left of the treasure buried at Vernell's feet?" *Maybe he and I ought to divide the rest of it? Lamont use his as he wishes for his family?* "Me? For mine? See if Dale wants to buy land or a business. Or go back to school." Brucie rubbed her palms over her eyes, then let out a long sigh. "And Memory's share? My daughter, if that's her heart's desire, could leave here forever." She shook her head. "Or is any of it ours?"

Brucie raised her hands as if asking for heavenly help. "I wish you were here to tell me what to do, Vernell. About so many things. God will always love you more than he loves me." She brushed her finger across her lips, then gently touched the picture of Vernell.

There was a rustling noise from just outside the parlor. Then, a faint voice. "Talk to Lamont."

Brucie drew in a sharp breath, leaned forward and looked toward the hall. She saw no one. "I think you just told me what to do, Vernell."

***

10:00

Memory stopped just before she came into the room, watching as Brucie set aside the family album that always sparked memories of yesteryear for her mother.

Off in the distance thunder rumbled. The weather seemed to fit the mood in the room. Memory noticed that her mother somehow seemed smaller, more vulnerable. Water beading on the windows could have been unwiped tears from her mother's eyes.

"I'll be going with Jenson for the day. We're driving to Jackson. Do you need me to shop for anything?" she asked.

"I don't know what we need yet. A good bit of today and tomorrow for me will be doing an inventory of what we have and what we don't have.

"Do you know where your brother is?" Brucie asked, her voice tense and anxious. "It's bad outside."

"I saw him in the kitchen. He said he had some errands to run," Memory said.

"It's storming."

"You and I both know Dale never pays much attention to the weather."

Memory spoke the truth. Weather had never bothered Dale much one way or the other. He had left on horseback and she suspected her brother would be wandering through the countryside doing who knew what. She was aware that her mother had great insight about some things but not when it came to her son.

"He said he might go to the courthouse. After that spend a few days looking up our property lines and titles. Then see what kind of shape everything's in. Getting an idea of what needs to be done; 'Lord of the manor type of thing.'" Memory half laughed. "He said it would keep him tied up for a day or two."

"Dale loves Redemption Ridge. He has a chance here," Brucie said. "It's in his bones, like it's in mine."

"That may be, but he's not making good choices right now," Memory said. "From what little I've seen of him, I have a feeling Topper may be one of those bad picks. For both of them."

"Your father will be here soon. I want everything to be as calm as we can make it."

Smoothing her hands down the sides of her brightly colored skirt Memory cocked her head. She stepped closer to her mother and when she did Brucie smelled the sweet aroma of magnolia-scented dusting powder.

"I don't want to argue." Brucie rubbed her eyes. "But Herschel won't be happy. Your father's of the old school as far as a lady's dress is concerned." Her body stiffened. "You just might want to dress a little more prudently when your father comes in. The way you're dressed now it looks like you're going to a social. You are a widow."

"Thornton's dead and buried," Memory said.

"You should still be in mourning for Thornton."

"We all have our secrets." For just a minute Memory was ready to slip back into despair. "There's a lot you and my father don't know. And it's best you don't." *Shank Potter...*

An awkward silence fell between the two of them.

"You brought us here to Redemption Ridge. You're my mother. I love you, but this much I do know; I'm not seeing myself as your reflection." Memory's words left the implication that like it or not, she was moving on with her life.

"Your roots are entangled in this soil. Your people are here," she said with a hint of anger in her voice. "If you loved this place so much, why did you leave it?"

But as soon as the words left her mouth, she knew it was an unfair question. It struck Memory that her mother had been through hell. *What had it been like? Those footsteps coming down the hall late at night belonged to the man you thought was your father. The nightmare of him. Crawling into bed with you. Getting you with child.*

Brucie glanced down at the floor. She sucked in a deep breath as if she had been hit in the chest then Brucie slowly looked up at Memory. When she did, she noticed something she should have seen before. Her daughter had circles under her eyes and a haunted look about her face. *Something's happened.*

A disturbing picture floated into Brucie's mind. She grasped her gold cross. She had the sensation of a cold damp breeze brushing the back of her neck and felt as if she were descending into another world. She closed her eyes, dropped her chin as if she were going to pray and she stepped into a painful nightmare.

Climbing a tree. Straddling a limb. Pine bark between my legs. The pine bark moved. I slipped. Yet, I still clung to a branch. I looked down. Saw, not mine. My daughter's twisting body.

"Last night. Something happened," she said. Head bowed, Brucie placed her hand over her heart. "The old well." *My shadow became one with yours.*

"You were hurt. The same way I was hurt." She opened her eyes and looked up.

Memory had left the room.

***

Memory went upstairs to her bedroom, sat in a slippered chair and picked up her pen. "I need to make me a schedule," she said.

But even though she said those words, there were other things on her mind when she sat in front of her journal and began to write.

A schedule:
Today? Jenson.
Friday? Shop or unpack
Saturday, rest and relax
Sunday-Church

Memory shook her head. "Not now. I don't want to write schedules and make lists of things to do." She twisted sideways in her chair, leaned over and dipped her pen into an ink well.

"Right now, while it's fresh on my mind, I need to try and understand a little of what's happened recently."

My mother's cries began here. As did mine.

And now, my brother echoes our cries. His came from far away shores. Ours, home-bred.

Scrabbling moments by the putrid, drowning waters of an abandoned well. Those memories. Fit only for slop waste; but, not yet yard-tossed from the back door. Hoarded, under skirted beds.

What did happen? I now remember.

There were unformed words, splintered dreams.

The devil had entered into me. As he did my mother, in what seems to be another age.

She and I. We fought a silent, lonely, war. Our tongues were tied. There should be a name for our feelings. My brother's has a title—shellshock. There is danger, dignity, bravery, mystery in those words. Mine. My mother's. Some would call it sin, some, shame-shock.

Memory felt a flush of anger burning her face.

"There is no dignity. Only condemnation. Ours. Others." She picked up the journal and pressed it against her chest.

"I am silent no longer—my mother—she has never, nor will she ever, speak of him; the devil, her kin."

Memory lay her journal down and shifted awkwardly in her chair.

"I may be snake-bit. But I won't forever be kneeling under the gently rocking waves, beneath the dying breaths of the ghosts of Redemption Ridge." Her eyes filled with tears as she picked up the pen.

Instead of naming, despair, anger and damnation, she wrote, Where do I settle my humiliation—I tried scooping out all the evil I could. My brother's battles. Still being fought. I could have lost my war.

Memory glanced toward the window, in the direction of the well. "I begin." She leaned forward and whispered, as if she were telling a secret. "No more. I do not care to listen to the ancient, gurgling echoes in those pulsating waves. No surrender. I'm done." She flung her pen to the floor and sprang from the chair.

"I start here." She bent over, raised the bed skirt and dragged out the chamber pot. She straightened, snatched up her beaded bag lying on the bed, reached in and pulled out her nail file.

She flung her pointed helper, piercing torturer, the jeweled nail file into the chamber pot. "You, my friend, my tormentor, are going out with my pee and body waste. I will gladly, thankfully, carry you as a sacrifice out back."

Grabbing the handles of the stained porcelain container Memory shoved her bedroom door open with her foot and hurried to the top of the stairs.

Her hand holding the slop jar she forced her legs to be careful as she made her way down the steps. She rushed through the house and out the back door. Holding the chamber pot as far away from her body as she could, she raced through the pasture. To the old well.

Heart pounding, breathing fast, Memory slung the chamber pot into the well.

"For the rest of my life. There may be more to be tossed. But there will be no more haunting of me. Not by these tainted waters."

CHAPTER 26

**In the coalescing attraction
of two outsiders,
Revenge coiled.**

Friday, March 26

The steady ticking of a mantle clock made Thelma Jewel anxious. Thirsting for revenge and ready to start claiming what she felt was her due, she sat in the parlor of Mrs. Netter's Boarding House waiting for Mudge Turnipseed and Liam McRae, the other man she had corresponded with but had never met.

Mudge Turnipseed had set things up for her at Mrs. Netter's Boarding House in Franklin.

She already felt somewhat of a kinship with Liam, who said he wanted to avenge the death of a friend and needed her help. Likewise, she also relished revenge. Revenge and money suited her to a T.

Although the Boston-bred-and-raised Liam McRae was a policeman, from what Thelma Jewel had picked up. He seemed to be a sophisticated man. *I'm a little further up the social ladder,* she told herself. *He's a policeman, and by blood, I'm a Redemption Ridge Claymore. Landed gentry. Like royalty around these parts. But McRae. Being a policeman, he can carry off a bunch of thieves and cheats in chains. Just might be what I can use.*

At the beginning of their correspondence, Thelma Jewel had high hopes that Mudge might be someone in Franklin who would court her. After all, he was from Tallouga County and probably had a certain status in the community. Once she saw Mudge, she rethought things a little bit. *Make sure he's got money. See what you can get out of him.* Back home in California, he would have been too countrified for her taste, but here in in Franklin, she could tell he was a man of means. That made a difference, and she was satisfied with the arrangements he'd made for Gertie Mae.

Boarding her with some orphans taken in by Mr. Turnipseed's church would get the girl out of her hair, and Thelma Jewel was more than ready for that; hopefully they'd keep Gertie Mae for a good long time. Maybe somebody might even want to take her in and make some sort of house servant out of her. She'd heard that was done down here. Sounded good to her.

She held a Blessed Rest Funeral Home fan taut between her fat fingers but laid it down when she saw Mudge bustle-walking into Mrs. Netter's parlor. The first thing she noticed, he was alone. "Where's Mr. McRae? I was told the both of you would be here." Thelma Jewel waved the fan up and down like a conductor's baton as she studied Mudge. "Let's get moving on something."

"As I tol' you, I hear tell your kinfolks've been busy settlin' in. He's taken a room out from town. Mr. Liam McRae an' I agreed it'd be best fer nobody here in Franklin to see him quite yet," Mudge said. "Quiet like, Mr. Liam's been doin' some detective work on the Claymore an' the Von Dieter families. An' he's makin' the acquaintance of a few folks from 'roun' these here parts."

"You mean Mr. Liam McRae won't be coming here?" Thelma Jewel asked. "Well, I never," she said before Mudge could answer.

"There's a few folks hereabouts we'd jest as soon not know he's here. I talked to him a short while ago this mornin'. He's gonter meet me an' you out at the Divine Deliverance Holiness Church and School for Boys and Girls. Thought you an' me'd ride out to the school where I had Gertie Mae sent so you could see fer yourself how she's bein' taken care of." Mudge nodded his head toward the front door. "I hear tell through the grapevine that it's taken some doin', but she's been broke in pretty darn good already. Scuse my cussin'," he said. "I don't oftentimes say darn in front of a bony-fied lady."

When Thelma Jewel lowered her head to set the fan down, her chin blended with her neck. She stood and pulled loose the lavender gabardine skirt that had lined the crack of her buttocks. She squared her shoulders and straightened the brim of her large deep purple velvet hat adorned with blue and lavender net poufs that looked like gathering thunder clouds.

"Well, it's good the weather finally decided to clear up."
Mudge opened the front door to Mrs. Netter's. "On most any other
day I'd a taken my roadster, but I had to put it in the garage," he
said. "But I'm gittin' it back tomorrow."   What Mudge didn't
elaborate on—Dedmon had gotten Tattler the Rattler to him and
he'd delivered the special snake to the Divine Deliverance
Holiness Church. He'd put the snake in an enclosure out back next
to Black Beauty, the harmless reptile he sometimes draped around
his neck. And Mudge even had a few words with the deadly snake
before he left.

"Okay, Taddler the Raddler," he'd said. "You stay in your
cage, an' come Easter Sunday, I'll see that you're the star in our
blest Brush Arbor Celebration an' Meetin'. Me an' you gotta ree-
spec each other. I'm gonter set you up front, a special place. Up
under the altar table."

But on the way back to Franklin, a yellow jacket had gotten
after Mudge. He flung his hands from the steering wheel, the
gravel road was slidy, and the next thing he knew, he'd crashed
into a tree. He'd snapped the left running board off and dented both
front fenders. Usually Shank Potter did any repair work that was
needed, but for some unknown reason he wasn't around. He'd have
somebody else fix it, but for now Mudge decided he wouldn't tell
Thelma Jewel he'd wrecked his automobile.

"So 'cause I ain't got my roadster back 'til tomorrow, we're a
goin' out to Gertie's school. Like I said, it's part of the Divine
Deliverance Holiness Church, in a carriage. If my roadster's got a
flat I usually hire Shank Potter when I need somebody to ride me
around," he said. "Nobody's seen hide nor hair of him since
Tuesday when he drove the Von Dieter's out to Redemption Ridge.
He may have fallen in the Big Black River or be on a drunken toot
as far as anybody aroun' here knows or cares. An' that reminds me.
He's got him a cousin name of Doot Potter who'll be drivin' us.
Same one what's fixin' my motorcar."

Mudge took Thelma Jewel's arm. When he walked her out onto
Main Street, the air was heavy, like being under some old quilt
that had been stored in mothballs. Winded before they got to the
carriage, Thelma Jewel had to stop for a moment and gasp for

breath. She swirled her hand in front of her face a minute, then they went on.

"You kin satisfy yourself as to how your dorter's doin'." He helped Thelma Jewel up. The carriage bounced when she plopped herself onto one of the two bench seats facing each other. The driver who had been sitting on the ground asleep jumped awake. When both Thelma Jewel and Mudge settled onto the outside seat he popped a whip.

"Well, I never," Thelma Jewel shrieked when the horses took off, her legs flying apart like something crawling between them had nipped on her private parts. Grabbing hold of one side of the wagon and clamping the other hand down so her hat wouldn't fly-off she hung on to the door handle with a death grip while the horses settled into a reluctant, head-bobbing, rough-riding trot. "We have motor vehicles where I come from," she grumbled. "And from my mouth to God's ear, when I get what's coming to me, I'll have me a Ford Touring car of my own." *With a uniformed chauffeur driving me. Like one of those I saw there in Hot Springs*, she thought. *I could get used to that Arlington Hotel and taking those baths. Having Gertie Mae around kind of held me back, though. Maybe I can take care of that someway. Easier to do here than in California.*

Thelma Jewel's large sagging breasts were bouncing and rolling like run away rubber tires come loose from a car. So she wouldn't be slung off the seat, she had no choice but to take off her hat. Holding her hat in place with her foot, she folded one arm under her sagging, bobbing breasts and she continued to grip the door handle with the other. It took all of her strength and concentration not to pitch forward into Mudge Turnipseed's lap, so she didn't bother to answer him.

They continued on out of town, veering onto a gravel road lined by fields which were being planted.

"It ain't too far out in the country," Mudge said. "Jest about a mile or so from town. Set out in a forest, with a hine leg of the Big Black runnin' through it."

In a short while they turned off the gravel road onto an even bumpier dirt path. Shards of coffee-colored corn stalks littered the ground. "I think they're runnin' a liddle behind on their corn plantin' this year an' they're gonter have to go whole hog to catch up. Them corn fields ain't quite up to snuff fer plantin' yet. But spare the rod 'n spoil the chile," Mudge said proudly, as if this were an original quote from him. "Earlier this mornin' you jest mighta been seein' Gertie Mae out there with some of our young'uns." He pointed. "Them chirren's. They work fer their food in the mornin's. Then if they do good with their chores, sometimes they go to school a half a day in the afternoons. If they don't, if they slouch off on their work, they keep 'em out in the fields. We take good care of what's throw'd our way."

"I should think so," Thelma Jewel hollered back.

"At the Divine Deliverance Holiness Church and School for Boys and Girls. We don't believe in spoilin' the young'uns. We even got a holt of one of them train chirren from up nawth here, got us a liddle money from him, but he died in the influenza. epidemic a couple of years back." He leaned forward as if to make sure Thelma Jewel could hear him. "I noticed Gertie Mae's got some black teeth in her head. Look like she been eatin' her some tar. We got us a dentist what comes 'roun' in his wagon. He's got him one of them foot pedal drills," he said with pride. "He can drill 'em down to nubbins, or pull loose a whole bunch of 'em at a time. An', it ain't gonter cost you much. Gertie Mae'll even work off the cost of most of it herself. We believe in young folks payin' their own way an' in learnin' readin', writin', an' 'rithmetic.

"We sen' 'em out to work in other people's houses an' fields. Along 'bout now the fields the chirren were working have done give way to weeds an' scrub brush. It's a money makin' deal fer us here."

Her body bouncing and sliding from side to side on the narrow bench as they made their way down the rough road, Thelma Jewel couldn't bother to nod. She was holding on for all she was worth. In just a few minutes, up ahead she saw a large, weathered building. "That air's the church." Mudge pointed to a large hand-painted, Divine Deliverance Holiness Church sign. "Out back, there's a barn. Tha's where them gol-darn, orphans"—He caught himself—"Scuse my cussin'. I mean them precious young folks live an' work an' learn to save their souls."

The church was as plain and stark as bones with the skin slipped away, and like the weathered barnlike schoolhouse behind it, was set on a patch of matted dry grass. Slightly behind the two buildings were freshly turned open fields where a few children could be seen, hoes in hand, chopping. Just beyond were woods of yellow pine and blackjack trees.

"What's that over there?" Thelma Jewel pointed to a tree adorned with large, multi-colored bottles.

"That air's a spirit tree. Evil spirits gits sucked up into them bottles an' can't hurt nobody no more." Mudge chuckled. "Probably some of them Claymores are hunkered down in there. If'n you've had a set to with somebody, you can set one of these here next to their house. I done it onct. Right after that, some of the people fell into the Big Black River an' drownded. Now, make of that what you want!"

The carriage came to a stop. The driver tied the horse, and before Mudge could get himself out, a courtly, handsome, redheaded man stood beside the wagon.

"I'm Liam. Miss Thelma Jewel, I presume," Liam McRae said, as he opened the door and reached up to help her down.

"Mr. McRae." Thelma Jewel could see the outline of Liam's manly build in the police uniform he wore. He gave off an air not only of self-confidence, but also of one who is very much in control of those around him.

Thelma Jewel shoved one of her saggy breasts back in place and batted her eyes. *Whooee. He is so good looking.* "Pleased. I'm sure."

"Pleasured to meet you in person, Miss Thelma Jewel. I think we both have very personal reasons to be in what I consider as this backward state. Mine, an old-fashioned cause. Revenge. Yours, personal and financial."

Thelma Jewel nodded her head.

Expressionless green eyes stared at her. It was as if those eyes could see right through her to any plans she might make and then he might try to take them over. She was on her guard.

237

The man gave her a quick smile.

You might not know it, she thought. *But I'll be more than a match for the likes of you.*

"I've thought about that poem you quoted to me over the phone," Liam said. "The one that was embedded in your memory."

Thelma Jewel held up her hand as if saying, "It's my turn now."

"When I was a little girl, Mrs. Bledsoe used to pray me to sleep every night. We'd start off with, 'now I lay me down to sleep,' and after she said those verses she'd change and say, 'and now to your namesake. Thelma Grace.

> 'Riches are there for someone to claim
> Finders are keepers, there is no shame.
> Look to her stone, dig it up good
> Search all around, don't be afraid.
> Sought by all, it's never been claimed
> For whoever finds it, there is no shame.'"

Thelma Jewel smiled smugly.

"And, she always added some words to that good-night poem about the despised Captain Bruce Claymore.

> 'His once good name, became undone
> He lived in sin, and he died by the gun.'"

Liam raised one eyebrow and bent his head slightly, as if to say, "That's how everybody ought to live and think."

Something shimmering in his eyes caught Thelma Jewel's attention.

I can't trust you, she realized. *You'd kill me or anybody else for getting in your way. It's probably going to be you or me, and it'll be over my dead body. I got a feeling you took care of that Irish maid, Elnora, because she told me she talked to you, and I never heard from her again. You didn't know we were in communication. You don't know it, but I'm one step ahead of you, buddy boy.* She flattened her hand against her chest as if trying to check for her heartbeat. *You think when we find this fortune, somehow you'll get it from me. You're dreaming, handsome man. You don't know it, but I'm running this show.*

Thelma Jewel grabbed her right brassiere strap.

You're not fooling me, mister. You aren't any the wiser. I can take care of you. She shoved her large breast toward the center of her body, like she was pushing a rock out of her way. *Like I took care of some other folks, Mrs. Bledsoe and the man who fathered Gertie Mae.*

"Charmed, I'm sure." Liam spoke the words with the nose-holding sound of a Boston accent.

Mudge shuffled to them. "The school's this a way." He led the three of them around back to an unpainted, barn-like building. He opened a large, sagging door and they stepped inside onto dirt floors. Stalls once housing animals were now covered by flimsy boards, partitioned off into small makeshift rooms for the children. A few slatted wooden boxes spilling over with clothes could be seen.

Sitting on a pair of benches and facing each other in front of a long narrow table, seven boys and two girls devoured small bowls of lumpy oatmeal as if it were the last meal they'd ever have.

"There's my daughter, Gertie Mae." Thelma Jewel pointed. *Whooee, it's nice to have somebody looking after her for a change. I'd like it to be for good.* "What's wrong with her face?" she squinted her eyes and leaned forward. "It's redder than a pin-stuck finger."

"She's jest a tad sun-burnt," Mudge said.

Head bowed, Gertie Mae sat off to herself. She seemed to sense she was being watched and slowly turned her head. When she saw her mother she made as if to get up, but a heavy-set, dirty looking boy who stood at the end of the table and seemed to command obedience from the other children stood and pointed his bony finger at her. A couple of the boys began chanting,

"Hey, hey, hey, Gertie Mae,

All of us boys are gonna pray.

That you'll be goin' out to play.

If you do, we gonna make you pay.

Hey, hey, hey, Gertie Mae. "

Her mouth open, one foot sliding back and forth, she slunk further down in her chair.

"They gotta learn some ree-spect," Mudge said. "Tha's the first lesson they git taught out here."

"This is exactly where that girl needs to be," Thelma Jewel said.

"What's happened to Gertie Mae's head?" she asked. "It used to be a shade drab looking to me, but now it's kind of white looking like she's been dunked into a flour bin. And what hair she's got looks like it's been cut with a pair of dull scissors."

"They painted her up fer lice an' nits. Tha's why it's white like. An', they got rules an' regulations here. My gut guess, her hair was lopped off," Mudge said, "'cause she musta done somethin' wrong."

"Well, I never." Thelma Jewel tilted her chin and brushed the top of her head as if for reassurance that she still had hair. "I can tell she's coming along," she said. "They need to keep her here." *And if I have anything to do with it, I'll see they do.*

"I want to say a thing or two to my precious daughter. First, I need to use the ladies facilities."

"You'll have to go back to the church. It's behin' an' to the side of it," Mudge said. "Ain't no flies on us. They've got a wadder bucket inside, an' some old newspaper you kin use."

Thelma Jewel wrinkled her nose as if she smelled something bad as she left the building and walked toward the church.

As soon as she left for the outhouse, Mudge motioned for Liam to follow him outside.

"I don't think too much of this motorcar you got for me to drive," Liam said to Mudge. "It's trying to shake my teeth out of my head, and it backfires all the time. It sounds like a team of farting mules."

Mudge hid a grin. *Tryin' to do a liddle bit a Mudge mockin' with your talk.*

"Jest you be grateful fer small favors." Mudge rocked a little sideways. "Don't forgit, city man. You ain't in no police force in Boston Town or New Yawk City. Pickin's kindly slim 'roun' Tallouga County," he drawled. "It's my spare motor. I'm havin' to do me some hoofin' it becuz of you."

"Why don't you and I make a deal right here?" Liam asked. "I'm not real fond of hearing you gas on about your car. What'll you take for this broken down, barely running automobile?"

Mudge gave Liam a crooked grin. "I can't take lessen seventy-five dollars," he said in a sad voice.

"Here's sixty. On the spot. Take it or leave it."

Mudge held out his hand. "We got us a right smart heap of bigger things to git on to. If this is handled right, both Miss Thelmer Jewel an' Miss Gertie Mae'll be comin' into a right smart amount of money an' property." Mudge walked to a pile of farm machinery and leaned against a rusty tractor with no wheels. He touched his finger to his lips, then smiled. "An' now, as to Miss Thelmer Jewel..."

Liam squared his shoulders and leaned toward Mudge. "I'll treat Miss Thelma Jewel like the lady she is, if she can help me get what I want," he said as if staking out territory. "My sweet revenge," he said, his voice as smooth as a water moccasin tail winding through a creek. "I'm all for doing whatever it takes. Then I can go back home." *I'll find some way to get hold of Thelma Jewel's money. Even if it means marrying that bitch quick. With her money and jewels in hand I'll be richer than Croesus,* he said to himself. *I took care of Elnora. Dumb as Thelma Jewel is, I can finish her off faster than you can say scat. And then, I might have to find some way to get rid of you, Mr. Mudge.*

"You kin rest easy," Mudge said, his shifty eyes reflecting the thoughts of what was going through his brain. *I'm on to you.* But what he said was, "We're on the same page. Now me. I am a dee-vout man. I believe in the Scripture. Here in the Divine Deliverance Holiness Church and School for Boys and Girls, we believe in savin' souls whilst they're still young. "'Suffer liddle chirren,'" he said piously. "I may see kin I hep Miss Thelmer Jewel an' save me some souls along the way. Course, I'd like to get shet of Gertie Mae. Might be some place fer her up in Boston. Miss Thelmer Jewel an' I could even buy her a one-way train ticket. If there is some place to put her in, it might be worth yer while." He rocked like an empty swing in a heavy breeze. "Truth to tell. I ain't too much on wantin' to raise little Miss Gertie Mae. Bein' as how she's from out west, she wouldn't fit into Franklin social circles." He stopped rocking. "An hefty as Miss Thelmer Jewel is, ain't no line gonter be formin' to marry her, what with them bowed legs an' all, an' that chopped off way she has of talkin'." Mudge licked his lips. "Now Miss Gertie Mae. She's young. If you can't git her to Boston, maybe Brother Tuggle kin hire her out fer some field an' kitchen hep."

"I need to go back to Boston in a few days," Liam said. "We might need to start taking care of the Von Dieters pretty quick. And it's best they don't know I'm here."

Mudge swayed from side to side. "Maybe that old house needs another mystery goin' on. Maybe we could use Thelmer Jewel an' resurrect some of them old ghosties." He giggled as if he knew a delightful secret. "I have me an ideer how to git all these folks together an' git them dancin' to our tune. Take care of a whole passel of 'em all at onct." He rubbed his chin. "I heerd Mr. Von Dieter's comin' in 'round Easter time."

He chuckled. "Now, to my way of thinkin', Bruce Claymore, the reviled an' traitorous Captain of Redemption Ridge, God rest his soul, ain't never been formally condemned nor honored. We got us a Celebration an' a Brush Arbor revival meetin' comin' up Easter, sponsored by the Divine Deliverance Holiness Church." Mudge changed his rock to a back and forth plummet. "Now, what with all the family back here in Tallouga County, better late than never to raise some questions about the dishonorin' done by most folks 'round here, or sanctifyin' done by some of Mistah Captain Bruce's family." He rubbed his hands together. "An we aim to either set that misstep straight or condemn him to everlastin' Hell fer good an' always. An' see as to invitin' all of what's left of the Claymore family. Hold a celebration in the Redemption Ridge Cemetery. Set up a small stage an' altar. Drape the flag of the Confederate States of America 'roun' it an' have all them dignitaries in a special, roped-off section. You never kin tell," he laughed. "You jest might meet up with some of them ghosties out there. Ain't nothin' like a faith healin' with a few snakes slidin' 'round to bring down the Holy Spirit an' have folks fallin' on their knees."

Liam's jaw muscles tensed. "Snakes?" he asked.

"It's a healin' service," Mudge rocked sideways. "Now, you're a big man from up east," he said, "but jest might be I'm a step or two ahead of you on some things. I got me an ideer how to rope all those folks in. We're talkin' about a three-pronged service. Honorin', savin' an healin'." He reached into his pocket. "I had me one of the ladies at my church write here up fer me. I thought I'd maybe have Topper give it to 'em out there at Redemption Ridge." He unfolded a sheet of creamy linen paper.

An invitation to the Esteemed Von Dieter family:

We'd be pleasured to have you as our honored and revered guests. To the descendants of the of the battle of Redemption Ridge, the Divine Deliverance Holiness Church is having a Brush Arbor meeting on Easter Sunday, April 4, at 11:00 a.m. on the Redemption Ridge battleground. Like the two headed serpent—once and for all, either, clear his name and revere Captain Bruce Claymore, or show his true colors—a hero to the cause or a traitor to our beloved southlands. As for us, we name him, Hero.

We would be honored to have you at this once-in-a-lifetime event. And bring any of your sick and ailing for the healing service. Dinner on the grounds will follow.

Liam grinned and nodded. "I like your plan," he said.

Mudge covered his mouth with his hand trying to hide his wide grin. *Okay city boy. You got the male Von Dieters in your sights. You're comin' to me with what I want.* Mudge gave a short side rock. *Maybe I kin git Thelmer Jewel fer me an' you kin take care of them Von Dieters. Lawd be pleased, an', that'll be the end of the Claymore family.*

He blinked his eyes several times. *Miss Thelmer Jewel. She kin be mine with all that Claymore money. An' them jewels to boot.*

He pulled a tobacco pouch from his pocket, rolled and licked a cigarette paper. *I have me a feelin'. I'll worry 'bout gittin' rid of Gertie Mae, an' this city slicker later. This here is my neck o' the woods he's in.*

Liam flattened one hand and jammed it into his pocket, up under his holstered gun. "I'd like to add something," he said. "As for all your military heroes. I think, whichever war they were in, it is so fitting for them to wear their uniforms. This ceremony will also honor them."

"I'll git that word out," Mudge said.

Snakes sliding around. Tormenting everybody with his shellshock. Liam smiled to himself. *His father wearing a German uniform. Senator Shields said he saw him in it once. Dale Von Dieter. Maybe I can make it look like he killed his German dad. That's where I'll start.* He eased his hand from his pocket and made small trigger pulling motions with his fingers. *These country folks won't know if they're coming or going when I get through with them!*

Mudge pointed to the school. "All this sounds like a good ideer to me, but Miss Thelmer Jewel done come out of the outhouse a couple of minutes ago, an' she might be missin' us. We best git on back inside. We do have us some bidness to take care of.

"You bein' a city policeman an all. You know a tad more 'bout takin' care of bad bidness than I do. An' I'll be there to hep you."

But his shifty eyes spelled a different story. They had no hint in them that he would be toadying to the Boston policeman, Mister Liam McRae.

Wiping her hands down the sides of her skirt, Thelma Jewel rounded the corner of the church building and came to where Mudge and Liam stood. "Le's us go on in so you kin visit with your dorter," Mudge said.

Mudge leading the way, the three of them stepped inside the barn turned schoolhouse. When Thelma Jewel saw Gertie Mae, she slowly walked to the bench where the girl sat, slouched over as if she were sleeping. Thelma Jewel pushed her daughter's shoulder. When Gertie Mae raised her head and saw her mother she grabbed the back of her head as if she'd had a sudden pain. "They're mean to me here," she wailed.

Thelma Jewel felt a familiar despair that quickly fed into anger. She shook her finger in Gertie Mae's face. "Our kin here in Mississippi have done you and me wrong," she said. Her eyes flared with spite. "I want my revenge. I want the money I'm owed from these people, and I don't care what happens to them. The devil can take the hindmost." *I took care of some other folks who did me wrong. Mrs. Bledsoe and that sailor man, your daddy.*

For just a moment she saw the reality of who she was, she felt an uncomfortable self-hatred, and it was not a pretty sight. Unaccustomed tears burned her eyes and slid down her cheeks. *I don't really have a mother. I don't have anybody.* She looked toward the floor and closed her eyes. Rejection lay at the center of her memories like a muddy pool of stagnant, putrid water. *I carry pain inside me. I cry. I cry. I cry.*

A jab of shame hit Thelma Jewel when she raised her head and looked at her daughter. *This dislike. It's passed on down to you, Gertie Mae. You whom I cannot love.* Then, the familiar self-protective anger took over. *That brace or that operation you need on your leg.* "It's all their fault," she whispered. "It should have been my money to begin with." She smiled to herself. "I got it anyhow. Somebody's going to pay for what they did to us."

"Who?" Gertie Mae whined. "I don't have me any money." She tugged on her hair as if she were pulling weeds from the ground.

"Shut up. I'm not talking to you."

Thelma Jewel's eyes narrowed. "That old Mrs. Bledsoe. She had a vision. Not long before she passed." *She was out of her head on that medicine I gave her. But I believe this.* "She was told by Cousin Sarah that something valuable was hidden in the Redemption Ridge Cemetery." Thelma Jewel patted her chest as to make sure her heart was still beating. "I think Mrs. Bledsoe was dotty in the head and her tongue was all twisted up at times. She did say a Sheriff Bramlett, hid something. Under where your auntie Thelma Grace is buried. That's what she thought.

"I believe those words she prayed on so many nights, 'Look to her stone, dig it up good. Sought by all, they've never been found'." Thelma Jewel felt powerful, energized and in control as she remembered how she took care of Mrs. Bledsoe. "Of course the old fool," she muttered. "She also thought I was poisoning her because she was Mary Queen of Scots and I was Elizabeth."

"My name's not Mary, and I'm not a queen," Gertie Mae sobbed. "Don't give me none of that bad medicine you gave to Gran Bledsoe," she pleaded. "It made her sick. And she died. I want to go home."

"That's enough out of you. I'm through talking to you." Thelma Jewel turned away and walked to where Mudge and Liam stood. "Gertie Mae doesn't know it, but she's staying here." She threw her head back. "Mr. McRae and Mr. Turnipseed, I'm ready to claim what's owed me."

Mudge tossed a cigarette he'd been smoking onto the dirt floor and ground it out with his shoe. "Come Sunday mornin', you an' me might wanter go by their church. So you kin see what your kinfolks look like. Later, we'll be making up a invite to our special service I tol' you about, Miss Thelmer Jewel. A ceremony honorin' your dead relative, Captain Bruce Claymore. An' a few more of our blest Confederate heroes." He made a little half bow. "We're gonter git your family together out at the cemetery with all them ghosties." He licked his lips. "We're also havin' us a healin' service. You git to see some of them snakes I was tellin' you 'bout. We might be takin' care of us several birds with one stone."

"Whooee!" Thelma Jewel said. "That sounds good to me."

"Now, while I got me a minute, I'm gonter go to the church office an' give this to our preacher man an' school director, Brother Tuggle," Mudge said. "Have them print this here up an' git it back to me by mornin'."

As soon as Mudge walked away, Liam pressed his fingers against Thelma Jewel's back. "Just talking to you on the telephone, I had no idea you were such an attractive lady. I'll tell you what. I've taken a room not too far out from town. Now, if we were back in Boston, in my old stomping ground, you and I might be courting, hot and heavy."

Thelma Jewel batted her eyes. "Well, I never. I'm staying at Mrs. Netter's Boarding House, and I don't know what's to stop you from calling on me here in Mississippi. I've been doing some more thinking since we've talked. I'm about ready to give that Von Dieter woman and those others I'm kin to something to think about."

She edged closer to Liam. "I'm here to tell you. I've got something on my mind. I could feather my nest. And yours too, if you do what I have in mind."

Liam frowned and stepped back. "I'm kind of my own man." His body stiffened. His eyes were suddenly a startling, translucent green.

"Don't trifle with me," he said. "I know how to handle women." As if thinking maybe he'd said too much, Liam dropped his head and rubbed the back of his neck. "I overstepped myself," he said. "We're in this together."

Thelma Jewel looked away, her lips curving into a half smile *Mr. Policeman. You might not know it, but I'm in charge. If you don't understand it, you're going to learn. If Mrs. Bledsoe was still alive you could have asked her. I handle things my way.* Thelma Jewel's eyes widened, her lips tightened. *No matter what it takes,*

I'm going to fix it so everything the Von Dieters have belongs to me. She felt her resolve strengthening. *I for one, don't care if they all get killed. If that's what it takes. And pretty boy. I'll probably need your help. And I'll also remember that something happened to Elnora.*

"Well, I never." She shook her head. "From my mouth to God's ear. I was woolly gathering a minute. But I'm back in the here and now." She cocked her chin at Liam. "That Von Dieter fellow, the one they call Dale." Her expression was grim as she said, "The one I'm sister-kin to. Did you get my note to him?

"Let him know that I'm out here?"

"I got it to him on the train," Liam said, "but I'm not sure he read it. He's pretty much staying blindsided by all that whiskey and the cough syrup he drinks."

"I want him to know I'm here in Franklin. Those people have some terrible things to answer for. Not just throwing me away, but also for money and stolen property. If worse comes to worst, you might have to take care of a few people along the way." She gave him a half shrug. *Like you did Elnora?* "Course, I'm teasing."

Thelma Jewel's face lit up as if she'd just recalled the words to an old tune. She gave Liam what for her passed as a shy smile. "We might need to go somewhere. And soon, I'm here to tell you."

"Let me guess where." Liam smiled dryly. "Does it have anything to do with jewels?"

She put her arm under one breast and lifted it as if showing off a flower display. "Jewels? Oh, yes, indeedy. If you've got the gumption, I'm here to tell you, they're there for the taking." She dropped her arm and stepped closer. "Enough to buy the whole city of San Francisco. Everybody in Tallouga County donated their jewelry to the Confederate Cause during the battle for Redemption Ridge. They're somewhere out there in the old Redemption Ridge Cemetery."

Thelma Jewel pressed her fingers to her lips as if to silence them, then took her hand down as if she'd made a decision. "And, I know some other secrets too. You might want to come calling on me tomorrow afternoon."

Liam folded his arms. "Mr. Turnipseed got me an old broken down motorcar to use around here." He tilted his head back and wrinkled his nose as if he smelled something rotten. "About the best I can say, it gets me where I need to go."

Thelma Jewel allowed herself a slow, half smile. "Sunday afternoon, after church, everybody around this country town will probably be sleeping." She swung her purse against her hip and felt the slight, reassuring lump of her pistol. "Why don't you and I take a spin out to Thelma Grace's grave at Redemption Ridge and look things over? I'll make our plans, and tell Mr. Mudge what we're going to do."

Looking at Thelma Jewel, a wave of revulsion shot over Liam. It was hard for him to hide his feelings. His hand shot out. His strong grip captured her wrist. But instead of showing how he felt, he got control of himself and put on the best face he could. He slid his hand into hers. "We'll make a good team."

Thelma Jewel had picked up on an air of arrogance and stiffened with resolve. She felt like she was pumping her legs on a high flying swing, getting stronger and higher with every lift. Soon she would take off flying.

I'm way ahead of you, Mr. Police Man.

CHAPTER 27

Cha- dot. Cha-dot. Cha-dot.
Left? I turned my head.
Right? Where?
Machine gun fire.
Raked the ground.
Double time they ran.
Cha-dot. Cha-dot. Cha-dot.

Cha-dot. Cha-dot. Cha-dot.
Bursting from the hills.
Charge! An order.
Out there they lay.
Suffocated in mud.
Baptized by blood and mire.
Cha-dot. Cha-dot. Cha-dot.

Cha-Dot. Cha-dot. Cha-dot.
Buzzards swooped and danced.
Bloody corpses littered the ground.
Stomped into the earth.
Bloated then and now.
For all eternity.
Cha-dot. Cha-dot. Cha-dot.

Sunday, March 28

"Memory's talked to Jenson about him driving out in their family car and picking her and me up for church this morning," Brucie said. "I'd love for you to go to the Dry Creek Presbyterian Church with your sister and me." An unopened Bible lay on the white wicker table beside her on the porch, white kid gloves rested in her lap and, as if to emphasize what she'd just said, she tapped a finger on the Bible.

The porch swing squeaked as Dale stood.

"I don't think I'm quite ready yet," he answered, pulling a pack of cigarettes from his shirt pocket. He struck a match, held the flame to the cigarette, then lit it. He leaned against the porch railing and watched wispy smoke coil into wings, then disappear. *My thoughts,* he mused. *They're there, then they float into nothing like smoke. Does a heavenly God see them before they're gone?* He shook his head. *One thing I do know, though. No more whiskey, cough medicine and pills from Topper. I'll go straight to the source. Dedmon.*

He took a drag on his cigarette. "And my guess is, Memory's newfound love affair with our old homeplace and Tallouga County, Mississippi, is mostly because of Jenson." He looked down. "It's almost as if she and Jenson were destined to be together."

"Thornton. It hasn't been long," Brucie said. But there was a question in her voice that Dale hadn't heard before.

"My sister and Thornton were as different as night and day. Thornton's dead. To me, it's almost as if they'd never been together."

Dale was torn up inside. Something was lacking in his life, something he thought he'd find as soon as he stepped foot on Redemption Ridge soil. But an old elusive longing hung over him for what, he didn't know. He wanted to think about Laura Lee, but memories of Samuel took over his feelings.

It had been less than a week, but it seemed to him as if they'd been gone from Boston for a long time, as if his growing up years had been someone else's dream. Only one thing was brick solid in his mind, The War. Those months in France seemed like yesterday.

"I'm not sure I belong here anymore." His jaw was clenched, his tone soft. "I'm just not interested." But then he thought of Laura Lee. *You're trying to fool yourself.*

"I wish you'd tell me what are you interested in," Brucie said. "I mentioned you taking over as assistant director of our funeral home. We could use some help." She pressed her hand to her chin. "If things work out like I hope they will, we won't just have the white and colored funeral home here in Franklin; we'll open them in other towns around the state. And have Lamont like he is now. A silent partner."

Dale heaved a sigh and turned his thumb down. "I've already told you, not no, but heck no. I've seen enough of death. I want nothing to do with undertaking.

"I may go back to school. To Ole Miss and study English. I majored in Liberal Arts. But I have a lot of English credits. Like my sister, I love to write. I like to write poetry." He lifted his chin. "This town could use a newspaper. But I also feel like I should study to be a business person. Leave the writing, poetry, and classic reading alone. That's for the young and free of heart. None of which I am now. I need to have other things on my mind. Buy more land, and be partners with Lamont and Jenson."

Brucie picked the Bible off the table and absentmindedly rubbed her hand over the Holy Book as if it were a magic talisman and would give her some answers.

"Everything happens in its own good time. And while I'm thinking about it, I won't be coming back home tonight. I'm spending the night in town with a friend, Sophie Blanton. We'll be visiting a few of our old friends later today." She set the Bible down and smoothed her hands down the front of her skirt. "There are some things I need to take care of. The wear and tear of time have caught up with our old homeplace. Sophie and I are driving into Jackson early tomorrow morning to look for furniture at Beidenhorns and fabrics at McRaes. We're just checking things out. I'll be back tomorrow afternoon." She looked like she was ready to say more, but just then the screen door squeaked open and Memory stepped onto the porch.

"Jenson's driving his family car to come out and pick us up. I wish you'd go to church with us, Dale," Memory said. "Laura Lee and another couple are meeting us."

Dale felt his face flush at the mention of Laura Lee's name. A few buried memories flooded back. Memories that didn't seem so long ago, her lips on his neck as he whispered, "This is how it must feel to fall in love." *Laura Lee,* he thought. His lips moved, but he didn't say anything. *The War. Everything changed. My brothers were wounded. My brothers were killed. Her brother. I don't deserve her.*

Memory halted his thoughts. "After church, we're riding in the hearse to Vicksburg for our Sunday dinner."

Dale shook his head as if he were trying to wake from a dream. "I'll try, but even if I can't go into the sanctuary, I think I'll have dinner with everybody. I wouldn't mind seeing Laura Lee. I'll carry a coat just in case."

Dale noticed that Brucie looked please with the thought that he might go with them. *And a ride into town,* he thought. *If church doesn't work out, maybe go by Dedmon's. Bypass Topper.* He pulled out his pocket watch. "Almost nine o'clock."

I haven't done much for her, he realized. *Since I returned from France, it's been me, me, me. Get over yourself. You're acting like your sister. Like you're the only one with problems.*

Memory took a tentative breath, as if she expected to be disappointed and was protecting herself. "I want you to go with us," she said softly. "I've missed the brother I used to know."

***

The white-washed Dry Creek Presbyterian Church had stood guard over Main Street since shortly after The War Between the States. Sometime in the eighteen eighties, money had mysteriously appeared in the church coffers and it had been extensively remodeled. At the same time, the colored church at the edge of town, Sweet Home Baptist, had been rebuilt from the ground up. There had been talk about where their money had come from; Lamont headed up the committee.

Because the street in front of the Dry Creek Church was filled with farm wagons, buckboards, surreys, tied-up horses, and a few automobiles, Jenson parked a little way down the street. When Dale got out of the car he noticed the sky was a sharp, bright blue, the March wind a little nippy. As he opened the door for his mother and sister, he glanced up at the sanctuary. *I may need to get my house in order spiritually. It's long overdue. Then, we'll see what happens.* He slipped on his coat.

"This could be what I need." Dale gave a shaky little laugh. "Getting out and catching up with old friends. I'm still not sure if I'm ready for a 'love thy neighbor' sermon though."

"Take these keys just in case you can't make it to church," Jenson said. "If that's the way you end up feeling, you might want to drive around a little. Just be here when church lets out."

"If you don't mind, I think I will," Dale said. "If I don't go to the service, I'll be here waiting for you all." *I'll make a quick run. Dedmon's.*

His heart beat faster when he saw Laura Lee waiting at the bottom of the church steps, her blue and green plaid skirt stiff with starch, belling around her ankles. Dark eyebrows curved over her blue-gray eyes. "Oh, Dale. I'm so glad to see you."

He bent from the waist, took her hand, and kissed it. "And if you all will have me, I just might come calling again. Do you remember?" He let the question hang.

"How could I forget? You're very cavalier." She laughed. "I do believe we're about to turn a Yankee into a Southern gentleman. We plan to eat Sunday dinner at Oakmont Plantation and then spend the afternoon at the Vicksburg park," she said. "Several motorcars from the church are going. We'd love for you to join us. There's room. Trestle Potter's driving us in the hearse."

A gust of wind caught the straw hat Laura Lee wore. She clamped her hand onto it. A wave of blond hair fell forward, brushing against her cheek. His heart beating faster, Dale looked down at Laura Lee. *It would be so easy to fall in love with you again,* he thought. *I was once. You are so beautiful. But not like I am now. I don't deserve you.* "Maybe this is where I should have started," he said. "With you. At a church." *Not with a ghost I saw in the graveyard,* he scolded himself.

Laura Lee's eyes carried the hope of good things to come. "I do declare. Whatever in the world are you saying to me, Dale Von Dieter?"

"I love your accent," he said. "But not just yours. I love the soft, rolling way our people down here talk. I'd love to study Southern literature. Write poetry. But that's a pipe dream. Whatever I study, needs to further me in making money. I'm thinking about catching a train to Oxford in the next day or two and check into going back to Ole Miss. I only lack a few credits."

"My, my, my," Laura Lee said. "Don"t even think about catching a train. Otis and I already have a visit planned with cousins. We're leaving on Tuesday. I'd love for you to go with us. There's plenty of room so you can stay at our cousin's house. And I can speak for Otis."

Dale's face brightened. "Well, if you'll let me buy some of the gas, I'd be honored to ride with you and Otis."

"I do think you're viewing us through rose-colored glasses, though," she said.

"Maybe so. Maybe not. But it's like you all have awakened from a comfortable, dreamy sleep and are having a hard time facing reality. The world may fall apart, but your lips still make a melody for the rest of us to hear." He reached out and took her hand. "I'm sure it's been this way, since our people first stepped off a covered wagon into the hot, Mississippi summer sun." Dale squeezed her hand. "I can just see it. After a long, dangerous journey, they slowly moved away from the mules and wagons and threw horse blankets under a limb-gnarled, shady, live oak tree. They sat down, plunged their feet in a creek, spread their toes and they said, 'Someday. We'll get started. Someday. When it cools off down here. In the meantime we'll talk it over and think about what all we should do.'"

Laura Lee raised her leg and straightened the strap on her black patent leather shoes. "Those were just everyday words coming from my mouth." She ducked her head then looked up at Dale. "My lil' ole' suthren' talkin' mouth," she teased. "And I've never been under a live oak tree on a scratchy horse blanket, or dabbled my feet in one of those creeks in all my life."

Dale wanted to bend over and kiss her, right then, in front of the church, his mother and sister, and anyone else who might be around. But before he could get into trouble, from out of nowhere Jenson Cooper bounded up the steps and clapped him on the back. "Be careful. You never know who's going to come into your rifle sight, Captain."

"Before we go into the church, while I've got the two of you together I have one thing in mind I need to take care of." He took a deep breath and then said, "I know Memory mentioned about Jenson and me bringing Samuel's remains home, Laura Lee."

Laura Lee eyes widened. "Yes."

"If you're willing, there's something I'd like to set up with you and Jenson. Is there any way we could have a small service for your brother tomorrow? I know everybody moves slower down here. I know this is rushing it, but it looks like we're doing a trip to Oxford, and my father drives in this coming weekend. There'll be lots to do before he comes and lots of changes when that happens. I don't know what's coming down the pike."

"Tomorrow's fine with me," Jenson said. "What about you, Laura Lee? Is there a space at Redemption Ridge you'd like for Samuel to rest?"

"Oh my goodness, yes," she said. "The Stantons have a large fenced-in family plot. And there is a space. To the left of Father. Mother will be on my Father's right."

"Jenson and I, we'll take care of everything and then have Scripture and a prayer."

"Otis and I would be honored to be there. Samuel would want that. What about sometime after lunch? Would tomorrow a little before one be all right?"

"That sounds fine," Dale said.

Jenson hitched his finger toward Dale in a let's-step-aside gesture. "I'll take care of Samuel's remains before she gets there," he said in a low voice. "Why don't I meet you early at the cemetery? We can have everything ready."

Dale gave him a thumb's up.

Just then the church bell pealed, marking time for the service to begin.

With a flourish and a half bow, Jenson took the arms of Memory and Brucie and they stepped into the church alcove.

"Let's go in," Laura Lee said. "I have so much to thank Jesus for."

"Just a second," Dale said. "Let me get rid of this." Just as he stepped back to flip a cigarette from his fingers a car ooged its horn.

Dale and Laura Lee whirled around to see a roadster rumble past and pull into someone's yard across the street.

"I've seen that car before," Dale said.

"That's that crazy Mudge Turnipseed." Laura Lee shook her head in exasperation.

They turned toward the church. Standing in an open door, an elderly gentleman welcoming the worshippers beckoned Dale and Laura Lee forward. Organ music wafted through the entrance. The opening bars of a well-remembered hymn assailed Dale's ears.

Warning notes thumbed in Dale's head. It was cool, but perspiration burned his eyes. He stiffened, as if at attention.

"Lead on, O, King Eternal.

The day of march has come..."

No. It's unbearable. Those words.

France. Cantigny

Dale froze.

The fields of France. We sang. We prayed. They trusted me, their leader. Sweat broke out on his forehead. He would never forget that hymn. It would haunt him, he knew, for the rest of his life. "I've heard that song before. We sang those words."

"Oh, I know, I know," Laura Lee said. "It's an old hymn. I've sung it many times."

But Dale was somewhere else, not in Franklin, Mississippi.

Church service. We stood. Water. Ankle deep. Icy. Filthy. A shredded haversack spread over a barrel. Held the host.

Without wanting to, Dale remembered how it was that morning.

My men took of the holy bread. Sipped the blessed wine. They sang.

"Henceforth in fields of conquest

Thy tents shall be our home..."

He thought the words, along with the melody the organist was playing

"Through days of preparation

Thy grace has made us strong.
And now, O, King Eternal,
We lift our battle song."
Dead man's alley lay in front. Charge! I gave the order.
Dale's body froze. He tightened his fists.
Cha- dot. Cha-dot. Cha-dot.
Left? I turned my head. Right? Where? Machine gun fire.
Raked the ground. Double time they ran.

I prayed. My men. They grabbed their heads. Clutched their
hearts. They stumbled, staggered. They fell. Their blood flowed
down. Crimson waterfalls pooled the ground.

"Lead on, O, King Eternal,
'Til sin's fierce wars shall cease…"
The organist pushed the foot pedals harder. The music grew
stronger.

"And holiness shall whisper
The sweet Amen of peace.
For not with swords, loud clashing,
Nor roll of stirring drums…"
Cha-dot. Cha-dot. Cha-dot.
Bursting from the hills. Charge! An order. Out there they lay.
Suffocated in mud. Baptized by blood and mire.

"With deeds of love and mercy,
Thy heavenly kingdom comes."
Buzzards swooped and danced. Bloody corpses littered the
ground.
Stomped into the earth. Bloated then and now. For all eternity.

"Lead on, O King Eternal,
We follow not with fears.
For gladness breaks like morning
Where'er Thy face appears.
Thy cross is lifted o'er us.
We journey in its light…"
Dale's eyes glazed. Scenes too painful to look at.

The usher opened the door wider. The bass and treble keys
pushed harder. The organ foot pedal pressed flat. The haunting
music swelled.

"The crown awaits the conquest;
Lead on O God of might."

Standing on the church steps, Dale flung his head from side to side. *Cha-dot. Cha-dot. Cha-dot. Christ rose. My men did not. No crown. No conquest.*

Dale's heart hammered. *Over there. Over there. Cha-dat. Cha-dot. Cha-dot.*

"Remember me?" A hand tugged on his coat sleeve.

Too wounded, he thought. *I'm too wounded.*

"Dale. Are you all right?" a voice asked softly. "I hope you don't mind me bringing you back to the here and now."

Over there. Over there.

He became aware of Laura Lee and of where he was. He had to rearrange his thoughts. *I'm over here.*

Dale pushed his hand against his chest as if trying to pump air into his lungs. "I can't go in." He backed away. "They believed." He thumped the side of his leg with his fist. "Over there. No cross was lifted.

"I'm not ready. I'll be back. After church."

"You're not in France. You're here. In Franklin. At the Dry Creek Presbyterian Church." Laura Lee smiled a small, tense smile. "You've come home. You're living at Redemption Ridge."

"I know. I know," he said impatiently. "I'm such a sinner. Unrepentant. I'm just not ready for church."

"Jesus forgives your sins."

There was a short, uncomfortable silence.

Dale whirled away from the sanctuary and bounded down the steps.

Cha-dot. Cha-dot. Cha-dot.

***

As Dale came down the sidewalk, standing at the edge of a yard on the other side of the road from the church he saw a stumpy looking man he'd seen once before. *It's that Turnipseed man. He was driving a green roadster down Old Farm Road. Something long and coiling hung around his neck.*

Today, a hefty lady stood beside Mudge Turnipseed. Although they were across the street, Dale could see her face clearly. Her hands splayed on her hips, the woman's smoldering eyes glared at him; she smiled, as if she knew a secret.

His mind on other things, he noticed but walked on and promptly forgot about the two of them as he climbed into Jenson's motorcar. He sat for a moment, rested his head against the leather seat, closed his eyes and became lost in thought.

I should have died over there in France, he agonized. *I failed my men.* "The past is too much with me. I'm not ready yet. For religion, or to give my heart to anybody." He felt for his syrup. "No. No," he said. "I need to relax. To let my misery, my shame go." But he shook his head as he said this. He was not ready to surrender his battles and was not sure if he ever would be. He would lose his men forever if he did.

Mudge and Thelma Jewel stood by Mudge's car. "Are you satisfied?" Mudge asked. "You seen your half-brother an' sister now." He did a short rock, then dropped his coat onto the hood. "It won't take me but a minute, an' I'm gonter run you on down to Mrs. Netter's. Then I'm comin' back to here. Soon's this preachin's done an' over with, an' soon's a few folks walk the aisle an' turn their lives around, 'amen', I got me some things to pass around in there. Invites to the Brush Arbor Celebration, mostly honorin' our fallen dead. Especially, Captain Bruce Claymore. An' I did say mostly honorin.' An' then we're havin' us a healin' service. With a feast to foller."

Mudge rocked from side to side. "An' since, from what I've done set up fer you, you're gonter be tied up with Mr. Police Man McRae all afternoon at the cemetery. He'll pick you up to Mrs. Netter's. Mr. Doot Potter's gonter hep y'all."

Thelma Jewel covered the side of the running board with her foot, grabbed a leather strap and breathing heavily heaved herself up and into the back seat. Mudge locked the crank in place and gave it a couple of healthy spins. When the motor caught, he shuffled into the car, stomped the clutch and shifted into gear.

Doesn't look like that Mudge man and that woman with him are going to church either, Dale thought as he saw the roadster jerking away as if it were a horse fighting a too-tight bit in its mouth.

He pulled out his pocket watch. He had an hour to kill while the others were in church. "Father's coming in. I'm putting Topper out of this. But better safe than sorry. I've got a few hard days ahead of me," he said. "Like it or not, just this one more time. Then I'm done. I'll either straighten myself out, or find some other way out of this hellhole I've dug."

Dale had a general idea where Dedmon lived. He cranked the car, pulled onto Main Street and turned off onto a side street on the outskirts of Franklin. The road narrowed, then twisted past a cluster of run-down houses and clumps of dead foliage. Dale stopped the car close to the end of the street. He got out, stepped around an overturned slop jar in the yard and walked up sagging porch steps. The windows were covered inside with what looked like old croaker sacks; the place almost looked abandoned. Dale knocked on the door. Standing on one foot and then the other, he waited a few minutes but there was no answer. Just as he turned to walk away, he heard a dog growling and saw a window covering raised. A few seconds later the door cracked open; a man's leg stretched across the opening held back a large, struggling, teeth-bared dog.

"Shut up, Boots," Lucius Dedmon hollered. He wheeled around, kicked the dog in the side, grabbed him by his scruffy neck and shoved him away. "Now, git." Howling, the dog sprawled in a heap.

"My dawg ain't did nothing," a child's voice whimpered from behind Dedmon.

"You shut up, or I'm gonna kick you so hard, you'll wish you were dead as that dog's mama. Looka there. And don't you forget it now." The man raised a fist and shook it toward the front yard. "I stomped her guts out, and throwed her out there in the woodpile. And I kin do it again."

"No," the little boy cried. "Doncha kill my dawg."

The sound of a slap was like a shot. The boy sobbed. Dedmon pushed the dog and boy back inside the house. He slammed the door and turned to Dale.

"Whatcha come here for?"

Dale noticed that Dedmon's eyes were sunk deep in their sockets, as if he hadn't had much sleep. He had to shake off a feeling of unease before he could say, "Topper said he was out of whiskey and syrup. And I need to tell you, I will not be using him anymore."

Dale came up with the only reasons he could think of. "I don't like his attitude." He tried not to look Dedmon in the face when he asked, "Do you have anything for me? If not, I've gotten word that I can get what I need in Vicksburg." There was an uncomfortable silence. *I'm not a good liar,* Dale thought. A crow cawed overhead. Dale ran a hand through his hair and stepped back.

Dedmon broke the silence. "My man I gits it from, he wants that Lamont's son, Mr. Topper should be the one selling it. Mr. Topper. He must have done did something. And I aims to take care of him.

"See is he going behind my back and using somebody else," Dedmon said. "I don't know what Topper done did to you, but I might have to teach him a lesson or two. I got me some snakes out in this backyard," he went on, "And I kin settle with him real good, if I needs to."

The skin on the back of Dale's neck crawled. "He hasn't done anything," Dale hastened to say.

 Dedmon rolled his eyes and swayed. "But for now, I gots to watch my backside," he said, a look of fear on his face. "There's some other bad bidness going on around here too. I been told, by somebody else from around these here parts of town, someone's out to git me. I done been told it has to do with that missing white trash, Shank Potter."

Dedmon leaned forward and seemed to be searching his yard. Satisfied, he cleared his throat, crossed to the edge of the porch, and spit over the loose railing. "Shank's brother Trestle is after me. Says I drowned Shank in a well, out at Redemption Ridge Thursday even'." He faced Dale and swiped the back of his hand across his mouth. "I won't have me none of what you're wanting 'til this afternoon. I needs me a little startup money. I won't make as much without Topper." His voice snapped like a fish taking a lure. "After this, I'm going to teach Mr. Topper a lesson. Then, I might just be leaving town. Let me show you something." He pointed to a pile of scattered firewood. "Looka there, on the other side of that there firewood."

At the edge of the overgrown yard, Dale made out a large dog's carcass with shreds of hair and skin hanging from its rib cage.

"That there dog you saw here in the house, that's his mother done been throwed over there. That's how I take care of things." He pointed to the woodpile. "That bitch over there. She growled at me. I don't rightly cotton to that. Anybody or anything what crosses me, I kin do the same to them. And I might have to teach Mr. Topper a lesson."

"He didn't cross you. Not in any way." Afraid he'd gotten Topper in trouble, Dale felt slightly apprehensive. He wanted to straighten things out for Topper, but he didn't know what to say and he was running out of time. "I've got to meet some people at church. I don't want to be late. I'll be back later."

"You want some more happy juice from me? It'll be in my hand later on today. Not 'til then. It'll cost me more, so it'll cost you more." Lucius Dedmon put his hands on his hips. "Lemme give you a little piece of advice, Yankee man." He harked, rolled thick saliva in his mouth, spit between his feet and Dale's. "You best better git on back up north, where you come from. Y'all left your peoples down here long time ago."

He spun around and slammed the front door.

He's mean. He's crazy. I don't like dealing with him, Dale thought as he walked through the overgrown yard, being careful to skirt around the woodpile, with the dog carcass lying on the other side. "The devil could make this place his home," he said, heading toward church where he would meet up with the others.

***

"Wives submit yourselves to your husbands," Jenson teased Memory. "You heard the minister."

"Well, we're not married," she said as they walked down the church steps. "And I found that scripture as tedious today as it was when Thornton and I were husband and wife."

"I'm picking at you."

"It's hard for me to trust males," she said. "And going along with that, to believe in love and forgiveness for all and for everything that happens." She tilted her head up so she could look him squarely in the eyes. "I guess a lot of my problems go back to all those years ago, Shank Potter and that well." *That one nightmare...it changed my life,* she thought. "You would think, as intuitive as my mother and I are, some of that dreadful night would have come back before it almost happened again. But no. It took another bad stink to make it come to mind. Old flesh. Rotten teeth." She put her finger under her nose. "A filthy body. What it did to me, is almost like a bad smell. Spell," she corrected.

"Together we'll break the spell and do away with the smell," Jenson laughed. "We're in front of the church and half the town would see us. Otherwise, I'd take you in my arms right here and now."

He patted his back pocket to make sure the small box was still there.

"There's the hearse across the street." Jenson pointed. "Another Potter drives for Lamont. Trestle Potter. He's a redhead, but in other ways, he looks nothing like his younger brother, Shank." He raised his eyebrows.

"And speaking of Shank, nobody's seen hide nor hair of him since that night he got after you." Jenson put his hands on his hips. "You know, Trestle Potter drives the hearse for the funeral home, so he's driving the six of us to Vicksburg for dinner. After that, I know he's taking you home and leaving the hearse at Lamont's."

Jenson linked his arm through Memory's and led her across the street. He combed his hair back with his fingers. "No matter what time we get back, my gut feeling is Dale will want to stay at Laura Lee's for a while. He can drive our family car home and leave it at your place. Then I'll have a ride back home. So why don't I ride out to Redemption Ridge with you?" He gestured to the hearse. "We'll all make a night of it," he teased. "I have a surprise for you," he said under his breath.

Jenson helped Memory into the back of the hearse where they waited on the other couple congratulating the minister on his fine sermon and Dale who had showed up right after the service to escort Laura Lee across the street.

Sitting in the front seat, eyes closed, mouth open, a gray line of dried drool streaking his cheeks, Trestle's chin appeared to be nesting in his chest hairs. He seemed to be in another place and time, unaware that anyone had loaded into the vehicle.

Jenson dropped into a narrow bench seat facing Memory. *We're not getting any younger. I hope you're ready for a ring.* He took a deep breath and slowly let it out. "Seriously, we'll make a night of it. You and I can see about burying those demons out there at that well," he said.

Trestle's mouth closed.

"Breaking that spell." Jenson leaned over, lifted Memory's chin and stared into her eyes. "I have an idea how to do it?"

"How?"

"It's a surprise. It'll start with the well. Again. We'll break the spell."

His body motionless as a dead rat, Trestle opened both eyes.

CHAPTER 28

An inverse marriage with
Lineage took place under
A bough of sweet olive
In a Mississippi cemetery.

As a relic disintegrated,
Fingers found two triggers.
of two outsiders,
Revenge coiled.

Sunday afternoon, March 28.

"We're almost there," Liam said glancing over his shoulder at Thelma Jewel. "This countryside is just about good for nothing. Except what it is. Burying a bunch of dead folks.

"Oh, oh. Hold your hat." Liam leaned on his horn and slammed on the brakes, dodging a horse and rider on Old Farm Road.

"Whooee," Thelma Jewel yelped, as the car fishtailed in the loose gravel.

Liam gave the wheel a quick steer in the direction of the slide as the motorcar arched sideways, like a proud, prancing show horse. Thelma Jewel gripped her large bag with one hand and held onto the seat with the other. Liam pressed the brake but had to pump it before the motorcar would come to a gravel pinging stop. "Nothing but a bunch of country hayseeds around here," he griped. He waited a minute for the dust to settle.

Thelma Jewel hiccupped, then patted her chest, trying to catch her breath. She cupped her hand to her mouth and partially stifled a loud burp. "You just about made me lose Mrs. Netter's Sunday special." Her gurgling stomach sounded like crunching crackers. "Her chicken and dumplings and water cornbread."

Thelma Jewel waited for Liam to come around and help her out of the car but he had moved away. "Well, I never," she muttered, flinging the door open.

"You wait there just a minute, Miss Thelma Jewel. I need to take care of some business," Liam called over his shoulder. He pointed to a man holding a shovel and a pick axe, standing under a tree, just inside the cemetery gate.

The man moved toward Liam with the lumbering walk of an old elephant. "Name's Doot Potter." He thrust his chin forward and squinted his eyes, as if something he saw hurt them. "You're hairs redder'n a burnin' liter knot."

And your face looks like an old fishing net hung out to dry. "Mudge told me you've done work for him and for the Claymores." A proud smirk pulled the corners of his mouth. "You know where the family's buried and they've paid you to clean the cemetery some."

"Them Claymores ain't never done paid me what they should. But I'll show y'all where they're at," the man said. "Mist Mudge tol' me to take y'all. You'd make it worth my while."

"Here you go." Liam reached into his pocket, pulled out a nickel, and handed it to Doot.

"'N' that ain't enough."

Up close, he smelled like wet dog hair. Liam stepped back, flipped another coin that landed at Doot's feet. Doot picked it up. He spit on first one nickel then the other, rubbed them on his coveralls and one at a time dropped them into a pocket.

"I might need you to do some more business with me." Liam searched the man's face as if he were looking for something he hoped to find. "You sound like you didn't like the Von Dieters very much."

"They're too highfalutin fer my blood," Doot whined. "An', way back when. Some of 'em Claymores, they done some of my peoples wrong." He cleared his throat and spit. "We Potter's are proud folks. We ain't likely to fergit. We keeps score."

"I have some ideas about how to take care of several of them with one fell swoop. I've got a long memory too," Liam said. "It's well known that Captain Dale Von Dieter, late of the United States Army, doesn't have much use for that German daddy of his, Herr Von Dieter. It's also a fact that the good Captain doesn't have his head on right. Claims he had some problems with mustard gas and he's overly fond of drinking and likes his cough syrup."

Liam shook his head. "A lot of other people went over there too. I don't hear them complaining about their bad dreams, burned lungs and dead friends." Once again he gave Doot a probing look. "I have a plan on how to get back with the father and the son for something they did up in Boston."

What Liam didn't say was, that he also had another plan. It was a known fact that Thelma Jewel was an unclaimed relative of the propertied Redemption Ridge Claymore family. Find those jewels, take care of a couple of Claymores, and it fell to reason that Miss Thelma Jewel would inherit a large estate.

Take her on for a short while. Get what she had changed over to his name. Then, he could get rid of her and that funny walking daughter of hers, Gertie Mae. He could do it in a way that no one would be any the wiser. And he would go back to Boston, a rich man. He might have to rethink Gertie Mae though. Look at her in a certain light and if it wasn't for her bumpy walk she wasn't too bad.

"We'll talk about some ideas I have later on," Liam said. "Right now, show me where she's buried. Mr. Mudge and I," he frowned. "We've got some different ideas about how to go about fixing things."

Doot's eyes narrowed. "These country folks may git you yet, city man," he muttered as he and Liam walked toward Thelma Jewel.

"Let's find those gems," Thelma Jewel called out shrilly. "I want them now."

"Follow Doot," Liam snapped.

"I haven't been to but one cemetery," Thelma Jewel gasped as she stumbled behind the two men, picking each foot up as though she were stepping into hot gravy. "I didn't like what I saw then. So, let's just get these jewels and high-tail it out of here."

With Thelma Jewel weaving her hips and high-stepping a short way back, the three of them wound through the graveyard, skirting fenced-in family plots, statues and wooden crosses and edging around marble markers. Doot stopped short of at a burial plot enclosed by an iron fence. "This here's where they plant the Claymore family," he said, shoving open a creaky rusting gate.

Low slung, weary looking oak branches drooped over the Claymore burial grounds. Someone had planted hydrangea bushes around the perimeter; their skimpy tattered leaves were brown now, but would be aflame with color in a few weeks. A throaty hoo-hoo became from an overhead branch as an owl flitted from one of the trees.

"Well, I never. I thought those birds just flew out at night when they come to chase ghosts, devils, and boogeymen. This place doesn't have a good feeling to it," Thelma Jewel said.

"Are you sure you know what you're doing about those jewels?" Liam asked. "Who in the hell told you they would be here?"

"The old woman who raised me. God rest her soul. Miss Bledsoe. I declare, she knew more than she let on," Thelma Jewel said. "As I've already told you, it's got to be close by.

"My namesake, Thelma Grace. She and I had the same father, Daddy Claymore, and she was known to be her daddy's pet. I always knew I'd come here someday," she said.

As Thelma Jewel stepped into the Claymore burial section, for a brief moment a noise rang in her ears, a sound like someone sawing a ham bone in half, and the air around her became flooded with a strong, sweet odor.

"What's that I'm smelling?" she asked.

"Sweet olive," Doot said. "It hangs 'round here most of the time."

Thelma Jewel looked away, over toward a fence that surrounded what looked to be another cemetery but didn't see anything.

"Miss Bledsoe always said she'd bet her life's blood on it, those jewels are buried under Thelma Grace' s headstone. She said an angel came and told her in a dream. Miss Bledsoe was kinda dotty at the end, but I believed her on that one." She shifted her hips from side to side and pulled her skirt forward as if opening a stuck door. "I had me the same dream one night. Right after I took Christian pity on a sick woman and helped Mrs. Bledsoe pass to the other side. I heard clear as a whistle those words she used to say to me."

Doot waved his hand to stop her, as if he needed to talk about something else. "That's where the Claymore's dotter's buried." He pointed toward the toe of Thelma Jewel's shoe.

Thelma Jewel wasn't done talking. Her mouth open, she looked down. She nodded her head and then in a chant-like voice said,

"'Look to her stone, dig it up good
Search all around, don't be afraid.
Sought by all, it's never been claimed,
For whoever finds it, there is no shame.'"

She reached into her purse and took out a paper fan nestled against her small derringer. She flipped the fan open and pointed it at the grave site. "There's her name. It's here." Her voice rose. "The jewelry's got to be here."

Doot jammed the shovel into the ground. Each time he punched the blade down, his shoulders jerked; streams of sweat slid down his reddish brown, crappy neck.

Thelma Jewel sat on a bench with the name **CLAYMORE** engraved on it, her bottom covering most of the concrete slab. She watched intently as, dig and throw, Doot tossed dirt at her feet.

"This here groun's hard'n a horse's shoe," Doot carped. "'N they got this here marble stuck deep. Goes almost to the gates of Hell itself, if you ask me."

Thelma Jewel's legs had turned numb, her feet tingled. "Dig up her headstone. I'm here to tell you, it's got to be there." Every now and then she stretched first one leg then the other, bent over and rubbed her thick, swollen ankles.

"Up under her headstone," she intoned. "Lord, I feel it. Lord, I feel it." She rested her hand flat against her chest. "That's where it is. I do believe. Thelma Grace is speaking. She's telling me. My fortune's right there. Waiting for me."

After about thirty minutes and a few stops for Doot to smoke a cigarette, the marker was tilted slightly back.

"One more time orter do it." Doot slid the shovel under the headstone. He spread his feet slightly to steady himself, put his foot on the shovel, and pushed down. Slowly, the marble marker came out of the ground.

"What do you see? What do you see?" Thelma Jewel cried.

Doot raised his head. He stepped aside and wiped sweat from his apish brow. "Ain't nothin' here."

"Stop." Thelma Jewel dipped her head, angling her thick double chins toward the ground. "Whooee, I think I see something. There. Right there under that piece of marble with Auntie Thelma Grace's name on it."

Doot pushed a pile of dirt aside with the shovel. The edge of what looked to be a small box was showing from up under the corner of the headstone still left in the ground.

"Oh, looky there," Thelma Jewel hollered. "Dig," she screamed. "Dig."

Liam grabbed the shovel from Doot. He toed it down furiously. In a few seconds he uncovered the top of a teakwood box.

"That's it," he said dubiously. "It's not big. Must not be as many jewels as all those crazy people around here thought."

Thelma Jewel stood unsteadily and spread her hands on either side of her large hips. Liam pulled a bone handle knife with steel blades from his pocket, flipped it open and sank to the ground. He rocked back on his haunches. He scooped dirt away, dug a little deeper, then lifted a carved wooden box from the ground.

"Give me that box," Thelma Jewel shrilled. "I wanta see them. I wanta see them."

Liam pried the top off with his knife and tipped the box sideways. A tortoise shell head comb, a string of red and black glass beads, shredded baby shoes, a pair of rhinestone earrings, and a tarnished silver bracelet spilled out. A lacy handkerchief with Thelma Grace Claymore embroidered on it caught in the red velvet lining.

"My God," Thelma Jewel said. "Surely there's more. The treasure. Where's the rest of it? This can't be all."

Liam turned the box upside down. A small, ivory colored object that had been folded in the handkerchief spilled to the ground.

"A finger bone. There wasn't anything else in there but this goddamned rotten finger bone," he said.

"Well, I never," Thelma Jewel sat down on the bench hard, as if her legs had given way. "I remember Mrs. Bledsoe saying something about that," she mused. *Thelma Grace wanted her mama's diamond and ruby ring. It was on her finger. She cut her mama's finger off.*

Liam stiffened his body in an all-over stretch, then caught his breath. He pulled out his pocket watch and checked the time. "Four o'clock." The temperature was dropping and even though it was cool, his cheeks looked flushed; he brushed sweat from his face with the back of his hand.

An angry sound escaped Liam's tightened lips. "Lady," he said under his breath. "If I don't get some answers pretty soon, there'll be more dead people planted around here."

Thelma Jewel lifted her chin. *Be careful,* she warned herself. "There's a lot going on around here, Mr. McRae. I'd better be ready for most anything." For reassurance, her right hand slid down into her tapestry bag and closed around the mother-of-pearl inlay handle on the small derringer pistol she kept hidden in her purse. *Wait your turn. It's coming. That's what you're here for. But not now*, she admonished herself. *You need him.* Thelma Jewel looked up into the sky a moment, as if she expected to see some answers written in the clouds

Her thoughts were interrupted by Doot's feet crunching in the brittle grass. "I gotta go pee," he said. His hand crept down his pants leg as he stepped behind a tree.

As soon as he was out of earshot, a look of cunning passed over Thelma Jewel's face.

"Mr. Policeman. Let me have that box and that finger. I'm here to tell you something. That finger was cut off my grandmama Claymore's hand. I bet you a penny I can use it for something. My Aunt Thelma Grace. She'd do anything to get what she wanted."

Liam took a small stick, pushed the finger back into the handkerchief with his knife blade. He rolled them together and gave the handkerchief and finger to Thelma Jewel.

"Well, things don't always turn out like we think they should," he said angrily. "And I'm one for making my own destiny."

For some reason when Thelma Jewel took the small bundle in her hand, her heart raced. The ground seemed to tilt, her head began swimming, her legs felt shaky.

Thelma Jewel's eyes burned; she shut them. She clasped the handkerchief to her breasts and when she did she could swear the bone throbbed like a fast beating pulse. The handkerchief began moving up and down, the finger rubbing her chest. She had a hard time breathing.

She heard a soft whisper, "Let them know you're here." Then, everything went still. The throbbing stopped.

"What the hell's going on?" Liam asked. "You were talking to yourself. Swaying your body back and forth like you were dodging bullets."

She shook her head and opened her eyes. She could have sworn she saw a gauzy green skirt gyrating just across the way but when she looked closer it was only bushes flowing in the March breeze. For a second she didn't remember where she was or what had happened. Nothing looked familiar.

She heard the faint words, "I did what I had to. Now, let them know you're here." Thelma Jewel felt weak all over. Her thoughts rolled around in her head like an unfinished sentence. Then she realized where she was.

The finger seemed to spasm, then it went still.

"What's wrong with you?" Liam asked

"A rabbit ran over my grave." Tenderly she raised the handkerchief and pressed it against the side of her cheek, then carefully set it into her purse.

Liam rubbed his chin as if it itched. "I'm not sure where this is heading."

"Me neither." She blinked her eyes hard, afraid if she shut them she might be in another place. "But I've got me some ideas. " *Keep that finger bone.*

Now she felt stronger. In control again. She shoved one foot forward, and when she did she stubbed her toe on the tombstone. On the name **THELMA.**

The sharp pain that ran up her was a sign to her.

"I'll take me a piece of that tombstone there. The part that broke off and says, 'Thelma.' You can still read it. I might have me a family calling card here." She paused a moment and nodded her head as if she had come to an agreement of some kind.

"I want somebody to deliver it. Not sure exactly when, where, or who. But I have some ideas. I might even want it tonight or tomorrow. What I'm going to do, they need to mull over it for a few days," Thelma Jewel said. "Before that Brush Arbor Meeting on Sunday."

Liam pointed toward Doot, who had stepped from behind the tree. "If you need anything done, Mudge said that for a little money, he'll take care of whatever you want."

Struggling to pull his overall straps up Doot shuffled over to them.

The shadows had thickened. By now it was nearly sunset. Liam's red hair stood out like a halo against a backdrop of the setting sun. "You're no saint," Thelma Jewel whispered, taking comfort from her hidden pistol and the finger bone in her purse.

"What?" Not sure what she'd said, but not liking the tone of her voice, Liam glared at her.

"Nothing." Thelma Jewel tilted her head sideways. "I was just nattering. You might want to just go on back to Boston," she said in a soft voice. "Bad things might be happening."

"No. There's more I need to do here." Liam leaned down, lifted the pick axe and slung it over his shoulder. "Unfinished business to take care of."

Their gazes locked for a moment.

I'd like to kill two birds with one stone, he thought. "I've got plans." *Maybe I can set it up so Dale kills his old man.* "Sweet revenge…it'll taste better on my lips than milk and honey." He raised one eyebrow. "I believe in speaking my mind. I'll kill to get what I want," he said, an implied threat in his voice. *You won't ever know her. But to get to you, I took care of a little Irish maid, Elnora. I can do it again.*

Thelma Jewel felt the impact of Liam's evil, something she was familiar with. "I won't make any trouble, Mr. Liam."

But I'm on to you, she cautioned herself. *You're a killer I can tell. Bet you killed that dumb Elnora, but you never knew she called me herself and had her eye on you. Fool. I'm no fool. If I have to, I'll get you first. I'm smarter than you. I'm a Redemption Ridge Claymore.*

The finger spasmed. Then went still. *Do what you have to. Look what I did.*

She peeped in, then folded open the handkerchief. The finger, was now nothing but dust.

But her namesake, Thelma Jewel had made her presence known. And now, she was ready to make hers known.

CHAPTER 29

**Two bodies huddled around
the old well;
reminiscent of
a pagan ceremony
from the ancestral country,
their cells caught
fire in the sunlight.
Several ghosts appeared
in Memory's second sight,
warning her of a malevolent
presence.
Two lovers fled like the tide of
Old Religion.**

Sunday afternoon, March 28

After they returned from Vicksburg, Trestle Potter dropped Dale and Laura Lee at the Dry Creek Presbyterian Church. The plans were that Dale would pick up Jenson's family car while Trestle drove Jenson and Memory to Redemption Ridge. After Dale visited with Laura Lee for a while, he would go home and leave Jenson's motorcar for him to drive back to town.

When Dale and Laura Lee sank down onto the porch swing, there were a few black-fringed shadows in the yard. "I can't wait until we leave for Oxford on Tuesday," said Laura Lee.

"Me either." He interlaced his finger with hers. "I look forward to being with you. *Forever? I wish.*

A comforting quiet between them was broken only by the gentle rasp of the swing chains. "Undying friendship," she said. "Why don't we start again by sharing our dreams?"

"I've never stopped dreaming of you, pretty lady," Dale said. "And for me. It wasn't just friendship."

"Me either," she whispered. "I prayed for you. For us. Every night."

He pulled her closer, raised her face to his. Her lips were moist, soft. Dale's heart pulsed in a machine-gun staccato.

"Undying friendship," he whispered. "In some ways it's akin to marriage."

As they lazily rocked back and forth snuggling under an afghan throw, the shadows slowly stretched then faded, as a bronze sun sank beneath a blanket of clouds.

***

A set look on his face, Trestle pulled the hearse up in front of the Claymore home. He was on a mission now since he had heard Jenson mention to Memory about the two of them going to the old well. Trestle opened the door for Memory and Jenson, then he backed the car away and drove to Lamont's yard. He turned off the motor and went around back of the Randall house. According to a pre-arranged plan with Lamont, a tied-up mule waited for him to ride back to his family house built in the trees along the riverbank. "You gonna have to wait on me a while fer that there ride back, Mr. Mule," Trestle said. "Driving them peoples over to Vicksburg, I heerd what they had in mind." Doubling his fist, he punched the mule's side, the animal wheezed and cut out a large fart. "I heisted myself on out here after I let them folks off. I got me some bidness to tend to 'round here."

Smiling to himself he climbed the fence onto the Claymore property and eased on around to the well. Trestle lit a match, stood on tiptoe and leaned over. He looked down but he couldn't see anything. An oak bucket sat on the side of the well. He shoved it forward; the handle spun wildly. When the water splashed, Trestle waited a minute, then he turned the handle. Once the bucket was raised he lit another match, then he smiled. "Goldarn it," he said. "First cast, an' I catched me something."

He spilled what was in the bucket onto the ground. "Only thang what's in there is part of your britches." Again he struck a match, spit on his finger and moved scraps of fabric around. "But looky here. Got them false toothies of your'n. What looks like a fanger bone, an' either part of a dead fish or one of yer eyes.

Goldarn that wench. I'll see to you an' scare the BeJesus out'n her." He harked and spit. "An' I'll git Dedmon. Yer my brother, Shank. A eye fer a eye. You gonna eat him up with those toothies. I'm gonna see to it."

Trestle moved closer to the barn and slid to the ground. From his position behind a pile of thick brush he had a good view of the well. He carefully set the coveralls and a small, creamy jellied chunk and a jagged row of false teeth into a cupping he had made with leafy branches. He pulled a greasy paper sack from a tattered jacket pocket and lifted out a pickled pig's foot. "I'm here to tell you. That air Claymore bitch is gonna be coming soon. An' I'm ready fer her." He sucked the tangy meat and with his teeth nubbins gnawed the pig's bones. Contented, he fell asleep.

***

At the house Memory cleaned up their late evening snacks, closed the kitchen icebox, and wiped the table. Jenson eased up behind her. His arms curled her waist, he rested his chin on her shoulder. "I saw a blanket on the porch. In case we get cold, let's pick it up, go on out to the well and confront your demons," he said teasingly.

"With your help, I'll bury those devils." Memory stepped back, lifted a creamy knit shawl draped across a chair and wrapped it around her shoulders. She felt warm and secure, but when they stepped outside a sharp wind brought tears to her eyes. A sense of foreboding took over and the nearer she and Jenson drew to the well, the stronger the feeling became. The sultry air smelled of stagnant well water. She shivered and pulled her shawl closer. It wasn't the wind making her shake, but fear, an emotion she was not used to.

"We've been here before," Jenson said when they got to the well.

Trestle stopped in mid-snore. He heard voices. Careful to make no noise, he checked the shredded pants that held the false teeth, and what could have been a slimy eyeball to make sure they were in place. Done, his hand patted the pistol in his coveralls, ready for whatever might happen.

"We have some real changes working in our lives," Jenson said. "Dale going to Oxford with Otis and Laura Lee." He sucked in a breath. "I expect something to come of that.

"And then, there's us."

Jenson spread the blanket he'd brought with him and then took the box from his pocket. His hands held to one side so that Memory couldn't see what he was doing, carefully, he eased out a small diamond engagement ring that was set in a gold, heart shaped mounting and slid it onto his little finger. "You're so beautiful." He pulled Memory close. "I want to spend the rest of my life with you."

"I haven't been a widow very long," Memory said. "We'd be breaking the rules."

Jenson put a finger to her lips. "To me, it's as if you were never married."

"I wasn't. Not really." She pressed her hand against her heart. "You've always been here. I just didn't know what to name you."

"Let's start over," Jenson whispered. "Forget everything that's ever happened to either one of us." It was as if he sensed the night would not turn out the way he wanted it to unless he headed off bad memories. "I'm of the old school. Before we go too far," he slid the ring from his finger.

"Give me your hand, pretty lady."

"Do you have something for me?"

"How did you know?"

"Like my mama, I've been told a few times I have 'the sight'," she said softly.

He raised her hand to his mouth, kissed the ring, then slid it onto her finger. "I, Jenson, will take thee—"

"Mrs. Jenson Cooper," Memory said. "What a lovely sound."

Jenson closed his mouth against Memory's, stopping any more words.

Her shawl fell to the ground. Slowly one by one, Jenson undid the buttons on her blouse and slipped it from her shoulders. She slid out of her skirt; he stepped out of his trousers.

"Forever," Jenson said. "Mine forever."

He and Memory stretched out on the blanket facing each other. Memory parted her legs, wrapped her left leg across his thigh. Jenson's hands stroked her breasts.

An intense longing surged through her; she was in a world she had never known. One she didn't even know existed. "Thornton. Never like this," she breathed.

She unbuttoned his shirt.

Neither of them heard the slight rustle and crush of dead grass and leaves as Trestle shifted his weight. "Watch this here that's gonna happen, brother," he whispered. "An' if he sticks it into her, I'm gonna kill her."

The air suddenly felt oppressive, a cold wind brushed Memory's body. She stiffened, and raised her head. She moved her leg and pushed up on her elbows. An uncomfortable feeling swept over her. Her heart hammered so hard she could hardly breathe. It felt as if something or somebody watched them.

Anticipation? Fear? Do restless spirits hover nearby? She shook her head. Enough had happened around this old well to entice them to stay. *No. No. I'm here with Jenson. Where I want to be. Exorcising my demons.*

As soon as that thought crossed her mind, she smelled a fetid odor. Rotten fish. *Are there rotten fish in the well?* She took a slow, deep breath. A tremor passed through her.

Memory pushed Jenson away. "I don't like the way it feels around here. I smell something evil." She sat up. "I feel like I'm sitting on the edge of that old well and about to be pushed in."

Close to Lamont's land, she saw flickering movements that slowly seemed to come together.

"Leave. Go."

Memory heard the words as clearly as if they had been the warning blast of a nearby train whistle

The shape toward Lamont's house slowly changed into a human form, a face.

"Now."

The lips moved slowly, like someone just waking from a dream. "Now."

Memory's ears rang. Although echoes of old evil whispered through the trees, something in the slow, undulating shape she saw made her feel as if she were being protected.

She made out an outstretched hand moving, the palm turned toward her, brushing her away, beckoning her to leave.

"If we stay here, bad things will happen," she said, her resolve to leave strengthening.

"Is this your sixth sense? "

Memory twisted away.

The hand waved faster, the face became clearer, and now she saw the image of someone who looked like Lamont and Bertha's daughter, an older, larger, Sassy.

"Leave."

Vernell, Memory thought. "We have to go. Someone's watching out for us. Near the fence. It's like they're waving us away." She grabbed her blouse and shawl. "She's telling us to leave."

"She? Who?"

"We just have to get away from here."

The form began to fade, like someone seen in a dream. When awakening, they're gone and you're not sure who they were.

To Memory's relief Jenson didn't try to convince her otherwise. They both stood and slid into their clothes. In her hurry, Memory stumbled over the blanket but managed not to fall. Jenson reached for her. Hand in hand, they ran through the back pasture toward the safety of the old family home.

As soon as they left, Trestle grabbed a small branch and pulled himself up.

"Goldarn," he panted, peeling his overall straps down. "I'd akilt her if he had stuck it into her." He spread his legs. "I'd akilt her dead. The both of 'em."

He lifted his flaccid penis toward the false teeth and what could have been either Shanks eyeball or part of a fish's guts. "Looky here. This here's from me to you, Shank." He cradled his now erect penis. He fell across the blanket trailing his nose along the spot where Memory's body had been, hunching himself up and down. Up and down. "Ahh,'" he yelled, spilling his semen onto the blanket.

Spent, he got up and stepped into his clothes. He pulled out his gun. "Bam, bam," he said. "I'd akilt you if he'd a had you, Miz Von Dieter." Carefully he picked up the ragged coveralls holding what could have been his brother's remains. "This here place's holy. This here's where my brother was kilt."

***

It was sometime after ten when Laura Lee's mother flipped the light on and off, a not-so-gentle hint that it was past time for Dale to go home.

Dale was relieved Jenson had told him he could use his old family motorcar. He would leave the car out front of his house when he got to Redemption Ridge, and Jenson would drive it on home.

After he left Laura Lee's, once Dale turned onto Old Farm Road, he was more relaxed than he had been for months. His thoughts turned back through the summers he had spent in Mississippi. To what Laura Lee had meant to him. The pedestal he had put her on. *And why did I?* he wondered. "It's time for me to reach up and lift her down."

Suddenly, in the glare of his headlights, he saw someone weaving off to the side. Dale slammed on the brakes and shoved the door open. He sprang from the car and wrapped his arms around Topper, just before he crumpled.

"What's happened?"

"Mist Dedmon," Topper whispered.

But even before he asked, Dale knew it had to do with Dedmon. He'd played a part in this when he told Dedmon he wouldn't use Topper anymore. He remembered that Dedmon had said his son-in-law, Passel Skinotes, would also be taking care of his business.

"Let's go." Dale slid his arms under Topper. "I'll get you home."

It wasn't long before the outline of the Randall house, usually surrounded by an aura of warmth and comfort, now stood out bleak and lonesome looking.

"You're home." Dale reached into the back of the motorcar. He grabbed Topper's ankles, gently pulled him forward and slung him across his shoulders. "I'm sick and tired of feeling weary. Of bringing heartache to people around me." He carried Topper through the yard, up the porch steps and laid him across a swing. He pounded the door with his fist. After a few minutes the front door swung open. Minyard stepped out, but didn't appear to be surprised.

Dale gestured toward Topper. "Do you need help getting him in?"

"No. I can handle it just fine."

"He's been to Lucius Dedmon's place," Dale said.

"Mist Dale. My daddy and my mama are right scared for Topper. Around these parts, we don't call that man, Lucius. We calls him, Lucifer," Minyard said.

After Dale left Topper he stopped Jenson's car at the edge of their driveway and as he had said he would, made sure to leave the keys where Jenson would see them.

Silvery moonlight washed across the front yard as Dale climbed the porch steps. He stopped to catch his breath, went upstairs and, without taking off his clothes, fell into bed.

He crossed his hands behind his head. It took some effort but he washed Dedmon and Topper from his mind and allowed himself to think about Laura Lee. How her inner beauty showed in her grayish-blue eyes. He not only allowed himself to think about Laura Lee, he cherished thinking about her. How the soft curve of her lips felt against his. How just a short while ago he had held her tight, his hands gripping her body to his.

"Ohh," she had whispered as he pressed their bodies together. "I've dreamed of this. For so long. I've waited. Kept myself pure for you."

"There's nothing like a southern girl," he whispered, half to himself, half to her.

Remembering the soft swell of her breasts in his hands, how her lips tasted on his, he sought his own release. He finally drifted off to sleep.

***

It had been a long day for Brucie. After a full afternoon of visiting with several of their friends, and a light supper at Sophie's house, she was secretly thankful when her hostess suggested they go to bed. "We'll have a heavy day of shopping tomorrow," Sophie said. "You have a lot of things to take care of and to look for." Worn out, Brucie had agreed and told her friend Sophie good night.

She breathed a sigh of relief when she lay down on the bed and pulled up the covers.

Sometime during the night, she jumped awake.

"Saved."

The word rang in her ears. Brucie sat on the side of the bed.

"Saved. Our girl."

A voice from long ago.

Vernell.

Brucie grasped the cross around her neck. "Thank you, God. I don't know how, but whatever was happening, they heard Vernell."

Brucie dropped to her knees. "Memory could have been killed."

Exhausted, she climbed back into bed and pulled the covers up. *All I have to worry about now is her and Jenson Cooper.*

Brucie heard a soft voice whispering.

"It's gone be all right, Miss Brucie. It's in the hands of the good Lord. Miss Memory and Mr. Cooper. They gone be together. Have faith. Them two. It's meant to be. He'll take care of our girl."

Brucie spread her hands and raised up. *An angel sang Memory away and saved her tonight. Jenson was there.*

Why? Why haven't I really seen? Jenson. He'll take care of her, she thought.

"Mrs. Jenson Cooper," she said. "The name has a really nice sound. A name that should be."

Drained, Brucie fell into a deep sleep.

CHAPTER 30

Sassy's mellifluous voice
Poured about the edges of the room,
Curls as dense as curdled sun.

Her coffee served as a warm reminder,
She had to help.

Monday morning, around 6:00 a.m., March 29

It was still dark when Memory awoke. She hadn't slept well. Then, she felt the ring. "I'm on top of the world." She lit a kerosene lamp, and careful not to make any noise, sponged off and dusted herself with magnolia scented bath power. She slipped into a navy gathered skirt and buttoned her long-sleeved white cotton blouse. The grandfather clock in the hall pounded out six times as she eased downstairs.

The light was on in the kitchen, and out of the corner of her eye she saw Lamont's daughter, Sassy, pouring coffee. "I guess you and I are the first ones up. This is going to be a wonderful day."

She did a gleeful turn, made a brief curtsy, pushed open the dining room door and sat down at the table. "I have some things I need and that I want to do." She spoke loudly, so Sassy could hear her. "If we're going to be living in this hot paradise, I need some light-weight clothes." *And as of last night, a wedding dress. Soon.* For just a moment, she shivered, remembering that other forces seemed to be at work, here at Redemption Ridge. A curtain of danger had been poised to drop over her and Jenson last night. Then, it was if someone raised a corner of the curtain and called to her. Nudged her to leave, to flee for her life. She shook her head, flinging her thick auburn tresses from side to side as if she were slinging unwelcome thoughts through the door.

"No matter," she said. "I'm engaged." She put her ring to her mouth, then took it down.

286

Sassy set a cup and saucer from the sideboard on the table.

"You're up and out early, Sassy," Memory said.

"That's the way I has to live my life."

"I'll be busy too. A friend of Laura Lee's and I are going into Jackson, probably tomorrow to look at patterns and dress fabrics. If I had my druthers, I'd maybe even catch a train to Memphis," she said, even though she'd been married to Thornton, once again imagining herself in a lacy wedding dress. "When you're dependent on other people for transportation you have to take what you can get and be grateful for it." She held her ring up to the light. "And when Father comes in Friday, I don't care what he says. I know you don't have any idea what I'm talking about, but I just had to tell somebody my good news. I'm going to marry Jenson," she sing-songed. "I'm going to marry Jenson."

There was no answer. Memory sensed either a deep unhappiness or a deep resentment between them. She couldn't tell which, but as she usually did, she reacted, not always in a good way. And this was one of those times.

She pointed to the coffee pot. "I hope it's good and hot. It was about half cold, yesterday. I could hardly drink it."

There was no answer.

"Did you hear me?"

Sassy cut her chestnut-colored eyes at Memory in a sideways look, moved to the table and poured a cup of steaming coffee. "Uh-huh."

Memory detected resentment in Sassy's voice. She flicked her hair back behind her ears. "It's not' uh-huh'. It's 'yes ma'am,'" she countered. She stirred in cream and sugar and took a sip. "By the way, it's hot enough, but it could stand to be stronger."

Sassy kicked open the door to the kitchen.

"Okay, okay," Memory said. "I'm sorry." She pushed her chair back. "But, nothing's going to take away from what I'm feeling on this day." She walked into the hall, lifted her gray gabardine jacket from the coat rack, draped it around her shoulders and went back into the dining room. Her saucer was still on the table but the coffee cup had been moved. A small piece of paper was in the saucer.

"Help."

This time Memory kicked the kitchen door open.

"Sassy," she called.

Her face tight with despair, Sassy leaned against the opening to the pantry. She laid both hands against her forehead, closed her eyes and raised her head.

> "My Lord, He calls me,
> He calls me by the thunder;
> The trumpet sounds within my soul,
> I ain't got long to stay here.
> Steal away, steal away,
> Steal away to Jesus!
> Steal away, steal away home,
> I ain't got long to stay here."

Memory spread her hands on the kitchen table and braced herself. "My God," she breathed. "I've heard the finest. The most talented. Never, never, a voice like this. My God, Sassy," she said again. "The world. The world needs to hear you."

She placed the scrap of paper on which Sassy had written the word "*Help*" over her heart.

It was as if the two of them were really seeing each other for the first time. Sassy locked eyes with Memory.

Memory looked away first. *I must do something. She needs help.*

She set the paper on the kitchen table and tapped it with her fingers. *Sassy looks like she's standing outside a room, waiting for someone to open a door and let her in.* "What can I do? Your talent needs to be shared with the world."

"Just help me." Sassy rocked to and fro. "'The trumpet sounds within my soul, I ain't got long to stay here.'" She raised her hands then dropped them to her sides, as if she were letting loose of something dear to her. "All I wants is to go to school. To sing. To learn." She reached over, wadded the scrap of paper, and threw it on the floor. "My father. He wants us to have good clothes. He'll give us some land on the place when we get married. Help us build us a house, in the shadow of his."

Her eyes closed, her face upturned, Sassy bit her lip. "I see you writing. I wants to write. My feelings. My family's story. Most of all, I wants to sing. I wants to write our story. I wants to sing our life. How it was. How it is."

Her feelings and her dilemma were a revelation to Memory. She had never allowed herself to think about colored people, but it only took her a moment, and she recognized what she had been offered in so many ways and what, through her own foolish choices, both in Boston and here in Mississippi, she had thrown out like waste from a slop jar. The choices she'd had that had never been offered to Sassy. The air between them was like the moment right before you say your prayers. The thought, *Do I confess all?* even ran through her mind.

Memory detected resentment in Sassy's voice.

"My daddy, he sees to it I can read and write. And do numbers. But come planting time, that's the end of it. That's about here. And that'll be the end of it." The girl's tone said, *Look at me. Listen to me.*

"That's not all what I want," Sassy went on. "What I want, I won't get none of it here at Redemption Ridge."

Memory was troubled. *I'm hearing Sassy's dreams.* Even though she personally had done nothing to thwart Sassy's hopes, her face flushed with a wash of shame for what she had failed to see. She was touched by guilt and compassion, but she also knew she couldn't sweep away all the loneliness and right all the wrongs in the world. But, maybe just maybe, they could start somewhere. *No, she could start somewhere.* She bent over and picked up the crinkled paper. "May I keep this?"

"Yes, ma'am."

Sassy needs help. A voice echoed. It seemed as if there were a presence in the house, as if another being had spoken to her. Whatever the spirit was, it seemed to be holding its breath, waiting for her answer. In an instant, from somewhere in the back recesses of her mind, she remembered hearing talk from Laura Lee about a school for the colored.

"There should be a place." Memory's fingers curled around the edge of the kitchen table.

"Have you ever heard of Cedar Woods?" she asked.

"No'm."

"I probably can't get in touch with Mr. Cooper right now. He and Mr. Dale are having a service at the cemetery later this morning for their fallen comrade, Samuel Stanton." Memory set her mouth and twisted her engagement ring. "I had a ride and a place to stay in Jackson, but my shopping program has changed. I'll hire me a driver there to get where I need to. I'm going to get this taken care of as quick as I can. Before Father"—Memory cleared her throat—"Mr. Von Dieter comes in."

Her mind made up, she laid her hand on the girl's thin shoulder, gave her a reassuring squeeze, then went into the living room. She sat in front of the desk, picked up the pen, opened her journal and began writing.

Dear Journal. Well, today I'm moving in a different direction. Doing something I never dreamed of.

Out in the front yard, a mockingbird burst into a shrill song as if he were full of questions.

Pale saffron early morning sun slipped through the living room windows as it slowly eased over the hills of Redemption Ridge. But if Memory had looked, dark shadows hung in the corners of the room.

CHAPTER 31

**Dale travels through a mined
Mindscape on a
Friends commandeered legs.**

**Behind him is a frothing
Platoon of souls.
Remembering home as a
New death.**

**Before him are the green
Trees of Redemption Ridge
Wild, withered headstones
That have escaped their
Dimensions**

Monday morning, early, March 29

A rooster out back of the barn announced a new day. Dale checked the time. Six o'clock. He yawned, turned over and buried his face into a pillow. Sometime later, he heard voices downstairs and smelled bacon frying. *Either Sassy or Bertha's here,* he realized. He forced his eyes open and once again, checked his watch. After seven. "More shuteye. Mother's in town with friends. Not meeting at the cemetery 'til right after lunch."

Once again Dale fell into a deep sleep.

***

He woke some several hours later from a troubling dream. He had a little over an hour before he planned to meet Jenson at the cemetery.

He sprang from the bed, shaved and sponged himself off from a basin in his room. He snatched his clothes from a chair.

"I'll dress, eat some bacon and be off." He opened the armoire. Immediately a strong odor almost overwhelmed him, a familiar fragrance he had smelled for years. A Bible lay on a shelf by itself, the aroma seeping from it could have been apricots, simmering on an open stove.

"Oh. Sweet olive."

His memory was sparked. "Coming from this Bible. It has to be the Bible Cousin Sarah told us about. Full of family secrets," he mused.

He thought about that day back in Boston before he went to war when Cousin Sarah had told Memory and him some disturbing family history and secrets she felt they needed to know. Proof of the same would be at Redemption Ridge Ridge in a Bible, she had said.

"This has got to be it. I was supposed to find it." Dale said, lifting the book. The cover had the slightly mottled feeling of an old person's skin. He noticed a thickening of the back page and slid his fingers along the inside edge. He felt a ridge, where the last page and the back cover had been pasted together. Old glue had loosened. He eased his fingers under it. A small bundle of yellowed papers slid out. Dale picked them up and carefully spread the first page open.

"I, Sheriff Homer Bramlett, have hidden this epistle in the back of the Claymore family Bible. For the time being, this Holy Book and this missive will be in the hands of a trusted friend, Miss Sarah Bowman. When I deem the time to be appropriate, I will so inform her to read the true story of what happened to Vernell, and the fortune in jewels. For all time, I will set the record straight on Captain Bruce Claymore.

Traitor? No. Hero. Yes!

Now, as God above is my witness, Captain Bruce Claymore of the Confederate Army did not abscond with nor steal those valuable stones. The tide of battle had turned. Not even a flea on the underside of a dog's belly could have gotten out of Tallouga County, to the Port of Orleans to purchase more arms and ammunition. The Yankees had overrun our countryside.

Bruce Claymore had given the jewels to Vernell for safekeeping. I know whereof I speak. Here in my office, I have held some of their weight between these, my very fingers.

At Vernell's demise, I, Sheriff Homer Bramlett, saw to it that most of the treasure was buried with her—some small part passed on to her father, Old Top, for a new church and to me, Sheriff Bramlett, for a new jail.

W. C. Claymore, known throughout this county as Daddy Claymore, killed his half-brother, Captain Bruce Claymore for jewels to be used for the Confederacy.

But did C.W. murder the Captain only for the worldly wealth he hoped to gain? Could revenge have also been in play? Bruce Claymore, and Brucie's mother, C.W.'s wife, Charlotte Caroline Tisdale, loved each other. To most of the town of Franklin this liaison was never known as fact, but daughter Brucie was born of that illicit love.

C.W. may have suspected this, and hatred may have festered in his breast. He was known throughout the county to be a dangerous and mean-spirited man. Himself, of unacknowledged parentage.

The one reason why I, Sheriff Homer Bramlett, an honest man, have not stepped forward at this moment in time is to protect those who are still living. In the meantime, Tallouga County harbors lies.

But, oh, how I wish these truths could be known now, in this, the year of our Lord, 1877. That Vernell Randall, beloved mother of Lamont was hung for the murder of Thelma Grace Claymore.

A murder Vernell did not commit. I have a signed confession below from the perpetrator of two heinous acts.

Dale remembered that Jenson had told him, that the Potter's had a long memory and a rabid thirst for revenge. When Vernell was hanged, the sheriff had made one of the lying Potter boys eat mouthfuls of mud in front of the whole town until the boy spoke the truth. For some months the Potters' desire for revenge festered like an unlanced boil in the summer heat. The inbred, treehouse Potter family were known for their vengeful ways. They bided their time, and then they struck. Jenson's grandfather, Sheriff Homer Bramlett, had died a horrible death. He had been tied and gagged at the edge of town, then carried to the Big Black creek bank and shot in both legs. The Sheriff's fingers were broken, spread apart and bound so that they formed a half circle. His fingers were held in place by sticks and nails that had been jammed into his hand. Each hand held a large clump of wet clay and his arms and hands were chained to his face. Mud dribbled from the Sheriff's mouth, down his neck and chest. He choked and suffocated on the muddy mass crammed into his mouth. "Payback," was written in black paint across his bare chest.

Dale realized that this message from Sheriff Bramlett had been a secret for over forty years.

He raised the other attached pages but set them down. "Enough for now."

"Read, now," he could swear a voice said.

"Later," he said. He laid the Bible on his bed and shook his head. His jaw slack, his heart thundering like a herd of runaway horses, he carefully slid the papers back into their hiding place and closed his eyes. Then in a minute he seemed to come to a decision and nodded his head. "Okay. I got your message from those long-gone days. But the rest can wait," he said. "What's in here, I'll worry about later. I have to bury my friend now. Father's coming this weekend. I need to get my head on straight. Before I can read any more of this and know what, if anything, I should do."

Dale put the Bible into his haversack. "I will read from you today at my friend's burial," he said, bounding down the steps.

He made himself a biscuit and bacon sandwich, and drank a glass of cold buttermilk. "Mississippi treats," he said. "In Boston, we'd toss this into the garbage." When he stepped outside, a chill was in the air. It was a slightly cloudy March day, the time of year when Mississippi weather can suddenly change. As Dale walked through the yard, he heard the clopping of horse's hooves and saw Minyard cantering toward him on a bay mare.

"Whoa, Nell." Minyard sawed the reins, wrapped them around the saddle horn and dismounted. "What's going on, Mist Dale?"

"I'm heading toward the cemetery. A small ceremony for my friend, Samuel Stanton."

"Topper, he ain't doing too well. Thanks for bringing him home, Mist Dale. He's his own worst enemy."

"Just like me," Dale almost said, but caught himself at the last minute.

"You wanna hitch a ride?" Minyard rubbed his horse's withers.

"I'll ride as far as your place. Then I'll walk on the rest of the way. I'm ahead of time. I need to do a little thinking."

Minyard grabbed the saddle horn and mounted the mare. Dale slung the haversack over his shoulder, walked around to the left side of the horse, gripped the back of the saddle. He slid a foot into the dangling stirrup Minyard had left for him, and swung himself up. The horse blew out a deep whoosh of breath, then clamped down on the bit in her mouth as if she were rearranging it.

Sitting tall and straight in the saddle, when Dale was settled, Minyard gigged the horse's flank with his heels. Dale grasped Minyard's waist as the horse bounded forward then settled into a loping canter, *Topper, Topper*, rang in his ears, each downbeat of his thoughts hitting the downbeat of the horse's pounding hooves. Dale didn't know if he was upset with himself or if it was a bitey breeze burning his eyes and causing tears to form.

Soon they were at the far edge of the Randall property. Minyard pulled back on the reins and stopped. Dale swung one leg over the horse's rump, gripped the edge of the saddle and slid down.

His eyes met Minyard's. His haversack suddenly felt heavy. *The Bible.* "It's time for Topper and me both to make some changes."

"Lessen the devil jumps back up onto him, I think he wants to be done with whatever business he and Lucius Dedmon was into. When you brought him home all beat up on, it musta made a chink in that hard head of his'n." Minyard bit his bottom lip. "But that Mist Dedmon, he's dangerous."

He paused a minute, then he went on. "A short while ago Mist Dedmon sent somebody around to tell Topper he owed him some money and he wants to see him. He's gonna make Topper pay, in more ways than one. My daddy, he says, none of that's gonna happen."

Minyard's voice was filled with anger. "Come this weekend, my daddy and me are going over to Mist Dedmon's to get a few things straight. Most everybody's scared of him, but not my daddy. He's going to tell him not to come around none of us Randalls again."

Dale rocked back on his heels as if he'd come to a decision about something.

"If I can, I'd like to go with you when you see Dedmon." Dale looked away from Minyard and said softly, "I've some things to make up for." *Only thing. Don't know what'll happen when my father comes in this weekend. Or if I'll even be here, or anywhere else on God's green earth for that matter.*

Dale touched two fingers to his head. "I'll see you and Lamont later."

He had just enough of his syrup left to last through the weekend. *I won't let myself need much in Oxford. When I get back, I hear I might be able to pick up some around Vicksburg or Summit County.*

He began a slow jog toward the cemetery. For some reason the gravel seemed thick and rough when he passed the black burial grounds, and noises from his feet sounded like someone was running close behind him, step for step. Slowing down, he glanced over his shoulder. *Nothing.* Then, for a split second Dale could swear he saw a long shadow stretching behind him. He stopped and turned. He saw no one, but he felt a presence. "Shadow you won't catch me. And if you're wanting something out of me, it won't happen."

Way off toward the back, and close to the white cemetery, it seemed as if he heard a faint voice saying, *Avenge me.* Dale

shivered. "Whatever or whoever you are, I'm leaving you behind."
He began running.

Up ahead, he saw a motorcar and Jenson leaning against the
gate, waiting for him.

Home. I'm home.   Again, he could have sworn he heard
someone speak; this time a different voice. *Samuel,* he wondered.
"You're imagining things."

Dale broke into a fast sprint. Winded, he made it to where his
friend stood. "Well, old buddy. My sister. Did you?" he managed
to ask.

"I never thought I'd see the day." Jenson's face spread in a slow
grin. "She took it."

"I had no doubt. I've seen it in her face." Dale gave him a half
salute. "Not just for months, but for years." He smiled. "Soon. My
brother-in-law."

"And my best man. Let's shake on it." Jenson reached out his
hand.

Dale pushed Jenson's hand aside and engulfed him in a hug.
"You've always been more like my brother," he said. "Especially
over there in France." He slapped Jenson on the back, then stepped
away. "I guess we'd better get to the business at hand."

Jenson nodded. He pointed to two shovels leaning against a
post. "I like your idea to go ahead and bury Samuel and spare Otis
and Laura Lee some pain.

"I've got his remains over there in the car. In that pine box I
told you about last night. It's on the back seat."

They each grabbed a shovel and went to the Stanton family
plot. In just a short while, with both of them digging, they had the
site to hold Samuel's remains scooped out.

"You carry our friend," Jenson said

When Dale opened the car door and saw the pine coffin, only
about the size to hold a child, he was overcome with emotion. "Oh,
Buddy," he said. "I promised. This is the best Jenson and I could
do. I wish I could have done more." Tears rolled down his cheeks
as he slid both arms under the box, lifted it, and carefully carried
it to the cemetery.

"Let yours be the last arms that hold him," Jenson said.

He picked up one end, while Dale held the other. They carefully placed the casket into the ground and covered it. They left a small pile of dirt nearby in case Otis and Laura Lee wanted to put more on top when they got there.

"Well, we're ready," Jenson had hardly uttered these words when they saw a cloud of dust coming down Old Farm Road. "Our timing's just right," he said as the car holding Otis and Laura Lee pulled to a stop. In a few minutes the two of them joined Dale and Jenson inside the fenced-in Stanton plot and the four of them gathered around the small, fresh mound of dirt. Dale took the Bible from his haversack, spread both hands and, careful not to let the papers fall from the slit in the back, let it fall open

He looked down. "The Holy Book opened to Job," he said. "We'll read from the seventh chapter of Job."

So am I made to possess months of misery
    And wearisome nights are appointed to me.
    When I lie down, I say
    When shall I arise and the night be gone?

Dale looked up, and then, skipping a few lines he read,
    For now I shall lie down in the dust.

"Samuel's night is over," he said. "He'll lie down at home now. And if he wants, he can rise and run across the hills and valleys of Redemption Ridge." He marked the place he had read from with a satin ribbon attached to the Bible. He pointed to the shovels. "Why don't we put a final covering from home over Samuel?" They each took their turn, scooping, then adding to the small mound over Samuel's grave.

"We'll close now with the Lord's prayer," Dale said. "And, Jenson, you and I will have finished what we started with our friend all those long months ago."

After they closed, tears streaming down her face, Laura Lee hugged Jenson and Dale. It was hard for Dale not to gather her into his arms, and soothe her tears, but he thought this was not the time or the place, so he held her close for a moment, as much for comfort for him as for her.

"Praise be to God that you could do this," Laura Lee whispered. "Oh, Dale and Jenson. Y'all have no idea what it means to our family. And I know, oh, I do know, that my brother will be at peace. He's home now." She slid her hand into Dale's as they walked away from the grave.

"Would you and Jenson like to go into town with Otis and me? As I told y'all, since Daddy died, Mother doesn't get out anymore. But she'd love to have you back at the house. Then we could have a real early dinner there. Or, we could go to Fly's Drugs and have a soda."

"Actually," Jenson said, "I'm a little pushed for time. I've got an appointment to see about a job."

"I have things I need to do too," Dale said. "There're some things at the place I need to see to." That really wasn't true. He just needed to be alone. "Give me a raincheck."

"That's fine," Laura Lee said. "Gentlemen. The Stantons are forever in your debt."

"You and Otis are more than repaying that debt by letting me ride to Oxford with you tomorrow afternoon. Maybe I can take you out again before too long, and you can repay a little of that debt in another way," Dale said, a half smile on his face.

"I'd love that. More than you know."

Dale gave Laura Lee a quick hug, and kissed her forehead. She stepped away. She and Otis waved goodbye, and walked to their car. "See you tomorrow," she called.

"If you want, I'll drive you on home, Dale," Jenson said. "I'm going to see your sister in a little while."

I'm not ready to go yet, Dale thought. "No, I'd rather walk," he answered. But even to him, his words sounded hollow, as if there were no truth or feeling behind them.

"Before you leave for Oxford," Jenson said, "I've spotted several acres of land close by for sale. The old Ferguson property, and it's cheap." He brushed his hair out of his eyes. "What about tomorrow morning? I can use my brother's motorcar. It might be something for us to look into."

"It'd have to be dirt cheap for the Von Dieters to consider it," Dale said. "I'm interested, but it'll have to be quick. Otis and I are going to Oxford, early tomorrow afternoon to see about getting back in school. And Laura Lee's riding with us."

Jenson raised his eyebrows. "Sounds like a good plan to me."

Dale extended his hand. Jenson took it, then slapped his friend on the back. "We're both moving on," he said, turning toward his car.

Dale waved goodbye as Jenson drove away, and then he walked back toward the Stanton burial plots. "Unfinished business," he said, glancing at the fresh mound of dirt. "That's what I'm feeling. Wish I'd been able to bring all of you back, Samuel. Not like this, in pieces. This is the best we could do though, friend."

CHAPTER 32

**Squeeze phosphene
From a poppy pod,
Ritual towards a
Caustic dream.**

**You see your mother's age
Suddenly your reflection breaking
When she shatters
Will your reflections break?**

Monday afternoon and night

After Dale had buried their comrade Samuel and his friends had left, he felt a strong need to stay in the cemetery a while longer. He went to the edge of the burial plot and snapped two small hanging tree limbs. Pulling off one of his shoe laces, he overlapped the branches and fashioned a crude cross. "There's so much missing, Samuel." For just a moment he forgot where he was. Dale stood at attention. "I heard no trumpet playing 'Taps,' no guns firing in your honor." His only reality, he was close to his friend, in a place they had explored together. "I'm sorry. You deserved more." He gave a snappy salute. "Here's to you, buddy."

He knelt and spun the cross down into the loose ground over Samuel's resting spot. Dale felt crumbly dirt, a few small stones under his knees and his cough syrup bottle pressing against his thigh. The past was still too much with him. He wasn't sure he wanted to get to his feet and go on with his life. He almost yearned to be back, not on this, a forgotten battlefield, but in France, to once again be with his troops and the best he could, protect them from harm. He found himself eaten up with guilt and with yearning for other chances in another time and place.

His heart beating a little faster, he shook his head. "Maybe I could have done it different. But I followed orders." He stood. He tamped the dirt down on Samuel's grave with his feet. "Enough. I guess that's it. I did all I could. Time to go."

He left the graves of one resting place, where he himself would probably someday be interred.

Dale stopped at the entrance to the colored side and took stock of what lay around him. The battlefield and cemetery. They were there, just like they'd always been. Taken for granted, like this state that he, in his heart, had always called home.

Since the turn of the century, most of the recent burials for coloreds and whites, were no longer on the battlefield, they were beside or behind churches. And now, the grounds of the Redemption Ridge Battlefield and Cemetery were not as well maintained as in the past. Even the once meticulously kept white side was sliding into disrepair.

Years ago, the white cemetery had been separated from the colored with a barbed-wire fence. It hadn't been long before some of the wooden posts had fallen, the barbed wire rusted. Even though most of the concrete markers and statues still stood, as if daring any enemy, even the elements, to harm them, tree roots and twisted vines had strangled many of the wooden crosses.

As they had for hundreds of years, live oaks reigned and seemed to have had their own temperamental way. Roots, thick and strong as railroad ties, had crept across and under sections of the ground, slanting markers, knocking others backwards, and even nudging caskets over sideways as if they were to be shunned, as intruders. A few of the smaller statues had fallen, crumbled and blended with the vines, dirt and weeds.

Shaded by a spread-limbed live oak on the border of the two cemeteries, Vernell's grave sat on a small rise close to the back, in a corner next to the white burial grounds. Only a few people knew this was also where Bruce Claymore, Daddy Claymore's half-brother, was buried. Captain Bruce Claymore, who many reviled and named as a traitor, the man rumored to have absconded with jewelry meant for the Tallouga County Confederates. In most of Bruce Claymore's family though, Captain Claymore was thought of as the unsung hero who fought courageously for his fellow soldiers. Known to the family, hoping to steal the Confederate fortune, Daddy Claymore had murdered his half-brother.

But the fact unknown to C.W. Claymore was that Captain Bruce had gotten the jewels to Vernell, and she had given them to Sheriff Bramlett for safe-keeping.

The truth had been well-hidden. Lamont and his grandfather, Old Top, had buried the treasure over forty years ago, at Vernell's feet. The secret fortune was to be used as Brucie Claymore and Vernell's son, Lamont, saw fit. This had been done.

Long ago some had gone to Sheriff Bramlett for a new jail and to Vernell's father, Old Top, for a new church in town. But that was graveyard talk.

When Brucie made her regular pilgrimage back home to Mississippi during the summers, Dale and Memory often visited this cemetery with their mother. More than once the old story about Bruce, the jewels and Daddy Claymore had been mentioned, and Brucie had always said, "When the time comes, the truth will out."

Very little had changed here for many years, and on this day, Dale had no trouble finding the mound where Vernell, Bruce, and Sunnie Flo, Lamont's long-dead twin sister, lay. Although Vernell's resting place was known to only a few, the site in the far back of the cemetery was marked by a wooden bench that sat across the top of the grave. The bench had been made out of the front door of the old house where Vernell, her father, and her two children had lived. The words, "He is arisen" were carved on the seat. At each end of the bench was a small armrest made of crutches belonging to Vernell's father.

Life wasn't kind to any of you. But, for as long as I can remember, I've heard good things about the way you all lived your lives.

After a short while Dale took out his cigarette case. He lit a cigarette and sucked deeply, as if it was his mother's breast and he was drawing solace and sustenance from it. His lungs burning, he choked and coughed, then lifted out his heroin cough syrup. The comfort he drew into his chest was stronger than his burning lungs.

"Do I want to come back to Redemption Ridge? Or return to Boston?" he mused. "Hanging around the waterfront pubs. Probably give in to despair. Stay with my thoughts of France."

Boston. Maybe reside in an insane asylum for the rest of my days? My nerves tingle, he thought. *When I breathe, my breath burns.*

He rocked back and forth.

What happened to justice and patriotism? he wondered. *Adulation of heroes? The war didn't turn out to be great and wonderful. No banners floating over the heads of its triumphant warriors. No.*

Shellshock? Yes.

Back here in the States, no one seems to care.

Instead of tootling horns, marching bands and confetti streamers, I can't get away from my thought-numbing realities. "The world is topsy-turvy."

Mottled green tongues, guts coiling on the ground, nostrils stinging as fiery tear gas slivers lungs away. Blood leaking from body holes. Digging men out before they smother in the mud. Not always making it. Friends and comrades left behind. He took a deep breath. *Rotting in unknown, unmarked soil. Perhaps to be next year's wheat crop of home baked bread. Served on wooden platters in French countrysides.*

Dale leaned over and dug in the dirt with his fingers. "I'm surrounded by my people in this soil. Not far away France. Good old Mississippi. Here at Redemption Ridge. It's all coming to a head." He let out a ragged, chest-burning sigh.

Do I look for heroes, demons or angels? Hovering spirits or, maybe, even gods? Or are you only old, dried corpses? Ghosts? Who knows?

Dale rose. "Now I'm here. At Redemption Ridge. Soon we'll be the past. The forgotten history."

His eyes dreamy, he gazed at the graves spread out before him. "All this happened a long time ago. How I'd love to hear some of your stories.

"When the gun's boomed, did you think of the shells falling, the body counts across the way?"

He looked toward the hidden site where Captain Bruce Claymore and Vernell were buried. "Or did you escape in dreams of peaceful, shady summers by Noble Creek?"

He tossed flecks of dust into the air and tilted his head toward the hidden spot that held the remains of Vernell and the Captain. "Sir, maybe even now I should clear your name. I'm out of causes. I just can't take on any more battles, though." Despairing, he desired more forgetfulness of the remains that lay in front of, and around, him here. Thoughts of what he had seen and lived through swirled through his head. He struggled to throw off feelings of failure that threatened to engulf him. He pulled out his whiskey flask, took several deep swallows, then rested his head against a tree and closed his eyes. A cool breeze with a tinge of moisture bathed Dale's face.

"Poetry. Mother, Memory, Me. All of us seem to have a yearning to be poets—writers. Maybe this is what I'm here for. In some way, to tell the story of Redemption Ridge. I could go back to Ole Miss. Finish my studies in English." He shook his head. "No. Von Dieter's coming in, and those are luxuries I can't claim or afford. And my sister's journal. It may well be, Memory will be the family historian."

I'll worry about my grandfather, Bruce Claymore, and old family stories later. I've got to make my way on around the next bend in the road before I can do anything for some disgraced ancestor, he thought.

Sleepy and tired though he was, he couldn't drift off; something he couldn't put his finger on disturbed him. He took another pull on a cigarette and tried to settle down. A sucking sound caught his ear. Then he heard movements nearby, near to Vernell and Bruce's grave. He blinked his eyes, sat up and looked around nervously.

Above him, tree limbs waved like arms, as if trying to get Dale's attention. It seemed as if thick, bloody red liquid, seeped from the ground, oozing around the tombstones, covering his feet. Dale shook his head. "You're hallucinating. The blood on this battlefield has long ago dried and turned to Mississippi clay."

A knot tightened in his stomach. "I am between worlds. Which one do I choose? Or do I have a choice?" He brushed dampness from his eyes. *Tears? No, a man doesn't cry.* "To defend the past. My grandfather. Maybe. Maybe not."

***

Late afternoon, the day's shopping expedition over, Brucie was worn out by the time her friend's chauffeur drove up in front of the homeplace.

When she got out of the car and started toward the house, she noticed that long shadows stretched across the yard and over the sidewalk. When she went to open the door, a folded piece of note paper fell out.

Brucie picked it up and read:

> *We needs to git together. Just you and me needs to walk through the cemetery. There's some important business has to be tended to.*
>
> *Tomorrow afternoon. Most of the times, my day eases off come around one o'clock in the afternoon. Why don't I just meet you there, then? If this ain't your satisfaction, let me know. Elsewise, I'll meet you come four tomorrow. At the cemetery gate. This here has been a long time comin'. I know my mama talks to you. Well, my mama done spoke to me too, and she says, "It's come time to take care of this, Lamont. Miss Brucie'll know what it is you're doin."*

Brucie folded the note into her skirt pocket. "And, oh, yes, Lamont. My half-brother. I can sometimes read your mind too. I do know what this is about."

She stepped inside. Brucie paused to catch her breath. The house was filled with the homey scent of food from the kitchen, but she wasn't hungry. She closed the front door and hung her cape over the hall tree. "There's too much going on in my life," she said, fretting over everything she had on her mind. And everything that needed to be done to settle into Redemption Ridge.

The parlor light was on. Brucie started to turn if off but changed her mind and went into the room. "I'm not sleepy, and I'm not quite ready for bed."

She picked up an old family album from a marble-topped table. "This is where it started."

She turned the light off and went up the stairs. Brucie slipped off her clothes, dressed for the night, then began going through the album.

She stopped turning the pages when she saw a small watercolor picture of Lamont's mother, Vernell.

Tears misted her eyes. Vernell had been more of a mother to Brucie than her own mother, Charlotte Caroline Claymore, ever had been. In this painting, Vernell was bent over, picking cotton. A sling across her back held Lamont. Even back then, a shaft of sun high-lighted, not the black of his hair, but touches of red. Behind Vernell, lying on a quilt made of old clothes was Lamont's twin, the sickly baby, Sunnie Flo. Vernell had made a shade for her from old gunny sacks and sticks.

Brucie closed the album but it had made her think of something else she probably should take care of. "It's time. Lamont and I should talk about our treasure buried there at Vernell's feet. I'm sure that's what he has on his mind." *Should he and I divide the rest of it? Him use his as he wishes for his family? Me? For mine? See if Dale wants to buy land or a business? Memory's share?*

"She could go away from here forever." Brucie lay down across the bed. "If that's still her heart's desire. Now, there's Jenson though. She may be changing her mind about leaving Mississippi."

She shook her head. "I wish you were here to tell me what to do, Vernell. About so many things." She brushed her finger across her lips, then leaned over and gently touched the picture of Vernell.

There was a rustling noise from outside the parlor window. Brucie sat up.

"You needs to know a secret, Miss Brucie. Miss Memory an' Mist Jenson. They done fallen in love."

"Oh, Vernell. I wish you were here. I'm tired. I'm old. There's so much going on in my life. My family in so much turmoil. What am I to think about Memory and Jenson? What to do about the jewels."

"Miss Memory an' Mist Jenson. But mostly I wants you to know an' be content with it." There was a slight hesitation, and then the voice continued.

"Talk to Lamont. You both my babies. You two decide."

Brucie had heard the words loud and clear. "Vernell. You always had so much sense. And God will always love you more than he loves me."

She raised her head, drew in a sharp breath and clasped her gold cross. "I think you just told me what to do, Vernell."

***

The air smelled of gunpowder. Lying on his stomach, his head resting on an out-stretched arm, Dale's heart hammered the ground. "Too much," he said. His throat felt tight. His skin damp with sweat, a sultry breeze filled with a familiar moisture bathed his face. He rolled over, coughed into his fists a few times. Not sure where he was, he looked around trying to orient himself.

Slowly he made out the swell and dip of remembered land. "Good old Mississippi," he breathed.

Dale had an uneasy feeling as if he were not alone. He felt as if someone or something was nearby, that he was being watched. He pushed up. "Is there anything or anybody there?"

Somewhere nearby he thought he heard sharp, heavy breathing, then a sound that could have been boots swishing through the grass.

"Clear. My. Name." A voice spoke as if each word were a measured pronouncement—there were just so many that could be said.

Ghosts?

"Your life needs me," the voice said, then slowly trailed the word, "Help."

Dale saw no one, but he made out where the voice came from. It was a little way off and to the side, where inch-by-inch overgrown trees and bushes slowly sucked the cemetery into its belly.

Dale's feelings were like wounds covered by old bandages. He didn't know for sure, but hearing those words he sensed that his life might become untethered and swerve in a different direction. Fear of the unknown and what might lie ahead crept along his spine, but also a fatalistic approach to what might be waiting for him.

"Maybe it's all coming to a head. Either way, if I do or don't survive, I may be ready for it." He frowned and tilted his head to one side. "I think I know who you are. Are you trying to tell me something?"

Palms damp, heart racing, Dale sighed, "My grandfather? If you are here, I don't think I can do anything for you. I don't know what you want."

"Abandon me not to the grave."

These words were clear and sharper than a hammer striking an iron bell

Was this some dark dream coming to Dale from death's forgotten background? Or should he pay no heed to what could either be his imagination, clouding his mind or, perhaps, a ghost in attendance who might upset his life more than he could stand?

"I need you to clear my name."

"I'm sick of causes," Dale said. "Useless banners will be the death of me."

Dale's heart quickened. He had always trailed in the footsteps of mystery, needing to find answers for evil, naively wanting to turn evil into hope and goodness. The mission in France, only misery, no glorious causes in the trenches.

Now, once again, the unknown and unjust, the need to struggle against wrong became a strong force for Dale to say, "no" to. Maybe, just maybe, he was being called to another mission, one close to home. A sense of emptiness was slowly being replaced by a desire to set things right. Mystery's footsteps had turned south, toward his grandfather and Redemption Ridge where the past is first cousin to the present.

"I will return." There were slow spaces between the words, air was sucked away and a feeling of emptiness spread across the ridge.

"Redemption Ridge," Dale said, his voice thick with emotion. "This is where I belong.

"Maybe I can begin my mending here. His cause was doomed. But I will not leave the eternal remains of my grandfather buried in disgrace. Misguided, yes. But, not a thief.

"Enough, for now. It's time to go home."

He tucked the Bible into his haversack, and tossed it across his back. Even though the day had faded, his steps never stumbled as he strode through the cemetery.

The far reaches of Lamont's land lay straight ahead, and his family home was not far beyond. He stopped at the edge of the cemetery and looked back toward the spot where he may have encountered his grandfather. "You can count on me, sir. I have things to do, but I will return soon. If I'm going to stay, I have preparations to make." He tightened his shoulders. "I have to move on with my life. Maybe school. Oxford tomorrow. Or business. We'll see, sir."

The moon was a bright silver slash across the front yard as Dale climbed the porch steps, saw a light in the parlor and glanced in. Back turned to him, he made out Memory writing in her journal.

"God bless, and good-night," he called from the doorway.

Memory glanced at her journal, set her pen down and turned. "It's almost past my bedtime, but I'm getting my thoughts on paper before I forget them."

"It was a good feeling to bring my friend back to Redemption Ridge," Dale said. "I kept my promise. Samuel made it home."

It was on the tip of his tongue to say more, but he changed his mind. He thought it best not to mention a ghost to Memory. Not yet. He'd sleep on it.

Memory almost decided to go on up to bed, but she changed her mind picked up her pen, and began to write.

BOSTON

The day begins; Boston bustles. Much energy is spent on getting to places on time.

Subways hum, streetcars grind as grim-faced businessmen run to catch their rides on trolleys, streetcars, trains and taxis. In the mornings it's off to work for the men, then later shaking off the shackles of their jobs as they head home for the suburbs of Dorchester, Brighton and Wellington Hill.

Faces are closed. Everyone seems to be on their own journey—I won't say to nowhere, but to their own private somewhere.

In the Boston Inner Harbor, I hear the sharp blast of ships' whistles as they enter and leave port. The voices of foreign-tongued sailors on decks ring across the streets as they load and unload their wares, then sail away to exotic faraway lands.

After Thornton's death, I had brief hopes of my life changing. I thought I might soon be on one of the large ocean liners, sailing across the ocean. Maybe have a glass of wine at a café in Berne, Switzerland, marvel at Michelangelo's sculpture's in Florence, Italy or visit Shakespeare's birthplace at Stratford-on-Avon.

Everything and everyone here seem to be in constant motion. As dusk steals across the harbor, cleaning crews and imbibers stroll in and out of the buildings and taverns, one of the many sights and scenes I can leave behind. But I'll miss lawn parties, art gallery shows, tea in homes on Beacon Hill, the Boston Theatre and dressing for dinner at the Fairmont.

In Beacon Hill where we lived, seasons are sharp. Fall leaves change to glorious colors, they curl as if trying to hold on to the Mother tree, and then shamed, turn loose and drift to the ground. Close behind, Jack Frost blasts snow and ice across the land. A breezy spring slips across the city and countryside and then summer is upon us. Not overwhelming, like the suffocating Mississippi heat and humidity, but milder, rather like a child on tiptoe, trying to hide.

Personal life seems to be less intense there than down South. Maybe there's just not too much interest in other people and what they have going on. Maybe it's because there's more to do. More to think about, claim, and be proud of. Perhaps our sense of pride, could be resting atop an open bottle of perfumed smugness because of our own special place in the country's history, culture and the arts. A touch of class, for want of a better name.

As of a few weeks ago, my Boston days are over and done; my life is on a different path. One I never imagined I'd make. It's a long ride from Boston to Redemption Ridge, Mississippi. In many, many ways

Goodbye to hustle and bustle.

MISSISSIPPI

The people are slow-moving and talking. They are fast to take offense, to cock the gun, but quick to forgive and to share whatever they have with others.

In Boston I often felt as if I were behind a fence, peering over at someone else's party, and I hadn't been invited. And how will I feel about Redemption Ridge? It's too soon to tell yet. There are two people who have made me see Mississippi differently. One is Jenson Cooper, my forever love. Feelings have always been there for Jenson. I just wasn't ready to accept them. Our tie is a thick one, going back to his grandfather, Sheriff Bramlett. He laid a God-touched path in front of the Claymore family.

There's another person. One I, hopefully, will help. Lamont's daughter, Sassy. I who have never done much of anything for anybody. Tomorrow, I will do what I can to see if that can change. When I heard Sassy sing in her glorious, God-given voice. "The trumpet sounds within my soul, I ain't got long to stay here."

And, the trumpet sang in mine. I am her hope. It happened
because of a cup of cold coffee and a slammed door.

Memory chewed the end of her pen a moment before penning
darker thoughts.

And the big unknown. Our half-sister, Thelma Jewel.
Maybe I'm pipe-dreaming like brother, Dale.

***

Album in her lap, Brucie wasn't sure if she was awake or
asleep when she heard footsteps going down the hall. Dale's door
closed. She slid down into the bed and drifted off to sleep.

Sometime later, cool air moved against her face, as if someone
had opened a window.

"Miss Brucie," a soft voice called.

Once again she felt a presence in the room. Someone who'd
protected her and had been with her most of her young life.
"Vernell?"

"Miss Memory doin' good. But, I needs to tell you 'bout
somebody else, who ain't. Miss Brucie. It's Miss Thelma Jewel.
She's 'round the place. She'll be comin' to you. Soon."

CHAPTER 33

She felt a dead recurring dream
Like bad rest in her out of body,
Waking around her glowing seams.

No fear, cool as placid water
Waiting for a heavy rain.

What recurred like a
Black, pumping heart,
Coming home to always been
Waking through her eyes.

Monday night, March 29

Brucie heard a noise downstairs. *Memory*, she thought. *It's past time for her to be in bed.* She turned on the lamp at the top of the upstairs landing and holding the hem of her flowing robe in one hand, she grasped the railing with the other and hurried down the stairs. She noticed the parlor light on and made out her daughter writing at the desk.

Memory sensed her mother in the doorway. "I know it's late. I was catching up on my journal. And I have some exciting news."

Brucie raised her hand with a blocking motion, then she smiled as if they shared a secret.

"It's Jenson," she said. "I know."

"Oh, mama. We're engaged."

"You have my blessing. You two were made for each other. A dear voice from back when I was a little girl came to me. Vernell whispered a secret. One I needed to hear." She smoothed her robe. "It was meant to be. I was so wrong. You and Jenson. Now and forever."

"I'll make you proud." Memory laid her journal across her arm and gripped it with her fingers.

"I'm already proud."

"There's one other thing. I told you I was going to Jackson tomorrow. But things have changed. It's not a shopping trip." Memory hesitated, then she went on. "I'm going to see if I can get Sassy in a school for the colored. There's one fairly close by. Between here and Jackson." She rolled her lips together then said, "Mother. Her voice. Untrained though it is, her voice is as fine as any I've ever had the privilege to hear. She needs to be trained. By the best. If she's accepted, hopefully, this will be the beginning of a different life for her. I just feel called to do this."

"I heard. We do what we need to." Brucie hesitated a moment, then she nodded her head. "And sometimes, what we should."

A comfortable quiet settled between them. Memory stood and began pulling her papers together.

Brucie felt a sudden flush of apprehension.

Trouble. Memory sensed it.

A loud crash shattered the stillness.

Papers spilled from Memory's arm onto the floor. "What was that?"

"It sounded like somebody threw something through the kitchen window." Brucie wheeled around. "I'll see."

"I'm right behind you. It scared me so bad I dropped my journal." Memory leaned over, but by the time she scooped up the scattered papers, Brucie was gone.

Memory flung the papers onto the desk.

"Oh God!" Brucie hollered. Her legs buckling like snapped matchsticks, she pitched forward.

Memory made it to the kitchen just in time to see her mother throw her arms out as if for an embrace.

Brucie crumpled to the floor and lay in a heap, her knees drawn to her chest.

Memory sank beside her. "Mother!"

Brucie lay on the floor, motionless. Then, "I'm all right," she groaned as if sensing her daughter might need reassuring. The velvet ribbon holding her comfort piece, the cross from Vernell was tight around her neck. She loosened it.

"Is anything broken?" Memory asked, urgency in her voice.

Dale burst into the room. "What happened?" He snapped on a light.

"I stumbled over something." Bracing both arms on the floor, Brucie made as if to get up, then she sank back. She slowly straightened each leg, testing to see if they worked.

Dale reached for her hand. "If I help, can you stand?"

"I think so."

"Be careful," Dale said. "I heard the noise from upstairs. Glass from the kitchen window is all over the floor."

He pulled a chair from under the table, bent over again, and circled both arms around his mother's waist. "Lean on me."

Easing Brucie to her feet, he was surprised at how frail she felt. *You were always strong. Not now. You're different.* Holding on to his mother, he helped her sit in the chair.

"This is what tripped you." Memory pushed at something with her shoe. "It's a piece of marble." She bent over. "It looks like pieces of a tombstone. It says, **THEL** and a **G**—" She took a step backward.

"My sister," Brucie whispered, "Thelma Grace. That's part of her grave marker." She rubbed her back and shook her head in disbelief. "She's been dead all these many years. Since before I left here for Boston."

"There's something else. Tied on with a piece of twine," Memory said as she untied the cord. "A note and a picture." She held a piece of paper toward the overhead light.

> *Every proper lady should have a calling card. And in spite of you, I was raised a proper lady.*
> *To the manor born? If only!*
> *Do you ever think about me? Well, I think about you. Oh, yes, I do. I left my calling card. We have a score to settle.*
>
> *Guess Who?*

"There's the picture," Memory said. "A goat pulling a little girl in a wagon."

Brucie drew in fast, shallow breaths. For a moment she had an," I can't remember where I am" look on her face and seemed to be in shock.

"You look like you've seen a ghost," Dale said, disturbed by his mother's appearance.

With those words, Brucie pulled herself together and reached for the photograph. She glanced at it, drew in a sharp breath and lowered her eyes as if she were ashamed to look in her children's faces. "Oh God. I didn't know when, or how to, but now I have to tell you this," she whispered. "There's another Thelma. Not my sister, Thelma Grace.

"You have a half-sister. I have another daughter, Thelma Jewel."

The false reality Brucie had created hung suspended over the three of them. An uncomfortable, shameful silence followed.

"You don't need to explain," Memory finally said. "We found out back in Boston. Before Cousin Sarah passed away, she thought we should know. She told us what happened to you. Dale and I have known for years. Oh, Mama, we understand."

Brucie looked off into the distance as if searching for someone far away, then she took a deep breath and reached for Thelma Jewel's picture. "This is your half-sister, Thelma Jewel, when she was just a toddler. Thelma Jewel's older than you and Dale. I haven't seen her since right after she was born." Brucie swayed, then as if she had found an inner strength, her body stiffened and she raised her head. "I gave her away. There was no other way for me to live here in Franklin, Mississippi. Some wounds never heal. They just form thicker scars.

"Thelma Jewel," she said the name quickly, almost as if it left a strange taste on her tongue, "was born out of wedlock. She was raised in California. I always wondered what kind of woman she would become. But what little I've heard about my elder daughter has been troubling. And Thelma Jewel has a thirteen-year old child. Gertie Mae. A child, who in some ways I've been told, is different."

A heavy silence filled the room.

Brucie set the picture down, took a deep breath and clasped her hands together. "There's a small voice in my head saying"— She began speaking as if the voice came from someone else— "'Yes, Miss Brucie, go on. Tell it all, girl. Let the Good Lord be the judge of who done right and who done wrong.'" She squeezed her hands together and moved them back and forth as if nailing something to a wall.

"My sister, Thelma Grace, died years ago. You probably don't know, but she was in the family way and may have been desperate for money."

She unfolded her hands and straightened her shoulders. "In my mind I see images of my sister. With child and not married. My mother on her death bed. My sister wanting those jewels you've heard so much about. Money. Her inheritance. Scenes of my sister struggling with our dying mother."

"My mind can't take in the picture of a daughter wrestling with her dying mother," Memory said. "Over money and jewels. Over anything."

"After our mother died and was buried, my sister, Thelma Grace, thought a fortune might be in our mother's casket." As if she were searching for unseen faces, Brucie turned toward the shattered window. "I wasn't there, so I don't know for sure what happened. But, hoping to find a fortune in Confederate jewels, Thelma Grace and a Yankee Carpetbagger, Warner Sledge, dug up our mother's grave. They opened the coffin. The jewels were not there. Only a valuable ring on my mother's hand." Brucie grasped her own ring finger. "And my distraught sister. She cut off our dead mother's finger and took her ring." Her face twisted, like a child who's ready to burst into tears. She paused, then went on.

"That same night, Thelma Grace was murdered. By Warner Sledge.

"The carpetbagger was the one who had gotten my sister with child. He murdered her and thought he could get his hands on the Confederate fortune and go back north a rich man." Brucie trembled.

"The story doesn't end there. Sheriff Bramlett, Jenson Cooper's grandfather, later got the ring back to my family. And the fortune in jewels that had been collected from all of Tallouga County for the Confederate cause. Your grandfather, not Daddy Claymore, Bruce Claymore, didn't steal them. I'm relieved to say, they weren't found by either side," Brucie said, almost proudly. "They were hidden." A small smile stole across her lips. "We know what happened. They didn't get to that no-good, lying Daddy Claymore. Sheriff Bramlett took care of them. Known only to a few, they were hidden in the cemetery with Vernell's body."

She laid a finger across her lips as to stop herself from telling secrets, then she took her hand down. "After the war, those jewels have been of some help to our family and Lamont's, but more to Tallouga County. In more ways than one."

Brucie didn't say anything for a few minutes, then she tightened her shoulders. "All those years ago. For a brief moment the whole town thought I was the guilty one and had murdered my sister. But no. Me, a little white girl? What an injustice. Here in the land of my childhood, that wouldn't do." Her words hardened. "But with the way it seemed to happen, it was easy, oh so easy, to switch over and blame our maid, Vernell," she said bitterly.

"I feel dirty," she whispered. "The truth came too late for Vernell. Oh, what sinners we all were." She lowered her head. *And now it's coming home. Here where it all began. Not just Thelma Jewel. I think lots of things may be coming to light.*

"What happened to me, also happened to you, my daughter, here at Redemption Ridge," Brucie said. "I didn't want to know. I wanted nothing bad said about my homeplace." She bit her lip. "I heard a familiar voice in my dreams. Trying to tell me that you too had been misused. I buried painful words. I denied you, my child." Tears streamed down her cheeks. She stared down at the floor.

"You had just turned thirteen. Vernell tried to tell me. No, no. I ran from her. Coward that I was, I denied your pain."

"It was down by the well." Head shaking, Memory clamped her hand over her mouth as if she might vomit. After a moment, she took her hand down. "By one of those Potter's. When I was thirteen."

Her eyes smarted with tears. "These are things good people like us don't talk about." She wasn't often at a loss for words but it was a minute before she could go on. "It was done. There was nothing you could do. He tried again." Her words hardened. "He has been taken care of."

Brucie stroked her daughter's cheek. "He should have been put away for life. However, I don't think it would have happened that way. Not in Tallouga County, Mississippi."

Dale laid his hand on Memory's shoulder. "It's 1920. This is too painful," he said in his clipped, no nonsense Boston accent. "We've all fallen short. Let's come back to the here and now. That damn tombstone," he went on. "Thelma Jewel is somewhere in Tallouga County. And, while we're being honest with one another, I need to tell you, she got in touch with me too." He scratched his forehead, like a child in distress, trying to answer a question he didn't want to. "When we were coming down on the train from Boston, a note filled with anger was given to me. It was written by Thelma Jewel." He glanced at the note. "Definitely the same handwriting."

"I felt it in my bones too," Brucie said. "On the train. Vernell spoke. Loud and clear. She told me Thelma Jewel was here."

Memory took the picture from her mother's hand and set it on the kitchen table. "There's no question where this picture and that piece of gravestone came from. Wherever she and her daughter are, somebody's up to no good. Dale and I both know. She may have murdered Mrs. Bledsoe, the woman who raised her. Two neighbors got in touch with us."

"They're here, somewhere in Franklin." Brucie bowed her head as if she were praying. "No matter what happens. Remember. They *are* family."

The clock in the dining room chimed one o'clock.

Dale drew in a long, shaky breath. "We're all worn out. We'd better go on to bed. We've heard about the murderer, Daddy Claymore, all our lives. Now, maybe it's time for us to know the one accused of being a traitor. Your father, and our grandfather, Bruce Claymore."

He leaned forward and wrapped his arms around his mother's shoulders. "And maybe, maybe together we can do something about Thelma Jewel and Gertie Mae."

"Who knows how it'll all play out? The sins of the fathers," Brucie whispered.

CHAPTER 34

There was a singing axe
After a faint, hollow moon, a
Dance of clockwork in a
Memory palace for revenge,
Deep as the even sky.

His teeth so long gone,
His thoughts meal-mouthed
Around a single, bright white
Oracle bone.

Another bunch of folks
Bump on down the road
But buzzards coast the wind
Save me, Thelma Jewel croaks.
Never again, never again.

Tuesday, 6:15 a.m., March 30

Trestle hitched his mule to a tree. He stared into the darkness; daylight lingered nearby but hadn't showed itself. In the backyard the dogs set up a howl. Trestle didn't let it stop him. He was sure these hounds barked at their own shadows and that Dedmon wouldn't be checking to see what had spooked them.

"It won't be yet a while, but I know you're gonnna come out fer a stick o' stove wood. 'Cepting for driving that air hearse some, I gots me all the time in the world. If not this day, then I'll git you tomorra," Trestle muttered to himself. Carrying the moldy, tattered coveralls he'd fished from the well, he eased to the edge of the yard. He slipped a pair of dentures and a small, gray jellied mass from the pants into the body of the rotting dog who had been left lying across the far end of the woodpile.

Trestle looked around then seemed to find what he wanted. Like a mole tunneling into a hole, he slid down into a thick brush pile. He hunkered down, set a wooden slat next to his hip, then lay the axe he'd brought across his lap and rested his hand on it. The afternoon before Trestle had sharpened the axe on a concrete block behind the funeral home.

He spit on his finger, touched the blade. "Sharp enough to skin a 'coon," he said. Taking comfort from knowing it was honed needle-sharp, he wiped a thin chain of sweat from his neck. "Yo voodoo spells ain't a-gonter save you now. An' you—I'm gonter git you, Mist Dead-Man.

Closing his eyes, his chin dropped to his chest.

A short while later, when there was just a hint of daybreak, the front door hinges creaked. Trestle raised his head. Breathing swiftly, he gripped the axe handle.

Lucius stepped onto the porch. He sank into a wooden rocking chair, slurping from a cup of coffee. He rolled a cigarette, licked, then lit it. Scowling, he spread his legs, scratched his balls and pulled on his penis as if he were adjusting a slab of bacon in a skillet. After a few minutes had passed, he leaned over and flipped his cigarette into a rusted tin tub. The morning sky was a timid golden haze as Lucius stood, went down the steps and walked toward the pile of split logs. He reached for a stick of firewood. He froze. His breath came fast and hard. Something had gone wrong.

The dead dog that had been thrown out still lay across the far slope of the woodpile. Maggots squirmed through the open, decaying belly. But something looked different. A pair of dentures sat in the carcass.

Mouth open, Dedmon flung his head around. He saw nothing, nobody.

Trestle threw caution to the wind. He sprang to his feet. He didn't care if anybody saw him or not. He was a white man in a black man's yard. *It'd be my word against a nigga's.*

"Mist Dedmon," he hollered.

Lucius Dedmon spun around.

Knee level, Trestle swung the axe.

"Aw Gawd," Lucius yelled.

The axe lodged in his knee bones. Fountains of blood spurted. Lucius pitched to the ground. Trestle braced his foot against the spilled pile of thick logs. Groaning, he strained, pulled the axe loose. He raised it again. "More than one way to skin a cat."

Dedmon shook, like someone having a convulsion. Tears poured down his cheeks. Eyes bulging, his voice came out a croak. "Give me a chance to live," he screamed, scrub crawling for his life.

Trestle raised his bullet-shaped chin. He spread his thin lips back from brown stumpy nubbins of teeth covered with thick spit.

"Like you done give my brother?" Axe held high, he lunged.

Dedmon's head snapped back. Trestle split Dedmon's chest and stomach. He fell against the log pile. His left foot twitched, as if it had a life of its own and wanted to flee. Red spurts of blood throbbed out. Dedmon's intestines spilled like large, greasy worms seeking escape from the light. Loud gurgling, "ahs" dwindled to one thick choke.

"Dawg gone your hide." Trestle moved the dentures from the rotten dead dog and placed them into Dedmon's open belly.

"Your choppers, Shank," he said. "Your dawg gone choppers are gonter chew on him. An here's something else to keep you sorry hide company." He reached into his back pocket and as he moved his hand up a rattling sound broke the silence. "It ain't your Tattler the Rattler. But these here rattles do you most jest as well," he said, placing the snake rattles to the side of his brother's dentures.

"An, jest so you won't miss none of it." He jammed the thin piece of wood he had brought with him into Dedmon's belly.

The early morning sky was the color of gray fox fur. If someone stood real close, there was just light enough to see a childishly scrawled name written in charcoal.

S
H
A
N
K.

At the edge of the yard, Trestle turned and looked back.

"Satisfaction," he said. "I seed to it. You gittin' your satisfaction."

***

6:45 a.m.

"No breakfast. And that's the best meal of the day," Thelma Jewel complained as she, Mudge and Liam pulled away from Mrs. Netter's Boarding House in Mudge's roadster which was up and running again. "I haven't even had me any sausage and eggs yet."

"Come early mornin' an' Mrs. Netter sets out some left over vittles. But, she don't put out the hot stuff 'til seven thirty on weekdays an' we're a little ahead o' that," Mudge said as he steered the car down Main Street.

"It's good to meet up with you again, Mr. McRae." Thelma Jewel leaned forward and called out over the noisy engine. "Well. And what do you think about Mississippi?"

Liam glanced at Mudge. He wanted to say, "Something or somebody in here smells like the must from old fruit," but he thought better of it. "I'm looking into setting up a little business in the town of Vicksburg," he said. Liam rolled his fingers together as if he were counting dollar bills. He had in his mind that he might go into some illegal whiskey running down the Mississippi River.

"After we git our bidness done with Mistah Dedmon, we'll drop Policeman McRae off, git us some grub, then you an' me'll motor on out an' pick up Gertie Mae. An' that shouldn't take us too long. We'll visit with Brother Tuggle, then we'll have us a good dinner over to Mrs. Netter's," Mudge said.

"It's good you'll be driving me out to pick up Gertie Mae at the Divine Deliverance Holiness Church and School for Boys and Girls," Thelma Jewel said. *Not really* she thought. *I'm tired of her. When I get some of that Claymore money, I'll make sure she's fed and has shoes on her feet. Then I'll pay somebody else to raise her. I might just move to Hot Springs, Arkansas, and mix and mingle with the hoi polloi. That's how I want to live.*

Liam slung his head and brushed his thick red hair back from his forehead. "Mr. Mudge, with all due respect, sir, that old motorcar you gave me to use won't go much faster than eight miles an hour. I wouldn't have come with you all to see about Mr. Dedmon's part in that church service you people are having, but he owes me some money. And as soon as we get through with our Dedmon business and you drop me off," he went on, "then I want to motor on to Vicksburg for a day or two. Maybe go through that world-famous park they have over there."

"Well, I never," Thelma Jewel said. "I'm from California. I haven't even heard of it, so it certainly wouldn't be called world-famous."

"Don't forgit, Liam," Mudge said. "You're expected to be on han' with the big church meetin' we have comin' up on Sunday."

"Oh, I'll be back."

Slowing for an elderly gentleman crossing the street, Mudge ooged the horn. "Celebration," he said. "I calls it a Celebration fer Captain Bruce Claymore an' the other heroes of Redemption Ridge. That's what I want it to sound like to them Von Dieters. Me, I got me some other ideers."

He made a quick turn off Main Street, slinging the three of them sideways as they began bumping down a dirt road. "An' along with honorin', we're gonter be doin' us a little savin' an' redeemin'. Git some of them sinners 'roun' here converted. Sometimes folks kin git outta han' an' a bony-fide policeman waitin' 'roun' will be a hep." He nodded in Liam's direction.

"After we git done here, Miss Thelmer Jewel, I wanna take you 'roun' to meet Brother Tuggle an' we can pick up Gertie Mae." Mudge jerked the wheel to the left, barely missing a scrawny gray cat crossing in front of them, then he steered back toward the middle. "Give the young lady a treat. Take her to Mrs. Netter's fer dinner."

"Well as to me, I want to see what's going on with my highfalutin rich Claymore relatives who won't even claim me." Thelma Jewel paused. "And certainly not Gertie Mae. Make sure me and my Gertie Mae are taken care of proper. I just might run into some of our kin folks when we're out and about Mrs. Netter's."

She's thinkin' 'bout gittin' her name on some property, an' gittin' a holt a them jewels, Mudge realized. With policeman McRae in the car he thought it best to keep his peace and not say anything about the Claymore riches Thelma Jewel might be coming into.

He also didn't let on that when he went to pick up Liam, while he was standing at the open front door waiting on him, he overheard a hall telephone conversation between the policeman from Boston and one from Vicksburg. It sounded like, even though Mr. Liam McRae might soon be going on back to Boston, he was interested in setting up a little whiskey traffic coming down the Mississippi River and was headed to Vicksburg to see about it. *It ain't a bad ideer, an' it'll keep him out of my hair fer a day or two,* Mudge mused to himself. *After I git shet of this here policeman, might think about it myself one of these here days. An' do somethin' about that dotter of Thelmer Jewels. Maybe see kin we find us a way to start gittin' rid of that chile. Let somebody else see to her raisin'. If we kin do that, then who knows wa's ahead fer me an' Miss Thelmer Jewel.*

"What are you gonter do about that tombstone you all dug up an' hauled off yestiddy?" Mudge asked.

"I don't know," Thelma Jewel lied, knowing she'd paid Doot Potter to throw it through a window at the Claymore house. *Won't be long before they all know I'm here and out to get what's owed me.*

"Lawd a mercy," Mudge called out, swerving toward the far side of the road.

With Mudge working the gears, pumping the brake, mashing the clutch and pushing the accelerator, the car bounded like a bucking horse.

Thelma Jewel's legs sprawled apart, as if giving fresh air to her privates. She grabbed the leather pull by the side of the door, and held on for what looked to her like dear life.

"Whoooee," she hollered, almost sliding off the leather seat. "Watch out."

"I come nigh onto hittin' that redheaded fool ridin' out there in the middle of the road on that air mule. It ain't even good sunup

327

yet. If I didn't know better, I'd swear it kindly looked like Trestle Potter. He's got him a weedy patch a red hair. Not as bright as yours, Mistah Liam, but mostly."

Mudge slowed as they dropped into pitted road bumps.

Thelma Jewel gripped a door pull and leaned forward.

"I've been thinking about our Sunday Celebration," she said, an awed sound in her voice. "And the snakes you've talked about. Sometimes they can get loose. Do you think we might get to see some of that at church on Sunday?

"We don't do things that way in California," she said, a regretful sound in her voice. "That's the way my grandfather Claymore died, I've been told. I heard tell he was in the barn at Redemption Ridge for a healing service and fell over dead."

Mudge licked his lips as if he had found a tasty morsel. "It jest might happen," he said. "Back then, somebody dropped the snake box. On purpose," he muttered. "An' it could happen again. Only the Good Lawd knows fer sure.

"Them snakes got loose an' then the barn caught fire," he said. *He an' that no good Book Turnipseed. All bit up. Then the two of 'em done caught fire. Both of 'em fried crispier than a piece of burnt toast.*

"Savin' souls. Snake handlin' an' all." Mudge's eyes lit up. "You ain't never seen the likes of it." As he said this, the motorcar dropped into a hole, then flew out as if it had been tossed by springs. The three of them slammed into their seats then were flung up almost to the roof of the car.

"Need to do somethin' about these here hidey holes," Mudge muttered. "But since the only ones that go this a-way are mostly jest colored, it don't matter none. An' like as not, most of the times they're ridin' mules.

"Dead ahead. There's Dedmon's house." Pumping the brakes, he hit the clutch, shifted gears and slid to a stop.

The three of them got out of the car and were quickly covered with the thin veil of dust swirling behind the car. Thelma Jewel patted her hands against her skirt. "Achoo," she belted out, as a light beige powder fluffed about her.

"Somethin' stinks to high heaven out here," Mudge said. "Over yonda by the side o' this place."

Penned up dogs out back of the Dedmon house had set up a howl but that wasn't the only sound Mudge heard. A loud rustling noise came from the far edge of the yard. He looked over to see a flock of buzzards running to take off, then flapping their wings, gaining altitude.

"Let's get on with our business here," Liam said. "I'm having to watch my time."

"It's too dusty out here for me," Thelma Jewel carped. "I'm just along for the ride. Since I missed the big breakfast, and only got me three cold biscuits and some molasses, it's good that you and I have a dinner date, Mr. Mudge. And truth to tell, it's probably past time for me to see to Gertie Mae." *Leave it up to him, and he might find her a place to move to forever. I can tell. He kind of thinks like I do.*

Mudge heard a whirring sound above. He noticed something moving over their heads; more buzzards than had just flown off. A steady stream of the big birds skimmed and dipped, riding the currents, almost as if they were waltzing to a tune only they could hear.

Somethin' don't look exactly right, he realized.

"I think I'll turn the car 'roun' an' smoke me a cigar while you tend to your knittin', Mistah Liam. Then, I'll take up my bidness with Mistah Dedmon, when you git done." He had no sooner gotten the words out of his mouth before Thelma Jewel laid her hands across her behind and arched her back.

"My legs are aching to beat the band," she said. She flung her body forward and bent over, stepping into the car.

Big as her butt is, Mudge thought, *if I had a need to, I could use it as a step stool.* He cranked the motor, crawled into the car and turned it around. Mudge angled the mirror so he could watch Liam.

When Liam got close to the house he glanced to his left. Instead of going up the front steps he stopped. He took a sudden turn toward the woodpile.

"Huh?" Mudge's chin jutted out. He saw a body spread out over the chopped up logs.

The screen door flew open. Wearing only his long John's, Dedmon's son-in-law, Passel Skinotes, stepped out. "White man," he hollered. "What chew doing?"

"I've come to get the money Mr. Dedmon owes me," Liam hollered back, "But..." he pointed toward the woodpile.

"You ain't gitting nothing."

Passel bolted into the house. A second later he kicked the door open. "Looky over yonder, you redheaded bastid." Passel ran his hand across his eyes. "Some redheaded sumbitch done kilt my wife's daddy," he hollered.

Passel raised, then shucked a shotgun.

Mudge saw the barrel.

Liam spun around. He ran. Spurts of dust nipped his heels.

A round of buckshot hit the rear bumper of the roadster.

Mudge slammed the clutch down, and jerked the car into gear. The engine coughing and smoking, Mudge floored the accelerator. He took off with Liam clutching the door handle. Liam jumped onto the running board, scrambling to get in. The car skidded, angled from left to right, barely staying out of the ditch on each side as the roadster jolted and wiggled down the dirt road.

"We don't do any of this in California," Thelma Jewel shrieked. A vision of Mrs. Bledsoe gasping for breath flashed through her head.

"Dear Jesus!" she prayed, her voice cracking with fear. "Save me, save me. I didn't mean to kill anybody. I won't ever do it again."

CHAPTER 35

**A seam held,
Suspended-like
On a rope
From the rigging.**

**These were natural forces
Too big for the mind.
No man's land was a
Blue green sea,**

Too big for the Colossus to straddle.

Tuesday, 7:00 a.m., March 30

Brucie nodded toward the busted kitchen window. "Dale, it's chilly in here," she said. "That broken window"—Her voice cracked—"was the doing of my child." She hung her head. "But I wouldn't know her if I saw her."

"I'll fix the glass for now." Dale pushed back his chair and left the room. He returned with a large tablecloth, shoved the remaining glass shards out toward the ground then stuffed the cloth around the wooden window frame. He poured Brucie another cup of coffee, then sat down.

She sighed, passed the sugar bowl to Dale and stirred her coffee. "We have some decisions to make about Thelma Jewel," she said.

"We have decisions to make about a lot of things," her son answered. "With what Thelma Jewel has done so far." He shook his head. "And knowing our half-sister and her daughter, Gertie Mae, are somewhere around here, isn't a good feeling for any of us. And something else not good, Jenson has it on pretty good authority that Liam McRae, the Boston policeman, may be in these parts."

An uncomfortable quiet fell between the two of them.

Brucie leaned forward. "My thinking is, Thelma Jewel will be getting back in touch with us. In her own time and way," she said. "Then, we'll see what happens. And there's something else. Before too much time passes we need to discuss our family resources."

"Definitely. We need look into our finances," Dale said.

A half smile on her face, Brucie tilted her chin and rubbed the palm of her hand across the kitchen table. "Our money and property situation is much better here than when we were in Boston. Lamont has invested wisely for us." She nodded as if that were a known fact. "With what he's told me, you should be in good enough shape to purchase land. Or maybe even buy a small business." She hesitated, then said, "Then there's always our funeral home business."

"Umm." Dale shook his head. "I want nothing to do with death. We'll have to discuss our finances later this week. Hopefully, without Von Dieter in the picture."

"Your father," Brucie said. "Not Von Dieter. We have his feelings to think about. He should be part of anything this family does."

"Oh, yes. Papa. Any of those things I want to do with my life will enrage the Kaiser." Dale gave his mother a hard look.

His jaw tightened. "Let's talk about something else. Don't forget, Memory's going to Jackson and checking on schools. I'm riding to Oxford with Laura Lee and Otis. First though, Jenson and I are checking on the old Ferguson property. It's at the edge of Main Street and close to the Presbyterian Church. They're running out of cemetery room and there's enough Ferguson acreage for a cemetery." He paused for a minute, then went on. "It's ironic. Things have really changed. For the most part, I'm looking. Jenson's buying.

"It'll probably be this weekend before we can get together for family and for this Thelma Jewel business. In the meantime," his voice trailed off as he said, "please be careful."

He massaged the top of his shoulder. "If I thought I had it in me I might re-enroll at Ole Miss and finish up with a degree in English.

"I'd really like to write, maybe start a newspaper here in Franklin, but the way things are now, it's not a moneymaker. And I have to think about that." He looked away a minute. "Maybe write some poetry," Dale said softly.

"Follow your dream," Brucie whispered.

Her heels making sharp clicks on the wood floor, dressed for the day in a pale blue jacket and skirt, Memory stepped into the kitchen. "Good morning," she said, pouring herself a cup of coffee.

"Never let it be said, that a southern gentleman doesn't respect a southern lady." Dale stood, spread one arm in greeting, then pulled out a chair for Memory. "And, I'm in training to be one."

"I'm glad last night's shenanigans are over and done with," Memory said. "I'll be going to Jackson after lunch but for a different reason than shopping."

Dale moved to his mother's side and gave her shoulder a gentle squeeze. "I hope you can help Sassy, Memory."

"I know. I'm proud of her, and hopeful for Sassy," Memory said.

Brucie shook out a folded napkin and wiped her lips. "Along these lines, don't forget the Easter Celebration honoring our Confederate dead. Maybe this will be not just a celebration, but a revelation. Surely, oh surely, this time around justice will be done. For Vernell. For my father, Captain Bruce Claymore. He was not a thief."

"That pot at the end of the rainbow," Dale said. "Those old jewels that everybody whispers about from time to time. I've heard about them all my life. But I've never seen hide nor hair of them." He almost added, "And the ghosts that guard them," but stopped. "What about those jewels, mother? My grandfather's Confederate fortune? Do they absolve, or condemn him?"

"What if they do neither?" she said softly.

"Right now, I don't have a Celebration in my mind. This weekend, when I return from Oxford," Dale said, a defiant tone in his voice, "my reality will be dealing with Herr Von Dieter. And the Boston policeman. Liam."

He heard the hurt in his mother's voice, as she said, "Your father. Your hard feelings seem to be getting stronger."

Dale's hands curled into fists. His mind went back to yesterday; digging a hole for his friend, Samuel Stanton. "It's not easy to forget. It was that man's army I fought against." His voice low and dark he took a step backward. "My friends were killed in France. I just laid to rest what was left of one of them. It brought so much back to me."

"The war's over," Memory said.

"There'll always be another one."

"You're angry at the wrong person, son. Don't blame your father."

Dale pressed his lips together, then forced a smile. "Maybe I need some help from the ghosts of Redemption Ridge." He wheeled around and ran up the steps to his room.

"A troublemaking half-sister's somewhere out there," he said, closing the door. "And Von Dieter's coming in."

He plunged his hand into his coat pocket. *Not quite ready to give it up yet.* He shook his head. "I'm getting low."

His fingers closed around a flask that held his cough syrup. Dale heard what sounded like a sudden blast of wind brushing a large tree limb against the window. He swung around. Nothing moved outside. Shaking his head, he narrowed his eyes and turned away.

A gentle tap at the window. Then words so soft, he wasn't sure if he imagined or heard them. "Abandon me not to the grave."

"Dear God." Dale bowed his head. "Will I always feel like I have my foot in two worlds?"

***

7:30

Standing on one foot then the other, Memory waited for Jenson under a large oak tree close to the road. A cool wind sang in her ears, carrying with it a faint, yet distinctive fragrance. It took her a moment, then, "Sweet olive," she said. *I've smelled this scent for as long as I can remember.* "Here. I only smell it here."

The wind died. From behind her Memory heard a sound like padding feet. Before she could turn, a warm hand touched her shoulder.

"Thanks, Miss Memory," a soft voice whispered in her ear. "I'm proud fer my granddaughter, Sassy. I knows you gone hep her."

Memory turned. No one was there.

A few minutes later she felt a sense of relief when she saw Minyard cross their side yard and carefully drape a large leather pouch he was carrying behind his horse's saddle.

"Sister Thelma Jewel. I know you're somewhere around here," she muttered. "I heard you were a troublemaker. And according to what your two old neighbors wrote and told us, probably a murderess. I just wish I knew what you looked like."

She shaded her eyes from the morning sun and looked down Old Farm Road. She and Jenson had made their plans for the day. Memory was spending the morning with an old childhood friend in Franklin. Jenson was taking her brother to look at the Ferguson property, and she would ride into town with them. He would pick her up later, and they would have a noon dinner at Mrs. Netter's.

Off in the distance she saw a thin trail of dust. She had told Jenson what little she knew about Thelma Jewel's background, and now she could hardly wait to tell him what had happened during the night.

When Jenson drove up, Memory was standing by the car before he opened the door. *I can draw strength from you forever*, she thought. "I'm so glad you're here," she said, as he pushed the door open. "We had an intruder at our house late last night." She gave a nervous laugh. "That half-sister of ours, Thelma Jewel, is around here somewhere. She left us a calling card."

Her hand shaky, Memory pushed loose hair strands up under her velvet cloche. "And Dale told me about a crazy note she got to him on the train from Boston. She told him we'd see her here at Redemption Ridge." She shook her head. "Late last night, part of my aunt's tombstone was thrown through the kitchen window. Minyard's carrying it away and putting it back on her grave. Like aunt, like niece." She bit down on her lip. "Both of them scary people." She pointed toward the driveway where Minyard and his horse sidled down Old Farm Road. "I'm sure Thelma Jewel was behind this episode too. There was another note and a photograph of her as a child with it." Memory reached into her pocket, pulled out a folded piece of paper, and once again read.

"To the manor born? If only! Do you ever think about me? Well, I think about you.

"Oh, yes, I do. I left my calling card. We have a score to settle."

"She sounds crazy," Jenson said.

A deep frown creased Memory's forehead. "Some time back, I heard from two of her neighbors. They were strongly suspicious that Thelma Jewel murdered the California woman who raised her, a Mrs. Bledsoe."

"You need to be very careful." Jenson's jaw tightened. "She's dangerous."

"Everyone here is aware of her. We're being very careful."

"And, she's not the only one. My friend, Zebulon, back in Boston did some checking for me. And it seems that Mr. Liam McRae, the crooked redheaded policeman from Boston is here in Mississippi. Intent on revenge for the death of Senator Peter Shields."

A cold wave washed over Memory. *I've seen him.*

Jenson reached for Memory's hand and kissed her ring finger. "Soon you'll be mine forever. I'll protect you from anything and anybody. I'm in love with you. And I'll also tell you, you need never worry about that Shank Potter scum again. He's disappeared from sight. The backyard talk is that he's gone to his reward," he said sarcastically. "Wherever that may be. But I don't think he's strumming a harp."

Memory looked at Jenson with a mixture of gratitude and relief. "Thank the Good Lord," she said. A small chuckle escaped her lips. "You're right. Most likely roasting on a spit.

"There's more going on here at Redemption Ridge, but it's not all bad. I'd better tell you about Sassy, and what I'm doing." Drawing in a deep breath, she exhaled slowly. "I told you I was going to Jackson shopping. And I still am, but this is no longer just a shopping trip. I'm spending the night. There's somebody I need to take care of." She tilted her chin. "I found out that Sassy, Lamont and Bertha's daughter, wants to go on to school." As she said these words, Memory felt a touch of unease. A short time ago she would probably never have thought to see if she could help Sassy. So much had changed within her. So much had needed to change.

"She wants an education," she said, a defensive tone in her voice. "Not only that, she has a beautiful voice and wants to study music." She straightened her skirt and looked at the ground. "Her natural talent is as good as anyone I ever heard in Boston.

"I'm no lady benevolent." Memory said. "But I'm going to help Sassy. I'm looking into a school south of Jackson for her. Cedar Woods." There was a moment of silence. Her blue eyes large, she stared at Jenson to see what his reaction would be.

He pulled her close.

"Good for you. I love you for being the feisty little person you are. And it warms my heart to see the softer side that I always suspected was there."

"Thank you," she whispered. "I should have known how you'd feel. My grip's packed. I have a ride from Franklin and a place to stay, so I'm leaving right after our meal at Mrs. Netter's. It's this side of Jackson, so it's not very far. I'll be staying the night with a friend of Mother. Her chauffer will carry me to the school." Memory stepped back. "They're seeing Sassy in the morning. Me, in the afternoon." She rubbed her chin against his sleeve. I worked out the details to get Sassy there too.

"I'm looking forward to our dinner at Mrs. Netter's." She smiled, then looked up at Jenson. "Mother knows about us. She says her friend, Vernell, told her." A look of relief on her face, Memory laid her head against Jenson's shoulder. "She's not only fine with it, she's thrilled. She says you and I were meant for each other."

Jenson circled Memory's waist with his arm. "Somehow I knew Miss Brucie would be fine with us. It's your father that concerns me."

For Memory, at this moment, standing close to her love, it was as if Shank Potter and her late husband, Thorton, and never been. She'd never had anything but good things happen in her life, and it would be that way forever. This man would see to it. This man had erased her past and would see to her future.

Dale opened the front door, and as he stepped onto the porch, he saw Jenson lift Memory's face and kiss her.

"God love them," he said. *They know*, he thought. *They know exactly what they want.* "They'll get it," he said. But with that realization, a wave of depression hit him. The sight of his sister and his best friend triggered a sore spot. Loneliness swept over him; he felt like burying his face in his hands. "Laura Lee. Beautiful, Laura Lee." He shook his head. "But Samuel," he said. "In my keeping. And dead."

Guilt took over. Dale drew in a deep breath. "Too many men." He exhaled slowly. "Your brother. His legs." *The Krauts. A prop for their goddamn latrine door.* Unconsciously, he reached into his coat pocket and felt for his flask. "My shoulders. Heavy with payback." *Laura Lee. I might hurt Samuel's sister. I might hurt her family.*

"My men. Dead."

"Hey, man," Jenson called out. "Dale."

Dale exhaled a long, painful breath. He felt slightly dizzy and gripped the porch railing. He clenched the railing a moment to steady himself, then bounded down the steps.

"It's been a long time coming for you and my sister," he said as he joined Memory and Jenson. "I could watch you two all day long." He doubled his fist and gave his friend a soft arm punch. "And, if we didn't have things to do, that just might happen. Don't forget. It's still early, but since I'm heading for Oxford with Otis and Laura Lee, I could be pushed for time.

Dale shook his head. "I might check with their English department. And, who knows?" He looked off into space. "I just don't know which way to jump.

"I probably need to come up with some type of business deal to make money." He rose up on the balls of his feet, stayed there a second as if trying to make up his mind about something then said, "But what I'd really like to do is write."

Memory nodded her head. "Yes. And me too," she said softly.

"I'm just not prepared for anything," he said. "Except for being there for my men. Which I didn't do as well as I should have." Dale glanced at his sister. "I haven't said anything to Mother. The old Tallouga County newspaper closed years ago, but the editor's son let me borrow the keys to the building. Thought I'd stop by there and go through their old ledgers and papers." He shrugged his shoulders. "But I'm not sure I want to stay in Mississippi."

"Well, maybe when you get to Oxford, you'll find some answers," Jenson pulled out his pocket watch. "For now, we'd better get moving. I'll leave your sister at her friend's house." He nodded toward Memory.

"The Ferguson place isn't far, and it shouldn't take long. We can check out the house and just drive by the land. There's over four hundred acres of land and it can be bought for a song. After I drop you off at the Stanton's, I'm picking up your dear sister for dinner at Mrs. Netter's."

Jenson reached for Memory's hand and led her around the car. Dale sprang into the back seat. Jenson opened the door for Memory, bent over and kissed the top of her head. He stepped away, cranked the engine, and jumped into the car. "We've got a lot going on today, y'all," he said, steering the car onto Old Farm Road.

***

9:00

"I'm glad you liked the Ferguson land. It's close by and is a bargain to boot. Something we might well consider buying together," Jenson said as he and Dale pulled onto Main Street.

Dale nodded but didn't answer for a minute. "I'm tempted. It depends on our finances. If it's dirt cheap I'm tempted to buy that old Tallouga County news building, finish college with an English degree and start my own paper."

339

"Look over yonder," Jenson said. "Lots of wagons and cars around the funeral home. Not much happens around here. Why don't we swing by there? Somebody important must have died."

Dale checked his pocket watch. "I still have about thirty minutes before I'm due at Otis's."

Jenson steered to the backside of the Blessed Rest Funeral Home.

Huddles of colored people stood around the yard and porch of the funeral home, most of them in their field-hand clothes, talking and milling around as if they were having an important meeting.

Jenson pressed down on the brake pedal and coasted to a stop.

Lamont stood at the funeral home door. When he saw Jenson and Dale, he beckoned to them. When he stepped close enough to be heard, Lamont whispered, "Somethin' bad happened out to Mist Dedmon's place."

"What do you mean?" Dale asked.

"What I mean is, somebody, or the Good Lord Himself, took care of Lucius Dedmon."

A sweat had broken out on Lamont's forehead. "I'm waitin' on Trestle Potter to come in with the hearse now. With Shank not showin' up anymore, he's our only driver.

"This here is bad business, Mist Dale. Dedmon was cut open and scooped out like a hog at killin' time." Shaking his head, Lamont stepped back from the car.

"Whoever killed Dedmon left a pair of false teeth sittin' in his belly. Ready to gnaw on his innards." Lamont ran a finger across his lips, as if cautioning himself to be careful of his words.

"And, whoever split him open. They threw in some snake rattles.

"Their knock-knock. That'll be the hymn he'll hear, on his one-way walk to Hell."

***

"I can't help but think that scum, Lucius Dedmon, got what he deserved," Jenson said as he and Dale pulled away from the funeral home.

"And Topper's safe from him," Dale said. "I'm glad it's been taken care of."

"What?"

"I was thinking about Lamont's boy, Topper."

"Everybody's safe from the bastard now," Jenson said as he drove up to the Stantons' home.

Dale sprang from Jenson's car and waved goodbye. Otis's automobile was parked in front of the house; he had a flannel cloth and was cleaning the front windshield. When Dale came up, he folded the cloth, laid it on the hood, and extended his hand. "We're ready if you are. Laura Lee's grips are loaded. We've got some decent roads and some rough roads ahead of us, but I figure we can make at least twenty miles an hour. We ate a big breakfast," he said, "so with just a few stops, hopefully, unless we have a flat tire or something else happens, that'll carry us 'til we make Water Valley. We're stopping there for a late supper with family friends, the Creekmores. Then we'll drive on to Oxford. It'll be a long day. You can spell me on a little bit of the driving."

"Be glad to."

Otis gestured toward the house. "Laura Lee should be right behind me." He gave Dale a meaningful look. "As I told you, we're staying with cousins in Oxford, and they've got a big house, so large you can get lost in it. I may be overstepping myself, but I think Laura Lee would like to be with you by herself some." He gave Dale a brief smile. "She's talked a lot about the good times you all had during your summers here."

"My visits to Mississippi were the best times of my life," Dale said. "And truth to tell, Laura Lee had a lot to do with it."

Wearing a white blouse, a blue cotton skirt with a matching blue and white plaid jacket, color high in her cheeks, a straw hat with a navy velvet ribbon looped around the brim, her blond hair cascading down her shoulders, Laura Lee looked feminine and dainty as she came down the sidewalk. When a breeze lifted her skirt showing her stocking-clad legs, Dale's heartbeat quickened. Each time he saw Laura Lee, the strong feelings he had possessed for her in the past were with him again.

For a moment they looked at each other; Dale took a slow, deep breath.

"A southern belle." He gave a half bow and opened the car door. "And, I must say, you lighten up a heavy heart."

"Will you be my Sir Galahad?" she asked.

"My pleasure. Get in Meh Lady," he pointed to the front seat.

"Oh no," she protested, "I'm not in the front. I'm riding in the back."

"I know you were raised with a chauffeur, but if it's okay with Otis, that's not the way it will be," Dale said. "I'll take the rear, you take the front seat."

Bent over, crank in hand and ready to start the car, Otis stood and dropped the crank. "We're not having this," he said. "I'll set the tone for this trip. You two had a lot going between you before you left for France, Dale. And you took care of our brother."

Ah, there it was again. That nagging sadness and guilt he felt about their brother, Samuel.

"I was his Captain. He died," Dale said.

"We're not having that kind of talk," Otis answered sternly. "This is a fun trip and I plan on being with two of my favorite people. Both of you, get in the back seat and play like you've never seen nor heard of me before. I'm nowhere in sight. Take up where you left off," he laughed.

Dale took a deep breath. To his ears Otis's laugh was like the sound of tin cans blown over by a shotgun.

He couldn't help the pain he felt when he looked at Laura Lee either, but the trusting way she cut her eyes at him reminded Dale of Samuel.

Settling in, Laura Lee straightened her blouse and removed her hat. She brushed thick curls from her face, fluffing the ends with her fingers.

These simple female gestures touched and calmed Dale. He reached for Laura Lee's hand and kissed it gently. "That'll hold me for the ride," he said. "I think I can behave that long."

"What?"

"Nothing."

But an understanding light seemed to flash in her blue eyes.

Once the ride began, Dale stretched his legs, then lit a cigarette. The hum of the car engine was loud in his ears as Otis turned north from Franklin toward Oxford. Dale rolled the window down, flipped his cigarette out, then wrapped his arms around his waist as if trying to hold in his feelings.

As they rode, every now and then, he glanced toward the front and without wanting to, when he saw Otis's profile, he felt a familiar knot in his stomach; it could have been that of Otis's brother, Samuel.

Thoughts of his dead comrade continued to gnaw at him. Filled with despair, he looked out the window. *His legs. Sliced. A goddamn trophy. Taken by Krauts. A latrine door stop.*

He sat with his head slightly averted, as if he expected a blow to the chin. *I wanted to save him. I couldn't. Samuel. Shot. In front of me. Guns raging. Ruddy, red guts splattering like hailstones from Hell.* Dale's head throbbed. *Got to him. Quick as I could. Samuel. Blinded.*

With the way he was feeling at this moment, in some deep, hidden part of him, he felt like he was between lives, one in France, the other in Mississippi.

As if she'd read his mind, Laura Lee reached for his hand. "You're a good man," she said. "An honorable man," she went on, her voice kind and encouraging.

Outlined against the pale golden light, Dale could barely see Laura Lee's blue eyes slanting slightly as she said, "Samuel wrote us. He was proud of being one of your doughboys."

"I couldn't save my doughboys. God didn't save my doughboys."

"God led them home."

"France was not their home."

"To their heavenly home."

Dale laced his fingers together and pressed down on his knees with them.

"We're here. Now. In Otis's car," Laura Lee said. "On the way to Oxford. You have new things to think about. Both of us do. I've prayed about it."

CHAPTER 36

**The mannequins in the window
Resembled wraiths, veiled in
The false memory of
Past unions.**

**Memory thirsted for her turn
To be a living mannequin,
To inspire the passersby
Into their own desperation.**

Tuesday, 11:00 a.m., March 30

"I'm kindly glad after that what happened to Mistah Liam McRae he got hisself headed on to Vicksburg," Mudge said. "We know it wadn't any of his doin', but folks likely to be kindly stirred up, an' lookin' fer somebody to blame fer the killin' of Lucius Dedmon. An' he jest might come up with him some whiskey running bidness.

"Now, you an' me. We seems to kindly think alike on some things, Miss Thelmer Jewel," Mudge said as he swerved the car around bumps in the dirt road. "Most especially when I hear you tell you're havin' some secon' thoughts about Mistah Liam McRae."

Thelma Jewel rolled to one side and slipped her hand over her right buttocks. She clutched a too-tight girdle, pulled it out then let it go. *I got onto him out there in the cemetery,* she reminded herself. *Looking for those jewels. He said just enough about that Elnora who called me to know he murdered her.* "Well, I'm pretty sure," she said. "Whoever gets in his way, he'll take care of them. I can play that game too. I'm onto him." *In more ways than one.* She clamped her foot down onto the tapestry bag holding her derringer.

"The mornin' ain't even 'bout over yet, an' you an' me, we've done been makin' a day of it, Miss Thelmer Jewel." Mudge hit a pot hole hard enough that it threw him partway across the seat and

Thelma Jewel had to grab the door handle to keep from being slung to the floor. "I been doin' lotsa thinkin'," he went on. "Miss Gertie Mae, she might need her a daddy figger in her life."

Thelma Jewel stole a look at Mudge. "Yes sirree, bobtail. That she does." *He's not all bad. I could do worse; he is a propertied man. And if you look at him in a certain way, and the light's not too strong, he's not too skunk ugly.*

"We'll stop here an' git Gertie Mae an' take her on to Mrs. Netter's fer a dinner." Mudge pulled his roadster to a stop on the stubbly growth of weeds and grass in front of the Divine Deliverance Holiness Church and School for Boys and Girls.

He unhooked a pair of driving glasses from his ears as he and Thelma Jewel got out of the car. She took out a lacy handkerchief, spit on a corner of it, then wiped a roll of sweat from her forehead. "It's the end of March, but I swear to goodness, California wasn't ever this hot. Not even in the dead heat of summertime."

"You ain't seed nothin' yet. Le's us go in." Mudge steered Thelma Jewel straight ahead. "Down front is the altar we done built out of planks from a hayloft, an' over here," he led Thelma Jewel to a small enclosed room just to their left, "is where Brother Tuggle gits down on his knees. He wrestles with the devil hisself," he said proudly.

Mudge opened the door with one arm and waved the other in a grandiose gesture. "Comin' in," he hollered, then he bowed his head as if in the presence of someone greater than he.

"This here's Durrell Tuggle, best known around these here parts as, Brother Tuggle."

A short, stocky, red-faced man sat behind a long, narrow desk made out of weathered plank boards resting on two sawhorses. His faded blue eyes were set far apart, as if each one had its own sights to behold and then report back to the other. Even though it was warm the man wore a frayed gray wool suit and a button down shirt. Brother Tuggle rose and gave Thelma Jewel a slight bow. "Miss Thelmer Jewel. I ain't had me the pleasure, but I do know Miss Gertie Mae, 'n' I'm here to tell you, she's a caution."

Although two of the preacher's bottom front teeth were missing, he talked through his nose, as if somebody had nailed his tongue to the roof of his mouth.

"An you know, the chirren are mostly in school on weekdays, lessen they're out workin' in the fields, earnin' their keep, an' praise the Lord, doin' a little fer the church missions. Tha's where they are today, out pullin' weeds out'n the field, an' earnin' a liddle money, so as we kin go to savin' souls. All 'ceptin' Gertie Mae. I sent out the word that y'all was comin', an' I think the wife's tryin' to clean her up some."

Brother Tuggle fingered a hickory bark brush on his desk, picked it up, then ran the brush across his back teeth. He spit into a dirty brass cuspidor.

"I told Miss Thelmer Jewel what kinda preacher you are," said Mudge. "Come Sunday, when we have our big Celebration, she'll be hearin' you fer herself."

The preacher gave Thelma Jewel a searching look. "Do you know about this here kind a ministry?"

Before she could say anything, Mudge took over. "Brother Tuggle," he said. "He heals the sick an' the lame. He's been known to lay hands on people an' cast out demons. Now me, I ain't much on hoodoo. But there are some commandments in the Bible what's done been fergot about."

"Jest let me have a minute or two," Preacher Tuggle said, swaying backward and forward as he spoke. "An' I can save me a whole raft of souls. Quicker'n you can blink your eyes." He raised a fist. "The Man Who walked on the Waters was heard to say, 'They shall take up serpents.'" Both the preacher's eyes seemed to slide sideways when he said this, as if there were things in the corners of the room they needed to note. "An' when I do, I feel the power in my hands," his voice trilled like a songbird. "Almost enough to move mountains. Got us some kindly high hills, but that ain't my callin'. We ain't got no mountain tops around these here parts. Me. I been called to save Tallouga County. I got me a big chanct at that Celebration what's been planned." The preacher smiled happily, as if he knew a wonderful secret.

As if they had heard their names called, both eyes seemed to slide toward his nose. "But the main thing I need to do is to convert me a mess a folks from the path of damnation they're on, to the one of true righteousness," he said. "I'm good an' ready to wrestle with the devil hisself. Praise the Lord.

"First thang we're gonter do is we'll hand out some of these here programs." He bent over, lifted a large piece of cream colored parchment and unrolled it across the desk.

Mudge steered Thelma Jewel around to where they could read.

"Hear ye. Hear ye. Celebration Day. Long overdue! A Special Service will be held honorin' The Redemption Ridge heroes. And the Long-Buried, Hidden Truth about our own Captain Bruce Claymore will be told!"

"An' come this Easter Sunday, startin' off we'll be actin' more like them churches on Main Street." Brother Tuggle leaned over and gripped a worn Bible that sat on the edge of his desk. "Out where everybody kin see, we'll have us a few of the women folks settin' up fer us to have a big dinner on the grounds followin' our services." Brother Tuggle spit into his sleeve, then wiped his mouth with his arm. "Come time church is over an' done with, then there'll be dinner on the grounds.

"First off there'll be the Celebration namin' an' honorin' our sanctified dead. Each name called out will be followed by a trumpet blast from our very own, Stalk Wheeler, my wife's second cousin. Then, everybody's belly full, 'fore we lets down the tents, there'll be one more call for souls."

"The healin' ceremony, an' I'll be helpin'," Mudge said proudly. "With now my own, Taddler the Raddler convertin' an' savin' souls."

"I got me a ideer. Why don't we let Miss Thelmer Jewel be part of the big healin' service?" Preacher Tuggle suggested. "Bein' as to how she's from California, folks from around these here parts are bound to take notice if the Spirit gits a-holt o' her."

Thelma Jewel nodded her head.

"It's okeydokey by her," Mudge said.

"Then, that's what we'll do," the preacher said. "I'm here to tell you"—He bent his head toward Thelma Jewel—"He controls some purse strangs around these here parts."

Brother Tuggle breathed hard, then, as if he were in the throes of some private religious experience, he shook all over and threw his hands toward the ceiling. "Now, jest don't you call her name before the healin' service."

Mudge reached into his pocket, drew out his watch and studied it. "If we're gonter make dinner at Mrs. Netter's, we'd best git a move on. She keeps the food out 'til after two, but it'll be mostly jest turnip green juice an' cold cawnbread if we don't git on down the road.

"After our dinner at Mrs. Netter's, we gonter make us a stop by the cemetery an' give it a quick look see as to some things that need to be done."

Mudge snapped his fingers as if he had something else on his mind that needed to be taken care of. "An' not only that. We'll need all of our brethren an' sistern to git together at Redemption Ridge come sometime before Friday. We got to make us our plans of what all to do an' where to put everything."

There was a tap on the door.

A short, dumpling-hipped woman with a donkey-shaped face entered. "This here's the wife," Preacher Tuggle said, brushing his hands across his large paunch. "Mother Bunny. She's on the mother board of the Divine Deliverance Holiness Church and School for Boys and Girls."

Right behind Mother Bunny, wearing a calico, long-sleeved dress with a dagging hemline and shoes with the soles flopping as if they were tongues lapping up water, Gertie Mae slowly came into the room. She peeped up and saw her mother. "They're not nice to me here," she wailed, cramming her fist into her mouth.

"Well, I never," Thelma Jewel said. "Hush your mouth. That's a bunch of hogwash. And right now, we're going to get us some dinner. But you have to behave yourself. If you do, you might even get you a fried chicken leg and some mashed potatoes. "

"I want me a vanilla soda," Gertie Mae whined.

"So, we'll do our savin' at the Celebration an' Healin' Service come Sunday." Brother Tuggle nodded in Thelma Jewel's direction. "Show 'em we can even save folks from up nawth." The trio left the preacher and his wife to go have a meal.

"It's gonter be kindly good for somma us to git our business done while Mr. Liam McRae is otherwise engaged over to Vicksburg," Mudge said to Thelma Jewel, as he, Thelma Jewel and Gertie Mae walked toward the car. "Brother Tuggle's had Miss Mealie Maude mostly do up the invites, an' we'll git them put out by tomorrow or Thursday mornin'. That a-way folks can make their plans. This is gonter be a really big thing fer the town of Franklin," Mudge said proudly. He went to the front, turned the crank handle, jumped into the car and, shifting gears, swung the car around, and they headed for Mrs. Netter's.

12:30

"Lord a mercy, something sure smells good." Thelma Jewel dabbed a thin streak of spittle from her cheeks as she, Mudge, and Gertie Mae stood in the doorway to Mrs. Netter's dining room.

"I want me a vanilla soda," Gertie Mae whined.

Thelma Jewel gave her behind a smart little slap. "Hush your mouth."

"Over there, there's three chairs vacant, at that air back table." Mudge pointed.

Thelma Jewel put her hand on Gertie Mae's shoulders. "You're not a country orphan. You're kin to quality folks. Tuck your skirt up, Gertie Mae, and hold your shoulders back," she said as Mudge led the way through the crowded room.

Three large round, wooden tables with a separate bottom and a spinning top were in a line in the long room. The bottom part of the tables were covered with linen cloths and were set with plates, tableware and napkins. The upper, spinning lazy Susans were loaded with platters and bowls of steaming food.

"She's got her usual spread out here fer folks," Mudge said as Thelma Jewel and Gertie Mae pulled out their chairs.

"I want me a vanilla soda," Gertie Mae said as they sat down, and an aproned black lady set glasses of iced tea in front of their plates.

"We ain't got no nellar soders," the lady said.

"They don't have vanilla soda. That's all I wanted. I haven't had me any vanilla sodas since you made us leave California. I want to go home."

It was a short-lived whine. Thelma Jewel popped Gertie Mae's leg, then she mounded food on Gertie Mae's plate. The three of them quickly began to lift platters of fried chicken, pork chops, sausage patties, pickled pigs feet, meat loaf, and roast beef and gravy from the top table and piled their plates high.

"Pearlie," Mudge hollered and beckoned their waitress over. "Git us all another plate," he said.

"My name ain't Pearlie. It's Opal."

"Well, it's Pearlie today," Mudge muttered.

They set the meat platters back, picked up the empty plates that had just been set down and once again gave the table a whirl. They loaded up on butterbeans, macaroni and cheese, fried corn, cabbage, mashed potatoes, sweet potatoes, black-eyed peas, stuffed eggs, homemade rolls and water cornbread.

They ate, spun and replenished, over and over again. Finally, Thelma Jewel sighed heavily and rubbed her stomach. "Well, after I have me some pecan pie, peach cobbler and ice cream, that ought to hold me until suppertime."

A short while later, desserts eaten, Thelma Jewel, Gertie Mae, and Mudge pushed their plates back. As Mudge turned his head over his shoulder he saw two more people, a young man and a lady had entered the dining room.

He erupted a loud burp. "Well I swan." He bumped shoulders with Thelma Jewel. "That over there is your half-sister."

Her face frozen as a mannequin, Thelma Jewel rolled her eyes toward the door.

A couple stood in the doorway.

Memory wore a pale blue jacket and skirt. Navy fringe dangling from her sleeves brushed back and forth like a feather duster caught in a breeze. She tucked strands of auburn hair under her velvet cloche hat. Jenson and Memory looked around for a second as if they were not sure where they wanted to sit.

Thelma Jewel raised her eyebrows and dipped her chin. *I know who you are,* she thought, as Jenson put his hand on Memory's shoulder and steered her to a table in front of the one where Mudge, Thelma Jewel, and Gertie Mae sat.

"You owe me, and I'm going to collect," she whispered as Mudge stood and the three of them got up to leave. "And you're going to know I'm here. But not who I am. Not yet."

Jenson pulled out a chair for Memory as Thelma Jewel, Mudge, and Gertie Mae passed by their table. Elbow cocked, Thelma Jewel stuck her foot in front of Gertie Mae and nudged her.

"Ow!" the girl squealed and spread-eagled on the floor just as Memory turned sideways to sit down.

"She tripped my daughter!" Thelma Jewel hollered, pointing her finger at Memory. "I saw it."

Everyone in the dining room raised their heads and stared. Halfway seated, Memory braced herself against the table and stood. "No, no, I didn't. But, I'm so sorry. I'm sorry she fell."

"You hurt my foot," Gertie Mae wailed, crawling to her knees.

"Well, I never. Some people," Thelma Jewel snorted. "Some people who think they're so high and mighty ought to pay more attention to what they're doing." She helped Gertie Mae to her feet. "My poor daughter," she called over her shoulder.

"Oh, I hope she's not hurt. I'm sorry she fell, but I didn't trip her," Memory said to Jenson as Thelma Jewel flounced away with the air of one who has just won an argument.

"That won't be the last time I get you," Thelma Jewel breathed under her breath. "You're going to get what's coming to you. All of you. And I'll see to it."

"That was strange." Jenson shook his head. "I don't know what happened, but whoever that girl is with a crooked leg, you didn't touch her."

Memory turned her head and looked toward the door as Mudge, Thelma Jewel, and Gertie Mae left the dining room.

"Hmm," she said. "I wonder. Something's funny about that woman and her daughter."

Her blue eyes flashed and a cold chill crept over Memory. Like a puzzle piece falling into place, she knew who the child and her mother were. The girl looked like a picture she had seen of her mother, when she was a young girl.

"Jenson," she started. "This is not good."

Jenson unrolled his napkin and spilled the silverware onto the table.

"Whatever it is that you have on your mind, you're leaving town and we won't see each other for a day or two. Why don't you just let it rest for now," he said. "You and I are here to enjoy our food and each other's company."

A smile played across Memory's lips. "You're right. I will." She breathed a forced sigh of relief. "Right now, I need to have Cedar Woods and Sassy on my mind." She leaned forward. "Don't say anything about my elbows on the table."

"I don't see them," Jenson said. "And there's something I really need to tell you. Please, be careful. I heard from a friend in Boston. There's a possibility that the Boston policeman, the one who we think murdered Thornton, may be in these parts.

"You're heading for Jackson in just a little while and I'll be tied up the next few days job hunting and land looking." He shifted uncomfortably in his chair. "You won't be here and I won't be around to protect you. No matter where you are, I want you to be careful." His eyes brimmed with concern. "Some bad things have happened around here lately."

He knotted his fists. "Shank Potter. That tombstone being thrown your window last night," he said in a firm voice.

"And having nothing to do with us, but a bad man named Lucius Dedmon was murdered today. He's been supplying whiskey and medicine for Lamont's son, Topper to sell." He reached over and squeezed Memory's hand. "And my good friend and your brother, Dale's, been buying from them."

Memory started to say, "I'm pretty sure we just met my half-sister, and, as evidenced by that melodrama we witnessed, I'm sure they mean us no good," but she stopped herself. She spread her napkin across her lap. "I'm going to be tied up with Sassy and Cedar Woods. I can't do anything about Dale and his past, but I do think Laura Lee can make a big difference in his life. If he'll just let her." She grasped Jenson's wrist. "It's up to him. But maybe I can help Sassy." She took a deep breath. "I plan to stay in Jackson for a day or two." She picked up a fork, then set it down.

Jenson leaned toward Memory. "You are now wearing my ring. You make me crazy," he said. "I'm speaking over the noise of these dishes and clanking of silverware, and I don't care who hears me. You are beautiful. Your blue outfit matches your eyes. Your lashes are so long they could swoop and dip in the breeze like a butterfly's wings." He looked, then he grinned. "Don't spend so much time on Sassy you forget about me." A smile spread across his face. "Even if you want to run away, because of what I'm about to say.

"'My love and I dined with Mrs. Netter
The meal was fine,
The company divine
But me a poet—it won't get any better.'"

He raised a finger, like a teacher instructing a student. "I want a wedding date set. Posthaste. Or I'll write you more poetry."

Memory met his smile with one of her own. "I think while I'm in the city, I'll go to the Emporium. Look at rolls of fabrics for my wedding dress." She paused, then nodded her head as if she'd come to a decision about something.

"Be home waiting on my bride's dress to be made." Laughing softly she tilted her head. "Won't the Kaiser be surprised when he comes in this weekend?"

CHAPTER 37

**Whose lineage affords
A chapel in the
Service of a mausoleum?**

**Memories are the cremated remains
Of ghosts.**

**And each strike under pressure
Glass caps transformers crowned.**

**And these are the family jewels,
Transitional, time travelling,
Random, crystallography.**

Tuesday afternoon, 12:30

Brucie glanced over her shoulder toward the hallway, then she set down the photo album she had been going through. "Vernell, Vernell. You meant so much to this family. Do you know how I feel? Somehow, someway, I sense you do. About a lot of things."

Just at that moment Bertha came into the parlor. She folded her hands against her chest as if they held something dear, yet unseen. "I want to thank you for lettin' Miss Memory see to some schoolin' for my girl."

"I have heard there are not many girls in school at Cedar Woods," Brucie said. A fleeting expression of doubt crossed her face. "I'm not so sure this is for the best for Sassy. She might be getting a little bit ahead of her time," she warned. "And in some ways, I'm of the old school.

"But I'll say this"—She raised her chin—"When my daughter sets that hard head of hers, she has a talent for getting things done."

"An' my girl. She wants Cedar Woods an' then to go on from there," Bertha said.

"More school? That will be a whole different way of life. She'll probably be leaving Redemption Ridge. And Mississippi! Are you and Lamont ready for that?"

Bertha turned away from Brucie. "Thank you, blessed Jesus, for what just might happen," she breathed, her eyes blurring with tears. "Sassy's a smart girl," she said, once again facing Brucie, an unacknowledged yearning in her voice. "She might get her a chance. I wants for her to get onto somethin' besides birthin' babies, scrubbin' clothes an' pickin' beans an' cotton." She rocked back on her heels. "Lamont said for me to make sure you know. Later this mornin' he wants that you should come to the cemetery. He's got him somethin' you might want to see to out there," she said, as she went through the pretense of dusting off a marble end table.

"He got in touch with me."

Earlier that morning Brucie went downstairs and picked up the family photo album. When she went into the kitchen for her morning cup of coffee, she had found a note from Lamont on the kitchen table that said he wanted to meet her at Vernell's grave around one thirty. He didn't say why, but she had an idea it had something to do with, not only her future, but also their children's. "Any other person and it would be strange to be meeting at the cemetery. But not Lamont," she said. Bertha either didn't hear her or didn't choose to answer.

***

1:00

"Minyard's already got old Maude hitched to the wagon," Bertha said as Brucie swallowed the last of her corn bread muffin, washed it down with iced tea and pushed away from the kitchen table. "He's bringin' it around front."

Brucie checked the Seth Thomas clock on the living room mantel. By the time she got to the cemetery, she'd be right on time.

She picked a pale green linen duster off a hall tree to protect her good skirt and blouse and went outside.

Minyard met her at the bottom of the porch steps. "I got the buckboard hooked up."

"I don't know how long I'll be. I'd kind of like to be alone and think about some things. I'll drive myself on over, Minyard," Brucie said, walking toward the wagon.

"Yes'um."

Brucie tucked up her skirt, Minyard took her arm, lifted her into the old buckboard and gave her the reins.

"Hoe down, Maude," he called, slapping a large hand across the mule's rump. Maude jumped and then she began a slow, wag-headed, swaying walk. Minyard ran on ahead of them and opened the gate.

"Memory. Dale. Young people." Brucie flipped the reins and the buggy rattled onto Old Farm Road. "Sassy. I need to realize. The world's changing." *And Bertha. She wants more for her girl.* Brucie let out a long, ragged breath. *I never had the chance for more schooling.* "Daddy Claymore saw to that," she muttered.

The years tumbled by like piles of fall leaves blown by a strong storm. The land was no longer the shadow of itself she had formed in her memory. Even with all of the heartache buried beneath the clay, it was real. "I'm back on my own land again. My beginning was here. My ending will be here."

Brucie shook her head. "But please, God, may I see my children with their lives straightened out first?"

Soon Brucie pulled back on the reins and halted Maude at the colored cemetery. She drew in deep breaths of the fresh country air. There was a purity here in the Mississippi springtime, something she didn't see or feel in Boston.

"Time to move." She swung her legs out and slid from the buckboard. Glancing toward the white cemetery she noticed that many of the wrought iron spears were leaning, some had fallen over and they were smeared with orange rust. *This is where our people rest. Until He comes again.* "It's in need of attention."

Lamont hadn't made it. Brucie waited inside the colored cemetery. A short while later he drove up in one of the funeral home wagons, stepped out and hurried through the gate.

"Sorry I'm late." He removed a straw hat from his head, tipped it to Brucie, then put it back on.

"Somethin' bad come up, and I thought I might not make it. Lucius Dedmon's done been killed. And he's down at our funeral home. But me, the likes of Mist Dedmon. I ain't gonna let him interfere with what I needs to do, Miss Brucie."

Brucie held her hand up. "Lamont. You don't have to call me Miss," she said.

"Well, if it was just me and you, no. But I might forgit. And that's why I have to say, Miss Brucie."

"Well it's for sure we don't want to get anybody riled up," Brucie said, "so we'll leave it be.

"I knew you'd be here," she said. "When I left Redemption Ridge, I never thought I'd want to be back." She raised her hands as if offering up a prayer. "But knowing you're here. Feeling as I do about this land, even with its memories. Now, praise be to the Lord, this is where I want to end my days. To rest next to my mama. Be close by to Vernell and my real father, Captain Bruce Claymore." Her feeling of nostalgia was replaced by one of determination. "But God willing, and I'll make sure my children see to it, I'll not be by Daddy Claymore."

Lamont nodded understandingly. He took her arm as they walked across the uneven ground, thick with twisted vines, heavy grass, and broken tree limbs, toward Vernell's final resting place. Graves had been slowly swallowed then tipped over by the restless ground. None of the old relics she remembered, the trinkets, seashells, were there anymore. Many of the concrete markers were cracked. Some had fallen over as if bowing to the ravages of time and weather. But she noticed that some of the wooden crosses looked as if they had been repaired; they were speared into the ground, proudly awaiting judgment day.

Lamont gestured with his head. "After Minyard, there ain't nobody left what's gonna tend to this here."

"All these years. It's fallen on you to take care of so many things."

"Thanks to old Sheriff Bramlett, we gots us a new church and a nice graveyard out back of that new church. This place here don't look too good no more. But you and me," Lamont said as they walked. "We'll come back to here.

"Now what's been done here, and that ain't much, my son Minyard has seen to. Come later in the spring, he mows it right regular. And, he's been setttin' up some of the old tombstones what's done fallen over. Nailin' up some of them wooden crosses and paintin' names and dates on 'em." He looked pensive for a moment. "Minyard. He mostly keeps his peace about things Any way you turns, he be's the caretaker now in this here family of ours." His face softened for a minute. "He kindly has a different walk from his brother, Topper.

"Topper. Now he's different. He might always be living willy-nilly. I gots me a bad feelin'."

"I pray that people and time will be good to both of them, Lamont," Brucie said. "We need more gentleness in this world."

Lamont took a deep breath.

"Now as to Sassy. If Miss Memory can make this here work, my girl Sassy'll be standin' on her own."

"I believe that's going to happen." Brucie put her hand on his arm and stopped for a moment. "I know you're an assistant preacher at your church. Someday I'd love to come and hear you preach."

"I'd like that too, Miss Brucie, but it might not be seemly."

Brucie stared at Lamont a moment and then gave him an understanding smile.

"That makes me think on to some things what needs to be said," he went on. "Let's us talk on other things. You best watch your backside with them Potters. They'll always and forever be up to no good."

A fond, protective look in his eyes, he glanced down at Brucie. "Now closer to home. You gots you that girl what's been hid away out there in California. And you may git hold of you a granddaughter. They're gittin' ready to come into all of this. You needs to think on what's to be done." The concern in his voice was touching. "You know I speaks the truth. You gots to watch out for yourself."

As if there were an unspoken agreement between them, they stopped walking. He shook his head. "You and me here at our old meetin' ground. Seems like the old days."

"You've always thought of others." Brucie gently rubbed his arm.

"And, looky over yonder."

They had come to a spot that held a special place in both their hearts. "There's where my mama's buried at."

No marker showed. A slightly raised mound on the border of the property, away from the other graves, was a place only the two of them and their children knew about—Vernell and Captain Bruce's resting place. Brucie sank down onto the old wooden bench at the top of Vernell's grave and ran her hand across the carved inscription: *He is arisen.* Both she and Lamont were quiet for a minute. The only sounds were wind sweeping through the tree limbs and off in the distance a quick harsh bray from the mule, Maude.

"My mama. She's here," Lamont said after a moment of silence. "Awaitin' fer Jesus. She's got company in there with her." He stepped sideways, then looked off into the distance. "And, that ain't all."

Old days rushed back as Brucie remembered her and Lamont burying their father, Bruce Claymore's, remains. *His bones, wrapped in a Confederate uniform, were laid to rest in Vernell's coffin.*

Brucie hid her trembling hands in the fold of her duster.

Lamont took a deep breath. "You remember, I'm sure," he said. "Them other bones that was here in that glass jar jamb up to my mama's coffin. It held my twin sister's bones. Sunnie Flo."

Brucie's eyes were drawn to the ground. "I remember," she said softly.

Lamont frowned. "All that time ago. Sheriff Bramlett was thinking ahead. It's good my mama was buried deep.

"Now, as to why we're here." He reached for Brucie's hand. "Them jewels."

Brucie stood and Lamont gave her hand a soft squeeze. He bent over and rubbed a finger across a thin layer of dust on the bench seat. "We did us something right smart when we moved them jewels. Up here. Under these here bench legs.

"We've used us lots of 'em," he said. "But mostly what's left, they may still bring a good bit of money," he said. 'Folks been searchin' fer them jewels since after The War. Everybody mostly looks fer them over around where the Confederates are at rest. I found some diggin' around where Mr. C.W. Claymore's bones are laid. But you and me. We knowed all the time where they was at."

"And, if they were to put up the whole town of Franklin on a market to sell, those jewels would probably still be worth enough to buy it lock, stock and barrel," Brucie offered. "Of course, practically speaking, the town may not be worth much."

Lamont smiled slightly when she said this. "Now me and you. We's it, Miss Brucie. Let's us see to each other. Like we've always done. They're right there close by to my mama. And Captain Bruce Claymore."

Brucie sighed. "For better or for worse. During the war, they may well have changed the tide for this part of the country if our birth father Bruce Claymore had gotten them through to the port of Orleans."

"Well, he didn't," Lamont said flatly. "And he was a good man. But more's the blessin' he didn't get them through."

"Every now and then we come to a crossroads." Lamont looked pensive for a moment and then went on, "And that's why I'm here. You all are back home. Fer good. Except fer you, other folks wouldn't believe me, but my mama talked to me last night. She reminded me, your girl, Memory, would be seein' to my daughter, Sassy. And my mama, Miss Vernell, I can tell you this. She wants you to know, she's right proud."

"The two of them might be getting into more than they bargained for," Brucie said softly.

"Sassy's my blood niece." She said the words tentatively, as if they were something she was just realizing. Her cheeks blushed with something like shame for herself and hope for Sassy. "My daughter's teaching me. Things I need to see." Her ambivalence toward Sassy's moving on with her life faded as she spoke these words. "Someday things will be different. Until then, hopefully the two of them will see to each other." She felt a soft touch across her shoulders; what could have been comforting arms encircled her. But there was just she and Lamont, and he stood slightly in front of her.

"Vernell, Vernell," Brucie whispered.

"Why I wanted you to come today," Lamont said, his voice barely above a whisper, "I'm gonna do what my mama asked me last night.

"My mama. She and I wants you to take the biggest part of these here jewels. They mostly belongs to your peoples. You can do the most good with them."

"You're my brother. We're together. And that includes these jewels. You've always looked after everything." Brucie felt an ache in her throat. "You stayed. I left."

"I've done used some fer my new church. And our funeral home." Lamont gave a soft laugh. "You've always been stubborn, Miss Brucie. We'll leave that be fer now, but that ain't the last of it. Miss Memory is seein' to my daughter. I just have me a feelin', between the Good Lord, and my mama, things are gonna work out. In ways I couldn't never have thought of." Lamont straightened his shoulders. "We'd best head on back," he said. "I've gots to tend to Mist Lucius Dedmon. Lots a folks wanted to see him gone."

Brucie lifted out her cross. "This was from your mama. The hairs, I was told, are from Bruce Claymore. I never take it off."

"Let me show you something else. It's in my pocket now, but I've kept it in my Bible," she said. "For over forty years. It was the last thing you gave me when we said goodbye. We thought, forever. I brought it with me today."

She wiped her eyes, reached into her duster, held up a yellowed and worn sheet of paper and began to read:

> **I writ some lines to you**
> **I know they ain't no good**
> **Since I ain' never dared to write.**
> **But I felt like I should.**

I don't know much good 'n bad
But in my heart I gots to stand
Close to Ol Top,
Near unto his hand.

My mama give you a cross.
It lays next to your heart.
Touch it. Think 'bout me,
An' our partin' ain't no loss.

Please, don't you grieve
'Cause you has to go an' leave.
I writ this, wishin' you good.
We been sealed by our blood.

Lamont

Lamont's eyes filled with tears. "My mama. She'd a been proud of what Miss Memory's doing fer my Sassy girl."

"She may even be part of what's happening, Lamont. And, I needed to rethink some things. I'm proud for both of our girls."

Hand in hand, as they turned away from Vernell's grave a chorus of birds seemed to fill the air with a blended, high-pitched song. Brucie noticed that the sky, which had been a vague shadowy gold all morning, seemed to flare crimson near the far end of Redemption Ridge. She blinked her eyes, then looked again. The sky had not changed. It was the same as it had been all day.

Lamont dropped Brucie's hand. He stopped walking. His legs stiffened. His eyes grew dreamy. His body began to move from side to side in a slow rhythm.

"Listen, Miss Brucie. Do you hear it?"

Hair prickled on the back of her neck. As if acknowledging an unseen presence, she crossed herself.

Voices.

"No. We're just getting carried away. It's our imagination."

A thrumming sound.

Then she experienced a moment of déjà vu. "I do. I do hear something. It sounds like a drum. Like it's saying, Kadom. Kadom."

"That's them old voodoo drums. We heard them before. You and me, Brucie. At a sanctification ceremony."

Brucie clutched her cross.

"I do remember," she said. "And wait a minute. Do you have a knife?"

"I do. I have the one."

Lamont reached into his pocket. He held a knife in the flat of his right hand.

"I've seen that wolf's head knife before," she said. "Here in this cemetery. You and I. We've used it. Back when we were children. Shortly before I left Redemption Ridge."

"Ain't nobody but me and you that'd understand this, Brucie."

"We should do this. It was meant to be. Both of us," she said.

Lamont gripped the knife. He bit his bottom lip. He pointed his left finger and stuck it with the knife.

Then he reached for Brucie's hand. He pricked it.

"My sister."

"My brother."

They pressed their fingers together.

Lamont put the knife back into his pocket. He gave Brucie a boost into the buckboard. "It ain't up to you and me no more. It's up to our people to make it right. Miss Memory and Mist Dale. My Sassy." He took off his hat and popped his hat against his leg several times. He put it back on his head, and turned away. "My Minyard." He closed his eyes. "And I pray to God, My Topper."

The heavy smell of sweet olive drifted through the cemetery. As if something or someone were trying to get Brucie's attention, a spiraling surge of warm air brushed her face, like someone blowing out a deep breath. One they'd held for a long time.

She turned and looked toward Vernell's burial place. "I could say, too much imagination, Brucie," she said softly. "But it's not."

Lamont turned away. Brucie suddenly felt as if there'd been a drop in pressure. She looked back toward the colored cemetery and saw wavering shadows, unformed shapes. A flutter of white appeared, then what looked to be the back of a woman's head and the flash of a tattered gray uniform.

The trees seemed to be breathing in rhythm as she heard the words, "Sassy gone make you proud, Miss Brucie. She gone do right by y'alls."

Brucie stuck her finger to her lips, sucked Lamont's blood, sprang from the wagon and hurried to catch up with him. "We'll always look after each other," she said. "And pray to God, our children will too," she whispered.

Their arms entwined, they walked away together.

CHAPTER 38

**A bioluminescent willow is
The nervous fountainhead,
The nodes of each words,
Drab berries of ache peppered
In the aurora wind.
Southern lights,
Secluded table,
Oxford, MS.**

Tuesday afternoon, March 30

Otis drove as swiftly as he dared. In some places where the narrow road gave way to stretches of concrete or to gravel the tires joggled, slinging Dale and Laura Lee from side to side as Otis held the wheel tightly and steered carefully. Hit the brakes too hard and the backside of the car could switch, like a fat woman's hips as she walked across far apart stepping stones.

Mile after mile much of the landscape had a forgotten, lost-in-time look. Mulberry and chinaberry trees spread branches over small, once white-washed homes that were now rat-fur gray and surrounded by scraggly, thick weeds. Their out-of-plumb porches were littered with broken furniture, kettles, and slop jars. There were abandoned cabins with sagging roofs, outhouses with loose hanging doors, as if someone had run out in a hurry, never to return.

Otis slowed, motoring in what he called "grandma gear" as he drove through a few small towns, past rambling old homes enclosed by picket fences, with wide porches stretching across the front. Through the open car windows they heard the sounds of trotting horse hooves, other puttering automobiles and the calls of small boys and dogs as they scootered and scurried down the streets.

Stands of trees, cows in fields, ponds, small hills, and barns lost their identity as cool shadows crept over the road and the sun slowly retired to the west. The scenes outside the window vanished. Night had fallen. Inside the car it was hard to see each other.

Long hours after they had left Franklin, "Water Valley," Otis sang out, relief coloring his voice.

He crossed a line of railroad tracks, turned a sharp corner and shoved the brake down. The car stopped with a jerk in front of a house set a little way back from the street. The front door flung open, golden bright lights illuminated the hallway. A porch light came on.

"Soup's served," a tall man called out as he bounded down the front steps. "I know y'all are ready to get back on the road soon's you can, so we'll make it a quick supper. Course, you're welcome to stay the night."

"Thanks," Otis laughed and shook his head. "But our plans haven't changed. It's not far as the crow flies, so after dinner we'll be heading on to Oxford. And Dale's got a full day at the school tomorrow. So, let me do this proper," he said. "Dale, this is Hiram Creekmore, a good friend of ours."

Done with supper, while they were eating blackberry cobbler and homemade ice cream, Hiram leaned back in his chair. "If you're re-enrolling in Ole Miss and thinking about taking more English courses," he said, "you ought to try to meet up with a young feller, a Mr. William Faulkner. He's a poet, short story writer, an artist and a member of The Marionettes theater group at Oxford. I know his people. Along those lines, The Marionettes are putting on a play this week. Mr. Faulkner's pretty active in that organization."

Hiram pointed to his son who had finished before the grownups. "Hubert. Run look on my desk and get the *Mississippian*. It has Mr. Faulkner's story in it and right next to it are some pictures he's done." He shook his head as his son scampered away. "And this fourteen-year-old scalawag son of mine. He has his sights set on writing too. Give him a few years, and he could be up there with the best of them." He laid down his spoon. "But me, I'm more set on him being a good soldier, like those of y'all who just came back from the war."

Hubert ran back and dropped papers on the table. Hiram waved them toward Dale. "This Faulkner. He's supposed to be a bit of a renegade. I'll keep the pictures, but you can take the newspaper with you."

Dale scanned the pictures. "Not that I'm an expert, but he's a darn good artist."

Hiram pulled off his gold rimmed glasses and gave Dale a meaningful look.

"Hear what I say. This man will make his mark in literature. Not just in this state. But in the world."

Otis yawned and pushed his chair back. "We don't have far to go, but we need to get back on the road," he said. "It's been a long day. Next stop, Oxford. Then we'll hit the sack. And we'll worry about school, plays and writers tomorrow."

Thank you's, goodbyes and see-you-later's rang out as the three of them got into the car.

"The house we're staying in's just off the square," Otis said as they pulled away from the Creekmore home. "I'll get you to the university in the morning. You can always hitch a ride back over here from the school. You'll probably be spending most of your day on campus, checking into things."

"Everything's a big maybe, right now," Dale said.

Once Otis, Laura Lee and Dale drove away from Water Valley, the only light breaking the dark were the beams of a few oncoming headlights. For long minutes, Dale and Laura Lee sat apart on the back seat. Then, Laura Lee moved closer to Dale. She stroked his knee, his hand fell over hers. A thick, expectant silence fell between them.

Dale had remembrances from the past, hope of things to come. "You're giving me hope, in spite of myself," he whispered.

His lips touched hers. Her lips parted to receive him. Dale's breathing grew shallow and fast. His hand slid under her skirt.

"Dead ahead. I see the lights of Oxford," Otis called out all too soon. "Almost there."

"I can't get out of the car like this," Dale whispered.

"Why?"

"Never mind," he groaned.

Laura Lee slid away from Dale, and by the time they drove thorough deserted streets and pulled to a stop in front of a stately, two-story white home, Dale straightened his pants and breathed a sigh of relief.

Wednesday afternoon, March 31

Otis opened the car door and let his sister out in front of J.E. Neilson's Department Store where Dale waited for her.

"I've got some decisions to make." Dale showed Laura Lee an Ole Miss catalogue tucked under his arm. "But I'll get into that later. What would you like to do, Meh Lady?"

"For now, let's walk around the courthouse square and after that do a little window shopping," she said. "Then we'll sit down somewhere, and you can tell me about school."

"I'd like that."

Even though it wasn't Saturday, there were a few autos, buggies, and some wagons filled with vegetables, bolts of material and old clothes parked around the courthouse square. "Wait here just a minute," Dale said. "I see somebody special over there. Blind Jim."

Dale touched the shoulder of a colored man leaning against a lamp post, then shook his hand. They talked briefly, then Dale rejoined Laura Lee.

"That man is a legend. The word is that he's been the official cheerleader for Ole Miss since around 1896. Or so I've been told. He's a tradition and a legend here." Dale felt an attraction. It was as if something or someone lured him to stay close to what lay around him. "But this is silly," he said.

"What?" Laura Lee asked.

"Nothing. Oxford has a good, comfortable feel to it, but I have things to take care of," Dale said, as they turned away from the courthouse and crossed the street. He gestured to a backless bench in front of Neilson's.

"I don't lack much to graduate," he said as they sat down. "If I do anything, I may pick up my studies in English. Not sure I want to, though." He shook his head.

"You mentioned starting a newspaper. There's none in Franklin. We could use one."

"I thought about it, but don't think I really want to. That means getting involved in the town more than I care to," he said crisply.

"Or really want to," he added.

Laura Lee put her hand over her mouth as if there were more she wanted to say but was afraid to.

"Let me show you something." Dale opened the Ole Miss catalogue and lifted a program from it. "There's a play by the Oxford Marionettes tonight. If you remember Hiram Creekmore mentioned William Faulkner. I had a cup of coffee and lunch in *Tom and Spiros Cafe* in the University Post Office Building. And I was introduced to the mysterious Faulkner. He did the illustrations for tonight's drama." Dale showed her the playbill. "It looks pretty good, and I was wondering if you would like to go?"

"I'd love to," Laura Lee said.

"Why don't we have an ice cream soda at the drugstore then I'll walk you back to the house. I'll catch a ride back to the University and check out more English and business courses. I'm keeping in mind though, I can always get a better paying job back east somewhere. And if I stay in Franklin, there's a lot of old family history I would feel a real need to sort through." Dale paused. He didn't know what, or how much to say. "Lay to rest some of our ghosts." His mouth tightened. "And there are some family members we might have problems with. Not just my father." He didn't call any names, but he had his half-sister and her little girl in mind.

Dale tucked the Ole Miss catalogue and the drama program under his arm. "Enough said." He stood, bent over and took Laura Lee's arm.

"I'll make the arrangements for tonight while I'm on campus. I think Otis would like the play too."

***

Wednesday evening/night

"I'm glad we went to the play," Otis said braking in front of his cousin's house. "Bachelor me. I'm meeting up with some stags. If I come in at all, it'll be late, so I'll see y'all in the morning."

"Don't get in trouble," Dale said. "If you get lost, don't forget. Your room's right across the hall from mine."

Taking Laura Lee's arm he escorted her down the dimly lit hall. When they got to her room, she stared up at Dale. He hesitated, tilted her chin with the tip of his finger and kissed her.

"Is this seemly, Meh Lady?" he asked.

"To me it is," she whispered. "I've waited."

He almost took a step through the door which she held open but decided not to. In many ways he was on shaky ground. They'd just buried her brother. She'd been hurt enough, and he didn't know which way he was going with his life. Dale smiled sadly, then stepped away.

Back in his room he took his jacket off and slung it onto a chair. It was quiet. He felt so alone. He knew he'd withheld himself from Laura Lee, that she wanted more. Dale shook his head. Truth to tell, so did he. Memories of his last summer in Franklin invaded his thoughts. He had been with her so much before he left to go fight a war, and he was beginning to think they had a future together. Even though he ached for her with every fiber of his being, he just couldn't seem to let go of his sad, guilty feelings. "I don't deserve her."

Restless, he shook off his wooly gathering and reached for his coat. He felt for his whiskey, but instead he pulled out the Ole Miss catalogue. He flung the catalogue into a metal waste can. He lifted out his flask, took a long, deep swallow and set the flask on the floor.

He turned off the wooden table lamp. Before he could slip into bed he heard a timid tap. Heart pounding, he slid the door open.

A smidgen of light from the hall framed Laura Lee wearing a thin, white satin robe and gown. Even in the dimly lit hallway he could see the outline of her sensuous body. Her eyes that spoke of love met his that spoke of sadness. Dale lowered his first.

"Sh." She put her finger to her lips. "I want to come in. I want to stay with you."

Dale let out a breath. *Maybe, just maybe*, he thought.

"I know you hurt," she said. "You saw horrible things in the war. I can help. If you'll have me. We're here to help each other. I've prayed about it."

Barriers he had erected around his feelings crumbled. Sorrow and guilt melted into hope. "Oh, God, yes," he moaned, closing and locking the door behind her.

His hands gentle, he stroked Laura Lee's hair, soft as corn silk.

She dropped her robe.

Dale lifted the gown over her head.

He stepped back. "Let me look at you," he said.

Her loveliness took his breath away. "Dear God. How beautiful you are," he whispered. His body melded with Laura Lee's as he took her in his arms and drew her onto the bed beside him.

He cupped her breasts. He slid down. His tongue caressed her nipples.

"Please," she begged. "Only you. I've waited."

Gently Dale pushed her legs apart.

She arched her back. "Oh, sweet Jesus," she moaned.

A brief finger of guilt tapped him. He almost pulled away.

"I don't have protection," he said softly.

"I'll protect you," she whispered.

You don't even know what I mean, he thought. Overcome with desire, he placed himself between her thighs.

"I will take care of you," he whispered. "I promise."

***

Dale jerked awake. He was alone. Laura Lee had slipped away sometime during the night. There was a dreamlike quality to what had happened. His spirits rose; it had to do with hope, with remembered love.

He got out of bed. "Come what may, Redemption Ridge will be my home."

He rubbed his head with the flat of his hand.

"I want a normal life," he said. "A wife. A family." He scooped the Ole Miss catalogue from the waste can.

"School. The paper. An editor.

"And, Meh Lady, Laura Lee."

CHAPTER 39

A sparrow swooping,
It's only family jewel
A bite of magnetite
Under the crown of keratin.

By the stars and weight of earth,
She dives home once a season,
Falling, chirping, screaming
Back to life.

Thursday, April 1

"Curse or blessing?" Memory asked herself. She pushed forward to the edge of her seat as the car turned into the back driveway of the Blessed Rest Funeral Home. The driver slammed on the brake and clutch, shifting, and steering to a stop. He opened the door, Memory paid him, then she stepped from the car onto the gravel drive.

"Tell me," Sassy yelled, running out the back door of the funeral home. "I'm just a girl. They mostly take boys," she said, her voice thick with emotion as if preparing herself for a let-down. "They said they had to talk to you first. After I left. Then they'd decide.

"Tell me it's true. You rang Miss Brucie. She told my mother." She flung her arms around Memory. "I just want to hear you say it."

"Yes." Memory pulled Sassy's head close, held her tightly for a moment, then pushed away. "You're as tall as I am. And you're just sixteen." She touched Sassy's cheek

Sassy flashed a tentative, then a proud smile. "They didn't talk to me long yesterday, but I knew they liked me."

"They made the decision late yesterday afternoon. You'll be a Cedar Woods student. Graduate high school. Maybe even college." Memory said the word college tentatively as if the thought had just occurred to her. "They not only thought your voice was beautiful." She hesitated. "But those tests they gave you—you're very, very smart."

Sassy's body froze, as if in a trance. She raised her right arm skyward and began singing in a crystal clear voice:

> "Whenever I am tempted
> Whenever clouds arise
> When songs give place to sighing,
> When hope within me dies.
> His eye is on the sparrow,
> And I know he watches me."

They were both dead still for a moment, as if a play had just ended and a curtain had dropped.

"His eye was on the sparrow," Sassy said softly, turning away. "I can sing. Go to school."

Off to the side, a car slid and braked to a stop in the driveway.

"I'm no sparrow, but you must have been watching for me," Memory said as Jenson drew next to her.

"You gave me a time and place; that's all I needed. But I'm not sure what you mean about a sparrow." He took her arm. "Anyway, as always, my love, I'm at your beck and call."

This simple yet profound statement from the man she had known most of her life and the one she had foolishly pushed away for so many years touched Memory. "You've always been there when I needed you," she said, an ashamed look on her face.

"It's done. I called Mother late yesterday afternoon. As soon as I knew. Told her to get word to Bertha. By the grace of God, Sassy's taken care of."

"No," Jenson said. "You went out on a limb, that's why the young lady's been taken care of."

"Well, whatever. Now, I think, I'll just sit back and enjoy the rest of the day."

"I've never known you to just sit back." Jenson opened the car door for Memory then cranked the engine. As the two of them drove away from the funeral home, she and Sassy waved happy salutes at each other.

"This was a good thing." Memory took a deep breath. "And yet I brood." She looked toward Jenson. "Coming home, back to our family roots, I feel like one of your bruised magnolia blossoms," she said as they swung onto Main Street. "In some ways, you are more honest about your feelings down here. You mull them. You ponder them. Up north, we endlessly and very logically explain them."

She sighed then gazed out the window. A few of the old homes they passed were once proud, grand southern manors, built before the war between the states. Now they were grim and spiritless, antique relics, victims to the ravages of time. No way to speak tales of their past, and for most of those who lived in them, no means to reclaim or restore their glory.

Memory cranked down the window and for a few minutes hung her head out and let the wind tease her hair. She moved away from the window, smoothed her thick, bobbed, auburn curls. "It's the end of March, not yet summertime, but already there's an intensity in sultry southern breezes," she said, turning toward Jenson. "For some reason, they bring an awareness of life and death I never felt in Boston."

"My free-thinking, Yankee female, this southland is soon to be laying claims on you," Jenson teased. "What depths you have sunk to."

Brow deeply knitted, Memory went on. "Life is more personal here. With its own unspoken rules. You have to be born and raised here to understand what they are." She dabbed at her lip with her finger. "Us Bostonians, we can be smug. We are prideful. We have strong opinions and a flair for expressing them." Conflicting emotions showed in Memory's eyes, then a wistful smile crossed her face. "But I'm finding out one thing. Our opinions are strong, but often, we speak as if standing on a podium, reading from a script. Sometimes, it's the first time we've seen the words, and we don't know what we're talking about." She gazed out the window.

"As to Sassy, time alone will tell if this was a good thing. For both of us."

"There was no way for her to realize her dreams without help," Jenson said. "Going to school, no. A career, no. But, you've given her a chance." He shook his head. "One she'd never have had. She's female. And colored to boot."

Memory gazed out the window. "I was accustomed to Sassy coming from the kitchen when I rang a bell. Her feelings hidden. Then I saw the expression on her face when I offered to help with schooling, her singing." Her eyes filled with tears. "All that I have, I have inherited, or should I say, will inherit. I never realized or even thought about how privileged I was."

She tightened her jaw. "And when my father arrives and hears about this, Herr Von Dieter will *not* be pleased. He won't like any part of Sassy going on to school, and me being a part of it."

"You turned her life around," Jenson said.

"No. She turned mine around. This could be a blessing, or it could be a curse,"

"I'm busy this morning and part of the afternoon, but let's, you and I, have us a private celebration later today," Jenson said, as they swung onto Old Farm Road.

'Yes. I'd like that," Memory said.

"Not just celebrating Sassy, but us," Jenson said. "Redemption Ridge. Here. Where it all began."

Memory hitched herself higher on the seat as if she had come to a conclusion about something. "l walked the aisle," she said. "I've already done it once. So, it may not be proper, but I think I'll do it one more time." She leaned over and smoothed her skirt. "I'd like to have Sassy sing at our wedding." Memory cocked her head. "Wouldn't that be something? Her voice is magnificent."

She began humming, "Here comes the bride." Then a comfortable quiet fell between them.

"Home, sweet home. I guess," Memory said as a short while later Jenson stopped in front of Memory's house.

"Home. Sweet sounding words with your Boston accent," Jenson said. "It doesn't sound like some of our old southern sopranos trying to sing with a mouthful of warm taffy." He came around, opened the door, and helped her out of the car. "I'd like to come in, but I'm still checking on jobs and property." He held Memory's arm with one hand and her grip with the other as they walked up the porch steps. "It seems like I've said 'good-bye' to you my whole life." He tilted her chin. "Soon, I'm saying 'hello' forever. Oh, my love," he said. "Someday I won't have to leave you." He shook his head. "Miss Memory Von Dieter, not Mrs. Thornton Percy Hastings. You're something else. You've made a new life for Sassy."

Memory brushed his words off with her hands as if she were swatting a fly.

"No," she said. "Sassy and I were in the right place at the right time."

Jenson leaned over and rubbed his cheek against Memory's. "I'll see you later this afternoon," he said. "I can hardly wait."

"Me either," she answered.

He bent to kiss her, but Bertha pushed the front door open before Jenson could finish the kiss. He gave Memory a quick hug then turned and hurried down the steps. "Around six thirty?" he called out.

"Yes, yes," she answered.

"Lawd love you, Miss Memory." Bertha wiped tears from her eyes, then held out her arms. "You done give my girl a new life."

"No," Memory said, leaning into Bertha. "Sassy did it. You wouldn't believe how impressive she was. I don't think she's going to be staying around this part of the country too long. Not with that voice she has."

Brucie waited just behind Bertha. "I'm so proud, for Sassy, and of you."

"It was all Sassy."

"You best git yourself ready," Bertha said. "Your mama done got word your daddy's comin' in tomorrow night."

Memory rubbed her head. "I'm tired. I'm going upstairs, change into something more comfortable, and probably take a nap."

She went up the steps to her room. Memory closed the door and looked out her bedroom window. Early afternoon and the sun rose high. She plumped up the feather bed pillows and pulled down a shade. She reached for her pen, inkwell and then her journal, which was now thick and tied with a gold satin ribbon. She set them on the table, sat in a small chair and dipped her pen.

Her skin damp with sweat, she let out a long ragged breath. "Where do I start? I've always pretended indifference and put a brave face on things.

"Now, thinking about Jenson, Sassy, and a half-sister and niece somewhere here in Franklin, Mississippi, maybe it's time for a true face."

She began to write:

Even with what little I know about the Von Dieter family, I should include my father.

Almost like the seasons, one moving and blending toward the other, the black hour hand has rolled forward; minutes, then hours have glided through their journey to this very day.

When I was a child my father would stoop down to the level of my brother and me. With his eyes narrowed, a heavy hand touched our shoulders. We were tracked to move in a straight line, our hours set to drum rolls. We had a formal education, there were no fantasy stories and we were not told to walk with a privileged swagger in our steps, but imitating our father and yearning for his approval, we did.

"First and foremost," he would say, "Your bloodlines are pure. Worth dying for. Courage is your heritage."

I felt strong when my father talked.

But there was a flip side to these admonitions. Our mother would say, "No. You are no better than anyone else. Get that out of your head. You are to pay him no mind when he talks like that. The man who delivers our ice may be a far better person than you will ever be."

Grown, I often stood while my father sat at his desk and talked. "We never tell our secrets. The Von Dieters have always been a family who kept our feelings in check. See that you live up to your name. You are better than most of those you pass on the street."

Superior me, it suited my fancies. I wanted to believe him. But I would be yanked back to earth by my mother. And in the summer, there was Redemption Ridge.

In this country our father was a self-made man, and in many ways, he passed on his vanity and the pride in his old-country heritage to my brother and me. Our mother, Brucie, bestowed upon us a love of language and of the land.

Memory set the pen down, stood and stretched. "But, when I think of where I am now, out from Franklin, Mississippi, it's hard for me to believe. I am in another world, still an upstart."

She yawned, covered her mouth with her hand, then sat back down.

Once again, she wrote:

Here, people are tuned into the drifting and rising timbre of familiar voices; they laugh at their own sad jokes. There are no military whistles to form straight lines, no drums rolling a time for things to happen. Not even towered clock chimes pealing for a beginning and an end to the day. Instead, train whistles orient and call out the hour. People listen to hear the crunch of buggies, mules and cars on gravel streets and often know who is going by, even if they can't be seen. In the evening there is a wait for the day to die down and cool off, for the sun to sink. Up start mosquitoes soon have their fill. Finally, when it's time to get up and go inside, the porch swing squeaks, like rusty nails being pulled from wood.

Although it seems like a lifetime since I left Thornton's bones in Boston, it hasn't been long.

She stopped writing for a minute and looked toward the window. "And thinking of that rusty nail sound, I remember the Bible verse, "'My bones are pierced in me at night, and my gnawing pains take no rest.'"

Memory shook her head sadly and once again put pen to the paper.

I can't help but think; we carry some wounds to our grave. Perhaps, we chose to do this, not as burden, but as penance.

Especially it seems to be so down here, where I have decided to live out the rest of my life.

I have already walked the aisle once. Thornton. Now, it will be times two. Jenson Cooper.

Maybe, just maybe, there will be a new beginning. But can he trust me?

A step in the right direction. I did well for Sassy.

I also think of my brother. And others out there. Thelma Jewel. Gertie Mae. What will be my chances with them?

I can try to do right. But will I? The thought that I might not strikes fear into my heart and brings tears to my eyes.

I need something tangible, a sign of my resurrection into a new world and a new life.

Memory looked up from her writing.

"Hopefully, a new beginning. Perhaps a symbol to myself that I have changed.

"I am tired." Like a comfort pulled across a bed by slim, lovely fingers, shadows began to stretch across the room.

"I'd better bathe and change clothes. Jenson will be here soon."

***

Memory was waiting at the edge of their yard when Jenson arrived. He had barely stopped the car before she pulled the door open and got in.

"Be careful, my lovely," he said. "You could hurt yourself."

"So much for that," she said. "This is a new beginning for me. I would like to move on with my life and go in a different way. With more courage, more kindness, more awareness of others. And tomorrow, it may become a little harder. My father comes in tomorrow night."

"It'll be a lot harder." Jenson shifted gears then put his hand on Memory's knee. "I want my life to be different too," he said. "I want to make love with you."

There was a short silence between them, then Memory nodded. "Yes. I pray to finish what we started the other night."

Jenson took a deep breath. "I know just the place."

Memory shook her head. "Not the old well," she said. "There's that talk of bodies in there. Miss Pet. And who knows who else? And, something could have happened to Shank Potter around there last week."

"That's not the place I had in mind."

***

A short while later Jenson pulled off the road into a wooded area. He and Memory stepped from the car. She glanced up toward the sky then looked toward the trees surrounding the countryside. Jenson moved to put his arms around her, but she pushed him away.

"I want something out of this." She took a few deep breaths then turned in the direction of Redemption Ridge. "Perhaps more than you bargained for.

"My life is changing and I need to recognize this. I want to be better. To first do no harm to another of God's creatures. To become closer to my God. To look after other people."

"You did. You helped Sassy," Jenson began.

"But more," Memory said. "I can make a fresh start at Redemption Ridge. Rebirth. A new sense of self and what I should be about. I feel a real need to be immersed in the earthy waters of Noble Creek." She laid her hand across her neck. "In our own holy ceremony."

Memory glanced at Jenson. "Then, you and I, we can celebrate." She lowered her voice. "You said, I might be the one to redeem Redemption Ridge. No. If there's any hope, Redemption Ridge will redeem me." She looked up toward the sky. "I just wish her grandmother, Vernell, were here to know about Sassy."

"Maybe she does know," Jenson said. "Let me say this. I want to bring us down to earth for a moment. It's cool. Before we go too much further, I'm going to have a fire ready to be lit when we get out of the water. It won't take but a minute."

Memory sat down and unlaced her shoes. She waited, while Jenson hurriedly gathered and stacked a pile of dried wood. Then, he walked close behind Memory, as she side-walked through heavy grass down the creek bank. They were covered by a green canopy of leaves as they wound their way down an unfrequented path and stopped at a small clearing. The roan-colored waters of Nobel Creek lay below.

Jenson moved to put his arm around Memory. She pushed him away. "First, this is a new beginning. This is not about us.

"I want you to dip, then raise and hold me."

He took a deep breath. "This may be a little bit of history in the making," he said.

Everything was still. No noise came from the rolling creek waters, no bird calls were heard as Memory stepped into the water.

Jenson stood beside her, his arm encircling Memory's waist. He placed his hand over her nose. "Memory Elaine Von Dieter." He lowered her into Noble Creek. "You are now a new creature," he said softly, raising her.

Memory coughed and wiped water from her face. Way off in the distance she made out a faint voice, "You can't see me. Can you feel me, Miss Memory Elaine? You done good fer my gran'girl. You gone do good fer your peoples."

"Yes," Memory whispered, covering her mouth with her hand. "You're here." Her arms out as if for an embrace, she murmured, "I do feel you."

"What?" Jenson asked.

She gave him a smile. "Just Redemption Ridge ghosts. They're hovering. Wanting to help us."

Jenson placed his hand firmly on Memory's shoulder and gently turned her around. "This has been a holy experience, but that's enough about ghosts," he said, "You're here with *me* now."

"Hallelujah! And yes! It's our time." Memory unbuttoned her blouse, slipped out of her skirt, then sat on the edge of the bank, swishing her toes in the short, choppy waves of the cool water. The rhythmic sound of the water splashing over rocks and fallen tree limbs was as relaxing as hearing the old childhood melodies her mother used to sing.

Behind her Jenson shed his shoes, pants and shirt. He scooped their bundled clothes, spread them across the ground and bounded down the steep slope.

"Here I come." Memory flung her arms wide and jumped into the muddy creek.

She bent, splashed water with her hands like a child enjoying a bath. Waving her arms in the air like a bird taking flight, her feet slipped on a moss covered rock. She pitched forward.

Jenson grabbed for her. The two of them tumbled into the cool, muddy, creek. They came up drenched and laughing, throwing water in each other's face.

Gasping for breath, Memory smoothed back her wet hair, then touched Jenson's cheeks. "I've known you my whole life, but I didn't know you."

"I want you." He scooped Memory into his arms. "I've always wanted you."

His arms cradling her, leg muscles knotted, Jenson carried Memory up the bank and gently laid her down on the makeshift bed he had made from their clothes.

While he lit a fire from the small pile of logs, she stretched out on her back, Jenson dropped to his knees. He stroked her breasts. She spread her legs.

A chorus of birds sang in the weeping willow branches hanging over Nobel Creek, followed by the coo of turtledoves. Memory sighed. "His eye is on the sparrow. I just pray it is so," she said softly.

"What?"

"Nothing. Us," she whispered.

He explored her with his fingers.

As the southern sun dried the muddy creek waters, their wet bodies slowly turned to a dusty haze.

Like a faint echo dying away, she barely heard the words, "You're hep'n me find my peace. My rest is a'comin'."

CHAPTER 40

**Mortality is the moral
Treasure buried away
By the Dieters.**

**Mortality,
The moral treasure-
Code of the single
Rite; mortality,
The curse by which a mind is quenched.**

**The Von Dieters assembled
Like strange hierophants,
Stippled in fog-soft hieroglyphics.**

Friday, April 2

"Is there any coffee left?" Memory asked, tightening the tie to her chenille robe as she stepped into the kitchen.

"Still got a little hot on the stove," Bertha said. "Your mama already done drunk her a mouthful of it. She's got a lot goin' on in her head, what with Mr. Von Dieter comin' in tonight." She rubbed her hands on the hem of her calico apron. "You looks different. Like you's carrying some secrets in your head. What you an' Mr. Jenson got goin'?" She gave Memory a suggestive smile.

"Doesn't everybody carry secrets?" Memory ducked her chin.

"Humph! An' all of 'em ain't so good." Bertha shook her head. "When's Mist. Dale comin' in?" she asked.

"Tonight. But I think he's spending the night in town with the Stanton's." Memory sighed in resignation. "And, my father will be here too, not long behind him."

She lifted the pot, poured herself a cup of coffee, then turned to the kitchen table to pick up the cream pitcher. Propped against it, she saw a folded piece of linen paper

"An invitation to the Esteemed Von Dieter family."

384

We'd be pleasured to have you as our honored and revered guests, was written on it.

She unfolded the paper and read:

To the descendants of the of the battle of Redemption Ridge. The Divine Deliverance Holiness Church and School for Boys and Girls is having a Brush Arbor meeting on Easter Sunday, April 4, at 11:00 a.m. on the Redemption Ridge battleground. Like the two-headed serpent—once and for all, either, clear his name and revere Captain Bruce Claymore, or show his true colors; a hero to the cause or a traitor to our beloved southland.

We would be honored to have you at this once-in-a-lifetime event; in uniform for those who have only just returned from The War. And bring any of your sick and ailing for the healing service.

"What's this?" Memory raised the invitation toward Bertha.

Bertha's lips twitched. "That there has to do with what's goin' on Easter." Her disapproval showed in the set of her shoulders. "Over to the cemetery."

"Oh, I remember hearing something about this. And as I recall, they'd be celebrating Easter and also honoring or dishonoring our dead relative, Captain Bruce Claymore." Memory blew on the hot coffee.

"Humph." Bertha said. "When I went to hang out the warsh, I seen a car an' a buckboard an' some buggies over to the cemetery. More'n likely havin' to do with that celebration on Sunday."

"Well, I'm at loose ends. Later on, think I'll walk over and check it out." Memory half-smiled. "If they have any fortune tellers, clowns or tightrope walkers, I'm going to be there. Not sure I want to hear any of their preaching, though."

"Huh," said Bertha. "With that holy roller church doin' it, no tellin' what they're up to. More 'n likely they're gonna have them some snakes crawlin' around."

"I'm going to do some reading. Later on I might take a walk over there," Memory said.

***

Liam counted out money for a ticket and laid it on the counter. "Before I leave here, other than that Easter Celebration for a bunch of dead folks that's coming up, there's one more thing to take care of. Dale Von Dieter," he muttered. "Easter Sunday."

"Come Sunday, are you gonna be celebrating our risen Lord with the rest of us?" The ticket agent thrust his head back and looked over his glasses at Liam. "They're having a big shindig out there at Redemption Ridge. Me an' the missus are gonna be right proud to go. An' be a part of setting some things straight around here. I hear tell they're gonna clean up our Captain Bruce Claymore's name. Might be they'll even give out some of them jewels people around here been talking about. For a long time."

"I hear you." Liam turned his head slightly. "I can't wait to catch the train back to where people don't talk like they have peanut hulls up their noses. Back to civilization."

The ticket agent's voice carried a challenge. "With that attitude you've got, I'd jest as soon get you back where you come from today."

Liam patted his coat and was reassured when he felt the thick wad of bills cramming his pockets. "Worth coming here, though," he said as he walked out of the station. "With that whiskey running, riverboat deal I've made, I'll soon be a rich man. I may have to do a little more checking on it."

He wrapped his ticket in a handkerchief and put in his pocket. He pulled out his watch and checked the time. "Ten thirty, and I'm hungry." He went down to the Lo-Sto, bought a sausage and a can of beans and sat down on a bench outside the train station to eat.

A short time later he was surprised to see a Packard, a car never seen around Franklin, pull to a stop. An older colored man, wearing a worn, too-large suit and carrying a tattered canvas suitcase got out of the car and went into the station. Liam noticed that the colored man had been riding in the front seat with a white man. *Not done in Franklin, Mississippi.* He couldn't quite see the driver's face but, suspicious of who it could be, ducked his head until the car pulled away. Then he went into the train station. He approached the man who was now seated in the colored part of the train station. "I've seen you somewhere before," he said. "Who are you?"

"You haven't seen me, but I'm Milton Birdsong, Mr. Herschel Von Dieter's chauffeur. I'm on my way home. Yes, siree, back to Boston."

"Where's Mr. Von Dieter?" Liam asked.

"Mr. Von Dieter's got him some business over in Hinds County. He's checking on some house deeds and other things. Then he's going out to his wife's place, Redemption Ridge."

I'm in the right place at the right time. Liam congratulated himself. *Von Dieter's here. Everything's falling into place.*

* * *

When Mudge came up on the part of the cemetery where the Confederate soldiers were buried, swinging the car over to the side of Old Farm Road and pumping the brakes, he jolted to a stop, throwing Thelma Jewel against the gear shift.

"That scared me," Gertie Mae cried.

"Everything scares you," Thelma Jewel snapped. "And I'm tired of hearing about it." She gave the child a menacing glare.

"Shut up, both of you," Mudge muttered. "Y'all git out." He flung open the door, then turned to watch as Thelma Jewel stepped onto the running board and heaved herself to the ground. *Your bosoms could have done double duty as a footstool fer me*, he thought.

"Le's us go on over yonder. I seen Brother Tuggle, Mother Bunny an' the others a-standin' right over there past the gate."

"Whooee," Thelma Jewel said. "This is gonna hurt my back."

Trying to keep up with the two of them, Gertie Mae stumbled and fell. "Help me, Mama."

Thelma Jewel beckoned to Mudge. "Mr. Mudge. You're closer to her than I am. If I bend down, I'm liable to jerk my spine out again."

She stopped walking. "When I pushed—when my daughter fell down the steps, I yanked my hip out of line trying to grab her." She raised her leg and hiked one hip up to the side as if to emphasize what she'd just said.

Mudge watched as Gertie Mae lurched to her feet. "We don't want no whiney bones nor no nonsense outta you." He pointed to a wagon on the road. "So, go set over there by that buggy an' talk to that air horse.

"Y'all got here a little ahead of us," he called out as he and Thelma Jewel walked toward Brother Tuggle and three other people. "You know Brother Tuggle, an' his missus, best known as Mother Bunny, Miss Thelmer Jewel." Mudge bowed his head as if he were paying homage to someone then he nodded toward the other couple. "This here's Deacon Harlan Sistrunk." A ruddy-cheeked, square faced-man bobbed his head sideways in acknowledgment.

"An' this here's my wife, Sister Mealie Maude." Deacon Sistrunk pointed to a small-boned woman whose chin seemed to have melted into her bony neck. A relieved look on her face, Sister Mealie Maude reached up and patted a ball of thin gray hair pinned to the top of her head.

"Where's Blackie the snake?" Harlan asked. "He's usually riding roun' with you."

Unconsciously, Mudge patted his neck. "Well, I thought as to how he might slow me down a liddle today." He glanced around. "An' I might orter keep him under wraps 'til Sunday."

"We're supposed to have us one more comin' out here to hep look things over. But I must say, even though Mistah Liam's a Boston man an' a cop, a heap a times, he's more trouble than he's worth." Mudge jerked his head like a dog tugging a bone away from another dog. "But I will hafter own up to this. He's drivin' an old flivver a mine an' sometimes it don't run too good."

He sucked his bottom lip as if he were tasting something sweet. "I have to apologize fer one an' all, but don't nobody know fer sure where Captain Bruce Claymore's bones lie. First off, le's us look fer Vernell's grave. I got me a notion. If we kin find

Vernell, we'll find Bruce. Been a while since I looked, but off-hand, I remember not seein' no marker settin' up fer Vernell."

He pointed toward the middle ground of the colored cemetery. "But I'm here to tell you. Bruce Claymore's spirit's gonter lead the way." Mudge ran his hands through his thinning hair. "When we find 'em, tha's where we'll unload us some poles to set up our brush arbor tent, an' mark where we're pitching tables fer our vittles. Mistah Liam kin find us if he wants."

He ran his hand across his nose, then wiped his fingers down the side of his pants. "We'll git us some of it done today, an' some tomorrow." He dug into his pocket and pulled out a cigarette and a match.

Unseen by anyone, hunkered close to the ground, Gertie Mae had edged up close to where Mudge and the others stood.

Spying her out of the corner of his eye, Mudge spun around, grabbed her shoulders and shoved her toward the gate.

"Ow!" she cried.

"An' don't you step away from that their buggy again," he hollered.

Mudge scraped a match down the side of his pants and lit a cigarette. "Le's us each go a different way fer a few minutes," he said. "Miss Thelmer Jewel an' me'll go on to'ard the back. See what you kin find off to the middle an' the other side," he said as he began walking along the edge of the colored and white cemetery.

"It's okeydokey by me." Trying to keep up with Mudge, her hands out for balance, Thelma Jewel walked with the rolling gait of a fat lady whose thighs rub together and chafe.

"Whooee," she said. "Well, I never. The cemetery I went to back in California was like a fresh-planted rich folks' lawn. This is like stepping on, then across trolley tracks. I don't think as to how I can walk over all these humps, ditches, and dead bodies," she griped.

Beads of sweat glistened on her forehead. She stopped, pulled her handkerchief out and dabbed her brow. "I'm here to tell you. You aren't supposed to step on dead people. It's bad luck. And besides, I don't think I'm up to going too much further right now. We've come a long way."

Mudge flipped his cigarette to the ground and stopped walking. Hands on his hips, he took a commanding stance. "If your butt wadn't big as a warshboard, you might coulda took more'n a step or two.

"Set down over there. We're 'bout at the end of the colored side."

He pointed to a shaded bench.

Thelma Jewel looked down. "There's something written here," she said. "'He is arisen,'" she read.

"Well, we're gonter raise us some folks," Mudge said, having no idea that Vernell and Bruce Claymore's graves were at Thelma Jewel's feet.

"Brother. Y'all come here," he called, waving the others over.

Still within the sound of Mudge's voice, Preacher Tuggle, Mother Bunny, Deacon Harlan Sistrunk, and his wife. Sister Mealie Maude. hurried to him.

"This Californey woman's done played out an' is gonter have to set a spell. We'll come back fer her in a few minutes. We're gonter look a little ways more fer Vernell's an' Captain Bruce Claymore's graves." He gave Thelma Jewel a hard look. "We ain't gonter let no city sissy slow us down."

"Well, I never. I just need to catch my breath a minute," Thelma Jewel said as the others followed Mudge toward the front of the burial grounds.

Turning around, she spread her legs wide, reached down for a wooden armrest that looked like it had been made out of crutches, hiked her skirt over her knees and plopped down onto the bench. In a few minutes her head drooped, double chins puffed out like blown up balloons. She began snoring. It wasn't long before off in the distance there was a snapping sound, as if a large tree limb had broken. Blurting out a snort, Thelma Jewel jumped awake.

The air around her seemed to have changed. Twigs crackled close behind her. Thelma Jewel narrowed her eyes and looked around. She saw nothing but she heard a rustling, like someone coming up behind her. She tugged her skirt down and stood.

"If you're some nigger woman hiding in some of those bushes, I'm going to set some folks on to you when they get back here."

She held her hands out for balance. "You'll be sorry you messed with me."

A sharp sound like a hand clap broke the cemetery silence. "You all needs to go on."

Her face creased with worry, knees shaky, Thelma Jewel swung her head around. Nobody. She tilted her chin and wiped away a slight drool. "I'm hearing things," she muttered, reassuring herself.

"We only wants our peace. We don't want none of you."

Thelma Jewel inclined her head in the direction the words came from. "I don't see anything or anybody," she said, her voice shrill. "Whoever you are. Just in case you're there, I don't want any of you either." Her body swaying, she tightened her shoulders. "But I want my revenge on the Claymore family."

She grabbed the wooden arm rest, bent her knees, hiked her buttocks and awkwardly sat on the edge of the bench. "I'm here to tell you something. I got me some business to tend to here. I came to take care of some people. And nobody, nor any ghost, is going to stop me!"

She pulled air into her lungs and when she did, something like rotten tooth breath washed over her. The odor seemed to come from under the bench. A cold feeling ran up her backside. She shivered.

"Mr. Mudge might want to look some other place than here, though, to set up that brush arbor tent."

* * *

The others trailed close behind Mudge. He hadn't gone far when, overcome by a strong sense of being in the wrong place, he clenched his fists and halted.

"The more I been thinkin' on it, I don't reckon Captain Claymore is buried with the colored. Somebody's gonter have done somethin' different fer him. An' I done looked in these here parts purdy good." Mudge halted and pointed to the barbed-wire fence separating the two cemeteries. "An' besides which, I heard a voice," he said. "Here inside o' me. A de-vine voice speakin'." He rocked from side to side. "The Spirit spoke. It said, the Captain's done been taken kere of. He's buried with his own kind.

"He's gonter be over crost the way. Where us white folks have our tombstones." Mudge nodded his head as if he'd come to a decision about something.

"Brother Tuggle. You come with me. The rest o' y'all stay here 'til I come back fer you. I'll let you know where the Spirit leads me."

The two men climbed the fence, stepped into the white burial ground and began wandering through knotted vines, dead leaves and kudzu, past gnarled hedges and spiny tree limbs. Many of the graves were sunken and grown over with weeds. Few names were readable.

Mudge's ribs and back felt out of kilter, like they might slip out of place. Blisters on his feet began popping and oozing, brittle toe corns pinched and crackled as he picked his way over the gravestones.

"Lawdy mercy. Don't know as to how I kin walk too much more," he said to himself. He stopped to rest and for several minutes rocked back and forth, staring vacantly across the burial sites. He spotted a large, flat area that had only a few trees on it and wasn't grown over with tall grass and weeds, and at the same time he noticed that his feet had stopped hurting,

He heard a voice in his head saying, "This is it. Where y'all needs to be."

Something in his back loosened its grip.

"I feel the Spirit callin' me. I see me a place. That right over there'll do fer us. Not too far from the hindmost edge. Set up everything comin' this away, an' it'll work out jest fine." His back loosened as he headed toward the place he had in mind. When he got there, Mudge stopped and surveyed the area. "An' we got enough room. I got me a picture in my head. Our young bucks kin drive sturdy poles. Then they kin nail boards acrost fer us to have a roof o' tree branches. Sides will be open. An' I want y'all to set Taddler the Raddler's cage a few feet away. Cover it up some."

Mudge realized he was standing on something and looked down. He had one foot across a grave; a cracked concrete marker lay at his feet. Ollie Potter.

He half-stepped back, then his face lit as if he'd had a divine revelation. "Ollie Potter. He's the man what hung Lamont's mama." Mudge rubbed his chin. "That colored woman, Vernell. This here's where I'm standin'. A sacred spot to me. Ollie Potter. He seen to it that Vernell was taken kere of." He nodded his head and took a deep breath. He didn't remind the preacher that Lamont was the son of Vernell and likely Captain Claymore.

"We need to lay our altar close by to right here where I'm standin'."

"I don't see nothin' bout Captain Claymore." Brother Tuggle pulled out a knife, dropped to his knees and cleaned off a large fragment of the concrete headstone. "All I see is Ollie Potter on here."

"Justice is gonter be done by us settin' up our tent here. I ain't gonter be wishy-washy about this," Mudge said. "I feel it in my bones. The Captain's done been here. An', tha's enough." His head bobbing up and down, he began singing in an off-key bass,

"Shall we gather at the River,
The beautiful, the beautiful river."

"Ain't no river here," Brother Tuggle interrupted, a bewildered sound to his voice.

His left eyebrow raised in a question mark, for a moment Mudge was speechless. He and Brother Tuggle stared at each other, but Mudge's recovery was swift. "Noble Creek ain't too fer from here. An' somewhere along the way it's gonter empty into the Mississippi River."

Mudge gazed toward the sky. He raised his arm as if giving a benediction. "Captain Bruce Claymore." He said the name as if he were laying a claim on it. "We're kindly runnin' outta time an' a voice tol' me this was the place." He nodded and pointed to the ground. "You an' me kin sanctify an' make this here holy ground. We'll put up our tent here." He wiped his brow then gave a low whistle. "It'll take us some doin' to git it laid out come Sunday. You git us some young bucks over to here from the church 'n the school. They gotta make hay while the sun's shinin'. Diggin' out holes fer them support poles. Cuttin' up boards to hold the leafy branches fer our roof. Bringin' in our already done made up pews, an' a altar. It's one of them ol' wooden musket chests from the War." He wiped his brow, as if the very thought of the work wore him out. "The ladies kin pick out where they'll set up food tables on the outside.

"Call the others over." Mudge put his hand on Brother Tuggle's shoulder, swung him around and pushed him forward.

Mother Bunny close behind him, Brother Tuggle swallowed hard, nodded his head and lumbered toward the fence. "Brother Harlan. Sister Mealie Maude, " he hollered. "We need y'all. Go bring Thelmer Jewel on over to here."

"Want me to fetch her daughter?" Sister Mealie Maude called back.

"Leave her be," Mudge said. "Ain't no need fer that."

In a few minutes the five of them joined Mudge gathered around Ollie Potter's grave.

Mudge licked his lips, set his hands on his hips and spread his feet. "Le's us have a little ceremony right here an' now, an' consecrate this here ground."

"That redheaded Yankee policeman ain't showed up yet." Deacon Harlan Sistrunk rubbed his ruddy cheeks and bobbed his head sideways.

"We ain't waitin' on Mistah Liam." Mudge clamped his jaw shut.

Brother Tuggle ran a finger under the sweat-stained collar of his button-down shirt, then pressed his hand across his forehead. His body quivered as if he had been struck with a high fever. "Joy. Joy. Unspoke of joy," he intoned. "Brother Mudge done found it. This here's the spot. Captain Claymore's done been here."

Sweat stood out on Mudge's forehead. A line of sweat coated his upper lip. He spread his arms out as if they were wings, and would lift him to the heavens. His eyes became unfocused. He began a rhythmic sideways rock.

"Bow your heads," he said. "An' git on your knees," he commanded. "An', slap your noses into this here holy ground.

"Hallelujah! Hallelujah!" he shouted, as their knees hit the ground and their noses scraped the dust.

CHAPTER 41

**Memory felt a flush
Of rage blossom up
Her spine,
This girl,
This girl,
He will hurt her, hurt her.
Gertie Mae her destiny?**

**Dale another fate
Beating drums
Shadows
Laura Lee
Or is it too late?**

Friday, April 2

Yawning, Memory walked back into the kitchen.

"You done missed lunch," Bertha said, "But we got some left over greens an' poke chops." She pointed toward the stove. "I saw me some buggies an' a car over at the old cemetery. Probably gittin' ready for that holy roller service come Sunday." She set her hands on her hips. "Lamont an' me. We don't rightly cotton to them folks."

Memory dipped a spoon into the turnip green pot, stirred them, then clanked the spoon down. "I'm not hungry, but I'm nosy. Think I'll see what's going on."

***

Gertie Mae had been told to stay by Mudge's roadster and a buggy while her mother, Mudge, and four members from the Divine Deliverance Holiness Church were looking for something. Bored, she left and went through the cemetery gate where she had seen her mother and the others go. She had walked only a short way when a tilted wooden cross caught her eyes. Written across from left to right, she could make out the letters; "B-a-b-y," She spelled slowly, pleased that she knew what the word meant. Something about the word baby made her feel like she needed to go potty. She stuck out her foot and pushed the wooden cross over.

"I gotta tee tee. I'm taking off my bloomers." She spotted a patch of daisies. "I'm going to wet me some flowers." She smiled to herself. "Make them grow bigger." She reached over and dragged the cross that said B-a-b-y up next to her, pulled her britches down and squatted. The wind teasing her bottom felt good. Done with her tee-teeing, her skirt still hiked, when she raised up a long, thick nail from the cross caught on her pants. Gertie Mae stepped out of her drawers and pushed the cross with her underpants clinging to them off to the side. She tucked her skirt up in her sash and began toeing the ground, edging away and enjoying the cool feel of a breeze across her bare bottom. "I haven't ever been outside with my pants off. This feels so good."

She heard a sprinkling noise and turned. A tall, thin, mangy dog, back legs splayed, was wetting Gertie Mae's thrown off pants. When the dog was done, her tail clamped under her belly the animal slinked toward Gertie Mae. Whimpering, she pressed her nose against the girls bottom and smelled.

"Stay here, stay here," Gertie Mae crooned, leaning over and petting the cowering dog. "You'll be my daisy, Dog." She kissed the dog's nose." You're mine. You're Daisy."

Out on the road, Liam's car sputtering, dust floated through the open windows, coating him and the inside of the car, as he pumped the brakes and coasted to a stop between a buckboard and a roadster he knew was Mudge's.

"Jesus," he moaned. "What in the hell am I doing out here in this God-forsaken Mississippi cemetery?" He shook his head. "Okay. Okay. I'm going to get some revenge against the Von Dieter family, and make some money along the way." He smiled when he thought about the whiskey running deal he had set up in Vicksburg.

Liam got out of the car, placed his hands on his hips, and stretched his body. He entered the cemetery and tramped a short way across uneven pitted ground, then he came to a halt, trying to decide which way to go. He heard whimpering sounds, looked over his shoulder and saw a bare bottomed girl, leaning over and grasping a dog's neck.

"Well, hot damn," he breathed. "Look what a treat I got. It's been a while. Girl or boy. One suits my fancy as well as the other. Right here in front of me. In the middle of a cemetery. And she isn't a ghost."

"Daisy, my Daisy," Gertie Mae crooned, kissing the dog's ear. "You'll be mine."

Liam wiped a thin drool from his mouth. He eased closer, reached into his pocket and pulled out a peppermint. "Little lady," he called.

Gertie Mae let go of the dog.

His green eyes flashed with lust. "Look what I've got for you."

"I don't want any."

"I've got jelly beans too."

"I want my mama," she howled.

Liam darted forward, clamped his hand over her mouth, gripped her under his arms. The dog snapped at his ankles, then howled as Liam kicked her in the side and carried Gertie Mae into a nearby thicket of bushes.

"Fun, fun, fun," he croaked. "Take it however you can get it."

Growling, the dog belly-crawled behind Liam.

***

Early afternoon

Memory saw several buggies and two cars on the side of the road. The skin on the back of her neck tingled as if she'd fallen into an ant bed. Her heartbeat fast, heavy breathing made her light headed. She remembered hearing about a man, Mudge Turnipseed, his green roadster, and that he often drove it with a large black snake draped around his neck.

"No," she said.

She spun around. Toward home. Toward safety. But she had only taken a few steps when she felt a change in the air. She sensed she was no longer alone.

Help me find my peace.

She had heard those words before. Vernell.

"No," Memory said. "I'm leaving here."

Somewhere close by she heard a voice that sounded like a baby's mewling.

Somebody needs you

Memory's fingers went cold, her hands flew over her face trying to blot out an old vision. *This happened to me.*

Another time, another place.

"No," a girl's voice wailed from bushes off to her right.

A dog growled.

A thumping sound. A yelp of pain.

A cry. "She's my Daisy."

"Shut your mouth," someone panted.

Memory ran toward the wailing. The grass beneath her feet was matted, skeletons of old wooden cemetery markers lay on the ground; gravestones stuck out at angles like rotten teeth. Images filled her head. Yellow stubs. Shank Potter.

Liam raised his head.

Memory glimpsed a tuft of red hair. *Husband Thornton! Bright red hair. No!*

The train station. When we came into Franklin. A halo from Hades in overgrown bushes. It is him. The Boston policeman. Liam McRae!

She tripped on the wooden cross Gertie Mae had dropped. Cross in hand, she got to her feet, raised and swung the grave marker, smacking the man's face full on.

Nose bones cracked. Blood spurted.

Gasping, Liam scrambled to his feet. Stumbling backward, his nose a bloody pig snout he jerked his pants up.

Memory raised the cross again. A rusty nail glinted in the sunlight. A sideways swing as if she were chopping a tree.

"Awww God!" Liam shrieked.

She jabbed his face. "I got you," she yelled. "An eye for an eye." A fleck of emerald green crowned the rust, covered the tip of her wooden spear.

A dog chewing his boots, bloody faced, one-eyed, driven by pain, Liam limped through the tangled scrub grass.

Memory dropped to her knees. The girl's clothes were blood soaked but she wasn't bleeding. The blood belonged to the man.

"You're all right. You're all right." She wiped Gertie Mae's tears with the hem of her pulled up skirt, then stretched the skirt down, covering the girl's nakedness. She circled Gertie Mae in her arms. It was not easy, she was almost as large as Memory.

Blood gushed in pulse timed spurts as Liam lurched toward his car. He raked his hand over his blood covered face.

"God! No!" he screamed as one finger slid into an empty, gummy, eye socket.

A stream of vomit spewed across his feet. He grabbed the wrench from under the seat, his hands slipping as he spun the vomit streaked wrench and cranked the car .

He fought the gears. Squealing tires drowned his screeching voice. Loose gravel spinning out from the fenders and running board made loud noises as the car jolted away.

***

Memory felt a strong affinity for the girl; she was struck by familiar feelings of despair. "You're all right. I hurt him bad. I'll take care of you."

"I want my dog." Gertie Mae's hands with chewed down nails reached out toward a tail-thumping, body-shaking dog, inching toward her.

"That's my Daisy."

She looked up at Memory. "I remember you. You bumped into me in the restaurant. You made me fall."

Memory pushed Gertie Mae back and looked at her. With all that had happened, and all that she had heard, she knew who this was but felt it was best not to say anything now. She held her niece. She started to say, "No, I didn't make you fall. You tripped," but thought better of it. The young lady's face was already etched with sadness.

"Where's your mama?" she asked.

"They left me here."

"Did you know that man?" Memory arched her eyebrows. "I think I've seen him before."

"He's a boogey man," Gertie Mae whispered, her eyes wide with terror.

"Gertie Mae." Memory heard somebody calling off in the distance. "You. Gertie Mae?"

"I have her," Memory yelled.

Gertie Mae stayed in the circle of Memory's warm embrace but she leaned over and petted the dog. "Daisy," she crooned, as if she had found comfort for everything that might be troubling her.

"Well, I never." Thelma Jewel loomed over them with Mudge and other members of the Divine Deliverance Holiness Church close on his heels. "What have you done to my child?"

"A man was after her. Something really bad was going to happen. Thank the good Lord. I got to them in time," Memory said.

A slight smile chasing across his face, Mudge eased closer. *This might could bring in some money fer Miss Thelmer Jewel. An' me to boot.*

"I recognized your daughter from Mrs. Netter's restaurant," Memory said. "When she fell."

She pushed away from Gertie Mae, who sank to the ground, holding onto the dog. *My half-sister. Don't let her know who you are. There'll be a better moment.*

"She ran the boogey man ran off." Gertie Mae pulled a knee up close to her chest.

"I hurt him," Memory said. "I got him back. It was divine retribution."

"There ain't no such a thing as a boogey man." Brother Tuggle stepped forward. "This is the devil talkin'. No tellin' what she's done been up to."

Rage bubbled inside Memory. "She speaks the truth. And I did. I ran a man off. She was by herself. He was trying to take advantage of this young lady."

"The truth ain't in her," Brother Tuggle answered. "This young'un ain't nothin' but trouble. She's gotta git back to the fields an' git to work."

Memory felt anger building up inside her. "How old is she?"

"Thirteen," Thelma Jewel said. "Not that it's any of your business."

"And she works in the fields?" Memory asked. *Something needs to be done.* "Where does she live? Does she go to school?"

"She lives at the Divine Deliverance Holiness Church and School," Thelma Jewel said, her mind churning. She had noticed that when they came up Memory's arms were around Gertie Mae. *This might be a fast way I can get into some of that Claymore money.*

Memory took slow deep breaths, trying to clear her head so she would say the right words. "A man was after her. I hurt him." Her body stiffened in resolve. *It's time.* "I know who you are. You know who I am. You're my half-sister. We saw each other at Mrs. Netter's Restaurant. You had that gravestone thrown through our window."

Memory shook her head. "I need to talk to you, Thelma Jewel," she said. "About a lot of things." *Remember. She can be dangerous.*

"Well, I never." A pitiful, poor-me look crossed Thelma Jewel's face. "It depends on what you've got to say." She laid her hand across her breasts, pushed against her chest as if she were massaging a pain.

"We didn't have a silver spoon in *our* mouths." She emphasized the word our and arched her back as if she had just proven a point that needed to be made. "Thanks to the Claymore family we weren't treated right. The cheap woman we had to live with, Mrs. Bledsoe, the one who was paid to raise me. She and our Redemption Ridge mother." She put her eyes on Memory's face and kept them there. "They saw to that."

Gertie Mae stretched a leg out and when she did she bumped Brother Tuggle's foot.

"You. Gertie Mae. Hoist yourself up," he said.

"I can't," she wailed. "I don't think I can get up from here."

"Now just look at that." Thelma Jewel's shoulders slumped as if someone had given them a hard shove. "My daughter. If she'd had just a little operation she could get around like other girls her age and you and me." *I deserved that money,* she thought. *And I had me some fun with it.* She wiped her eyes as if she were crying.

"An operation?" Memory asked.

A sly smile crossed Thelma Jewel's face as if she had an idea what Memory was thinking and was a little bit ahead of her.

Memory started to say more, but stopped herself. *Watch what you say. Later. That doctor friend in Boston. Bone surgery and braces?*

Mudge rocked sideways and licked his lips. He thought Memory might offer to volunteer something about money for an operation. When she didn't, for the moment he'd had enough. Besides, he was getting hungry. "We gotta git on with our bidness here at hand," he said. "See to settin' up fer our Easter Brush Arbor Meetin'. An' we ain't goin' nowhere with all this palaver."

"Brother Tuggle. Hoist up that air girl," he said.

"I want to take my Daisy with me," Gertie Mae's voice was tiny and high with fear. "She's my dog."

"We ain't barely got room fer you, much less got room fer no dawgs," Brother Tuggle said.

"Daisy's mine. She came to me. I love her," Gertie Mae sobbed. "She loves me." She closed her eyes.

The girl's cries rang in Memory's ears. She felt as if her life was about to change. *Will this girl become my destiny?*

Although she trembled inside, Memory patted Gertie Mae's shoulder. "I'm your friend." For some reason, her words, seemed to settle the girl and she took a deep easy, breath.

She bent over and rubbed the dog between her ears. "Let me take Daisy home for now. I'll keep her for you. You can come see her or I'll bring her to you when it's okay. Daisy will be yours."

The dog inched closer to Gertie Mae and licked her cheeks as if in agreement with what was said. With that, the girl looked up at Memory with something akin to hope.

Memory slipped her sash through loops on her skirt, pulled it through and quickly fashioned a make-do collar, slipping it over the dog's head.

"Let's us go," Mudge said.

"I'm getting up," Gertie Mae said, her voice quivering. "Daisy, Daisy," she whispered over and over as if that would give her a cause and the strength she needed. She curved one leg and began to rock sideways. Memory noticed that Thelma Jewel made no move to try and help her daughter as struggling, she shoved with the other leg,

Memory felt a bitter sorrow for the girl. She grabbed Gertie Mae's arm and helped lift her.

The dog moved against Gertie Mae's heels and tried to follow but Memory held the sash tight.

Somebody needs you.

Memory had heard those words a short while ago. Then she had heard Gertie Mae's cries.

She almost felt compelled to run toward Gertie Mae and try to rescue her, but with Mudge leading the way, the church group following and Gertie Mae limping behind her mother, they were moving toward the front of the cemetery.

"I did two good things. I saved my niece. And I got some payback for what was done to Thornton."

The sun was low in the sky as Memory and the dog slowly made their way out of the Redemption Ridge graveyard and on back to the house.

***

7:30

The car headlights cut through an early night filmy darkness as Otis dodged potholes and swung the motorcar along the flat, curvy Tallouga County road. Dale removed a cigarette from a pack of Murads that Otis had given him, tapped it on the car door, then struck a match. "I see the hometown lights ahead," he said as they rounded a final bend onto Main Street in Franklin.

"All in all, I'd say, it's been a good trip," Otis said. "And before too long we may be saying, Herr Professor, or Editor Dale Von Dieter."

"We'll see," Dale answered. *I'm not sure I'm ready to let go of the past. Abandon not my men,* he started to say but stopped himself.

Unconsciously he tapped the Ole Miss catalogue in his lap.

"What you need to say is, 'I fought the good fight and now I'll move on,'" Otis said, his tone authoritative. "Truth to tell. If this goes in the direction it seems to be heading." He raised his hand and crooked his finger to the back seat. "Man to man, let me say something. For your ears only."

Dale leaned forward.

"I think you got a lot done at Ole Miss. And that, especially, includes my sister," Otis said in a low voice. "I have to confess. I had a few ulterior motives in mind about this trip."

"Your sister brought out a new side of me," Dale said. "No, actually, an old one, that the war almost snuffed out. And, of course, she and I go way back."

Otis nodded his head. "All things considered, some would say I didn't make a very good chaperone." A sly smile crept across his face. "But in this case, and from where I sit, that was a good thing."

"We'll see what comes down the pike," Dale glanced over his shoulder to make sure Laura Lee couldn't hear him then he leaned closer to Otis. "I treasure your sister. I have for as long as I've known her. You were kind to let me ride to Oxford with you. It would feel so good to think I can move on now. In more ways than one," he said in a reflective tone. For a moment, he let himself hope.

Laura Lee. She could be the difference. As God is my witness I'm going to do my best to come back. He laughed to himself. *With the ghostly voice of my grandfather and with this sweet thing here by my side, I just might make it.*

Dale leaned back, pressed his head against the seat and picked up Laura Lee's hand. A shadow crossed his face.

"Both of you. I have to keep one thing in the front of my mind though. Things may change pretty quickly. Von Dieter—my father will be coming in soon. As a matter of fact, he may well be at Redemption Ridge when I get home tonight."

He drew on the cigarette as if by the act of inhaling he might also draw in some answers.

"I just hope he and I get along okay. I have to talk to him about Ole Miss. And if that's what I decide on, I may have to eat more than a little humble pie. See if he's willing to put out anything."

He looked pensive. "I'll also need some form of transportation." Dale pushed his smoldering cigarette out against the car door. "If I toady to my father, which galls me to even think about, he might help me get something to drive."

"From what I've heard of the old geezer, you'd be lucky to have a spavined mule," Otis said. "And speaking of transportation. Y'all are out there in the country with no way to get around except a horse and buggy. We've got another motorcar at the house. My father's old Oldsmobile. Why don't you use it for a day or two? Until you see what the lay of the land is," he offered Dale.

"Let's just stop at our house and you take it. It could stand to be run. It's filled with gas, there's water in the radiator, and air in the tires. I'll crank it before I go in and make sure it starts. The keys stay on the front seat."

"That's too much trouble."

"We owe you. In more ways than one."

"Not so."

"Well, that's our feeling." Otis said as he turned onto their gravel drive and swung around back of the house.

Dale stepped from the car and moved close to Otis. "I'm going to marry her. Someday."

"Have you asked her?"

"Not yet. I have to earn her love.

"Her brother died," Dale said under his breath. "Your brother. Come get me, I heard him calling. I couldn't get to him."

I don't deserve her. I don't deserve her, staccatoed in his chest like the beating of a military drum. For a short time war had been only a distant memory. In a flash the shadows in his mind floated back in, his reality had returned. Samuel's legs. Sliced off. Used as a latrine door stop.

And now O King Eternal, we lift our battle song.

Dale's head ached. His mouth went dry as the song once again invaded his brain.

"Stop it," he said, not realizing he had spoken out loud.

"What?" Otis asked.

"The war still gets into my head. And for lots of reasons, I need to earn your sister's love."

"Bull crap." Otis looked baffled. "You're sounding more southern than I. And I'm from Mississippi, so that takes a lot of doing."

Dale flipped his dead cigarette butt into the yard, opened the door for Laura Lee and helped her out.

"I'll make sure it starts," Otis said. I'll drive it around to the front. Then I'll turn off the motor, and go on to bed." He raised an eyebrow. "You can tell my sister goodbye. Take as long as you want," he said walking toward the house.

Dale raised Laura Lee's head with the tip of his fingers, took her face in both his hands, and kissed her. Then he held out his arms. She slid into his embrace. They leaned against the car as if they were being pushed by a strong wind, and needed propping up. Laura Lee cradled her head against Dale's chest, his hands stroked her back. One hand slipped forward, cupping the soft fullness of her breast.

"Let's make love again," she said. "That was my first time. My only time. I liked it. No, I loved it—YOU." She broke off her words. "God's already forgiven me," she whispered. "So, it's all right."

A pang of conscience hit Dale. He stepped back.

Take it easy. Take a deep breath. "I have to earn your trust," he said. "I violated it the other night."

"No!" She rested her forehead against his chest. "I've waited. For you." She raised her head.

"You're the best person I know. You are what I've hoped for. What I've dreamed of. What I don't deserve," Dale said, his voice thick with distress. "If you're feeling guilty because of our love, and what we did, I won't get you into any more trouble."

"I've said this all wrong." Laura Lee looked him up and down as if she were searching for something yet to be found. "I've wanted it to be you. For as long as I can remember."

"I'm sorry," Dale managed to say, before he pushed her away. "I'm just not good enough."

For the longest time Laura Lee looked up at him as if there were more she wanted to say. Then she ducked her head down. "I'd better go check on Mother."

Dale walked her up the porch steps and set her grip by the door. He turned and hurried to the end of the driveway where Otis had left the car.

"Will you keep me sane? Can you end this war in my soul?" He mashed the clutch and shifted the gear into reverse. "Can I bury the ghosts of Redemption Ridge? Redeem them?

"I pray so," he whispered. "I just hope I don't drive you insane. I've got to finish fighting my wars before we can have a life."

Dale backed out, turned the car, and stopped in front of the Stanton house.

Laura Lee stood in the doorway. She waved goodbye.

"I'm ready to see the preacher," she called out, but there was no way he could hear her words. She turned off the lights and stepped inside.

When she closed the door, Dale felt himself vanish with her.

CHAPTER 42

To write the bead of blood
Is to speak the first word in private,

A mirror is her compass,
Vanity the only magnetism
In a wilderness of responsibility.

Later Friday

"It's too dark to see what I'm doing." Memory twisted the socket key and turned on the back porch drop light. "You're now Gertie Mae's Daisy Dog," she said, tying the dog she had brought home from the cemetery to a chair leg. She fed her water and table scraps, and spread an old burlap bag for the dog to lie on. Brucie had settled into a rocking chair and she watched, keeping time to Memory's movements with an up-and-down creaking rhythm.

"Daisy Dog," Memory said softly as the dog curled into a contented ball. "You're mine until she takes you."

"Who?" Brucie asked.

"The dog. And Gertie Mae. What a week this has been!" she exclaimed. "Especially today!"

Brucie shook her head. "That must have been a nightmare. I'm sorry you had to go through something like that with that horrible policeman. But it's good you were there for Gertie Mae. You saved my granddaughter's life."

"Yes. Your granddaughter. My niece." Memory's face lit up when her mother said this, but she shuddered inside thinking about what had happened to Gertie Mae. And it would have been so much worse if she had not been there.

"That policeman from Boston." Brucie gave Memory a pointed look. "Herschel always believed he had something to do with Thornton's murder. I can't believe he followed us all the way down here to Mississippi."

"Revenge," Memory said. "For the death of Senator Peter Shields. Nobody murdered him. The good Senator ran in front of a streetcar."

"Yes. But Liam McRae blamed your brother," Brucie said. "I pray to the good Lord he goes on back to Boston. Something needs to be done about him."

"He may need help getting there." A satisfied smile spread across Memory's face. "I told you." She gave a sharp but painful sounding laugh. "I'm pretty sure I took care of him. For this, I was in the right place at the right time." Her eyes narrowing, Memory paused a moment. "Even though our marriage left a lot to be desired, I would never have wanted Thornton dead." She threw her head back. "I'll always believe he was the one who speared my husband on a fence. And I. In the Redemption Ridge Cemetery, I speared his eye," she said, proudly. "With a piece of broken cross and a rusty nail. '"Vengeance is mine,"' saith the Lord.'" After a moment's silence, "Well, vengeance was mine today. And I claim it."

She straightened her shoulders. "I think we need to stay away from Thelma Jewel. But hopefully, we'll all be able to help Gertie Mae. Better late than never."

The rocking chair stopped creaking. "The sins of the fathers." Brucie's eyes showed the hurt she was feeling. "No, the mother's."

"Yes, but Thelma Jewel. She wasn't your sin," Memory murmured. "Daddy Claymore had his way with you."

A painful look on her face, Brucie nodded in agreement. "And then, I was with child. I should have gone against Herschel's wishes all those years ago and been in Thelma Jewel's life." She cupped her knees with the palm of her hands.

"Not just taken care of my daughter financially. My cousin Sarah and I saw to it she had a life with a faraway relative, Mrs. Bledsoe. But I should have been there for her in other ways. She barely knows her own mother. What she does know, she hates," Brucie said, a tone of regret in her voice.

Just be careful, Memory thought. She went back over the letter from Thelma Jewel's neighbors. Their suspicions about her murdering Mrs. Bledsoe ran through her mind again. "From what we've heard, Thelma Jewel hates everyone, even her own daughter. Except, of course, herself." She spoke in a calm voice, but that was not the way she felt inside. "We both need to remember. She could be dangerous. Maybe our part in this redemption will be to protect a little girl. Gertie Mae. And that would be from her own mother."

Brucie closed her eyes, remembering more from her own past than she cared to. "My daughter and granddaughter are somewhere here in Tallouga County with us." She drew in a deep breath. "By them coming, and with us back here at Redemption Ridge, we have a lot of changes in our lives. We'll handle them the best we can. I do see some hope, though." She began rocking again. "We have some pleasant things to think about. You and Sassy may be a little bit ahead of your times, but I for one am pleased about Sassy. Her voice. And that she'll be going on to school."

"I am too," Memory said.

"There's more." Brucie's face softened. "The life that's ahead for you and Jenson." Frowning slightly, she rubbed her forehead. "Of course there's Dale and Laura Lee."

"I have my fingers crossed for them," Memory said in a thoughtful voice. "For Dale, life could go either way. My brother. The watches he stood with his men. In those trenches. When he came home, to live, he had to allow whiskey, that cough medicine, which I heard was banned, and pills to soothe his soul. But, oh, I do see a chance for him coming out of it now, with pretty, slow-talking, Laura Lee Stanton."

She bent over and stroked the dog. "After Thornton's murder, even though I couldn't see it at the time, I needed to move on in a new direction." She felt a surge of happiness. "And, oh, how lucky I am! Now, there's Jenson. I'll be with him for all our forevers. So much good is ahead." Her thoughts swung back to the night before, when they had made love by Noble Creek. "Thank you, God," she whispered.

"Your father," Brucie said. "You and I both know, he never really liked Thornton."

She stopped rocking for a moment and lifted her shoulders in a slight shrug as if she wanted to say more but thought it best not to.

"And speaking of your father. He rang earlier. He'll be here later tonight."

Memory looked out toward the backyard. A dark feeling crept over her. If it had been daytime, she could have seen the old well. Evil seemed to pool there. She shivered.

As if she too had heavy thoughts on her mind, it was several moments before Brucie spoke. "Redemption Ridge. So different from Boston. But this is my home. Everything will change when your father joins us." She cleared her throat. "He's been here for many summers on short visits. But living here?"

She stared at her daughter, then her voice filled with uncertainty. "He'll have to give the town of Franklin a little time," she said.

She nodded toward the sleeping animal. "You might want to do something about this dog. Find a place for her."

Memory raised her hand in a stopping motion. "Her name is Daisy. The dog stays," she said firmly. "We've got that pen where Dale used to keep his bird dogs. And there's an old dog house out there."

She yawned and rubbed her back.

"It's got to be getting on up in the time," Brucie said. "A lot has happened in the last few days. Why don't you go on to bed? I'll wait up for your father. I know you're worn out."

"Yes, I am." Memory bent over, and kissed her mother goodnight. She took Daisy from the porch, settled her in the dog pen, then went upstairs.

When she got to her room, she turned on a table lamp. "I am worn out. I feel like an old woman." She slipped off her clothes and looked at herself in the chifforobe mirror, but to her relief she saw no bulging thighs. She put on her gown and stepped closer to the mirror. She brought a hand to her face and was reassured that at twenty-eight there were no crow's feet yet, nor turkey wattle neck skin.

But she was apprehensive because of all that lay in wait for her and her family outside these walls. She was filled with uncertainty for her brother. With what would happen when her father came in. She was disturbed over Gertie Mae, and she would never forget what she had done to Liam's eye and was fearful of what might happen because of that. He could still be here, lying in wait.

And her half-sister, Thelma Jewel, might be the most threatening part of their lives right now.

Danger loomed.

With all she had on her mind, and after everything that had happened today, Memory was torn up inside. She desperately wanted to go back to her old routine, to cut herself. To feel the pain. To feel alive and in control of her destiny.

Without thinking, she reached into her purse for her silver fingernail file but quickly flung her purse to the floor. "Oh, no," she said. "Of course, it's not here. I threw it away."

Unable to relieve herself by cutting, she pulled a chair near a bedside table. "Second best." She took several deep breaths to calm herself, then she lifted her journal and began to write.

> My father comes in tonight, and I have mixed feelings. I loved my papa, but his rules governed our family. In our heads we marched to his tune, the sound of fifes, whistles and drums. I must say, our father grew more rigid as the cursed war continued. I think if my brother had not been fighting for this country, our father may have left his American family for his family in Germany. No longer Mr. Von Dieter, but Herr Herschel Von Dieter.
>
> By name I am a Von Dieter. What I know of our German relatives, they have always been a family who kept thoughts and feelings in check with silence. We never tell our secrets. They are hidden like the underbelly of a night sliding opossum. What if someone slits the belly open—do the secrets spill out of the open wound, writhing unlovely baby opossums, for all to see and abhor? I don't know.

Although my mother never said it, there were times she thought I favored the Von Dieters. No, I did not. It was just my way to goad, prod, and grow up and away from her, an annoying habit. Now, am I, at long last, in the process of outgrowing this? I pray to God it will be so.

There is still so much uncertainty in my life, why I'm like I am. Those tainted old days. Shank Potter—did he put a blade into my hand? Would this have been my comfort had there been no Shank Potter? Or was he just my excuse to hurt myself? I'll never know. But, oh, what relief those jabbing slices gave. I was alive. Powerful. In control.

When it comes to my brother, there are reasons for his distress. Will Dale ever let loose of his dead comrades' boots? Those he carries in his memory and his soul. I pray the sound of the marching dead will be beaten down by the strumming of angel harps. Streaming notes of redemption across these Tallouga County hills and valleys.

And now there's this confrontation with Liam. The truest feeling I have for this is that old Bible verse, "an eye for an eye." Although I probably shouldn't admit to this, I swell with pride. I feel in some small way, justice has been done for Thornton. Avenged. Revenged. How ironic is it that I speared the man who speared my husband? Liam McRae. No proof, but my second sight tells me it's true.

A dark feeling came over Memory. "I didn't kill him. And yet, I may have killed him in other ways," she said.

"With that, I have folded the pages shut on Boston." She rubbed her chin. "I'm in Mississippi."

The barking of a dog startled Memory and brought her back from the past, to her room, to the here and now. She looked toward the window.

"Daisy," she said. "Right now you're Gertie Mae's maybe dog. If I have anything to do with it, soon, you'll be Gertie' Mae's forever dog."

As if the animal sensed someone was talking about her, the barking changed to a plaintive howl. The dog seemed to call to the moonshine, appeal to the stars, wailing of all the anguish and sorrow pulsing through her blood stream, washing across her fragile bones. Then the cries died, and, as had happened to her in the recent past, Memory felt the nearness of someone close by. She looked around, but there was no one else in the room.

She picked up the pen to begin where she had left off with her journal writing.

> **Will our forever death be here in the old Claymore burial plot? Surrounding the murderous Daddy Claymore?**

Memory heard a tapping sound, a noise like a dog lapping water from a can.

No, it seemed to come from the chifforobe. Her heartbeat quickened. She lay her pen down and held her breath. Out of the corner of her eye she saw a flicker of movement by the side of her bed. She saw no one, but she felt a presence with her.

Soft fingers brushed her cheek.

Another hand turned her hand over. Placed the pen in it.

Slowly the pen began to move. It was not Memory's handwriting.

> Miss Memory. It ain't yet the sweet by an' by, but I'm with you. I ain't forgettin'. You took care of one of mine, an' you be's right. It's gone come full circle. An' you an' me. We'll be standin' side by side.

***

Gravel spun into the ditches and trees as Dale sped down Old Farm Road. What he had said to Laura Lee had not come out the way he intended. Now, shaken over the feelings he had when she turned away and walked into the house, an unhappy Dale headed back to Redemption Ridge.

"Chaste. Until you slept with her." Shame, like sweat from their love making seeped into his pores. "They'd call you white trash down here," he scolded himself. "Sex with a virgin."

The car slid. *You took advantage of her innocence.* Dale snatched the steering wheel to the left, straightening the car just before it left the road.

You pulled away, an unspoken voice countered. *You did not spill your seed in her.*

"Earn back her trust. If you haven't lost it forever."

"I'll apologize. Set it right," he vowed. *Do that southern gentleman thing of protecting her.* "Whatever I need to do."

He fought a sudden urge to turn around and go back to the Stanton house. To see Laura Lee and promise never, until they were man and wife to make love to her again. S*he wanted it that first time too,* he reminded himself. *She wanted it tonight.*

The back wheels skidded. Dale jerked the car just before it dropped from the edge of the narrow road into a ditch. "Otis's car," he reminded himself, turning his attention to the road ahead. "Slow down."

A strong yearning came over Dale when he spotted the gates to the Redemption Ridge Cemetery. He had felt this attraction where his dead ancestors lay on more than one occasion; it was as if a siren song called to him. He thought back to an old poem. "Follow! Oh follow! To be at rest forevermore! Forevermore."

"'The Sirens' by James Russell Lowell," he muttered. "Get hold of yourself Dale."

He needed to get his thoughts straightened out; Dale pulled to the side of the road. The car idled and sputtered to a stop. He lit one of the cigarettes Otis had given him and unwound his window.

The cemetery was bathed in pale silver moonlight. He drew in several deep breaths, lay his head against the seat, and closed his eyes. He allowed himself a moment to move away from Laura Lee. To reflect on other things.

"The war is over." Almost forgotten faces swirled through his mind. *And yet, I feel a need to learn from my men.* As soon as he thought those words, it was as if he felt comforting arms drape his shoulders.

"They were brave. They did what they had to do." *So many of them will forever lie in the deep dark fields of foreign soil.*

His jaws clenched as he allowed himself to think about the recent past and what lay ahead. He finished one cigarette and took out another. "My father's probably here now. Will I be on another mission? Fighting battles? Creating battles?"

I don't know what it is I'm supposed to do. Dale shivered in the cool spring night air. "What I want to do."

He lifted the Ole Miss catalogue. "I think this is what I want." He shook his head. "But knowing my father, he probably has other ideas. Maybe return to Boston for college and a career. Move back east somewhere. Away from Mississippi."

Low sighing noises came from the cemetery. It could have been the wind picking up and rustling tree limbs, but Dale didn't think so. It had a more rhythmic, musical sound than random gusts of wind and rustling tree limbs.

The ghost of Bruce Claymore? For a moment his breath caught in his throat; thoughts galloped through Dale's mind like a horse racing to a finish line.

"Do I need to clear my grandfather's name?" He swallowed hard and rubbed his brow. "I'm just home from one war. I'm facing battles with my father."

He flipped his burned-down cigarette out the window. *I've got to make my way on around the next bend in the road before I can do anything for some disgraced ancestor.*

Dale looked out the car window. He saw a flicker of movement near the fence.

"Abandon me not." He heard a distant voice, as if coming from a deep tunnel. A shadowy shape flitted across the mounds and gravestones. He made out a silhouette, one he had seen before.

"Captain," Dale called. "Is that you?"

Once again he saw the straight proud body of his ancestor. He wore a tattered, blood soaked coat. His brooding blue eyes were fixed on Dale.

"My tears fell for my men. They suffocated in slimy mud. I had to leave them in dark, foul soil," Dale said. "Yes. I will not leave my grandfather in disgrace. Bone of my bone, I will not forsake you."

A shadow of a smile crossed the ghost's face. He dipped his head, straightened his body, and saluted.

Dale heaved several deep breaths.

"Home," he said with longing. *Sometimes I wish to hell I could just walk away from all of this. I might have done that in the past.* But those thoughts didn't fit his feelings. "Now, there's Laura Lee. If I can just get myself together, hopefully there'll be a life for the two of us."

He got out and cranked the motor. It was late when he made out lights on in their house. Once again driving too fast, he cut sharply and almost missed the turn into the driveway. Barely missing the front gate he steered with the slide, stopping just before he slammed into his father's touring auto.

"Damn!" Dale hit the steering wheel with his fist and got out of the car. "I knew it. He's here." He took a step backward, raised his arms and leaned against the door frame.

"It's time," he said after a moment. "Am I ready?"

***

Parlor lights shone through the leaded glass panes of the front door. Dale gripped the handle for a moment, then very quietly opened the door. He held his grip in one hand, the Ole Miss catalogue under his arm. When Dale heard his father's voice, he paused in the entry hall.

"I vas around many of my Von Dieter cousins and nephews on my recent visit home," Herschel's voice strutted.

For a moment Dale's legs went weak on him. *Get hold of yourself. You need to hear what else he has to say.* He leaned against the door jamb and carefully set his grip down.

"They vere too young, but if Germany had had a few more like them in The Var, the outcome may vell have been different, Brucie."

With those words, Dale had heard enough.

Physically worn out, but his mind cocked like a trigger finger on a loaded pistol, he eased on up the stairs to his room.

He untied his shoes and flung them to the corner. He unbuttoned and stripped off his shirt. When he bent over to step out of his pants, Dale smelled an odor, one he had smelled before. Sweet olive. He quickly associated it with the old Claymore family Bible and turned toward the bed. Propped up, pridefully the Bible lay against a pillow, as if it were on a podium, and ready to be read.

"I didn't put you there," Dale said.

He remembered that a few days ago, as now, the peculiar aroma of sweet olive had drawn him to the armoire. When he lifted the Bible, a packet of yellowed papers had slid out.

He felt an attraction that day and had started reading what Sheriff Homer Bramlett had written those long years ago in the eighteen seventies. But due at the cemetery shortly to bury his friend Samuel, he had run out of time and had not read all of them.

He had folded, the yellowed papers and slid them back into their hiding place. He put the Bible into his haversack and carried it to the cemetery. When Dale buried his friend, Samuel Stanton, as part of the service, he had read a chapter from Job.

"And after the funeral I took this Holy Book from my haversack and left it here it in the armoire," he said. "The night before I went to Oxford.

"I'll take a look at what I started before we went to bury Samuel."

Sighing, he turned on the oil lamp, crawled into bed, and pulled a quilt over his legs. He opened the Bible, eased out a packet from the back and glanced at Sheriff Homer Bramlett's words, written all those years ago.

August 13, 1877

I will approach the crippled and infirm C.W. Claymore and attach his signed confession to this missive. Matthew Stanton, Attorney at Law, is here as a witness.

This was not easy. My fingertips are too big. I used one of the new type writer machines. I have finger-punched in the below, and I am reading it to you, Mr. C.W. Claymore. I need to keep straight in my head what I have said to you, in case someone ever again needs to know what I am doing and why.

"I'm tired, and after hearing my father, depressed," Dale said. "Can't do anything about it now. I'll finish this later."

CHAPTER 43

A cool, damp nose
And a kind presence;
An alien ghost given form
In kindness.

This friend can't hurt,
Won't hurt—its fierce spirit is sizeless,
Wicked against the wicked.

Saturday, 9:30, April 3

"Mr. Von Dieter's already dressed an' in the parlor," Brucie said to Bertha as she stepped into the kitchen. "He and Milton, our Boston chauffeur, drove straight on through. Herschel left Milton in Franklin. He'll catch a train sometime today and start on back to Massachusetts."

"An' what do you want me to be cookin'?"

"We'll have a big breakfast and then an early dinner."

"As I recollect, Mr. Von Dieter"—Disdain rode in Bertha's voice—"He don't cotton too much to fried chicken or cawnbread. He likes to have him some red cabbage, crispy roasted chicken." Her eyebrows drew together. "An' somethin' I ain't never heard of. Hot tater salad."

"Since we're going to be living here from now on, I'm turning over a new leaf. We're not doing anything special, for anybody. And that will include Mr. Von Dieter." Brucie released a long breath.

"Just do the best you can, Bertha. I think we're all tired. Most anything should be fine."

"Um-hum." Bertha tightened her back and rolled her lips together as if there were things she wanted to say, but thought better. "You go on ahead with Mr. Von Dieter. I'll tote some coffee on in where you all's at an' then start frying some bacon. Grits is done made. Biscuit dough's rolled out."

When Brucie came into the parlor, Von Dieter rose, then sat back down on the sofa. "It's the first of April, and it's already hot as Hades down here." He pulled out a creamy linen handkerchief and wiped his forehead.

Bertha set a silver tray with coffee, cream and sugar on a marble-top table at the end of the sofa.

"Easter's tomorrow. And speaking of Easter, we've got that big Celebration coming up," Brucie said. "Honoring Captain Bruce Claymore."

"There's too much of the supernatural and vhat you people call spirits and haints down here. Vell, if I go, I'm going to vear vhat I vould have vorn to a celebration back home. My uniform. I brought most of my clothes vith me."

Brucie poured their coffee then sat next to her husband.

Von Dieter blew on the hot coffee. "I'm not sure this is vhere I vant to live out the rest of my days," he said. "All things considered, I should have stayed in Boston. That unpleasantness about Senator Peter Shields vould have died down. Here, it's the same old scenario all over again. Nothing ever changes."

There was a moment of silence, then he went on. "Ve'll start vith vhat you told me about our daughter and that man, Jenson Cooper. I'm not in favor of vhat our daughter's doing. Maybe, just maybe, Mr. Cooper thinks he can step into this family and come up in the vorld." Von Dieter cleared his throat in a scraping noise as if he had something caught in it.

"I'm sorry you have doubts about Memory and Jenson, Herschel. To me, it's almost Divine Providence."

"That's vhat I'm talking about. Changes. From the minute she steps off the train into Tallouga County, our daughter becomes a different person."

"Our daughter is a strong woman. She avenged Thornton's death. She does a lot of good. In many other ways. She's helped Sassy," Brucie said proudly. She blew on the hot coffee, then took a sip. "And there was someone I should have done so much more for. She helped her too.

"Gertie Mae," she whispered.

Von Dieter pulled a pipe and a packet of tobacco from his coat pocket.

"And helping Sassy?" he snorted. "You think that's a good thing? From vhat you've told me, she and Memory have overstepped themselves. It vouldn't go over so vell in Boston, and certainly not down here in this God-forsaken, God-haunted, part of the vorld."

"Speaking of God, I don't believe much in coincidence. If it works out, it's Divine Providence. And, I would say, God-touched," Brucie said proudly. A heartbeat of silence fell between them.

"Dale was due back from Oxford yesterday," she said. "We'll see what happens. I thought I heard him upstairs a little while ago. I'll feel better when we find out what his plans will be."

"Vhen my son comes down here, I hardly know him. He acts like the Mississippi Claymores." Von Dieter tapped his empty pipe on a table, then filled it with tobacco. "Vhite trash people. They chicken-pluck and dirt-farm."

"Well, well." Brucie and Herschel turned to see Memory, hands on her hips, standing in the doorway.

"Please stop! Brother's close behind me. You're into the same old, tired song of blame and shame." Memory sat on the edge of the sofa facing her parents. "Welcome home, Papa."

She smiled brightly, but there was unhappiness behind her words.

Von Dieter, took a sip of coffee, then struck a match to his pipe. "Thornton's not been dead a year. There's a proper and an improper vay to act. Unfortunately for us, you've chosen the latter."

Dale stood in the doorway. Even before he walked into the room he sensed an undercurrent for something he couldn't name, the closest word in his mind was arrogance. "I see you're back from Germany." For a moment all attempts at conversation ceased. There were a few muffled sounds, as if they were heard through a thick cloth: moving fan blades. chattering squirrels, the slipping slide of a clock's minute hand. "Let's start over."

"No velcome to Mississippi for your father?" Von Dieter asked. "You seem to have gotten a cockier attitude since you've been down here vith your people. Be a man. Tough that your men got gassed. But that's the roll of the dice."

Dale spread both his hands in an I-give-up movement. He shook his head and walked away.

"Not a vone of those doughboys is vorth my boy losing his mind," Von Dieter muttered.

Close on her brother's footsteps, Memory grabbed the edge of his door just before he slammed it.

Dale let out a ragged sigh. "The war is too much with me," he said. "I wish my tears would dry. I don't need to be around the Kraut. We're not good for each other right now." He dropped his shoulders.

Memory started to agree, but stopped herself. For her brother's sake, she tried not to give in to the anger she also felt for their father. *Easter is a time for forgiving,* she reminded herself.

"He was probably tired from his trip."

"He seems to be angrier than before he left the country. I was doing better," Dale murmured. "Why, oh why, didn't Laura Lee and I stay in Oxford? Why did I come home?" His eyes narrowed. "And thanks to me, things are not good between the lovely lady and me."

Memory realized she would have to be the one to get things moving between Dale and Laura Lee. That meant more right now than this confrontation between her brother and their father. He needed Laura Lee in his life. For many reasons. "You came home because you had to. Calm down. Catch your breath. There's a lot going on. We'll worry about Father's attitude later. She put her hand on Dale's arm. "I didn't have a chance to say anything," she said, "but Jenson's motoring out here in about an hour. I'm having a jacket altered and a green and white gingham skirt made for the Easter celebration. We're driving to Jackson to pick them up." She dipped in a saucy, half curtsy. "Thought I'd dress a little more like Tallouga County folks.

"Why don't you and Laura Lee join us? We could pick her up as we go through town."

"I don't think she'd go with me."

"You're wrong. Laura Lee rang me. She sounded distressed. Stubborn brother of mine, she loves you."

Dale leaned against the wall as if he needed propping up. "And I her. I didn't leave on the best of terms with her last night. It was my fault. I have some making up to do. With her, and probably Father, too."

"Our father." The shadow of her father's behavior in the past ran through Memory's mind. "He marches to a different drummer, especially when he returns from his homeland. He needs some time to settle in. And on the other side of the equations"—She smoothed a lock of hair from her face—"There's something about Redemption Ridge. You change when you come here. There's none of the 'be a man' you always heard from Father and often tried to parade march to. It's more as if, there's a long, long trail a-winding into this land of your dreams, and they come true when you return to Redemption Ridge."

She drew in a deep breath. "You should see Laura Lee and make amends. You've been wrong about some things. I think she'd love to see you.

"Jenson's bringing me back before dark. Call Laura Lee. Go with us." Her eyes widened as if she were going to say more, but an eager barking from the back yard got her attention.

"Oh, Daisy Dog. I nearly forgot. I need to feed her and she's telling me about it. I'm going out back to feed her."

Dale gave a slight nod. "If Laura Lee says yes, I have to clean up."

"I think she will. We'll meet Jenson down by the road."

Once in her room, Memory slipped on a jacket, smoothed her hair, pulled a hat over her head, and checked herself in the mirror. She ran her tongue over her lips to moisten them, then hurried down the steps, stopping in the kitchen. "We won't be here for dinner, Bertha. Dale and I will be eating in Jackson. We'll be back around suppertime."

"I'll set what ain't eaten back on the stove," Bertha said, "for you all to have whenever you come in."

Memory took out a greasy sack of leftover food she had put in the icebox. When she stepped outside it was warm. The sun was shining, but a few clouds drifted overhead. The trees were in full leaf and a breeze brushed Memory's hair back.

Daisy Dog howled in greeting as Memory walked to where the animal was penned.

She emptied the sack, leaned against a tree and sank to her knees. She spread her skirt and watched with satisfaction as the dog devoured the scraps. "I have a little time before Jenson comes."

Done with her food, the dog licked Memory's hand in what could have been gratitude.

Memory gave a sigh of contentment and stroked the animal.

"Daisy Dog, My journal helps me think things through, but I need to talk to somebody. I wish you could tell me what to do." Memory put her hand over her mouth a moment and then took it down. She raised the animal's chin and looked into her eyes. "I stabbed somebody yesterday. I never thought I'd be violent."

She drew in a painful breath. "But you know what? It just may be that God's in His Heaven, and all's right with the world. I saved the life of my half-sister's daughter.

"It took a while for me to realize who he was. And then it came easy. I have seen him before. But I wasn't ready." For a moment Memory couldn't speak, she had to clear her throat before she could go on. "It was him. That red hair. Those green eyes."

A sense of power came over her. "A stabbing for a stabbing. He was with Thornton that night. Father thought I didn't see." She shook her head. "He impaled Thornton. I *know* it. I stabbed him." She wrapped her arms around her waist. "I don't know where the man is now. I really don't care. I just want him to leave us alone."

She lowered her eyes. "I can only guess what kind of shape he's in."

She gave a wistful sigh. "If I write the story of Redemption Ridge? Do I include this? Me? Stabbing?

"I need to know what to do. About a lot of things. Where I'll start." Memory reflected a moment. "Vernell," she whispered. "That's where I'll start."

Her tail wagging, the dog licked Memory's hand.

She raised her arm and rubbed the ridge between the dog's ears. Memory felt comfort and calmness creep over her. She hadn't thought much about animals. Until now. But she found it easy to talk to Daisy Dog, who looked at her as if she understood what Memory was saying and agreed with her.

"My half-sister and I. Someday we may be on the same path. Will we be able to walk together through the woods of Redemption Ridge? Or will one of us shove the other into some mud-filled ditch or raging river waters?"

The dog stared at Memory, tucked her tail and dropped her head in an attitude of what could have been either submission or boredom.

"And the redheaded man. Will he seek revenge? Or will he tuck tail and run away?

"I fear I already know the answer." *Think about something else*, she told herself.

"And my brother, Dale? The War." Her heart skipped a beat. "He hurts so much. I see Redemption Ridge and Laura Lee as his salvation.

"The same as my mother. Redemption Ridge." Stroking the dog made Memory feel calmer inside. Soothed her. "And Lamont." Except for the quiet panting of Daisy Dog, the silence was deep. "Jenson and me. I didn't know it for so long, but he'll be mine. I'll be his."

The dog rolled to her side and folded her legs as a child often does before drifting off to sleep. "Daisy Dog." Memory stroked the dog's soft belly. "Someday you'll be Gertie Mae's dog. I'll see to that. Somehow.

"And where will I be then?" She slipped her hands under Daisy Dog's neck and cradled her in her arms.

"I've got to leave you now." The dog licked her hand. Understanding of what Memory was saying and also feeling her pain seemed to shine through a pair of glossy dark eyes. "And the ghosts of Redemption Ridge? Oh, Daisy Dog. Will we be able to help them claim their peace? Or will they steal ours?"

CHAPTER 44

**Home is a ghost
In the lineage,
A gene turned
Off and on by
Impulse, memory,
Déjà vu.**

**The family approaches,
Their odyssey of longing
Hardening into prehistory.**

Late Saturday morning, April 3

Mudge heard a thundering whistle as a train pulled from the Franklin station. "Is Mistah Policeman on that train?" he asked himself. It was not often that Mudge was unsure of himself, but he had mixed feelings about Liam McRae.

As if reading his thoughts, "Where's Mr. McRae?" Thelma Jewel asked Mudge as they walked toward his roadster.

"I ain't heerd nothin'from the Boston policeman, since he high-tailed it from the cemetery," Mudge said. "Here one minute, gone the next. I was already 'bout to warsh my hands of the man. He an' I jest didn't see eye-to-eye on thangs. You can't depend on much of nobody but yer own self nowadays. Nobody knows fer sure where Mr. Liam McRae has run off to."

He ran his hands down the sides of his dirt-splotched linen duster. "I knew from the first, he was a stuck up coxcomb. An' I thought you an' him jest might be sparkin' a liddle bit."

"Well, Mr. Mudge. I figured him out. I think Mr. Liam McRae had some ulterior motives in mind. For you and me both," Thelma Jewel said.

"I heerd somethin' you might orter know," Mudge said. "He might coulda been on that train what jest left from here. I did hear tell somebody thought they saw him down by the train station buyin' him a ticket." Mudge gave a short sideways rock. "He bought that air ole' car a mine, but it was jest about on its last leg." He smiled. "Made me a liddle money off'n that air policeman."

A thought settled into Thelma Jewels brain. *If Mr. McRae's left town, that leaves Mr. Mudge as my only choice.*

"I smarted up. I ain't exactly piss ant poor 'n' I'm thinkin' he jest mighta been wantin' to git his hands on anything o' mine he could. Any way he could. An' I'm a few steps ahead a him." A foxlike smile crossed his face.

Thelma Jewel drew in a deep breath. Mudge's remark stirred up thoughts of sudden wealth, if she and Mudge were to become Mr. and Mrs. In her mind's eye, she began to see some of the homes people here in Franklin had before The War. Before they ran out of money, and the homes began to settle in on themselves like pans of warm biscuit dough.

Mudge nodded his head slightly, and covered his mouth with his hand. "Mmm," he said. "From the git-go, you'n me. We kindly think alike on some thangs."

"And you know what?" Thelma Jewel said. "With what we have going on with that cheating family of mine and with that service tomorrow, I could most likely come into my inheritance. What I've been denied," she said. *Put that with what Mr Mudge has, and I just might could be the richest woman in Tallouga County, Mississippi.*

"Whooee," she said, wiping a slight drool from around her mouth. *And then I could mostly likely pay somebody to take Gertie Mae off my hands.*

"Le's us go ahead on 'an' go out to see what them church folks has got done," Mudge said when they got to his car.

He shifted the gears and mashed the clutch. Mudge toed the accelerator, jerking Thelma Jewel's head forward, then popping it back as he jolted away from Mrs. Netter's. Turning off of Main Street, he stomped the accelerator and sped up. Rubber tires dropped into buggy tracks, digging into the gravel as if chewing it up and spitting it out. Thelma Jewel was flung sideways on the loopy, bumpy Old Farm Road. Dropping her bag, she gripped the curve of the seat with both hands. "Well, I never," she moaned several times.

"Looky there," Mudge hollered, slamming on the brakes. Her body sprawled halfway off the seat, Thelma Jewel grabbed the door handle so she wouldn't be flung all the way to the floor as they skidded to a stop. Mudge pointed to the far side of the white cemetery where a wooden arbor was being built. "That air's where Brother Ollie Potter's buried. A lot's already been done. I had them set it up right over Brother Ollie Potter's restin' place. We honor our dead in holiness, Brother Ollie Potter. I done tole them not to drop them poles onto his coffin. But if'n they do it on somebody else's, so be it."

Members of the Divine Deliverance Holiness Church had been setting up for the Brush Arbor Meeting since daybreak. Upright poles had been driven into the ground. Open on all four sides, long thin boards were ready to hold a roof made of green, leafy tree branches that had been cut and stacked. Benches from the church had been carried in wagons drawn by mules and had been unloaded off to the side. A platform was being built to hold the altar, a small table and an old wooden musket chest from the war.

"There's Brother Tuggle in his wagon over yonder," Mudge said, springing from the car. He grabbed a canvas bag from the back, tucked it under his arm and then, hips swishing, swaggered toward the wagon.

Thelma Jewel hesitated, pushed the door open, and slowly swung one leg out and then the other. Lightheaded and breathless, she stood, gripping the hood. When she caught her breath and looked over, she saw Deacon Harlan Sistrunk, his wife Sister Mealie Maude, Brother Tuggle and his wife, Mother Bunny, standing next to a wagon hitched to the fence. Gertie Mae peered over the side.

"Mama!" Gertie Mae screamed.

"Well, I never," Thelma Jewel said in a wavery voice. "What's she doing here?" But nobody was close enough to hear or answer her question.

"Looks like some good work's been done, but we still got a ways to go," she heard Mudge say as she drew closer.

Sister Mealie Maude scratched under her armpit. "I hate to say, but it looks a bit like rain."

"It's in the hands of the Lord," Brother Tuggle said wisely. "He takes care of His own."

"He's here 'n' He'll take ker 'a us," Mudge said. "We'll make it jest fine but we'd best heist us a leg. We'll make our dead brother, Ollie Potter shirt bustin' proud. I done brought our blest flag from The War. The only one what counts. An' don't fergit to cover our altar table with our honored Confederate flag."

He turned to Brother Tuggle. "You needn't have brung that air young'un, Brother Tuggle."

"The wife, Mother Bunny, tole me to git Gertie Mae outta her hair fer a while. That young'un ain't been doin' nothin' but whinin' 'bout that there dog she wanted 'n' wantin' to see her mother." He nodded toward Thelma Jewel. "Drivin' them other chirren an' my missus out'n their heads," he grouched.

"Well, maybe she'll shut up some now she sees her mama," Mudge said.

"Mama!" Gertie Mae cried again. The wagon creaked as she turned and began to carefully crawl over the side. She dangled, then, right leg twisting, she fell to the ground in a heap like a bundle of clothes.

Thelma Jewel shook her head in disgust.

"I need to convert me a mess a folks from the path of damnation they're on, to the one of true righteousness," Brother Tuggle said. "I'm here to set you straight on a few things. I'm good an ready to wrestle with the devil hisself."

He put his hand on Mudge's shoulder. Mudge shrugged it off.

The Preacher's eyes slid sideways. "I've been called to save Tallouga County," he said, his voice trailing away.

"You bes' lissen to me," Mudge said. "An' I'm gonter tell you what we're doin'." His lips took on an arrogant, I'm-in-control smile.

Preacher Tuggle spit into his sleeve, then scrubbed his mouth with his arm.

"Startin' off we'll be doin' more like them churches on Main Sreet. A liddle gospel singin', an' a short sermon. Pass the collection plates.

"Out where everybody kin see, we'll have us a few of the women folks settin' up fer dinner on the grounds followin' that air short service. After dinner, we'll start us havin' the Celebration."

His voice blaring like a trumpet, Mudge pulled a cream-colored parchment from his duster and read:

> *Hear ye, Hear ye. A Celebration Day. Long overdue. We're standing here by Brother Ollie Potter's grave, who always fought for the right. As he knew it. An' we feel in our heart of hearts, our brother, Captain Bruce Claymore is layin' right here beside him.*
>
> *This is our Special Service honoring the Redemption Ridge heroes. And the long buried, hidden truth about our own Captain Bruce Claymore.*

He folded the parchment back into his pocket.

"We was gonter call out the names of all our saints, there'll be the namin' an' honorin' of our sanctified dead, followed by a trumpet blast from our own Stalk Wheeler, but that may take too much time from our healin' service. So, I done cut that down."

He pointed to Thelma Jewel. "We're gonter let Miss Thelmer Jewel be part of the big healin' service. Bein' as to how she's a Claymore an' from Californay, folks from around these here parts are bound to take notice if the Spirit gits a-holt o' her. An' I think it will be then when we have our snake ceremony."

"I'm not sure what you mean, by spirits, but it's okeydokey by me," Thelma Jewel said. "Only thing is, the last time I took spirits, they made me sick to my stomach." She licked her lips. "I want to see those snakes." *Not sure as to what I'd do, though if one of them is to get loose,* she thought. She touched her bag to make sure the derringer was still there.

"The healin' ceremony, an' I'll be helpin'," Mudge said proudly. "With my own, Taddler the Raddler convertin' an' savin' souls. Snake handlin'. You ain't never seen the likes of it.

"Y'all go ahead on an' start hepin' our brothers an' sisters," Mudge said. "I need to have me some quiet prayer time fer jest a minute."

"Tha's what we'll do. I'm here to tell you, when Mr. Mudge speaks, we do like he says," Preacher Tuggle said. "Le's us git movin."

"Mama." Gertie Mae pulled on her mother's skirt as Brother Tuggle, Mother Bunny, Brother Sistrunk and Sister Mealie Maude flowed away.

"Come on, girl." Thelma Jewel huffed over her shoulder. Gertie Mae limped behind, stretching her head forward and back, like a pecking chicken, as if by doing this she could speed up.

As soon as the others left, Mudge turned his back to the fence, and pushed his duster open. He spread his legs, unbuttoned his pants and aimed an arc of yellow toward the road. As he buttoned his pants, Mudge heard a motor. Looking toward the road, he spotted a car pulling away from the Claymore house. He scuttled to his roadster, opened the door, and leaned into the car, checking to make sure he had a snake cage.

Saturday evening

"I'm glad you and Laura Lee made up," Memory leaned forward from the back seat and spoke to her brother. "What a lovely sister-in-law I'll have. Please don't mess it up again."

"I'm just grateful she took me back."

"They're doing a lot over at the cemetery, getting ready for tomorrow," Jenson said, slowing down as they neared the cemetery.

He pointed. "Well, Lord love us. Look over there." A little way ahead and off to the right, they could see shimmering torch flares and in the motorcar lights, a few mule-pulled wagons edging away from the cemetery.

"It's almost nine. It looks like they just now finished getting ready for tomorrow," Dale said. "The Divine Deliverance Holiness people have had a long day."

"I'll be back for their Easter Celebration," Jenson said. "And to say the least, it should be interesting."

"We plan to be there. To say the best, it could clear my ancestor, Bruce Claymore's, good name." Dale rested his arm against the back of the seat. "And I have some evidence to back it up."

It occurred to Memory she had mixed feelings about the Easter Celebration. Maybe they shouldn't go. *No,* she admonished herself. *You will be a part of this community. Starting tomorrow.*

"Believe I see that no good Mudge Turnipseed," Jenson said.

"Wonder what mischief he's up to?" Dale asked. "As usual."

"He's shrewd and acts crazy minded. But I think he likes to throw people off with that," Jenson drove slower. "He's doing something over there in his car."

Bent over into his car window, only Mudge's backside showed.

"Ooga. Ooga. Ooga." The horn blew over and over. Mudge whirled away from the motorcar and flung his arms toward the sky. "Glory, glory, glory," he hollered.

"The man is crazy," Dale said.

Jenson shook his head. "Memory. I'll feel better if I stay out here with y'all tonight." He raised his voice. "That Liam McRae. I have a feeling it's far from over with him. As God is my witness, I will not let him harm you. In his mind, it could be, an eye for an eye. Thanks to you, he has only one." Jenson pushed in the clutch, shifted gears and swung into the driveway. "You still have both of yours. And beautiful ones they are."

"This is my fight now," Dale's voice was full of assurance. "We're in my territory. I'm Lord of the Manor here." He cleared his throat. "From what I know of McRae, he's a coward and a weakling. He's probably on his way back to Boston. And good riddance." He inhaled quickly. "I'm here. You go back to town tonight. I'll protect my sister." He looked back and forth between the two. "Don't rile Father."

Jenson pulled to a stop in front of the Claymore house and set the brake. "Aye, aye, Captain." He gave a quick salute with his hand. "Old habits are hard to break. You're still my superior officer."

Memory couldn't help but smile at this banter between two competitive males.

"Home again. We've had a lot happening in our lives. No matter what it takes, I'll make things right with my father," Dale said.

Jenson swung from the motorcar and opened the back door. "While you're doing that, you be sure and take good care of your sister." He took Memory's hand, lifted her from the back seat and pulled her close.

"Good night, my love," he whispered, pressing his lips against Memory's. "I'll see y'all tomorrow." He gave her another quick hug and stepped away.

For a moment Memory stood there, then she nodded and turned toward the house.

She heard tires crunching across the gravel and the rumble of Jenson's motorcar pulling away as she and Dale climbed the porch steps. Although she hated to admit it, a certain amount of her security drove down Old Farm Road with her lover. She wished she felt half as confident as her brother that things would be all right. *It's a male trait. Control. But sometimes men are not as tough as they think they are,* she reminded herself. *Especially when you're dealing with a mad man. The Boston policeman. A man to be feared. Especially now that I've blinded him.*

"One eye," she reminded herself, as if she were reminding him too, that all was not lost. She took off her coat and hung it on the hall hat rack. Ahead of her, Dale had already stepped into the parlor. Soft lights were on in the room, a fire blazed in the fireplace, giving an atmosphere of warmth and welcome. But to Memory it felt to be a temporary warmth. She paused in the doorway; in front of her she saw her mother and father sitting opposite each other on facing sofas.

Brucie stood, her arms extended in welcome. "Glad and relieved you're back and in for the night."

Slowly Dale walked to his father's chair.

"Welcome home."

"Home!" Von Dieter snorted. "I don't call this home."

Von Dieter pulled a pipe from his coat pocket. He tamped tobacco into it then laid it on the marble-topped table at the end of the sofa. Next to the pipe was a silver goblet. He raised the goblet, threw his head back and took a long sip of port.

"Forget the wars," Dale said.

"I don't care to forget the past. Or our conflicts. Armaments. My people have alvays dealt in veapons. Ve're proud of it, and ve're a proud people."

"As are we here in Mississippi," Brucie answered. "We're a proud people. Also a God-fearing people."

"I don't see any shovers of blessings coming down on this part of the vorld," Herschel said

"You just a lost a world war," Dale said. He shook his head. "I'm sorry. I want us to all move on with our lives. Start over."

"Be a man, son." Von Dieter spoke in an authoritative voice.

He is a man, Memory was on the verge of saying.

"I'm trying to be careful of what I say." Dale took a deep breath.

"I am your father. Say anything you please. You seem to have gotten a cockier attitude since you've been down here vith your people," Von Dieter answered, a hard look on his face. "If that vould be possible, I might add."

Her eyes flickering with anger, in a show of strength, Memory moved over and stood by Dale. *There's more bluster in Papa. He's higher and mightier than he was before he left the country with his tail tucked between his legs,* she thought.

Von Dieter's face remained impassive.

Brucie's head was bent. She ran her hand down the front of her creamy silk blouse and clutched the revered gold cross from Vernell.

"I'm like my brother," Memory said, noting the pained look on her mother's face. "Let's start over."

A pall-like silence hung over the room.

"You are my father and whether you like it or not, I am your son," Dale said. "With those words, I'll go upstairs. Before we both say something we'll be eternally sorry for."

"Be a man. See if you can sleep on that."
"Sweet dreams to you too, father."

CHAPTER 45

A Bible, open face,
Lay like a projector,
Bright apparitions
Reenacting deaths
And humiliations.

Dale, a moviegoer
To his own mind
And memory sets out
To slay his saints.

Early Saturday night, April 3

Even before Dale reached his room, a sweet, tangy fragrance assailed his nostrils. He yanked the door open. A soothing aroma that was in contrast to the restlessness he had escaped from downstairs flooded his room. "I keep smelling this. Only here at Redemption Ridge. And usually something happens. Things change."

The odor came from an afghan-covered trunk at the foot of his bed. He had a feeling that someone or somebody was trying to communicate with him and felt as if he had a foot in two worlds. It was as if their lives were being shaped by unseen hands. With those thoughts, he half-laughed, then shook his head. "Maybe I have more of my mother in me than I like to claim," he said. "She perceives things more than most people. Sees. Or so she says. And as I've been told. And as I believe."

Dale tossed the afghan to the floor and lifted the trunk lid. Lying on top of a stack of old clothes he saw the Bible he'd read from when he'd buried Samuel. He picked the up Bible, and as he did, he thought he heard a faint voice speaking from the trunk. "Find your peace." His legs weak, he sat on the edge of his bed.

"Wherever or whoever you are, you make it sound easy to find my peace. Which way do I go? Tell me," he asked. "Do I start with mein vater?" *In our house. No marching drums. No flags or music. No pride. I found those with my men.* He shook his head. *Now. I brood. Nobody will say it. Shellshock. Still with me.*

"And what to do with my life? Time is not my friend. If I don't change, I may be running out of it." He took a deep breath. "Laura Lee." *Hope stirred in the back of his mind.* "Can she be part of this?" *I see love and need in her eyes.* "Will I let her down?" Guilt tapped his shoulder. "Like I did my men." He leaned forward. "Those I couldn't save."

Even though they had just had a confrontation, once more Dale felt a need to make it right with his father. "But maybe I can save something else. Never too late." Grasping the Bible he slid to his feet. "Go down. Try again. Make things better."

"Vhen my son comes down here, I hardly know him."

When Dale heard the guttural tone in his father's voice, his skin prickled. His feelings of reconciliation wavered. He hesitated before stepping into the parlor.

"He's not a Von Dieter," Herschel went on. "He acts like a dirt farmer. A Mississippi Claymore. "

Forgetting his good intentions, Dale confronted his father. "I fought for the United States. My country. *And You.* You just now came back from collecting Deutschmarks for the money you made off of slaughtering them."

Brucie clutched her hands. "You're wrong, son. What little was left of your father's business before the war was gone. None of it was made off of the blood of our soldiers. "

"Be a man. Tough that your men got gassed," Von Dieter said. "But that is the nature of var. People die. And you're no hero now." He took a long pull on his pipe. "You're just a bloody drunk."

Dale took a deep breath. "I came down to tell you something pleasant for a change. And it has to do with Mississippi."

"Vhat's pleasant about this cotton-picking state? I vish I knew something."

"You may have a new daughter-in-law soon."

"Vhite field-trash. Marrying vhite field-trash."

Dale thumped the Bible against his hip. "Do you know how much I've come to dislike what you stand for?" he asked. "You're a bloody Kraut. Gas tortured my friends. They died in hell."

Von Dieter stood. His blue eyes blazed with anger. "Don't you cuss in my house."

"Your house? I don't think so!"

Dale pivoted on his heels and bounded up the staircase, missing his mother's words.

"I'll never leave here again. If I have to make a choice, I know who and what I will chose." Brucie's voice held a threat. "So, stop it, Herschel."

"Let me say something, vife. That so named 'celebration' tomorrow. I'll add class to it they've never seen around these parts. I told you. I'm vearing my uniform."

"That's ridiculous," said Brucie. "1914. Germany was going to invade Paris. And they didn't. And you were living in *Boston*!"

"I vas ready then. As I am now. They are to respect and honor their proud heritage from me. The father."

Von Dieter rhythmically kicked the floor. "You left Redemption Ridge, but it never left you, Brucie."

Upstairs in his room, Dale was filled with pulsating anger, energy and anxiety. His heart beating fast, he flung the Bible on his bed and slammed his fist into his bedroom wall. "I can't stay around here with the Kraut. Where are my men? Where is redemption? Mine? My father's?" He slapped his head with the palm of his hand. "My ancestors?"

He opened his chifforobe and took out an old German Luger his father had given him when he turned seventeen. He lifted his haversack and shoved in whiskey and his cough medicine. "I have to do something."

"Read the Good Book," came a quiet utterance.

"Captain Bruce. I am the one. I can redeem you," Dale said. "I hold it here in my hands."

He took out the Luger, put the Bible in the haversack, slung the kit across his shoulder, and loped down the steps. He ran from the house and jogged through the yard.

He heard a dog barking frantically, as if trying to warn him of something. Or somebody. "No, Daisy Dog," he called, swinging onto Old Farm Road.

At the entrance to the cemetery he stopped. A warm breeze brushed leaves that had burst out, covering the once bony-barked tree limbs. Dale ran his hand over the rusted gate spokes.

When he got to the resting place of Vernell and Bruce Claymore, he sat on the bench that was over their grave. He lifted the Bible from the haversack, set it beside him, and caught his breath.

"Captain Bruce. I feel you're here. But I must say this. Before anybody or anything else. I have to come to terms with my father. Herr Von Dieter's my reality right now. Von? Some noble patrilineality that no longer exists? I don't know that there's room for both of us in Mississippi." For a minute Dale didn't know whether he was reassuring himself or laying an ultimatum down for dealings with his father.

A rustling sound got his attention. He smelled the scent of fresh-turned earth.

"Avenge me." The speaker's voice was clearer and sharper than a hammer striking an iron bell. Dale saw a patch of moving shadow, a tousled mane of lion-like blond hair.

"Help me find my peace."

Out on the road, the rhythmic sound of wagon wheels intruded on the voice. Lights flickered. There were clicking noises. A horse neighed.

Dale heard creaking wagons grinding to a halt by the white cemetery.

"Oh, no. That Brush Arbor Meeting," he said. "They must be working on it some more."

He turned to the spot where he had seen the ghost, apparition or whatever it was. He saw only the blurred outline of an outstretched hand.

"Hup!" a call from across the way.

Dale reached for the hand, but it was beyond his grasp.

Then, another call from across the way. "Whoa up."

Again, he reached for the hand. It was gone.

A shiver went through Dale, he closed the Bible and slid it into his haversack. Once again he wished he had found a quick, easy answer here from the ghost of his grandfather.

"I'm not sure what I'm doing here. I may need to find my answers somewhere else. I'll worry about my grandfather, Bruce Claymore, tomorrow. For now, I've got to make my way on around the next bend in the road."

Dale thought about the evidence that had been hidden in the back of the Bible. *It's probably pushing against my cough syrup bottle, but thank you Sheriff Bramlett. For all those years ago. Putting Daddy Claymore's confession for Bruce Claymore's murder and what had happened to the jewels in the back of this Holy Book.*

He took a deep breath and walked across the graveyard, toward the gate.

"Help…"

If more was said the voice was lost in the sounds of wagons being unloaded for tomorrow's Celebration.

Dale felt as if he needed to reassure his grandfather he was not abandoning him. "Sir," he said. "I don't know what I'll be doing the rest of the night, but I plan to be there tomorrow. For you, my Captain. And for me."

CHAPTER 46

A breeze caught my attention,
The smell of fresh cut grass;
Like a tiny emblem on a cigarette pack,
Parked in the habitual sector of my memory:

A warning poster: A man silhouetted,
Grasping a mask.

"Warning, phosgene smells like fresh cut grass.
Don your mask and clear your pressure!"

Saturday night

At the entrance to the colored graveyard, Dale stopped and ran his hand over rusty spikes then closed the gate behind him. Hearing hammering noises from the far side of the other cemetery, not sure what he wanted to do, Dale headed home. "But bed? Hell, no!" he said as he crossed Old Farm Road. He went on around the house, stopping for a moment to pet Daisy Dog. When he walked away from her, Daisy Dog threw her head back and began barking as if she were warning him of something.

Silhouetted against a copse of trees, there where they used to tell ghost stories, Dale saw the outline of the old well. Something beckoned him to their childhood meeting place. He walked to the well and stopped. Lots of strange things had happened here; maybe some answers would come to him. He reached out and touched the craggy stones. For long moments there was silence, then something slithered away from the other side of the well, toward nearby bushes. As if on cue he heard the lonely sound of an owl hooting, a plaintive, questioning cow moo, then a more keening howl as if Daisy Dog were sending questions toward the moon.

For a moment he was transported to another time, to summer nights at Redemption Ridge, there where they had told ghost stories. Tonight the air had an expectant feel to it. "I believe something's going to happen," Dale said. "The well. Those tales. The things that happened here. Maybe the ghost of my grandfather, Captain Bruce Claymore, will cross the road and speak again."

An oily stench, as if dead fish had been rotting underwater for a long time floated from the well. Dale slid the haversack from his shoulders and reached into it for his medicines and his whiskey flask. He took a quick look back toward the house. "No. You need to stop. Not tonight." He drew his hand away and sank to the ground.

***

"Oh God," Liam moaned, touching the right side of his face, covered with blood-stained gauze. Liam hobbled from Dr. Verner's home. His breaths coming in short gasps, his legs trembling like willows in a wind, he made his way to the car. Liam leaned against the door, and, pulling a small pewter flask from his coat pocket, he unscrewed the top. He turned the flask up, and guzzled down several mouthfuls, a few drops dribbling down his deadened cheek

Pain racked his head, as swaying and reeling he cranked the car and pulled away. Barely holding the car steady in the road, Liam made his way back to his room at the edge of town. Once in his room, he raised the whiskey flask again, drinking down several gulps. He weaved his way to the back corner, fell to his knees, held on to the sides of a rusty spittoon, and began retching. Done, he rolled a blanket into a pillow shape. Coughing, he sank onto a spindle-legged cot, and eased his head back onto the makeshift pillow.

The deadening the doctor had injected into the side of his face had begun to wear off, as had the laudanum.

"I'll kill her. I'll kill her. I'll kill her," he said. "She'll pay," he whispered, wiping his mouth with the back of his hand. "I have to get there. I have to get up and make myself do it."

He rested a few moments, took several deep breaths, then stood. "Help me," he sputtered. "In the name of my Senator Peter Shields, I can do it," he moaned. "And I don't have much time." Bracing himself against the bed post, he yanked his bandana from his pants pocket and tied it across his forehead. The best Liam could, he pulled the right side down, covering his blood-stained, stuffed, gauzed eye socket.

"I've got it in me to do it. She'll beg to die. Him too. I'll take care of the both of them."

He picked up his holster and gun and lurched out the door.

Liam managed to shift and steer the sputtering, smoke-belching car out from town, down Old Farm Road and toward Redemption Ridge. Several times he had to stop, get out, hold onto the car door, lean over and vomit. Curving around a switchback, he slid in loose gravel and skidded to the edge of Noble Creek; for a brief second one back tire hung over a steep embankment, but he managed to jerk back onto the gravel.

Close to Redemption Ridge, Liam spied torchlights, mules and wagons where tomorrow's Celebration would be.

"Goddamn. Those fools are still working. It's almost Easter."

He jerked the car off onto a wagon trail running alongside the cemetery, and braked behind a stand of trees. He removed the bandages and heavy gauze from his face and squeezed some of the ointment Dr. Verner had given him into his eye hole. He taped the patch back on, then stepping away from the car, slowly began to make his way toward the Claymore home. He had to be careful. Since his balance was off, he hobbled like a lame mule.

"I'll get him and her," he muttered. One-eyed though he might be, he swore to take care of his debts. *They'll pay.* "I'll show them."

He'd take care of these Mississippi people, then ditch the junky car; it wouldn't make it to where he was headed. He'd catch the train to New Orleans. Get him a good glass eye then maybe see about a whiskey running business, from New Orleans to Vicksburg.

Thinking about New Orleans, a shaky smile crept across Liam's face, and the depression that had almost overwhelmed him since the night before lightened for a moment. He'd heard some wild stories about The Pirate's Alley. That gutted eye-socket of his. He might find him a way to use it. He might just tie him a red bandana around his head, sew on a black eye patch, wander that famous alley and find him a gentleman friend or two.

He pushed his hair back from his forehead. Or he might go down another track. Even better known was that red light district. From what he'd heard about ladies of the night in the New Orleans red light district, he just might have him some unusual carnal pleasure. He'd think about the men, but that eye hole might really light a spark in some of those street ladies—especially if he could get a patch made to match his red hair. Maybe find some way to bloody it up a little and they'd even think he was a war hero.

He'd touch the patch. "A surprise, pretty lady," he might say to entice them. "One you'll like. From the Battle of Belleau Wood."

And when they raised the corner, they would see a one dollar bill.

"Just show me where to go, pretty lady."

He'd have his fun. Then, he'd make them pay.

He'd get his one dollar bill back, and maybe some more.

But for now he had to be strong. Get his revenge.

***

Dale's head was full of images as he leaned his head against the well. Childhood days swam back as he thought about those sun-dipping, night-dropping hours they had spent here, in this very spot. Their stories always started with wondering what had happened to the bones of Miss Pet Binkie, the spinster lady old Warner Sledge had murdered, then tossed her body in the family well. Miss Pet—she always set the mood for their tales.

He moved his head, the sharp ridges of the damp, uneven, mushroom-colored stones jabbed, breaking his reverie, bringing him back to the present. He jerked forward.

Miss Pet. She wasn't all. Evil still lurked and bided its time. It had happened again. Here. Some years back. His sister.

"Memory."

Speaking his sister's name, his mind went back to that terrible time she had lived through. Because of a violence filled encounter with Shank Potter, Memory was a different person. It was painful to think of what that must have been like and how it had affected his sister.

And now, thanks to Dedmon, he suspected something else. A smile spread across Dale's lips as if he knew a delightful secret. Shank Potter. His body could be moldering in these waters in front of him. And word was, Dedmon had done it.

"That chap. I hope it's true. It just may be so." Once again he reached into his haversack; this time he lifted out his medicines and the whiskey flask.

"Even though you might not approve of some of the things I do, this one's for you, Memory."

The comfort he would draw into his being was stronger than his desire not to indulge, he was not quite ready to give up this part of his life. He unscrewed the top from his syrup bottle, turned the vial up, and hands shaking, poured the thick liquid into his throat. He swallowed, waited a moment then placed three pills on his tongue. He raised his flask, threw his head back, and swallowed once again.

Dale lit a cigarette, sank back down and sucked in deep, lingering breaths. Disturbed and distressed, a strong craving for more solace filled him.

There's a lot to take care of here. My sister. That Ceremony coming up in just a little while. He took another quick taste of his syrup, but even before he finished swallowing it, an odor of fatback almost choked Dale. He rose and stepped back as an image seemed to float out from the well. Wearing a shredded lacy top, an over-skirt of puffed lavender silk edged with violet fringe and trimmed with rosettes of pansies, he saw a snub-nosed, apple-cheeked woman with a pinned-on chignon of false yellow curls.

"Good God. Not Miss Pet?"

He closed his eyes. Shook his head. When he opened his eyes, there was nothing, not even the smell of fatback.

Dale poured more whiskey. Rolled another pill on his tongue.

"I may have dreamed you, Miss Pet. But I know who I didn't and will never dream of again." Dale cleared his throat, then leaned over and spit into the well. "I baptize you into hell, Shank Potter."

***

Dale stretched out on the ground. A sultry breeze filled with a familiar moisture bathed his face, his skin became damp with sweat, his breathing slow and shallow. The woods around him were hushed, as if waiting for something to happen. His thoughts turned to his friends and the world he had left behind. Everything shifted from the here and now to the then.

It didn't take long before a feeling engulfed him; death was in the air here, as it had been in France.

The breeze picked up, and when it did, Dale heard sounds of muffled feet, then mournful voices carried on the wind blending with the rustling, stirring leaves, weeds and tree limbs. The musical sounds of the night, singing songs. Sad songs.

"Lead on Oh King Eternal," they sang softly.

Emotions overtook Dale. "I'm fracturing," he murmured. "In my head.

"Chateau Thierry," he moaned. *Eyes. Blood-red eyes. Tongues mottled with greenish goo.*

Cha-dot. Cha-dot. Cha-dot.

Sucked in blood-drenched mud. Gray-lipped men spit lungs, gut pink. Loopy lungs. Bloody globs. A blood bath.

Cha-dot. Cha-dot. Cha-dot.

Twirling ears flew through the air. Hands flapped like pancakes tossing in a skillet.

Cha-dot. Cha-dot. Cha-dot.

Dale swung his head from side to side.

"Machine guns! Machine guns!" he hollered.

Quiet.

"Incoming?"

No. Still.

Quiet covered the battlefield. The end is death.

448

A howling dog smacked the silence. Dale's cheeks slicked wet with sweat and tears, his throaty sobs blended with the baying cry of the dog, and a pleading echo. "Help me find my peace."

Cha-dot. Cha-dot. Cha-dot.

"Avenge me."

CHAPTER 47

A bullet crackled into existence
Spanning war and war and war
Building its thrush tail
Seed of blood

Generations folded
And folded to trap the wind
And Herschel's breath
A novel of papercuts

Later Saturday night

Liam crossed the road and leaned against a fence post at the edge of the Claymore yard. He wiped sweat from his forehead, straightened the patch over his eye socket, then, bending over made his way up the driveway.

The car was there. He made out Von Dieter's Packard pulled up next to the house. It was the same car he had seen in town, not one driven around these parts. He propped against the front fender on the side away from the house, pulled a large cotton ball from his pocket and wiped away a stream of eye ooze. He dropped the cotton to the ground, urinated on it, then leaned over the cranked-down car window, and smeared the secretion across the velvet front seat.

Moving like a hunchback, he made his way to an oak tree, and hunkering down, he sheltered beneath streams of gray moss, hanging from low-slung branches like an old man's beard. Liam prepared to rest his wound and to get some respite while he could. It would be daylight in just a few hours.

Then, a short while later, the front door creaked open, to his surprise and delight, Herschel and Brucie walked out.

Liam spread several mossy fronds, making a small gray curtain across each side of his face. He could see Brucie and Von

Dieter and tell they were talking, but he couldn't hear what was said.

Herschel walked toward the porch door, raised a glass and faced his automobile. He rolled his head back and tossed a shot of whiskey into his mouth. "Prost," he toasted loudly. He then turned and said something to Brucie. She shook her head as Herschel shoved the screen door open with his foot.

Liam pushed a thick sleeve of moss aside and watched as Von Dieter went down the steps and through the yard to his car. Liam covered his eye socket with his hand, focused as hard as he could on what he was seeing with his one eye as Von Dieter opened the car door and carefully lifted something out. Liam made out what looked to be a uniform on a coat hanger.

"I'm going to find my son," Herschel called to Brucie. "Make him man up. I'll show him a thing or two."

He closed the car door. "I heard that hound dog barking a vile back. Something stirred her up. I'll bet my son's somevhere out back. Maybe by the barn or that vell the young people all used to hang around."

Head down, he brushed the uniform with his hand. "You're nothing but a cry baby, son. I'll find you," Herschel said. Although he was talking loud enough for Brucie to hear, she was out of earshot. She had gone into the house.

"I'll show you vhat a real man looks like." He draped the uniform over his shoulder and thrust his chin out. "And how he should act."

"And I'll be right behind you," Liam whispered. "I'll have you both in my sights."

He felt for his holster, ran a long forefinger over the mother-of-pearl grip on his Colt pistol, and pressing his tongue against the roof of his mouth he made several metallic clicks.

***

Not sure which way Von Dieter would go when he left to find Dale, Liam moved to the side of the house so he could see both the front and the back. Restless, he consoled himself for a moment

451

thinking about the train ticket to New Orleans he had bought. *Done here. Get yourself to the train station.* His eye socket burned. It throbbed. The longer he waited the more it hurt and the angrier he grew; sweet revenge would taste better than milk and honey on his tongue.

He forced himself to be patient and stretched out on the ground.

***

Von Dieter checked himself in the hall mirror. Wads of skin bulged over his uniform collar. He threw his head back, raised his chin and ran a finger between the collar and his neck. "Tight. If I do say so myself. But I think I could go to var. And defeat any enemy that gets in my vay."

He blew out a deep breath, sucked in, then tightened his belt buckle. He pulled a flashlight from his jacket pocket and checked to make sure it worked. "Not too late. Make my son see vhat a real man looks like."

Forgetting he had on his leather army boots, Von Dieter tried to click his heels but lost his balance and nearly fell. His booted feet made heavy thumps as he swaggered through the house, and down the back porch steps.

***

A noise from the back of the Claymore house got Liam's attention. He sat up and slapped his hand across his covered eye socket. A jolt of nausea hit. He leaned over and retched. Easing to his feet, he swiped the back of his hand across his mouth. This was too important for him to let pain and the loss of his eye get the best of him and not to go through with his plans. "Get your ass moving." He dabbed at the seeping eye secretions and began edging to the side of and slightly behind Von Dieter, making sure he stayed hidden.

"Damn." Von Dieter tripped over a tree root. He caught himself, squared his shoulders and lit a cigarette. He inhaled deeply, blew smoke out of the side of his mouth, then moved forward again.

Liam blended into the trees and underbrush, tracking as close beside Von Dieter as he dared. He spotted the stony gray well, and made out a form sleeping next to it.

Von Dieter stopped. He flung his cigarette to the ground and swiveled his boot heel over it.

Liam knew he would have to shoot from the front or the side so it would look like Dale fired the shot. He bent over double, circled the well, and sheltered himself beneath a tree limb.

A dog barked. Dale jumped awake.

"Where am I?" He moved his head slowly from side to side. He saw no scattered body parts. No feasting pigs. No slathering wolves.

Off to his right side, a waving tree limb seemed to beckon Dale.

A German officer was silhouetted in the moonlight.

Dale thrust his hand into his haversack. Reached for his pistol. Grabbed the Bible.

"Damn," he cursed. "No gun!"

Liam eased his gun from its holster. "They'll think you did it, soldier boy Dale," he whispered.

He cocked the gun, bit his bottom lip. He aimed.

He had a hard time focusing his one eye.

A shot rang out.

Blood sprang from Von Dieter's abdomen. He spun back, reeled sideways and slammed into the side of the well.

Muttered words sprang from Von Dieter's lips. "Vhy, God? Vhy?"

Dale's head cleared. He knew where he was. Not Chateau Thierry. Redemption Ridge.

"No!" he screamed. "My father."

***

Memory was resting in bed when she heard the gun. "That was out by the back pasture."

She hurriedly took a moment to use the slop jar, then pulled a long gray skirt and a chamois top from the chifforobe.

"Something's wrong." Brucie sat up.

"Dale!" She swung her legs to the side of the bed and leaned over to turn on the lamp.

A soft touch brushed her cheek.

"No," a familiar voice said. "No, Miss Brucie. This ain't fer you to take care of. Lamont. He'll be on to it. You jest git yourself ready fer what's comin' later on this mawnin'. It's almost here. Easter. Redemption."

"Vernell," Brucie whispered. "Always. You're here. Yes. I'll wait."

On this night Lamont had gone to bed early. He had been lulled to sleep by the familiar chorus of throaty bullfrogs, the symphony of buzzing insects and the occasional bass call of a hoot owl.

A blast shattered the quiet. Lamont snatched up his coveralls and hitched his suspenders. "Over there by that well. Ain't nothin' good never happens over there."

***

Liam stumbled away from the well. "I've done it. Von Dieter. I've done it," he bragged to himself. "His son. It'll be on him. Now, I'm getting away from here." In spite of hurting and feeling weak, he began thrashing his way through high weeds, tangled bushes and twisted underbrush. "New Orleans," he gloated.

***

Dale scrambled to his feet.

"Son," a weak voice moaned. "Help me."

"Father," Dale cried. He grabbed the haversack and ran toward Von Dieter. "You're hit. I didn't. I didn't."

"I know," Von Dieter gurgled. "I know. Oh, God. I don't vant to end like this," he cried. His eyes were locked on his son's face in petition and supplication. *Help me. Help me*, they seemed to plead.

Dale heard the fear in his father's voice and saw the apprehension in his eyes. All anger gone, he looked hard at his father's face, and for a moment years of built up resentment drained from his feelings; the now had become like a dream from the past, when his father was his hero.

"You won't die," he said, feeling a need to reassure, not only his father, but also himself.

"I'm here." Lamont sank down by the two of them. "I heard it."

Looking at Von Dieter and seeing the pool of blood over his lower stomach and his urine soaked pants, Lamont shook his head. "We gotta git Mist Herschel to the doctor.

"I got me the hearse." He stood and placed his hand on Dale's back. "It's at my house. Le's us git on to Dr. Verner's house, Mist Dale."

Dale slung the haversack over one shoulder, then circled his arms around his father's chest. "We'll take care of you." Lamont picked up Von Dieter's legs, and as fast as they could, the two of them carried him to the hearse. They gently laid him on the floor where coffins were usually placed as they were being carried for burial.

Dale in the back of the hearse, holding his father, Lamont cranked the engine, jumped in and sped down the rutted path toward Old Farm Road.

Liam heard the rattly sound of a car cranking and then gravel crunching as the hearse drove away. He took a moment to enjoy his victory and gloat; he clenched his fist and raised his arm in triumph. "And I've got me a train ticket to New Orleans. Away from this cursed place. Mary, Joseph, and Jesus!" Pleased with himself, he took a jaunty, parade marching step; his foot caught on a gnarled tree root, his ankle twisted, he wind-milled his arms, then sprawled to the ground. Something sharp jabbed his face. The other eye. The eyelid was pierced.

Liam heard a deep growl, then loud, warning howls. "Dog," he moaned. "Get up. Get away."

Memory was descending the back porch steps when she heard Daisy's alerting calls. "Daisy Dog. I'm coming."

Numb with weariness and pain, his head swimming, almost blind, by sheer force of will, Liam made it to his feet. Trying to stay upright, he crept away. A small stream of hot liquid bled down his face. Afraid of the dog, barely able to see where he was going, some minutes later, he once again found himself at the well.

Hot fluid drained from Liam's throbbing eye socket, a knot of tears clogged his good eye. "Oh, Jesus. I can wash my eyes out," he moaned, taking several deep breaths. He gathered his strength, reached for the handle, and twisted. The handle wouldn't turn.

Memory made it to where Daisy Dog was penned, and when Topper appeared by her side, she wasn't surprised to see him. No. The way so many things happened here at Redemption Ridge, it was meant to be. Not sure where she was going, but knowing things were in motion that she had very little control over, she unlatched the dog and let her loose. Daisy Dog bounded forward. Memory and Topper followed, and with Daisy Dog leading the way, the two of them drew close to the well.

Craving relief from pain, hoping to clear his eye, Liam pulled his handkerchief from a pants pocket. His New Orleans train ticket was wrapped in it. He set the ticket on the well rim and again tried to twist the handle. It didn't move.

Stretching on his toes he hung over the well, trying to free the bucket. Liam had no luck.

Dizzy, he stood straight for a moment, to let his head quit spinning.

In the flare of Memory's lantern she and Topper saw a few wisps of bright red hair. They paused.

"I'll push," Topper breathed. "Him. He don't need to live."

Memory grabbed Topper's arm. "No," she whispered.

The bucket still caught, Liam crawled up onto one knee on the stony circle and leaned over. Still no good. Breathing heavily he spread both hands and slowly, painfully hoisted both his knees onto the rocky, slick edge and looked into the well.

Daisy Dog was still as a stone. Then, hackles raised, she growled low in her throat. She bared her teeth. She took a flying leap and sprang onto Liam with her all fours.

He pitched forward.

Topper and Memory heard the splash. They rushed to the well.

Daisy Dog fell back, then scrambled to her feet and scooted away.

Topper grabbed the handle to lower the bucket and throw a lifeline to Liam. His hand brushed a piece of paper.

The blocked bucket didn't move.

Her ears raised, Daisy Dog's tail thumped as if proud of herself for pleasing her people.

A New Orleans train ticket floated down into the murky waters.

CHAPTER 48

An antecedent face
Makes for a strange surgical light.
Only a squirreling knife
Can create one into that.

Lineage is the gleaming scalpel
Drawing upon Death's pound,
Circumstance the ginny hand
Of the interlocutor.

Late Saturday night

Lamont swung into Dr. Verner's yard which was at the edge of town. He darted from the hearse, banged on the doctor's side door then ran back to the hearse to help Dale.

An outside light came on. Screen-door hinges squealed as the door flung open. The two men lifted Von Dieter and carried him to Dr. Verner's treatment room and laid him on a covered wooden table.

The office smelled of old cigar smoke, dried blood and the tangy odor of pine trees after a heavy rain.

"You'll be fine. You'll be fine," the doctor soothed the patient as he donned an apron and prepared to exam him.

"I don't vant to end like this," Von Dieter moaned.

"You won't," Dr. Verner assured him. "But we've got to put a few things back in place and sew you up. The bullet went clean through your left side. From what I can see, nothing vital was hit. You are one lucky man."

"I von't let you touch me doctor." Von Dieter took a deep breath. "Unless you make me a promise."

"What's that, Herschel?"

"Ven you're done. I vant to go home. Not to the hospital in Vicksburg." He made a whisking motion with his hand. "To Redemption Ridge. No hospital."

Dr. Verner drummed his fingers on the table for a moment. "It's your life. I'll do as you say.

"I've been busy," he said. "I took care of a feller who'd had his eye poked out. And now, Mr. Von Dieter's been gun shot."

He shook his head then went to work with scissors, cutting away the trousers to Von Dieter's uniform and throwing the scraps of wet, heavy material to the floor. He cleaned urine and blood from his lower body and swabbed the wound with alcohol. "I can do what we call a cadaver stitch," the doctor said softly to Dale. "He's gonna hurt like hell, but he'll make it."

"Vait a minute. Is there a Bible in this house? First, I vant something read." Von Dieter raised his hand in a stopping motion. "Vords I used to hear from my own father." Tears slid from his eyes. "Ephesians six, verse four."

Dale slung his haversack from his shoulder and dropped it on the floor when he came in. "I have it here." He reached into the haversack, pulled out the Bible and turned to the pages his father had asked for.

"And, ye fathers, provoke not your children to wrath..." he read.

"I am so sorry, son," Von Dieter whispered. "I vas so angry."

"All is forgiven and forgotten." Dale leaned over and kissed his father's forehead. "We'll make a new start."

"Let's get this done." Dr. Verner laid a gauze mask across the patient's face and began dropping ether over it.

"We're sending him to dreamland," he said as Von Dieter sighed, then grew limp.

"Will he be okay?" Dale asked.

"He's one lucky bastard. Unless something unforeseen happens, I'd say yes." The doctor bent over and began suturing.

Dale couldn't watch. He looked out the window, off in the direction of Redemption Ridge.

Help me find my peace. The words of the ghost echoed in his mind. Now, maybe, just maybe, he'd helped his father. This could be a new beginning.

Oh dear glory! It's almost Easter, he realized.

And what will this day bring?

***

Yellow lights flickered near the old cemetery; in the stillness Memory heard a few noises that seemed to be coming from the white burial grounds.

"Somebody's at the graveyard," she said. "Probably getting ready for the Celebration. And from what little I can see, the weather could go either way." Bathed in the soft front porch lights Memory and Brucie stood arm in arm, watching the road.

"Vernell came to me, " Brucie said. "Herschel will be all right. It's all according to plan. I feel it in my bones."

Memory stepped to the side. "I see car lights. I'm glad the doctor rang and told us what happened."

"Yes, and here they come. They made it home." Brucie had held back her feelings for so long, on so many occasions. Her voice was thick with emotion as they watched Lamont make a slow turn and carefully steer up the drive.

Lamont and Dale slid Herschel from the back of the hearse, then one on either side, they made a chair with their hands and arms and carried him up the porch steps.

"Oh, dear God," Brucie breathed as she led them to the parlor and nodded her head to indicate the sofa. "We've made a bed. Lay him down here."

"He started coming to on the way home," Dale said as he and Lamont lowered Von Dieter.

Von Dieter moaned slightly. "It's nothing. I'm okay. I'm a man."

"You're a wounded man," Dale said. "And it *is* something. But Dr. Verner assured us you'll make it just fine."

"Lamont, I need to tell you." Brucie raised her hand as if expecting someone to reach down and hold it. "Your mother came to me. That's how I knew you were with Herschel. She said for me to just let go and wait. She told me you would take care of him."

"And Lamont did," Dale grasped his hips for a moment as if his back hurt. "Dr. Verner said to just let Father rest for now. If there are any problems we are to drive him back to his home." He bent forward, straightened up and dropped his hands from his hips. "We know who did it."

"So do we," Memory said, a grim smile on her face. "Mother, Topper, and I all heard the gunshot. Topper and I went to the well. We saw your car lights when you left with Father. A few minutes later we saw the Boston policeman. And we know what happened to him. This is the beginning of peace and redemption for our family."

"From the time Liam McRae murdered Thornton, and we know he did even though the authorities never proved it, and he came to Mississippi, all was foreordained." Brucie placed her hand across her heart. "It was all set in motion. He came here to make trouble. That was his undoing. From what Memory told me about his ending, maybe the ghosts of Redemption Ridge took care of that murdering Boston policeman."

"What do you mean about his ending?" Dale questioned, a bewildered look on his face. "Where is he?"

Unspoken words of what had come to pass lay between Brucie and Memory. Then, a smile she couldn't have stopped even if she had wanted to crossed Memory's face. "He had an accident," she said. "With a little help from one of God's creatures, he fell into the well."

"Sweet Jesus," Dale said. "The well? That God-haunted, devil-calling well?"

"Yes," Memory said. For the time being, she thought it best not to mention Daisy Dog. And looking back on it, and the way things seemed to come to pass here at Redemption Ridge, she had a feeling the same thing would have happened to the wicked Liam even had Daisy Dog not sprung and knocked him into the well. It could have been she or Topper. Better, the dog—or he could have just slipped.

For a moment Memory stood still, then she reached down, picked a pitcher of water from the table and poured it over a washcloth that lay in a small crystal bowl. "We got there just after it happened. Topper and I couldn't do anything. We came back here to the house. There was no way we could get him out. That's all I know for now."

She wrung the rag out, bent over, and wiped her father's forehead.

Von Dieter opened his eyes. For a brief second he gave the impression of being his old braggadocio, but it was for just a moment. He took a deep breath then let it go.

"Thanks," he murmured, the look on his face a combination of shame and hope.

He turned his head toward Brucie. "It's been a long journey, but I feel like I've come home." He spoke deliberately, as if the words he uttered were very important and no one would ever say them again, exactly as he had. He reached for his wife's hand, brought it to his lips and kissed it.

"Let's carry Father upstairs and to bed," Dale said.

"No!" Von Dieter raised his head. "I vant to be here." Tears came to his eyes. "Around my family. I feel so very different from vhat I did." He lowered his voice from his usual gruff, manly tone. "Vhy don't ve have us our own private, Easter service? Here vith our family. In a few hours."

"I don't feel that's what we're supposed to do. It will be a special day here at Redemption Ridge. It is Easter. The day He arose," Brucie breathed. "Pray to God. His will can be done.

"My father. My wish is he could be redeemed. He's waited a long time."

She bent over and placed her cheek against her husband's. "The rest of us need to get some sleep, then we'll go to the Celebration. Who knows what might happen?"

"Yes. You are correct, my vife." A peaceful smile on his face, Von Dieter closed his eyes.

"Except for your father, let's all be at the service," Brucie said. "And that means you too, Lamont. Vernell would want you there." Her words hung in the air as if they were amening a sermon, and there was nothing left to say.

The comforting aroma of coffee drifted through and then filled the room. Bertha appeared, holding a large silver tray with a coffee urn and cups. "I got some cinnamon toast on the stove," she said.

"I'll have a sip or two," Brucie said. "But we all need a couple hours of sleep. It's been a long, hard night for all of us. I'll make myself comfortable on the other sofa, and stay in here with Herschel. It won't be long until we need to get ready for the Celebration."

"I think I'll get a cup of coffee and go on upstairs," Memory said.

Lamont moved toward the door. "Topper an' me gonter git on home."

"I want you there at the service, Lamont." Brucie took a deep breath. "Next to me."

"And me on the other side," Dale said.

"What'll folks think?" Lamont asked. "I'm supposed to be in the back. With the colored."

"Who cares?" Dale asked.

Lamont looked dubious for a moment, then nodded his head. "See y'all after a while then." He tapped his forehead with a finger, and reached out his hand to Dale, who brushed it aside. He wrapped his arms around Lamont's shoulders, drew him close, then walked to the hall with him.

"Father will be fine. I feel like it's a new day with him. And, perhaps, with all of us here at Redemption Ridge. We owe you," Dale said. "In many ways."

After he closed the door behind Lamont, Dale stopped by the parlor. "I'm going to get myself a little shuteye," he called to his mother.

"It's gonna be full up mawning before too long," Bertha reminded them. "Y'all best git yourselves together. It's Easter."

CHAPTER 49

**As through a glass,
Flowing; diatom-aceous
is the lymph
Tiding the old with new.**

**Grabbed by the shirt;
Tensile, tumbling colors
Whipped into the frame
Of a descendant.**

**My name is round;
My name has corners.**

Easter Morning, about five o'clock, April 4, 1920

Up in his room, Dale flung the haversack toward a chair but missed. His cough syrup and a small bottle of whiskey hit the floor; the syrup leaked, and bourbon ran onto the floor. The Bible lay beside them, spilling the letter from Sheriff Homer Bramlet. "This isn't over yet. There's still the captain. The grandfather. Later, though. For now, it is time to catch a little shuteye. And I'm tired. "

Dale flopped onto the bed, stretched out and quickly fell asleep.

***

A determined look on her face, Memory shook her head, turned on a lamp and sat at her bedside table. "I saw a small miracle last night. Brother and Father. It's been a long time coming. Yes."

She untied the ribbon, opened her journal and dipped her pen into the ink pot.

I have a blank piece of paper here in front of me, And, I have so much on my mind, she wrote.

I witnessed the death of the evil man who tried to have his way with a helpless little girl and who slew my husband Thornton, though he covered that crime well.

Policeman Liam McRae no longer walks the face of the earth. Am I sorry? I don't think so. Could I have done anything? I don't think so. But I ask myself, how does his death play out in the grand scheme of things here at Redemption Ridge? Could I have lowered a bucket? Saved him? I don't think so.

And yet—retribution. Will redemption ever be mine? I pray God it will be so. For now, I have to let it go

And me. In my mind's eye I passed from a new land, into an old world, a different life. I left my familiar world behind. Now I ask myself. What did I accomplish there?

As always, we traveled south on a rail line. Leaving Boston this time, because I sensed I would be lost in dreamland forever, I began no final list, with a well done, good and faithful servant column. Truth to tell, I didn't always do it so well during the past.

As has happened before, my heartbeat quickened when we crossed into Mississippi and I revisited the same images I have passed by and seen so many times. I soon became part of another world going back to another era, but Massachusetts, the forgotten world of my childhood should always be part and parcel of who I am. Or will other, already-lived lives take over? I'm not sure.

Riding the train, I was now in a different time and place. From early morning and on through the day and night, I hear noises I never heard in Boston. There are no cock-a-doodles, clucking chickens, cows lowing to be milked. No trundling of horse and buggies or the creak of mule-pulled wagons in Boston.

Although I was sitting in a train seat, in an enclosed compartment, with what I was feeling and thinking, and the way I was seeing things, with the intake of a breath, it could have all been different.

I could well have been flung out the window and been jolting and slinging sideways in a covered wagon with wailing children rolling across the wooden boards, a mooing cow tied on behind and handheld shotguns at the ready. For robbers, bears, or who knows what.

Mississippi creeks and rivers meander through flat farmland that's often broken by muddy swamp bottoms or the swell of rolling timbered hills. Country roads are rough and twisted. Sharecroppers' land; old cotton fields give way to brown broom-sedge and fallow fields. Stumpy corn rows sit either sideways or to the back of sagging houses perched on decaying tree stumps or stacks of thin stones. Outhouses the color of, and as fragile as, rotten sticks floating in a creek, lean close by wells that are halfway between a barn and a house.

Just around another bend in a Tallouga County road, I see smooth, winding gravel drives, lush lawns enhanced with sturdy oaks, magnolia trees, gardenia bushes, boxwoods and day lilies.

There are glimpses of balconied, porched, sturdy homes. Homes with brick chimneys and inside toilet facilities.

The stars are the same ones I saw in Massachusetts, but somehow in this southland they seem nearer, brighter. Their sparkle hints of secrets. Mississippi seems to be a mythical land, still in touch with past glories but underneath the bragging talk, dark shadows of hooded men and old injustices linger. Many atonements are yet to be made.

Where is my place in this grand scheme of life here at Redemption Ridge?

When I was younger, my mother and I both had the gift of sight. My mother more than I. Now I wonder, was it real?

The Presbyterian in me crawls out. Or was it all just part of a Master plan?

Was all this foreordained? For me? For us? Will they, we, roam these hills and valleys forever, searching for peace and redemption? Will I hear soul voices wailing for their unfound peace?

Or am I here, hoping to settle old scores? Captain Bruce Claymore. Sunnie Flo. Thelma Grace. Vernell. Daddy Claymore. Shank Potter.

Even before I settled into my family's old homeplace, dipped my pen and began to write words in my journal, an unsettling feeling brooded within me

Will there be a gateway and a path to an earthly Eden? I helped a colored girl. Lamont's daughter, Sassy. And too soon, the Good Lord has placed someone else nearby. Someone who needed me in a different way from Sassy. What happened to me with Shank Potter—just yesterday, I stopped it from happening to another little girl. My half-sister's daughter. Gertie Mae. My niece.

Now there is the Easter Celebration. If I am called, will I caress or will I deny Gertie Mae? A new chapter begins. I wait for the yet unknown.

***

Too soon, Dale's ears filled with roaring noises, a storm raged. He jerked awake

"Avenge me." The words rang in his head. Emotions threatened to overwhelm Dale. He took several deep breaths. Distraught, he rolled from one side to the other.

The smell of sweet olive seeped across the room, stronger where the Bible lay. Strangely, the bourbon and syrup had no odor.

Dale tossed off the covers and sprang from the bed. He turned on an oil lamp, picked up the spilled papers and glanced at the top page.

My intention in due time is for Lamont or a descendant to make this a public document.

I will now prepare and have ready to be revealed for the future generations, the role Mr. C.W. Claymore has participated and perpetuated in these events. My hope is that his child, Brucie, or her offspring will see to this being set right.

He folded the pages, put them back into the Bible.

"I'll finish this later. I've got things to take care of."

He craved a drink, but instead of reaching for one he set the Bible back into the haversack, pulled out a flashlight and checked to make sure the battery was still working.

He flung the haversack over his shoulder, ran down the steps, and out the front door.

***

The front door slammed. "Dale's not catching up on sleep. Not quite sunup yet."

To this moment. A short while ago I heard the front door slam, Memory wrote as white curtains drifted through her open bedroom window like lacy skirts caught in a breeze.

My brother crossed the road to the cemetery. Since he came home from the War he's fascinated with death. His men in France; Chateau Thierry, Belleau Woods. Back home at Redemption Ridge, to the bones of his childhood friend, Samuel Stanton, haunted him until he was able to get Samuel's remains buried in an old family plot.

I do feel hope for Dale. He and Father last night. In many ways they set to rights old, built-up resentful feelings. There is also his longtime girlfriend, Laura Lee, who has come back into Dale's life. She and this father-son change may chase away the demons and be my brother's salvation.

She rubbed her eyes. "I think I'll nap just a minute." She set her pen down, smoothed the bedside table covering made from one of Vernell's old quilts and, a smile on her face, fell across the bed. *Soon my walk will be down a church aisle as a bride. Jenson, Jenson, Jenson,* sang in her dreams

***

His eyes fixed on the land that lay in front of him, Dale crossed Old Farm Road and entered the colored cemetery.

The ground smelled musty, of rot and decaying tree limbs and leaves. As he carefully picked his way between burial sites, some were marked by crumbling tombstones, while others were only small indentions to step over.

After a few minutes he came to the familiar spot at the far corner of the cemetery, Vernell's grave. Known only to a few, under there lay the bones of his grandfather, joined with those of Vernell for all eternity.

The wooden bench at the head of their unmarked graves beckoned him to sit.

Maybe I can say goodbye here. To the past. Maybe I can weep and wail for my dead and maimed men in faraway France. Lay them to rest.

He ran his fingers across the words carved on the seat, *He is arisen.* "This is where I am. Good old Mississippi. For now and for what will be my eternity." He gazed at the graves spread out before him. The early morning air had a troubled feel. It seemed as if the ghosts of memories past seeped from the ground, unheard and forgotten stories all around.

"If I listened hard enough, I could probably hear you," he said, imagining cries from slaves and the long-dead phantom soldiers who had once fought and died on Redemption Ridge.

"Am I called to redeem a ghost? Or myself?" He brushed his hair away from his face.

"I'm here. My real home. Life has a rhythm here you don't find in the city."

Dale wrapped his arms around his body as if trying to hold his feelings in. "I want to sit in a flat-bottom John boat. I want to face the evening sunsets. Not hearing death cries, but the moaning of a full-titted cow. Gut fresh catfish caught in a slough of the Big Black River. Then go home to my love, Laura Lee. Hear the creak of a cane-bottomed rocking chair, listen for the ring of a dinner bell.

"Take swigs of bourbon whiskey from a jug. Satisfied that I have done all I could for her brother and for my men. Henceforth and forevermore."

He squinted his eyes as if he were lining up a gun barrel and gazed over the ridged cemetery. "Those of you in front of me now. I can only imagine what you went through. You all lay under the same night sky as my men. "

Disturbed by feelings of anxiety and depression, his thoughts drifted away to France, where so much of his uncertainty about good triumphing over evil began.

I wonder what it feels like to die, Dale wondered. *Many of my men found that answer. I came close many times.*

His heart beat faster.

The trenches. Eardrums burst with the spit and boom of gunfire. Bombs explode. Rolling, thick gray smoke. Hot swaths over our heads. Screams. Burning bodies.

"I was their captain. I sent my men out." Dale clasped his hand across his mouth and cleared his throat. "I saw them. Held them. They begged for home. They coughed their lungs out. I struggled to breathe for them."

He took a deep breath and tried to let go of the memories, but it wouldn't happen; recollections were in control. *The smell of wet ground.* "Blood soaked, red carpet.

"I heard their death sighs. Breathed them."

His heart skipped a beat. "What helped was not caring. But I couldn't stop. Even down to this day.

"Nightmares will never leave. I left the best part of my heart in foreign soil.

"Oh, God." He hit his chest with a balled-up fist, then grabbed the edge of the bench. "My men dreamed of peace—of family."

He leaned forward." They're over there. Across the ocean. Forever." Dale contemplated the scarred, bumpy ground in front of him. His head pounded. "You're here. Forever."

Again, his eyes filled with tears. "I'm weary with bringing heartache to people around me. I sent my men out to die."

He bit his lower lip. "Will part of me always be buried in Chateau Thierry? Even if I begin a new life with Laura Lee?"

"Easter." *The day of redemption?*

"Will this day tell the tale?

Dale opened the haversack, took out the Bible, but realized there was not quite enough light to read the confession written by Sheriff Homer Bramlett. He wanted a cigarette. Instead of reaching for one, once again he ran his fingers over the carved words, *He is arisen*.

He leaned back on the bench and crushed the Bible to his chest.

The papers from Sheriff Bramlett that he had folded back into the Bible scratched his neck, like long, sharp fingernails trying to get his attention.

"Okay, Sheriff," Dale said. "I guess you mean for me to finish reading this now." He lifted out his flashlight and began to read more of what the Sheriff had written.

A rustling noise in a nearby tree broke off Dale's reverie. He looked up and saw a thin human shape hanging from a rope tied to the high branches of a live oak. He angled his hand across his forehead, trying to bring the form to focus. The best he could make out, it was a woman, her body swaying in the early morning breeze.

In a voice strangled with agony, he barely heard her choppy words, "The chirren are a-gatherin'. Even Daddy Claymore's lay-by."

Bony fingers kneaded the air. "Some of 'em was bad, murderin' peoples. But I done looked after Miss Brucie. She be's liken to my very own.

"This be's the second chance."

Although she spoke, the woman's voice seemed to be strangled with what Dale thought was pain. He palmed his hand against his chest as if to still the beating of his heart.

"Evil done called. It done reared its ugly head again."

Skeletal fingers reached down. There was no sound for a moment, then in a voice Dale could barely hear, the hanging body said, "This here is where redemption begins."

She tugged at the rope around her neck, her words spoken haltingly, as if they were hard to get out. "Then, I will be set free. To join my God in heaven."

"This is Easter Sunday," Dale said, "As God is my witness. The truth will be spoken." He drew in a deep breath. "I'll do what I can to bring you peace on this day, Vernell. "

Long, narrow shreds of a tattered skirt swished back and forth, waving goodbye. "I'll stretch out my arms to you, Jesus."

A scent of sweet olive floated through the air.

The soft words were spoken haltingly, "An' be with my loved ones again."

Dale's vision blurred. His eyes stung. He bent over and wiped them with the edge of his sleeve. A sharp crack broke the stillness. A low limb had snapped. When he looked up, the woman had disappeared. "Where did you go?" he asked. *Where?*

Daylight crept across the horizon, showcasing the hulking trees guarding the graveyard.

"Were you here? Or was I imagining things?" Almost as if to answer his question, the underbrush crunched and a thick tangle of bushes parted. In the rising shaft of sunlight Dale saw a shadow slide across the ground.

A tall man with broad, squared shoulders and military posture blocked the rising sun. The man wore a tattered gray uniform riddled with bullet holes, a felt hat tipped at a rakish angle. A tousled mane of lion-like flaxen hair spilled over his shoulders and down his back. Legs spread, arms crossed, the figure looked at Dale.

"You are a soldier. I was a soldier. Help me find my peace." His voice was clearer and sharper than the ringing of the Dry Creek Church bell. The soldier stepped closer. Dale could see that his cheekbones curved like a saucer, his skin was tanned like the bark of summer trees. He saw his own reflection in the unblinking eyes of a weather beaten replica of himself.

"I know who you are, Captain. You were murdered." Dale nodded his head. "You are not guilty of theft and absconding with the Confederate fortune."

The ghost shook his head. "I'm here for my name to be cleared. Of murder. Of being a traitor. Vernell's name. For my rest. For her peace."

"Your story and Vernell's will be heard on this Easter Day. You will not go down in history as a traitor.

"People from our family and from Tallouga County may not choose to believe it, but they will hear the true story of you. And of who killed Vernell. Her name will be cleared. And more than that. Honored."

Dale reached down, and slid papers from the Bible. He held them up.

"I hold the proof here in my hands. Of who killed my mother's sister, Thelma Grace. And of who hung Vernell for a crime she did not commit.

"Daddy Claymore's signed confession. Our people will hear this today."

With those words, the sudden bright gold of a luminous morning sun burst forth, blinding Dale for a moment.

When he could see again, as mysteriously as he had appeared, the ghost disappeared like a snuffed-out candle.

Dale closed his eyes, took a deep breath and willed himself to calm down. So much had happened in the last two days. He was physically and emotionally exhausted.

He was a strong man, but for long months he had fought his own raging, inward battles. For a moment he soaked up a welcome stillness.

"I need to lay them all to rest."

The quietness was broken by the neighing of a horse. Dale shook his head and squared his shoulders. He turned back to the bench, bent over to pick up the Bible and papers from Sheriff Homer Bramlett.

Across the way, on the other side of the fence, he heard buckboards and wagons clanking. He walked to the edge of the colored cemetery. He could make out men propping up ladders, a few of them carrying leafy branches to bind across the top of the brush arbor shelter to help shade people coming for the celebration.

> "Fairy tales have ended
> Ghost stories laid to rest.
> I will set the record straight.
> For my grandfather.
> Within myself.
> I will gird my loins.
> It is past time."

***

Memory jumped awake when she heard the front door slam and someone hurrying up the steps.

"Dale's home." She shoved the covers back, got up and used the chamber pot. She pushed it back under the bed, and once again, picked up her pen. "Not much more to say." She dipped the pen firmly into the ink pot, as if she were ready to write down answers to troubling questions that were never talked about.

> All things may come full circle. I feel as if I've made my way through a long stretch of woods, not to an unknown land, but to a beloved home. I must own this. I have spent my life looking for my true love. And he was in front of me the whole time.
>
> Soon, my walk will be down a church aisle as Jenson's bride.
>
> I have come to believe Redemption Ridge is not only a place, it is somewhere here within us. There is Lamont. Vernell. My grandfather's ghost. They have always been there.

Maybe if I am still and listen, I'll hear what they are trying to tell me,

For whoever cares to know, if anyone ever reads my once-proud, now-humble words, I feel a need to continue telling these, our stories. Why? I don't know. I don't know.

Someday maybe someone out there, family friend or even foe may pick up these pages.

Some of our stories are not pretty.

I am a woman.

No, I'm in the south. I am a lady.

So, because I am of the female extraction, will anyone be inclined to read these, our stories?

Ladies are supposed to write pretty stories. Sweet.

Not those speaking of colored folks' and white folks' feelings. Of caring and of love. Or of frustration and dislike. Bodies tossed in wells. Father's having their way with their daughters. Hangings.

Memory set her pen down and walked to an open window.

"Easter morning," she breathed.

"Maybe we all have work to do, if, when and before we become angels. If that is the plan. If there is one."

CHAPTER 50

**Eyes to tail in a widening gyre,
A burning, glimmering ring of flesh.
Is this the crown of faith?**

**Slipping through orange leaves of time,
Garden to forest to the crest of the mind.**

Setting up, 9:00 a.m.

Mudge checked to make sure the door to Tattler the Rattler's cage was securely tied with thick string. "Okay, Taddler," he said. "You stay in your cage, an' later on this mawnin,' you jest might be the star in our blest, Brush Arbor Celebration."

He called to Preacher Tuggle who had been loading supplies from back of the Divine Deliverance Holiness Church into a wagon. "Fore y'all leave here an' head fer the Celebration, I need to tell you where to put Mr. Taddler up."

Mudge rocked forward. "Sister Mealy Maude done made us a big flag honor'n' our glorified dead. It's gonter set under our gun box that we done made an altar out of, an' it'll cover the table. You're to set Mr. Taddler an' his cage up under there."

Preacher Tuggle scratched behind his ear. "Not so sure that all's a good ideer," he said. "Me an' the Missus, Mother Bunny, had us some other things on our mind."

"You jest never know when things might git outer han'. Thas' what the Lord done tol' me to do," said Mudge.

Preacher Tuggle shook his head as he walked away. "I ain't got no answer fer that," he muttered.

"Hiss, hiss," Mudge spewed. "Might be comin' at some o' y'all. 'Fore it's over an' done with, I jest might need Taddler to take ker of Brother Tuggle fer me."

He dragged another cage over. He set it into his roadster, then lifted Black Beauty out and draped her around his neck. He cranked the motor and fell into his roadster. "We're on our way to pick up Miss Thelmer Jewel."

Singing to himself, "Standin' on the Promises," Mudge headed to town driving in time to the marching beat of the music.

"It's all comin' to a head, my pet," he crooned a short while later, pulling to a stop in front of Mrs. Netter's Boarding House. He had already telephoned Thelma Jewel, so she was waiting out front, propped against the white picket fence. Thelma Jewel was dressed finer than Mudge had ever seen her. She wore a bell-shaped skirt, the color of elephant skin, a white satin blouse with lace collar, a raspberry colored linen jacket, and a navy straw hat large enough to be a church bell clapper.

"There she be, Black Beeyoutee," Mudge said. "After our liddle talk, I kin count on her to do like I say."

Although Thelma Jewel wasn't happy about it, she and Mudge had had a conversation the night before about what time he'd pick her up and what he planned to do.

"Now, Miss Thelmer Jewel," he'd said, "All ya gotta do is to let me drape Black Beeyoutee 'roun' your neck. I got her trained real good. Then the folks'll see you touchin' her an' not bein' harmt nor hurt, cuz you done jest give up a lifetime a' sinnin'.

"They'll put a purty penny in the hat fer that. An' it'll be fer the both of us." He grinned to himself as he got out of the car and held the snake up. "I won't never be poorer than no church mouse," he laughed.

Although Thelma Jewel had tried to prepare herself, when she caught sight of Black Beauty, twisting in loopy circles and thought about the squirming snake, for a moment she froze hard as a rock. She drew in a shaky breath and raised the collar to her linen jacket to cover her neck. She pulled her straw hat further down over her ears, then bolted backward so hard she caught her jacket on the picket fence. She jerked forward, there was a ripping sound, the collar tore away and the loosened fabric hung down like a stuck out tongue.

"Oh, glory me. Well, I never," she moaned.

"Git a move on. We're gonter meet Brother Tuggle, his wife, Mother Bunny an' Gertie Mae. She's gonter tear at their heart strings," Mudge said. "An' right about now, them sisters orter be unloadin' some vittles. So, git a holt of yourself. I hear tell a passel of them highfalutin folks what belongs to other churches is gonter come on out to Redemption Ridge an' see fer theirselves what's goin' on." As he slid in, settling the snake around his shoulders, he motioned for Thelma Jewel to get into the car. "If not fer nothin' else, they'll show up fer them vittles."

Her guts roiling and churning, Thelma Jewel plunked herself into the seat. She spread her legs, placed her hand on her thighs, and leaned as far away from Mudge as she could.

The reptile began to writhe and twist. Thelma Jewel drew her legs up and together as if she were afraid the snake might crawl between them and get up under her corset.

"We're gittin' there a little early. Got us some settin' up to do," Mudge said, his voice cackling with delight and anticipation.

The car in gear, steering with one hand and stroking the snake wrapped around his neck with the other, he motored down Main Street at a reasonable rate of speed. Once on Old Farm Road, Mudge gripped the steering wheel with both hands and drove faster, as if he took pleasure from hearing the ping and clunk of flying gravel. As he made one final curve before they got to the cemetery, he spied Lamont walking on the far side.

He blared the horn and slammed the accelerator to the floor, "Gotcha," he yelled. The roadster whirled sideways, sending rocks and dust flying. Mudge jerked away at the last moment as Lamont jumped and rolled into a ditch to keep from being hit.

"'I'll shout an' sing,'" Mudge hollered over his shoulder, "God loves you, an' them other coloreds, an' all the sinners there be."

He wheeled the car back onto the road, so fast that Thelma Jewel was flung forward and came close to striking the glass.

Mudge pumped the brakes, cut through the open gate into the cemetery and skidded to a stop between a line of wagons.

Thelma Jewel slammed against the seat back.

"You set here fer jest a minute," Mudge said. Holding onto the snake he pushed down on the handle, shoved at the door with his shoulders, and climbed from the car,

Legs shaking so she could barely stand, her puffy cheeks blazing red, clasping her tapestry bag Thelma Jewel hoisted herself out and leaned against the car to keep from losing her balance.

"By now they orter be done finished settin' the brush arbor up," Mudge said. "You wait here a minute." He pulled the snake's cage from the roadster and dragged it to a small patch of bushes close to where tables were being set up and food was being cooked and put out." He walked back over and motioned for Thelma Jewel to come to him.

"The good Lord gonter swoop down from His throne today. Here where we're at, at Redemption Ridge."

Black Beauty wriggled and writhed in Mudge's hands, it's tongue flashing out as if searching for something to eat or to strike.

Rocking from side to side, Mudge fastened his eyes on Thelma Jewel. "Best you be careful with her." He held the snake high, like she was a prize he had just won. "Fore this day's over and done with, everybody's gonter sing praises to Black Beeyoutee. Jest don't you let them 'howlin'' storms of doubt an fear assail.'" He carefully tossed Black Beauty toward Thelma Jewel.

"Lordy mercy," she screamed, her arms flailing the air as the snake flew from Mudge's hands and landed across her shoulders.

Heart pounding, gasping for breath, Thelma Jewel grabbed the car door to keep from falling.

"'By luv's strong cord,'" Mudge sang, snatching Black Beauty away.

Thelma Jewel jammed her hand into her bag reaching for the derringer.

"We're gonter make us some money," Mudge warbled.

Thelma Jewel caught herself.

"Money," she breathed. "Black Beauty's going to make me rich."

"'We're gonter shout 'an' sing,'" Mudge trilled, stroking the snake.

CHAPTER 51

On resurrection day
Was this family resurrected?
In defiance of the demiurge
Did they lay claim to their lineal
Tract.

This inheritance is guaranteed
By the transformational
Power of the trench.

Only in grime and gore is a man a spirit
Of its own mastery.

Easter, 9:00 a.m.

Although it had been good daylight for a couple of hours, the parlor lamps were still turned on and a fire slowly burned itself out in the fireplace.

Bertha set a silver coffee urn on a marble-topped table at the end of one of the sofas. "You wants more, Miss Brucie?"

"I'll have one more, then I'm done."

"Miss Brucie." Bertha stepped back and looked at Brucie like she hadn't seen her for a long time. "You sure do look fine," she said.

"It was a long night. I hope I look fine enough for a brush arbor meeting." Brucie tilted her head and ran her fingers through her silver streaked, glossy hair. "Well, I don't know. This Mississippi humidity makes my hair frizzle." She lifted her head and sniffed. "Do you smell that?"

"I smells bacon fryin'," Bertha said.

"No. A tangy sweet smell." Brucie's hand strayed to her neck and touched her comfort piece, the cross from Vernell. "One that speaks of secrets. Sweet olive." She took a deep breath, held it a moment then said, "My father. Captain Bruce Claymore. The man I know so much about, but never saw."

"You dreamin' again," Bertha said.

"All those long years ago. He's still here." Brucie said softly under her breath. "So many times I have felt his restless spirit roaming through the hills of Redemption Ridge or his voice calling to me across the Big Black River. I did last night. When I was asleep here on the sofa a fragrance like a bowl full of apricots woke me. Sweet olive," she said wistfully. "And then I heard him call my name. I rose up. I could swear I saw him through the parlor window."

Bertha seemed uncomfortable with the way the conversation was going. "You always could see things other folks couldn't," she said. "But you might jest a heard Mist Von Dieter callin' after you," She nodded toward the couch where Von Dieter snored softly.

The two women stared awkwardly at each other; both were relieved when they heard the soft tap of shoes and Memory swept into the room breaking the tension.

"I'll have some coffee," she said. "But I'll pour it myself."

Brucie's unease diverted, she couldn't help but chuckle when she saw how her daughter was dressed. Memory had selected a pink chiffon dress with flowing chiffon sleeves, a rosy satin scarf encrusted with gold and pink beads encircled her small waist; the hem of her skirt stopped just below her knees.

"Memory! I thought you had that green jacket and gingham skirt altered for today."

"I changed my mind."

"Don't forget, you're going to a brush arbor meeting. In Tallouga County, Mississippi," Brucie reminded her.

"Don't say a word. I'm here to show them how uppercrust Boston dresses," Memory said.

Yawning, Dale entered the room as Bertha asked, "What fer you all want me to fix fer a late breakfast?"

"The service starts at eleven." Dale glanced up at the mantel clock. "It's just past nine. I can't speak for anybody else, but with the food they'll probably be serving at the Celebration, coffee's all I want right now and maybe a strip of that bacon I smell," he said.

Bertha nodded and bustled toward the kitchen.

"Besides, I've got a lot more things than food on my mind. I have some things that need to be taken care of. Today," Dale said.

"Laura Lee?" Memory asked.

Dale's face softened. "Oh, yes." His lips tightened. "But that's ongoing. And a pleasure." He scratched his head. "Among other things. The air needs to be cleared. The truth about Captain Bruce Claymore and Lamont's mother, Vernell, needs to be spoken. To be heard and honored."

As if he had heard his name called, the front door which had been opened to let the cool morning air in, slammed shut. Lamont usually made a quiet entrance from the back porch into the kitchen, but today he came into the parlor, stomping his feet, and brushing his clothes with his hands. He shook his head in disgust. "I'm not so sure this here what's goin' on over 'cross the way is a good thing. That crazy Mist Mudge Turnipseed almost run over me a liddle while back. He had him that woman from out west with him."

"He's not only crazy as a loon, he's dangerous," Dale agreed. Bertha returned, holding a platter of thick, crisp bacon. Dale snagged a slice.

The front doorbell chimed, the sound of familiar voices came from the hall as Bertha let Otis, Laura Lee and Jenson in. "Lots of wagons and folks over across the road," Otis said. "And I saw several members from the Dry Creek Presbyterian Church. Most unusual to come out this way. Guess they want to see what's going on out here."

"And maybe to get themselves a good Sunday dinner, cooked by somebody else," Memory said sarcastically.

"Happy Easter," Laura Lee said, her eyes shining with pleasure. "Whatever the occasion, I'm just glad to be with y'all." She cocked her chin at Dale, as if sending him a message. "I believe this will be a day to remember," she said.

For a long minute the two of them looked at each other. "I remember other days." Dale drew in a deep breath, stepped closer and brushed Laura Lee's hair back from her face. "You're lovely," he mouthed.

"What?"

"At this moment, I'm not in France. I'm here. In Tallouga County, Mississippi. In the land of the living. What a lucky man I am."

Von Dieter raised his head. "I'm still living," he said in a weak voice. "And like father, like son."

"Amen, Father."

Dale stepped away from Laura Lee. "I'll go on upstairs, shave and finish dressing. You all visit a few minutes. Who knows? We may all see some of our ancestors today." He rubbed the back of his neck. "Gird your loins and get ready for a Brush Arbor Service." He snagged another strip of bacon.

The last noise Dale heard before he returned to his room was the faint sound of Laura Lee's drawl. Her voice was as uplifting to him as what he imagined a heavenly choir could be.

It seems I've come back from the grave. The Good Lord willing, I'll be part of my grandfather's redemption.

"Dale should be down in a minute. Why don't you and Jenson go on ahead, Memory?" Brucie said. "I'll wash my hands, then I'm ready. Bertha, Lamont and I will leave."

"I ain't goin,'" said Bertha. "I'd feel better off stayin' where I'm at, here with Mr. Von Dieter."

Swooping his hands in a gentlemanly like gesture Jenson opened the front door for Memory. "It looks like they're having a crowd at the Brush Arbor Worship Service." He held her arm as they walked through the yard and toward the Celebration.

"I saw a good many buggies, wagons and a few automobiles when Otis, Laura Lee and I drove by," he said. "I guess the Celebration's a pretty big event for Tallouga County."

Involuntarily, Memory caught her breath. "Wait up," she said. A warm breeze brushed the wild flowers, budding leaves and dogwood blooms that had burst out, covering the once bony tree limbs. Forgetting the stifling summer heat she knew would be ahead, right at this moment, Memory loved the southern weather.

"The air smells so clean. The trees so fresh."

She threw her arms out and twirled around, her chiffon skirt rippling above her knees, her thick auburn hair flowing like rushes in a breeze. "I feel a beginning. And an ending. Here in Mississippi. I feel as if I am in two worlds, the now and the past."

"Always remember, we were made for each other. You're ahead of me, in so many ways." Jenson glanced sideways. "I've felt that way since we were children. No matter what world you seem to be off in."

Memory drew in a deep breath. Her gift of insight had come from her mother. *But is it a gift?* "There are troubled souls here yearning for release," she said softly. "I sense them so strongly."

This was now her forever home. She felt the history and stories of Redemption Ridge settle in her chest like a lodestone

What is my role, my place in all of this, she wondered.

As always, still not sure of other people's feelings, searching Jenson's face she found love and trust in his eyes. Until Jenson, she thought she had lost the ability to fall in love forever. She wound her arms around his neck, and when she did, she heard the dull thud of his heart, a normal, comforting sound. In his arms it would be easy to regain that trust and love she had lost those long-ago years at the well.

"Let's go on to the Celebration," she said. "We have people here to take care of. Whatever is ahead, we'll go through Redemption Ridge together."

***

"Dale's taking a little longer dressing than I thought he would," Brucie said.

"He's gittin' hisself spanked up for Miss Laura Lee." Lamont laughed softly.

"Either way, you and I will be moving a little slower, so I'm glad we went on ahead of Laura Lee, Otis, and Dale." A gusty breeze blew Brucie's ankle length skirt. She pulled a matching navy linen jacket closer over her white long-sleeved blouse and then tugged her suede gloves further up her arm. "It feels good to be with just you for a short while," she said to Lamont as they walked down Old Farm Road.

She fingered the gold cross around her neck. "Who knows what this day will hold?" she asked, a touch of uncertainty in in her voice. "I wish I could go back and relive part of my life."

"You done right, Miss Brucie," Lamont said. "The best way you know'd to."

"We both did."

When they got to the border of the colored and white cemetery, with neither of them saying a word or asking if this was what the other wanted, Lamont lifted then shoved the sagging rusty gate. The sun shone brightly overhead. The day was warm, but an unexpected gust of wind spiraled the leaves and branches as they stepped into the colored burial ground. Brucie pushed her navy felt hat further down on her head as she and Lamont carefully walked single-file through ankle-high weeds and across uneven grounds scarred by sunken graves, crumbling headstones.

Brucie felt a gentle touch on her cheek from an unseen presence. *I feel closer to Vernell here than anywhere,* she thought

"I felt like your mother was with me last night." She pointed to the small unmarked mound close to the back. "Your mother, your twin, Sunnie Flo, and our father. Waiting for the truth. So they can have their rest.

"I would like for Vernell's and our father's names to be cleared. Today will be an end and a beginning."

The smell of sweet olive drifted across the burial ground. There was a sudden shadow over Brucie's head. She looked up. A large hawk, riding the currents, tucked its wings. He slowly drifted over the mound and settled onto a low lying tree branch sheltering the grave.

The bird bent its head, lifted a frayed tattered rope from a bent, crooked tree limb, then pumped its wings. There was a fluttering noise, the hawk flung the rope at Lamont's feet, then flew away.

Lamont drew in a deep breath and reached for Brucie's hand,
She removed one of her gloves.

Lamont raised her hand to his lips and kissed it.

"She was here. I knew Vernell was here."

"And him too. Blood is bindin'," Lamont said

CHAPTER 52

The waltz was a lying dirge.
A disembodied music seized
As tarantism as an ill altar
Was fussed over.

A tingling spine and trembling
Fingers receive the echo of the
Eerie tune.

Easter, almost time for the Brush Arbor Celebration

Horses and wagons and a few automobiles were stopped along both sides of Old Farm Road; Mudge drove a short way past them and stopped at on the far side of the cemetery. Mother Bunny leaned against the rear of a wagon that was covered with a piece of tied down canvas.

"Be patient, Thelmer Jewel," he said. "I gotter see Mother Bunny fer jest a minute before we go in to the meetin.'"

"You done like I tol' you?" Mudge asked drawing next to Mother Bunny.

"She's in there." She nodded toward the wagon.

"Be patient. You stay right here, Mother Bunny. 'Til you hear my signal. Three horn blasts from Stalk Wheeler. Then you bring her an' come ahead to the meetin' ."

"An' she won't git out til then, Mr. Mudge," Mother Bunny assured him.

Mudge turned the car around and swung through the open cemetery gate.

He stopped close to the food tables, where Preacher Tuggle waited. "I got somethin' to do real quick like, 'fore we git started," he said to Thelma Jewel. He picked up a burlap sack he had brought with him, and went into the brush arbor shelter.

He had made a cross out of two sword pistols and tied them together with a pair of thick shoelaces. He propped the pistols against the gun box then hurried outside.

"Brother Tuggle. We needed us a cross fer Easter," he said. "An' I set one up on the altar table."

"Where's Black Beeyoutee?" Preacher Tuggle asked. "She's usually ridin' round with you."

"She's homed down in some bushes off to the side. Whar it's cool. She's under wraps 'til the Spirit moves me." Mudge rubbed his neck. "An' you took care of Taddler?"

"I did like you ast."

There were hugs and handshakes as worshippers and curiosity seekers gathered around and drifted into the brush arbor shelter.

Mudge surveyed the crowd. "If any of the men folks have on hats, they kin keep them on their heads if they've a notion to. An' some of 'em got the head lice." He scratched behind his ear. "You an' the deacons be sure the cigarettes an' cigars are stepped on an' put out 'fore folks settle in. We can't let us catch on far. They kin chew on tobaccer. Long as they don't spit on somebody's feet." He cocked his head toward a nearby open area where cooking kettles filled with water and food boiled and grease-filled skillets sputtered. "Looky yonder at the spread them ladies are puttin' out. Bet you ain't seen nothin' like that in Californay, Miss Thelmer Jewel."

Tables covered with sheets were being filled with food by busy, important-looking women. "We got us chicken an' dumplin's, ham, sarsage, squirrel, deer, blackeye peas 'n' hog jawl, sweet taters, an' mashed taters. Angel food cake, peach cobbler, peecan pie, an' lots more that they're cooking," he said proudly.

Mudge stood on his tiptoes "An' looky over yonder at who's comin'," he said as he saw the Von Dieters and a few people who were with them picking their way through the cemetery. He rolled back on his heels and made a slow, deep rock.

"I'll go give 'em a Divine Deliverance Holiness Church welcome."

***

"Are you sure this is what you want to do?" Laura Lee asked Dale. The two of them were a few steps ahead of Brucie, Memory, Jenson, Otis and Lamont as they carefully made their way through the cemetery where the old battle had been fought. Dale gazed at the grass mounds and crumbling tombstones spread beneath their feet. He wondered if the words he would be speaking today would be like those fragmented, forgotten shards of graves and head markers.

A sadness swept across Dale. *Like those in front of me now, who remembers or cares about the past? Who will hear the truth about what I have to say?* He let his thoughts return for a moment to his friends interred in faraway France. *My buddies. They can be, "A lamp unto my feet."* Feeling stronger he turned to his family and friends. "As God is my witness, the truth will be heard today," he said.

Brucie pressed the gold cross she wore to her chest, and Memory nodded her head in agreement.

They were nearing the crowd gathered around the brush arbor setup, when Mudge Turnipseed strutted toward them.

"Y'all are our blest guests on this Easter Sunday," he squeaked, slapping Dale's back in a man-to-man gesture. "Foller me. Y'all are to set up front on the second row. An' you, Mistah Dale, since you're our honored, speakin' guest, you take the outside."

He gave a short rock. "Brother in Christ, Dale," he said. "You an' your people, git you a fan 'fore you go in." He waved his fingers toward a large, rusting metal barrel where people were picking up handmade cardboard fans with printed-on pictures of Jesus rising to heaven. "It can git a liddle bit heated when the Spirit gits to movin' 'mongst the brethren an' sistren."

Mudge noticed Thelma Jewel edging up and he took a step backward. His hands like a pair of claws, he gripped her shoulder. "You set in the back," he whispered. "God knows best. An' He's talkin' to me. I'll let you know when it's your time to shine. 'Til then, you keep your mouth shut."

As the Von Dieters and their friends and Lamont and his family moved into the overhead covering a smothering scent of damp leaves wafted down. The tangled limbs and vegetation overhead lay like a shroud. Dale's body stiffened. He remembered telling his men, "Pass the word. When I say charge, we go over the top."

And to a man, they were wiped out.

Moving to Dale's side as if he sensed a need to reassure his friend, Lamont gave his shoulder a squeeze. "Mist Dale. My mama an' your grandfather needs their peace. An' you been called to give it to them. It's a-happenin'. I feel it in my bones," he said.

"Yes, Lamont," Dale said. "It will be done. For now and all time, on this Easter."

"Le's us start on down," Mudge said. "Y'all come with me. We got us a pianer up to the front an' will have us a liddle music."

Lamont stepped away. He stood at the back with a few coloreds who were already in attendance as the Von Dieters and their friends followed Mudge.

Dale shook hands and heard messages from a few well-wishers, real or otherwise, as he and the others slowly moved forward.

"I see a row of people from our Presbyterian church here," Otis whispered to Dale. "The men look like their shoes hurt their feet, and they'd rather be somewhere else. But their lady folks look curious; they want to see what's going on out here." He pointed. "They're there. Up close to the front. "

Dale looked in the direction Otis indicated and saw the people he referred to. He also made out a small platform with a table covered by a Confederate flag. A wooden musket box sat in the middle with a cross made of pistols propped against it. *An altar*, Dale reasoned. He saw a man standing by the side of the table glance around suspiciously. He sank to his knees, and lifted a corner of the Confederate flag, making motions with his hands, as if he were arranging something.

Instinct told Dale something was wrong.

"We got red ribbons 'round your seats," Mudge said, waving them to a bench at the front adorned with satin bows. "You're the special, honored guess of The Divine Deliverance Holiness Church on this Easter Sunday. Since you been named a speaker fer the dead, what needs redeemin', you set there on the edge Mistah Dale. You're gonter speak after we hear from our own Brother Tuggle who's standin' up there next to our blest altar." Mudge nodded his head and rocked. "An' we're gonter show you city folks what the Gospel is all about, here in Tallouga County, Mississippi."

As soon as they were seated, Mudge made a bee-line to the front

"Le's us git movin'," he yelled. He pointed toward the back. "An we're havin' us some vittles after this here service. We'll be celebratin' some truth that's been tol', do some healin' an save us some souls. Then we'll have us some bonfires lit so we kin stay, long as the Spirit's with us."

Mudge took a deep breath, stood on tiptoe, and waved to someone in the back.

"Hallelujah?" he hollered, his voice a loud question.

An offkey horn blasted an answer through the brush arbor enclosure.

Then, a trumpet clutched in his hands, an overall-clad, bow-legged boy with carrot-colored hair ran through the tangle of people to the front. The milling crowd hurriedly found seats, filling benches, leaving standing room only.

"Stalk Wheeler. Le's us hear it again," Mudge called. "Hallelujah?"

The boy wiped the horn down his pants leg, shook out his spit, then raised his trumpet. He tooted another blast.

"He's the wife's cousin's son," Preacher Tuggle tapped his chest. "An' he can beat a drum too."

Fat hands clasped over his large paunch as if he were holding it in place, Preacher Tuggle stepped onto the platform. He nodded to Sister Mealie Maude, who sat in front of an upright piano. She banged out three off-key chords. "Here they come," he called out.

"'When the trumpet of the Lord shall sound,'" Sister Mealie Maude sang, her breath whistling through her gap-toothed mouth like a steaming kettle. A small group of ladies clad in scarlet robes moved to the middle aisle as they chorused, "'and time shall be no more.'"

The congregation joining in song, "'When the sons of earth shall gather,'" the ladies marched to the front. "'Over on the other shore.'"

Dale noticed that except for him and Memory, and they were not singing, no hymnals were necessary. Everyone knew the words. Even his mother, who with her hands raised high never missed a word or a note.

"'And when the roll is called up yonder, I'll be there.'" With these closing words, the sisters took a seat on a short side bench.

Preacher Tuggle cleared his throat and stepped slightly in front of Mudge. "Le's us all bow our heads.

"Now, Jesus. This is your day, an' I'm here to pray." Preacher Tuggle gripped the table. "To redeem you evil doers, what's gone astray," he intoned.

"An' all them sinners will hear, what I have to say."

Preacher Tuggle beat his leg with his fist. "An' now Blest Jesus, show me the way."

"Amen, Brother," Mudge shouted. He gave a nod to the trumpet blower. The boy sprang to his feet and tooted out a note.

"Huh!" Preacher Tuggle jerked his head up. "I ain't done givin' my call-to-all sermon yet."

Mudge shouldered Preacher Tuggle to the side. "Hallelujah! Amen!" he cried.

His eyes glistening with anger, Preacher Tuggle looked down toward the altar table. "I'm ahead of you, Brother Mudge," he muttered. "I done loosened that there string you done tied 'round Tattler's cage. He an' I might jest git the best o' you yet."

Mudge raised his arms. "Le's us do a liddle foot-stompin', han'-clappin' an' fan-waving' fer the Lawd."

For several minutes feet pounded the dirt, Mudge rocking in time to the rhythmic sounds.

"Hallelujah." He stepped onto the platform and raised his hands. The stomping stopped. Mudge cleared his throat.

"We're gonter fight us another battle. We'll have us a healin' service after this man from up nawth is over with. When I'm done, they won't be no doubtin' Thomases left in this here meetin'."

He rocked back and forth, in time to the rhythm of his own voice.

"Now hear me out, brother's 'n' sisters. Mistah Dale Von Dieter has him some Talllouga County Claymore blood flowin' through his veins. An' he has him his own words to say about, Cap'n Bruce Claymore. Many good folks hereabouts thought him a traitor, a few folks a hero." Mudge ducked his chin and rolled his eyes heavenward as if he and God shared a joke.

"Mistah Von Dieter, he has him a Yankee name," he said with a sly laugh. "When he's done, then I, Brother Mudge Turnipseed, will lead us in a savin' some souls meetin'. An close with a healin' an' a gift givin' to the Lawd, so we kin continue our blest work." Mudge raised his shoulders in a let's get this over with shrug. "An' it's come to yer time, Mistah Dale." Then he added, "In Jesus name."

Dale stepped to the front but he didn't mount the platform. Even with that he stood as tall as Mudge; with his military bearing he looked taller. *Well, I may have been setup for a hometown firing squad*, Dale thought as he faced the crowd.

He stood at attention, determined to see this through.

"On Easter, I am at my family's birth place, Redemption Ridge, Mississippi. Now my home."

With those words a hush fell over the building; light slipping through the brush ceiling could have been coming through stained glass windows in a cathedral.

"It is a privilege for me to stand here before you," Dale said. "Some of you I know, and many I don't."

The crowd that had been restless, moving and talking, were now still, looking for Dale to speak of a moment in time from the past and maybe truth for then and now.

Mudge stood on tiptoe and pointed to the back.

Stalk Wheeler, who had kept his eyes on Mudge, jumped to the center aisle. He threw his head back, raised his trumpet, and blew.

"Shut up an set down, Stalk Wheeler," Deacon Harlan Sistrunk cupped his hands around his mouth and called out. "Le's us hear what Captain Claymore's kin has to say."

492

Dale had heard, not an offkey horn note, but a bugle call. Time crumpled away; he had a sudden remembrance of his men in France. He drew strength from them now; he would not be here were it not for their protection. The world of everyone in front of him would be different.

Dale pulled the Bible from his haversack. "I returned from the War a few short months ago." Shadows from the past blended with the faces in front of him. "A changed man; once again, I have been called to fight a battle." He felt a hot rush of tears. "For honor. For decency. For truth." He choked for a moment, then got hold of himself.

"I hold here in my hand words and truths never heard."

When he said those words, Lamont moved to the center of the back aisle. He raised his hand.

"Mist Dale." A torn and tattered rope hung from Lamont's fingers. He swung it slowly back and forth, his body moving with the rope.

"This here choked my mama to her death," he said. "We needs our peace."

Dale's face twisted in sorrow. He had to wait a moment before he could go on. He walked down the aisle, took the rope from Lamont's hand and returned to the front. He draped it around the cross that Mudge had made and set the Bible on the table. "There is history here on Redemption Ridge," he said. "Each step we take in this dust, someone else has already stepped in.

"You shall hear the truth about Lamont's mother, Vernell, and my grandfather, Captain Bruce Claymore," Dale said.

Dale's proclamation was met by many gasps.

He went on, "As well as that lying, murdering"—He bit his bottom lip—"degenerate, W.C Claymore."

Mudge slammed the altar table with his fist. Then stepping around Dale, with Preacher Tuggle following he hurried down the aisle.

People stood up to see what was going to happen.

"I surrender. I surrender all," a pimply faced teen jumped up. "An' it ain't here, listenin' to this nawthin' liar."

A shriveled faced old man called out, "In His name he will cast out demons. We got us one right here. An' I'm leavin this house o' sin."

His wife, a stoop-shouldered woman, her gray hair twisted into a tight top knot and two of the women clad in scarlet robes fell into step behind him.

A few people scattered throughout the shelter stood and left. "We're waitin' fer Brother Mudge to come back," someone called.

Mudge beckoned Thelma Jewel to follow him as he passed by her.

She tugged on the sides of her skirt, grabbed her tapestry bag, patting to make sure her derringer was where she could reach it and then moved out behind Mudge. Stalk Wheeler met them at the back.

Not sure what to do, the rest of the brush arbor crowd who had risen to their feet, took their seats.

Outside, Mudge was once again in control. "Brother Tuggle, it's 'bout time fer me an' you to have us a healin' service."

He knew it would take Mother Bunny a while to get Gertie Mae moving and to the shelter. "We'll git started in a few minutes.

"Stalk Wheeler. When I say so, you toot yer horn three times," he directed.

"The rest of y'all, git by your wagons. When you hear a three-blast call come back here.

"Miss Thelmer Jewel, you an' Brother Tuggle don't move from here."

His eyes glistened like something hidden under a rock. "That trumpet toot's Mother Bunny's signal to haul Gertie Mae to this meetin'. An' you come down the aisle when I give the call," he whispered to Thelma Jewel. "You gonter have you a spell. I'll tell you what to do. But lay it on. We gonter be passin' out collections plates an' kin make us lots o' money. Fer the glory of the Lawd," he said quickly.

"I'm gonter start with Black Beeyoutee," he muttered to himself. "An' finish up with Taddler the Raddler."

***

A tall, wiry man in the back came forward with a glass and a pitcher of water. "You might need this, Mr. Von Dieter."

Dale nodded his thanks. "I'm Dale, not Mr. Von Dieter, " he said. "Henceforth and forever more, just plain Dale."

Three blasts of a horn startled everyone in the shelter.

This time Dale was not reminded of his men in France. He had another mission now.

He raised both hands. "I'm not surrendering," he said. "I'm just beginning."

He lowered his hands and picked up the Bible.

CHAPTER 53

A confession, read like a chime
In clotted blood.

A gaunt, disheveled veteran
Presents his evidence to the contrary.

Easter, time to set the record straight

"I hold in my hands a signed confession." Dale raised the Bible above his head then set it on the altar box.

"First, I shall read to you what Sheriff Bramlett wrote and read to my great-uncle, the murderer, C.W. Claymore, as he lay paralyzed and awaiting death."

He carefully lifted out yellowed typewritten pages and began to read:

> *C.W.*
> *I have seen where you have various bruises. A broken toe on one foot, and toenails ripped from the other. Book Turnipseed, who was hired as your caretaker, has also been your tormentor.*

Dale set his lips in a tight line, studied the crowd a moment, then went on:

> *You will pass on soon, Daddy Claymore, but you will not spend your last days in the agony to which you have been subjected for the last few months."*
> *There are matters, C.W., of which you had knowledge but chose not to speak of. The murder of Thelma Grace Claymore by one Yankee, Mr. Warner Sledge. And the hanging of Vernell Randall by one Ollie Potter.*

Dale glanced at Lamont. He held up the shredded rope he had draped over the cross of pistols, then continued reading:

> *Vernell Randall had no part in the death of Thelma Grace Claymore.*
>
> *I will make sure the record of what happened to Bruce Claymore and the Confederate jewels is set straight for all time. Traitor? No. Hero? Yes! I am putting this into the hands of Cousin Sarah Bowman, with instructions to pass on to Lamont Randall when he is older.*
>
> *And for the ages to come the fortune that would have been spent on a lost cause, will be used for good. A new church will be built for the colored people of Tallouga County and a new jail for the town of Franklin.*
>
> *What remains of the jewels will be buried at the feet of Vernell Randall. And near to the bones of Captain Bruce Claymore. They were joined in life. They are now one for all eternity.*

Several heads in the congregation pivoted toward Lamont. Dale read on:

> *When you sign this confession, then I will see to the dismissal of Mr. Turnipseed. You know me to be a man of my word.*
>
> *My intention, in due time, is for Lamont or a descendant of his to make this a public document.*

Dale nodded toward Lamont, then continued:

> *Also, I, Sheriff Homer Bramlett, have alerted the family friend, Vernell's father, Old Top. There have been some threats on my life. If any misfortune of fate befalls me before I tend to this matter to my satisfaction, first of all, look to the Potter family.*

Dale set the paper he had been reading on the table. "I have it in good authority that Potter and his boys murdered Sheriff Bramlett." He glanced toward Jenson Cooper.

"Sheriff Bramlett was the grandfather of Jenson Cooper, from right here in Tallouga County. Jenson went through The War with me and saved my life on more than one occasion. And he is now engaged to be married to my sister, Memory."

Dale drew in a deep breath.

"I was told by Jenson Cooper, that not long after Vernell Randall was hung, his grandfather, Sheriff Homer Bramlett, died a horrible death.

"Some months before, the Sheriff had made a couple of the lying Potter boys eat mud in front of the whole town until the boys spoke the truth about a matter involving Brucie and Lamont.

"The Potters shot the Sheriff in both legs. They tied and carried him to the Big Black River. The Sheriff's fingers were broken, spread apart and bound so that they formed a half circle. His fingers were held in place by sticks and nails that had been jammed into his hand. Each hand was smeared with clumps of wet clay, some had been crammed into his mouth. Mud dribbled down his neck and chest. He choked and suffocated on the muddy mass crammed into his mouth. Payback, was written in black paint across his bare chest."

Dale covered his mouth with his hand for a moment, then he took it down and went on. "Would everyone join me in a moment of prayer. I have heard, on more than one occasion the words from my grandfather, "Abandon me not," so I shall not abandon justice for him. Neither for Vernell. Nor for Sheriff Homer Bramlett."

Dale called out in a soft voice. "Would you all bow your heads, for only one moment." He looked down.

"God bless, absolve, and sustain these dear, good and innocent souls. Henceforth and forevermore. They were ours, now they are Yours."

He saluted, then raised his head.

"Amen."

He carefully unfolded another page. He held it up, then began reading.

I have printed the below with a typewriter. I will now hold your hand, C.W. Claymore, and lead you in signing this typed, written document of confession.

The below is the legal and binding confession of C.W. Claymore:
"I murdered my half-brother, Captain Bruce Claymore, for the Confederate jewels. They were not on him."

C.W. Claymore

I, Lawyer Matthew Stanton Esquire have witnessed the above on this date, August 13, 1877

Blood will tell. May God forgive us our sins.

Sheriff Homer Bramlett

In this the year of our Lord, August, 1877.

Dale folded the papers and returned them to the Bible.

"The names of two people were dishonored. Vernell Randall, the mother of Lamont Randall, was falsely accused of murdering Thelma Grace Claymore. The murderer was one, Warner Sledge. Vernell was hanged for a murder she did not commit."

Dale paused for a moment to let the full realization of what had been done to Lamont's mother sink in. He cleared his throat.

"And, my grandfather, Bruce Tisdale Claymore, was accused of thievery. Of being the one who stole the jewels all those years ago." He lifted his chin, turned and looked toward Bruce and Vernell's grave.

"He was murdered by his brother, C.W. Claymore. The jewels were not on him. They had been given to Sheriff Homer Bramlett."

Dale pointed toward town. "A new jail and a church were built. And the money said to be stolen? What is left, has been buried in a grave. What is still there will be given to this community."

One of the men in the audience sprang to his feet. "Let's us hear a halleluyar fer Brother Dale," he called.

"Amen." Most of the crowd roared and rose to their feet. A few shook their heads as if they didn't believe anything that had been said.

A ruddy-faced, paunch-bellied man bounded close to the platform. He raised to his tiptoes and pointed his finger. "I ain't straddlin' no fences." He tossed his head back and opened his mouth like he was waiting for manna from heaven, then shouted out, "I think we needs us to git this devil on the run."

A few people scattered throughout the shelter followed him out.

Dale took a deep breath and looked toward Lamont, who stood at the back of the shelter.

"Let me repeat. My grandfather, Captain Bruce Claymore was murdered for a fortune that was to have been used for the war. Vernell Randall, Lamont Randall's mother, was hanged for a crime she did not commit." Dale held up Daddy Claymore's written confession. "And now, may their souls rest in peace.

"I'm sure Mr. Turnipseed has further plans for this Easter service. That's all I have to say." Dale folded the confession back into the Bible, put it into the haversack and sat beside Laura Lee. "I feel like I'm home at last." He picked up her hand and raised it to his lips. "Henceforth and forevermore."

Lamont came from the back, slid in next to Brucie, and touched her shoulder in a protective gesture. Seeing a colored man sit with a white woman, a few wives poked their husbands and nodded toward the front row; the men raised their eyebrows and shook their heads, but no one said anything. This was a holy day, an Easter Celebration. And the Claymores home property was Redemption Ridge.

Several people came to Dale and his family, pleased with what he had told them about his grandfather and Vernell.

Memory shook her head and took Jenson's arm. "Hold on. Here it comes," she said.

"What? Everything's fine."

"We're waiting for a two-headed serpent to strike."

Sunlight filtering through the leafy roof threw black shadows across the room. There was an expectant quiet as before a brewing storm waiting for a thunderclap and a lightning bolt.

CHAPTER 54

**Remanded to the living
Real for reeducation,
Dale was at himself again
As through a lens, darkly.**

**The Easter dirge pulsated
Like a creeping fusillade
In his crackling lungs.**

**His eyes were two soft blue
Orbs of light, good for nothing
Save setting fog alight.**

Easter, "He Is Arisen"

Mudge and a small group of people stood just outside the enclosure. "Did you put them spent bullet casin's in there?" he asked Preacher Tuggle.

His eyes sliding sideways the preacher held up a lidded straw basket that was on wheels. "I did, an' they're rollin' an' rattlin'. Jest like you wanted."

"Keep 'em clackin'. It won't hurt Black Beeyoutee none."

He beckoned Thelma Jewel closer. "Miss Thelmer Jewel. You gonter be a queen." Mudge smiled. "I'm gonter make you a necklace out'n Black Beeyoutee. I'll kindly make sure them folks see only a speck o' my frien'. They won't know it ain't a raddler."

He wiped his hand across his mouth. "An' you ain't gonter have to take no more care a that gimpy-legged girl of your'n.

"I'm savin' Taddler the Raddler fer Mistah Dale." Mudge set his jaw. "You know what I tole you to do," he whispered. "I want that you should hike up your skirt and kindly stumble down the aisle. Act like one leg's shorter'n' the other.

"We have us our plan." He smiled to himself, licked his lips and rocked. *But mine an' yours ain't nearly bout the same. What you don't know ain't gonter hurt you*, he reasoned. *That there snake is gonter nest by your bosoms.* His smile deepened. *You put on your highfalutin show. An tha's when I step in.*

"We got us some rich town folks in here today," he chuckled. "You let 'em know I've done healed you. Then we're gonter pass the hat.

"All fer the glory of the Lawd," he added.

Thelma Jewel's eyes narrowed with suspicion. "I get my half as soon as we're away from here." *For the glory of me.*

Mudge turned toward several people who huddled next to the food tables. "Stalk Wheeler," he called.

When the boy came over Mudge punched his arm. "We're goin' on up to Zion." He swung his arms back and forth. "Le's us hear some marchin' music. Kin you git hold o' your drum."

"I set my horn and my drum under the tater an' dressin' table." Stalk Wheeler bent over. He reached under the table, picked up some drumsticks and a drum, draping a cord over his neck.

"Le's us go." With a small group following, Mudge stepped into the brush arbor shelter.

"Y'all take you a seat. This here's a Easter Celebration," Mudge boomed. "Not a church social," he said, a hint of reproach in his voice.

The room buzzed and rustled with anticipation. Sighs and thumps were heard throughout the shelter as the crowd sat down on their benches. Not sure what was going on, some shrugged their shoulders, while others shook their heads. A few "amen's" and "glory's" echoed throughout the enclosure.

A steady *Thump, Thump, Thump,* rhythm was heard as Stalk Wheeler began throbbing a dirge.

Mudge rocked to the beat for a moment keeping time, then he moved like a stalking animal as he led Thelma Jewel and Preacher Tuggle who was holding a thick, covered straw basket in a slow forward march to the music.

Close on their heels Mother Bunny pulled a drag-footing Gertie Mae.

A scent of lemon and cloves seeped through the room.

Thump, thump, thump.

Dale heard what sounded like the hollow sound of tromping boots, or the thundering thuds of hoof beats. Once again he stepped toward the smothering world of the dead. *Sent my men to their death,* he agonized.

Before he could sink into his troubled past, a soft, gentle touch returned him to the land of the living. Laura Lee raised his hand to her mouth, and rubbed it against her soft lips. Dale looked into her eyes. His thumb traced her jaw. He took a deep breath, then glanced down at the haversack holding the Bible and Daddy Claymore's confession. He shook his head. *I can't follow. They're in the past now. I cleared his name. For those who listened.*

All through the shelter, hands clapped in time to the drum beat.

Mudge stopped. He faced the Von Dieters, Jenson, Stantons and Lamont. His teeth nibbled his lips. Sweat popped out on his forehead, rolled over his heavy eyelids, dripped onto his eheeks "There she sits, Mrs. Von Dieter from up nawth." He rocked.

"'Scuse me, I means. Missus Brucie Claymore. Of Redemption Ridge."

Thelma Jewel did a slow turn. She put her hand over her heart, looked her birth mother in the eyes and then recited the words Mudge had told her to say. "This man of God will save me."

As if she couldn't help herself, Thelma Jewel stuck out her tongue. "Payback," she mumbled. "It's time." She slipped her hand into her purse. She cocked her derringer. *You never know.*

Preacher Tuggle jiggled the basket, shells rattled.

Her heart thudding, Brucie slumped forward. "My daughter."
Thump. Thump. Thump.

"Now, let me put out a call," Mudge said. "To Miss Thelmer Jewel. Another lady from up nawth. One who has come here with her crippled dorter, Gertie Mae. A angel chile. If'n there ever was one," he breathed. Smiling, he rocked back and forth.

"What's been treated lower than a snake in the grass. By her fambly. Right here at Redemption Ridge." He let his words sink in then he gave a forward motion with his hand.

Thump, Thump, Thump, the beat chorused as Mudge and his group moved toward the small altar platform.

Mudge turned and faced the gathering. Preacher Tuggle stood next to Mudge. He set the basket down, and Stalk Wheeler and the singing ladies stepped to the side. The music stopped.

"I hear me a raddler buzzin. A black raddler," Mudge said reverently, as if the snake were worthy of worship.

"There was a snake in the garden of Eden.

"We got us some snakes with legs here," Mudge intoned. "Some of 'em got the devil inside. Snakes slither an' slide." His voice shook. "They got raddles. They strike."

Mudge flailed his hands. He threw them in the air. "I kin heal. I kin save!"

Preacher Tuggle bent over and rolled the basket, the loose bullets rattled.

"We got us a snake here. A poison raddler. Hold up that air basket," Mudge called. "The one what holds a devil snake."

Mudge's body plummeted back and forth. "I got 'em in my pocket." He waved his hand and jerked his head forward. Preacher Tuggle moved next to him and raised the basket.

"God can give me victory over serpents," Mudge called, turning to Thelma Jewel who stood next to the altar. "Woman, even though you from up nawth, you kin have victory in your life."

"Oh, Lord, I need healing," Thelma Jewel called out the words Mudge told her to say.

Everyone stood so they could see what was going on.

Mudge rocked from side to side. Outside, there were no bird calls. No rustling leaves. Inside, no one was clearing their throats and spitting. The silence was deafening. Mudge leaned toward Thelma Jewel.

"Miss Thelmer Jewel. You an' me, we're gonter be rich," he murmured. "This here ain't no rehearsal. It's gonter be believed. I kin make that happen."

He leaned back, folded his hands and looked as pontifical as he could.

"On your knees," Mudge hollered, his voice pealing across the crowd.

Her face flaming, Thelma Jewel's eyes blinked wide, her lips pulled high over her teeth.

"No," she hissed.

Mudge plunged to the side. He dipped his hand into the basket and cocked his arm sideways, in a throwing position,

He gave Thelma Jewel a sharp kick.

Her legs shot out. Her corset popped loose. The top to her blouse flew open. Mudge flung a coiling, curling and hissing snake.

Black Beauty landed between the mountains of Thelma Jewel's breasts.

Shrieking in terror, she knocked over the snake cage under the altar.

A loud pop. Her ankle snapped.

Thelma Jewel flung her arm. The small Derrringer flew from her purse. With a clomp it hit the ground, discharged a bullet, whizzing into Mudge's leg. He fell.

Tattler writhed and slithered from under the altar.

A wounded bleeding Mudge looked Tattler the Rattler in the face. "Help!" he screamed.

The crowd was frozen with awe and fear.

Dale sprang from his seat. He grabbed Thelma Jewel's derringer from the floor, and with one quick motion, shot the snake.

The crowd was stunned.

Dr. Verner who sat close to the front, ran to Mudge and Thelma Jewel. He pulled a knife from his coat pocket. "Handkerchiefs. I need to make bandages," he said, ripping open the leg to Mudge's pants.

"Who did the shooting? How many been shot?" Someone yelled.

Dr. Verner looked up. "Need some calming down in here."

"I got me my gun!" a deep voice bellowed.

"Sister Mealie Maude. Stalk," Dr. Verner called to the two who were standing close by. "Gotta have us a call back to worship."

They both understood. A heavy bass piano thrum and a loud blast of sound from the horn got everyone's attention.

Dr. Verner nodded in Dale's direction. "The hospital. Need to get them there. Both of them."

"The doctor needs help," Dale announced. "Everyone calm down."

Several stout older men and a couple of hefty younger ones rushing to the front quickly made chairs with their arms. They lifted a bleeding Mudge and a fainted Thelma Jewel. A loud thud got everyone's attention.

"Oh glory, she's heftier than a spavined mule," one of the men shouted, as Thelma Jewel rolled from their arms and hit the dirt floor. "We need us one more pair of hands to lift this here hunk o' lard."

A young lad jumped forward.

Nobody watching them, Preacher Tuggle and Mother Bunny slipped out, leaving Gertie Mae .

"You best move this here gathering on along," Dr. Verner said to Dale. "It could get outta hand."

"One, two, three," four men lifted Thelma Jewel.

"Hallelujah. Brother Dale's gonna take over this Easter celebration for y'all, and to the glory of God," Dr. Verner called out, his voice crackling with apprehension as they left the meeting.

Dale took a deep breath and stared at the faces in front of him. *My name is not printed on a stone slab in France. My name, my bones, will be here for eternity,* he thought. *All I want is peace and good will.* "Let this be a new beginning," he challenged himself.

He mounted the small raised platform and placed his hand on the cross. "This is Easter. The day of our Lord's resurrection. I would like my brother in Christ and my dear friend, to be here at the front with me," he said in a firm voice. "Lamont Randall. Brother to brother. I need you."

Lamont's body stiffened. He hesitated a second, gritted his teeth and moved forward. "A long time ago, my mama told me that someday the chirren are a gatherin'," he said quietly. He leaned toward Brucie.

She grasped the gold cross twined with Captain Bruce Claymore's hairs and raised it as if it were an offering to Lamont.

It seemed as if for one magic moment Vernell was beside them, her goodness a beacon to follow.

"Miss Brucie. Lamont." Their names were soft, coming from unseen lips.

"She's here. With us," Brucie whispered.

"I heard." Lamont slowly let out a breath and placed his arm across Brucie's shoulder. "My sister."

"My brother."

Lamont helped Brucie to her feet. She turned and reached for Memory's hand. "Come with us."

There was an unsettled murmuring in the crowd as the three of them moved to the front.

"Y'all show us the way, Brother Dale," one of the scarlet-robed choir ladies sang.

"Not me. Jesus will show us the way," he said. "And He will bring us all together."

"Amen," someone called out.

"Lamont is my brother in Christ. I want him and my other loved ones to kneel here with me and when we do, I ask that the whole congregation say the Lord's Prayer."

A hush fell over the building.

A shrieking childish voice pierced the uneasy solemn quiet.

"Be my mommy."

Her eyes fastening on the one she wanted to see, Gertie Mae lurched toward Memory.

"Yes." Hot tears pricked Memory's eyes. "Yes." She held her arms out to the child.

Dale held up the Bible. "Today, the truth has been told," he said, stepping down from the platform. Brucie, Lamont, Memory, holding Gertie Mae close, and Dale faced the crowd; as they knelt Laura Lee and Jenson eased up beside them.

There was a rustle through the whole building as people dropped to their knees and said in unison:

"Our father, which art in heaven.

Hallowed be thy Name

Thy Kingdom come.

Thy will be done, in earth,

As it is in heaven.
Give us this day our daily bread.
And forgive us our trespasses,
As we forgive those that trespass against us.
And lead us not into temptation,
But deliver us from evil,
For thine is the kingdom,
The power, and the glory,
For ever and ever,
          Amen."

"There is a balm in Gilead," Brucie sang softly.

From somewhere back in Dale's memory, words from old revivals and hymn singing in Mississippi came back to him. Facing the congregation, one arm around Laura Lee, the other around his mother who was also held by Lamont, he joined Brucie, then everyone began,

"If you cannot sing like angels,
If you cannot preach like Paul,
You can tell the love of Jesus
And say he died for all.
To heal the sin sick soul."

With Lamont by his side, together they reached up to the cross made of pistols and lifted the rope that had hung his mother. Lamont and Dale raised and held it.

"Peace to a loving soul," they said in unison.

They spit on it then threw the rope across the still writhing, but dead snake.

Dale felt a rush of air brush his neck; it seemed as if he smelled the scent of freshly turned dirt. He turned and faced the altar. Just above the cross he saw a ghostly form in a tattered uniform. The soldier snapped a salute, the figure shrank inside his tattered clothes.

"You sir, may have lived only in my dreams," Dale whispered.

Blue eyes melted into a heavy skull.

And then he was gone

"But, we've had a unforgettable ride.

"I hope to do you proud."

EPILOGUE

Easter, 1921

"With this being Easter, and our church having dinner on the grounds after the early morning service, I'm glad we made it back as quick as we did." Dale's voice carried a tone of relief as he stepped into the kitchen. "My car had a flat, and we all rode home from church with Memory and Jenson."

An uncomfortable look on their faces, Lamont leaned against the icebox while Bertha wiped her hands on her apron.

"You got my message from Topper." Dale smiled. "We're here for something of a surprise on this Easter Day." His eyes widened as if he saw something they couldn't.

"By the way, Topper's doing a good job at the funeral home. Mother did us all a favor when she fired Trestle Potter. I just wish we'd been able to hire Topper to do the hearse driving too." He squared his shoulders. "He's colored, so it wouldn't do for him to drive. That day's coming, though."

Dale arched his eyebrows. "But right now we have something special to do. Let's go to the parlor."

"We got to git on home shortly," Lamont said. "Sassy's comin' in from Cedar Woods later this night."

With a resigned set to their shoulders, Bertha and Lamont followed Dale to the hall, but when they reached the parlor, Bertha hung back.

Dale pointed to one of the two dining room chairs that had been brought in and were facing the fireplace, Brucie in one of them. Rolling her lips together, Bertha looked at the chair next to Brucie as if there might already be someone in it.

"Here's your place," Brucie said, her voice warm and sincere, but leaving no room for argument. "With us." She pointed to the chair next to where she sat.

Bertha gazed at the floor, slowly took a seat and crossed her ankles.

"What you got up your sleeve Mist Dale?" Lamont asked.

"It's Dale," he said. "And I'm not saying, *Mister* Lamont to you."

"Ye suh. If'n if you say so." A half grin on his face, Lamont shook his head. "You gone git us in trouble."

"Trouble is my middle name."

Memory, holding Jenson's hand, her other arm around Gertie Mae sat on a sofa, facing Herschel who lay across from them.

"Lamont, you sit on the sofa with Jenson, Memory and Gertie Mae."

Lamont half shook his head. "That ain't done."

"You mind my son," Brucie said.

Dale moved over to where Laura Lee sat in one of the wingback chairs. His face gleaming with tenderness, he bent over, and cupped her chin in his hands. "It's time," he called out, a small smile on his face. "My wife and I have set the stage a little."

He moved away from Laura Lee and unhooked thick ties holding the swagging velvet drapes on either side of the fireplace.

Herschel pulled himself higher on the sofa and tucked a red quilt closer around his shoulders.

With a barely perceptible head nod, Dale raised the top to a large Victrola sitting on one side of the fireplace then cranked the handle.

The air in the room was heavy; the grandfather clock in the hall ticked to the slight grinding of a turning record.

"This is a recording by the Boston Symphony Orchestra. Someday, maybe somebody we know may be singing with them. If I have anything to do with it, she will. Those who know, say she's that good."

Dale raised the arm, then set the needle on the spinning record.

A violin began a melody; in the space of a few breaths the violin was joined by a harmony of oboe, then a cello, softly carrying the tune.

In the background a voice was barely heard, beginning with the words, *Deep river, my home is over Jordan.*

Bertha's gasp could be heard through the room. Dressed in an ankle-length white flannel skirt and a loose jacket, a willowy young lady appeared in the hall doorway. Everyone turned toward the singer.

There was a moment's hesitation, then Sassy slowly entered the parlor. She stopped in front of her mother and threw a lavender velvet cloche covering her thick black hair into Bertha's lap.

Arms outstretched, her deep, soulful contralto voice slowly swelled as Sassy walked on through the parlor and sang,

> *"Deep river, I want to cross over into campground.*
> *Deep river, my home is over Jordan,*
> *Deep river, Lord, I want to cross over into campground.*
> *Oh don't you want to go to that gospel feast,*
> *That promis'd land where all is peace?*
> *Deep river, my home is over Jordan,*
> *Deep river, I want to cross over into campground."*

A prayerful mood engulfed the rooms as the music and Sassy's voice drifted away.

"That's mahvelous," Herschel burst out. "You're going to be heard all over this country."

Lamont's head was bowed. Tears streamed down the faces of Memory and Laura Lee. Dale smiled proudly, as if he'd put something over on the world. He held his arms in the air, both thumbs raised upward.

Memory caught her breath. "How beautiful you are," she said softly. "Your voice is a treasure." She pressed her fist to her mouth

"I hope," Sassy whispered.

Gertie Mae kicked her braced legs as if she wanted to get up and run toward the singer. "She sounded good. Like the birds I hear outside my window in the morning. And I smelled something good when she came in."

"Sweet olive. Not everybody can smell it, Gertie Mae," Brucie said, her face beaming. "But I smelled it too."

She nodded toward Sassy. "I have been to several Easter concerts by the Boston Symphony Orchestra. I have never heard a song sung better," she breathed, gripping the gold cross twined with Captain Bruce Claymore's hairs she wore round her neck.

Pride showed in Sassy's dark brown eyes as she held out her arms, embracing Memory as Dale lifted the metal arm and needle from the record, spinning like a merry-go-round.

"Her talent is beyond anything we've ever heard around here. Your daughter's on to bigger and higher things than she would ever have around Redemption Ridge," said Dale.

"I jest wish my baby gurl wouldn't never leave me," Bertha said, her voice thick with emotion. "It's done been a while since I've seen her."

"I'm homesick, and I'm ready to go home," Sassy said.

Brucie stood. "First thing. I'm going to claim Lamont for a little bit," she spoke up. "Topper and I took care of something together, and he needs to see it. It won't take long."

"We're goin' on to home, girl," Bertha said, pulling her daughter into an embrace. The hall clock chimed out a deep note for the half hour as she and Sassy waved goodbye.

Dale pulled out his pocket watch. "Later this afternoon Laura Lee wants to check on her mother. But my car's in town with that flat."

"I'll be glad to run to you all to town after a while," said Jenson. "I need to meet with Topper and Minyard for a short while. They want to show me something about that well they're digging for our new house. We can go when I'm done with that."

"I think I'll just stay here," Memory said. "I'm a little tired."

Jenson put his arm around his wife and smiled as if the two of them knew a secret.

"Y'all is blesst, an we all is leavin'," Bertha called.

"I want to cross over campground," the words echoed from the back door.

***

"I have something special to show you," Brucie said as Lamont gave her his arm and they walked out of the house. "Look around," she said. "Everything has taken a fresh, deep breath; this world wants to live."

A bright blue sky splotched with cotton ball clouds was an overhead canvas. The front yard was a latticework of green bushes and black shadows, leaves rustled lazily in the trees.

Walking down the road, clusters of thick weeds waved, birds chirped and caroled as Brucie and Lamont crossed the road and into the cemetery. Wildflowers had come to life; white blossoming dogwoods spotted the graveyard; squirrels chattered overhead.

As they stepped into the colored cemetery the woods seemed to draw their tree limbs together in a protective shield, sunlight filtered through the branches.

"What for you wanted us to come out here?" Lamont asked as he followed Brucie toward a familiar spot, one he hadn't been to in a long time.

"I hope you're okay with something I've done," Brucie said. "It's different. Topper's come a long way. And him working in the funeral home helped me to get it taken care of. I wanted you to see this, before anybody else."

Lamont stopped like he had been jerked by a chain.

Where there had once been a rotting wooden plank scarring the ground there was now a white marble tombstone.

VERNELL AND BRUCE
WE REST IN PEACE

"This was my Daddy," said Brucie. "And yours."

They both felt, rather than saw, a presence. Dale stood beside them.

"It's all come full circle, Uncle Lamont."

As if in agreement, haunting coos came from the tree where Vernell had been hung. A flight of mourning doves took off as if they were no longer on a mission of caring for the dead.

"Amends have been made for our father, Captain Bruce Claymore," said Brucie. She lay her head against her son's shoulder. "And his soldiered grandson has returned."

"On this Easter, in this place, there is peace at Redemption Ridge," said Dale. "I'm home. Here with my people."

Lamont reached out a hand. He laid it on Brucie's cheek for a moment, then kissed his hand and pressed it against the tombstone.

"Praise Jesus," he breathed. "They can sleep now."

Brucie cocked her head. The trees, they whispered an old song, a lowly fading echo. *Peace I leave with you.*

"Do you hear them?" she asked, but no one answered.

***

Memory was relieved that everyone was finding something to do, and as much as she loved him, that Jenson would be gone for a short while. It had been several weeks since she had found, not the time, but the inclination to write in her journal. To bring their life up to date, so to speak.

"I'm almost done with what I have to say," she told herself, holding onto the railing leading upstairs with one hand and clutching brown wrapping paper and twine with the other hand. Many old wishes and hopeful dreams draped in the house corners and out in the fields like ghosts. Memory didn't want to lose them. "Words that nobody at Redemption Ridge may care to hear. But maybe someone else would like to read."

She closed the door to her room, turned sideways and looked at the growing round of her stomach. "Girl or boy. It doesn't matter," she said. "But a girl, and her name will be Charlotte Caroline. That will please my mama. Her mother's name. A boy, and it will be Claymore Tisdale—Clay Cooper. I don't know if I'll have the time, or the inclination to pen my thoughts after the arrival of this little one. That has yet to be seen. So, I need to go ahead, put pen to page and finish our story."

"Daisy Dog, Daisy Dog." A pleased smile on her face, Memory looked out the window. One of her legs in a brace, Gertie Mae was walking with her dog. Unexpectedly, moisture filled Memory's eyes. "'Suffer the little children.' You're mine now," she said. "No one knows for sure where Mudge and Thelma Jewel are. And no one cares." She nodded her head. *Louisiana. That's where we heard. Mudge's started a church there. The Bourbon Street Born Again Believers.*

She gave an unseen hand wave in Gertie Mae's direction, moved from the window, and opened the chifforobe. She lifted out a large bundle of papers tied with a gold satin ribbon and laid them on her bed. Memory untied the ribbon, lifted a few pages from her journal and then sat down. She picked up her pen and dipped it into an ink well. One word following another she began.

March 27, 1921

Redemption Ridge used to be my nothing. Now, it is my everything. Hopefully, someday some of my loved ones will thank me for writing this history. Then again, maybe they will wish I had left well enough alone.

The names, tales and misdeeds of those who have hurt and misused my family are penned throughout my journal. I have told the story of Vernell, of Captain Bruce Claymore. Of Lamont, Brucie, and Dale. My family. And me, who in many ways view myself as the least of the least.

With the help of my Heavenly Father, and I believe with the whispers from one who is not too far away, I have pulled together the happenings, stories, and, perhaps, some fantasies of my family, and of those who have impacted them.

Thank you, Vernell.

And now we have come to another Easter. Perhaps, in some small way I have honored the memory of Vernell. Of Bruce Claymore. I will not name this Easter a Celebration. No. It is A Redemption.

In some ways we have made a full circle and returned.

Memory set the pen down. She added the pages she had just finished to the bundle on her bed. In a flash she remembered the telephone conversation she had had with an old family friend of her father who owned the company, *Auld Lang Syne Book Publishers*. "He said he was interested. I'll worry about what family thinks later."

Once again she bound her papers with the gold ribbon. This time it was hard to keep the smile off her face as she wrapped her journal in brown paper and tied the bundle tightly with twine. She dipped her pen into the ink one final time and addressed:

Attention: Mr. Austin Lange
The Auld Lang Syne Publishing Company
Number 16 Red Bird Drive
Boston, Massachusetts

She would have Jenson drive her downtown to the post office tomorrow and get it in the mail. *Or, if he's busy, I'll drive myself.*

ABOUT THE AUTHOR

Lottie Brent Boggan has a knack for finding humor in the worst of circumstances. She's been a long-time contributor to the *Northside Sun*, a weekly newspaper in Jackson, Mississippi. Lottie has had numerous accolades, winning The Eudora Welty novel competition, placing at the Faulkner Wisdom Competition, and receiving newspaper column awards. In addition to her novels, she has also compiled multiple anthologies of short stories with Judy Tucker and served as editor to several critically acclaimed authors besides herself. She is one of the founders of The Red Dog Writers and is a member of Middle Mississippi Chapter of the Mississippi Writers Guild.

Lottie's family is somewhat of an icon in Mississippi, with her father having started Brent's Drugs, which was featured in the movie, *The Help*. Her late husband was a founder of River Oaks Hospital, now Merit.

Lottie is a resident of Jackson, Mississippi, and has been an avid skier, golfer, and tennis player throughout her octogenarian life. She is a dog lover and staunch supporter of rescue dogs.

Lottie jokes that she hopes to live long enough to complete the Redemption Ridge trilogy with a third installment tentatively entitled *Redemption Ridge Redeemed* with a story focusing on World War II and pilots, including a Tuskegee Airman, and loosely based on the actual experience of her late brother-in-law, Lt. Robert Thomas Boggan.